Mo's Mix Series

MO'S MIX
MO'S MIX: QUEEN-DOM

By: Javanna Plummer

MO'S MIX

Published by Kindle Direct Publishing, a trademark of Amazon.com Inc.

410 Terry Ave. N Seattle, WA 98109

First published in the United States of America by Kindle Direct Publishing, a trademark of Amazon.com, Inc., 2015

Paperback Published by Kindle Direct Publishing, 2016

Copyright © Javanna Plummer, 2015

ISBN-16: 9781535037242

Foreword – *A novel is more than just the characters, the plot and the novelist. A novel is too those whom inspired the characters, the plot, and the novelist.*

ACKNOWLEDGMENTS

First off, I would like to thank God for being my personal advisor and confidant as I prepared the novel you are about to read. Next, I would like to thank my family and friends for being so supportive. Without them, there would be no "Mo's Mix." Then, I would like to give thanks to those whose works inspired the work you are about to dive into.

First up is Scandal (written by Shonda Rimes); this a show that showcases a black career woman and I would be lying if I said Monique Ross didn't possess some traits of Olivia Pope.

After Scandal is Parenthood (created by Ron Howard); this show got down to crux of some real life issues and watching the show helped me tell a real story.

Thirdly, there's "Zara and Gibson," a story written by my sister Justice Plummer that discussed a rapper's claim to fame. A few years back, my sister sent me that story and about 2 years later I drew on the fast-paced, witty, and realistic nature as I wrote Mo's Mix with some elements of Justices' piece. So, I would like to thank her, Mr. Howard, and Ms. Rimes for their inspiration.

Finally, I would like to give a special shout out to my father, Ronald V. Plummer. May this novel and any others I write reach you in Heaven. Rest peacefully.

Prologue – *Mo's Mix was the epitome of Monique Ross' success; it won over many hearts because of Monique's unique tale about her journey with natural hair. 5 years later, she was preparing to lecture fourth graders on the value of hair care.*

5 YEARS LATER

Monique sat there manically brushing, over and over again. Yet, there were no results. "Mo?" Dre, Monique's boyfriend, came knocking at the door. "You ready to go?" "No; five more minutes, babe," Monique replied. Somehow, she knew this five minutes would turn to fifteen minutes, which would inevitably lead to another half hour. "You said that 20 minutes ago. They're expecting you there soon, baby."

"Don't rush me!" Monique snapped. So Dre backed down. He knew it wasn't the time nor the place to start an argument. *This is a really nice hotel,* he thought to himself as he tried to wait patiently. Monique, realizing the truth in Dre's statement, finally settled on a style. "Scarf it is," she told herself as she began to pick one from her suitcase.

Dre made a face when he saw Monique. "Don't tell me you're wearing those again." "What if I am? Would that be a problem?" Dre came closer. "You're beautiful the way you are. Why do you feel the need to hide behind a scarf?" "I'm not hiding. I'm…" She couldn't think of an adequate excuse so she snatched the scarf up. "Don't question my decisions."

Dre threw his hands up. "You know what? Do whatever pleases you." Monique rolled her eyes. "Do you have to say it like that?"

"How else would you like me to say it?" "How 'bout you try not scolding me because I want to cover up my hair?"

Dre sighed. "If I'm scolding, it's because you're the genius behind 'Mo's Mix.' You created these hair care products so that African American girls, teenagers, and women wouldn't feel the need to deny their natural hair. Your punchline is 'Natural locks rock!' So, I don't get why you're putting that scarf on."

Monique sighed this time. "My hair fell out again." "Could it be because…?" She shot him a look, which meant he was not allowed to say whatever he was thinking. "Monique, what's going on?" She rubbed her head. "I don't know, Dre, but we gotta go." "Now, who's rushing?"

Dre kissed her cheek and grabbed a jacket. "Whenever you feel like talking, I'm here, okay?" She smiled and put on her heels. "Okay, Dre. I love you." He was rushing out but he still looked back and smiled. "I love you, too." Hand in hand, they exited the hotel room. "Are you excited that you get to speak to these students?"

Monique held her journal closely. "I couldn't be any happier."

"Class, quiet down. As you all know, Black History Month commemorates African-Americans for their various achievements. To get you all excited, I decided to bring in a special African-American guest each month. For this month, I've called upon my old friend who founded Mo's Mix. Please give a warm welcome to Monique Ross!" The fourth graders exclaimed as Monique passed out candy, a ruse to get them excited for what she was about to say.

"How many of you like stories?" Almost every hand shot up. This made Monique smile. "Great. Boy, do I have a story for you all." She pulled out her old journal. "You see this journal?" They nodded. "This was a journal I kept when I was you all's age.

Would you like to hear one of the entries?" The students nodded again.

Monique opened the book. "September 14th, 2005: 'Dear Diary, it's the first day of fourth grade. I'm so excited. Mom's made me a PB&J just the way I like with the peanut butter lined up perfectly to the crust and jelly oozing from the sides." The students made an "Mmmm!" sound as Monique described it.

She grinned and kept going. "Then, dad's going to let me ride my bike through the neighborhood after school. I'll get to zoom past the trees and let the wind catch my pigtails in the breeze. I'm so happy mom finally let me get cornrows. A lot of older girls in my school wear them and they make me feel so grown-up. I like feeling grown-up.'"

The girls with cornrows seemed to feel pleased with Monique's statement. She took note of that but continued, "Still, I always think of how my grandma reacted. She called mom all types of mean names when she'd seen I'd gotten braids. She called them a disgrace." The self-assured girls suddenly seemed to feel small.

Monique still proceeded. "I don't understand why grandma would say such a thing. I love my braids. They make me feel older. I really like that feeling. This is going to take some getting used to, huh, diary? Sincerely, Monique'." At this point, Monique closed the journal, since the entry was finished. "How do you all feel about that?"

One of the girls with long hair shot her hand up. "I think your grandma was right. If you have short hair, you have short hair. You shouldn't hide beneath some braids." The girl cocked her head back at her classmates. Monique countered, "You're right. You shouldn't *hide* behind anything but sometimes braids aren't about hiding; sometimes they're about protecting. Did you all know that braids are actually considered a protective hairstyle?"

The class shook their heads to say "no."

"Well, they are and they were much easier for my mom to manage."

"Well, maybe your mom was lazy."

"Morgan!" Ms. George shot the fourth grader a scolding look but Monique just smiled. "It's fine, Ms. George. Maybe my mom did sometimes feel lazy. But, your mom doesn't seem to be lazy, Morgan. You have beautiful natural hair." Morgan shook it in her classmates face. "That's right. My mom says that my hair is my best feature."

"What about your personality?" Morgan scoffed, "What about it? All my friends just *adore* my hair." Monique, while not wanting to scare the child, didn't want Morgan to suffer in the long run. "But, what if all your hair goes away?"

Hearing this, Morgan's eyes started watering. "Th-that's never gonna happen, is it?" Monique slowly pulled the silk scarf from around her head. "Unfortunately, it could." The children gasped to see the bald spots on her scalp. "What happened?" They all wondered. Monique shook her hair out.

"I was careless with my hair and it suffered. Now, Morgan, I don't mean to upset you. I just don't want your hair to make up who you are." Morgan looked down. "But what if my hair is all I have?" Monique said, "Look at me." The child did.

"You're beautiful, okay? Not because you have long hair, but because you have a unique personality. No one is like you, Morgan. You have gifts that other people can't even *dream* of having. I want you to take that with you."

These compliments made Morgan smile. Then, a boy named Skyler's hand shot up. He was the class trouble maker, due to his outlandish questions. "Excuse me, Ms. Ross?" "Yes, sir?" "How do you have a line of hair care products but you don't even have a full head of hair?"

"I made some mistakes," she responded. "I think you're a fraud," he stated. "Skyler!" Ms. George got up. "Go to the corner. We *don't* call our special guests frauds." Speechless, Monique removed herself from the classroom. After getting an apology from Ms. George, she left the building.

"What if that little boy was right, Dre? Am I a fraud?" Dre pulled out the seat so that Monique could sit down. "No, you're not. He's just a kid. They say the first thought that comes to mind." "Sometimes kids are actually the most intuitive, though." Dre rubbed Monique's hand as he sat down. "When you started Mo's Mix, your natural hair – in its natural texture – is what endeared so many people to the brand. Now, you've run into some issues. But, that doesn't change the Monique Ross who started it all. You had a vision, baby."

Monique nodded. "You're right. It's just…I created this entire line of products that are supposed to support the growth and development of *our* hair and *our* self-esteem. Yet, I can't even properly take care of my hair so I hid it in a scarf because I didn't want anyone to see its state." Dre's hand came into her scalp. "So you'll work on your hair, Mo. You'll fix it. I know you will."

"Oh yeah? How do you know?"

Dre kissed her head. "I believe in you and everything that you stand for." Once he said this, Monique could feel the longing in Dre's voice. He wanted to marry her. "This is a nice lunch you set up. I'm sure it cost a fortune." "No amount of money is too much to spend on my lady."

"I realize that." As they ate and chatted up a storm, Monique began to wonder if she was ready for a long term commitment. After all, she loved Dre and they'd been together 5 years. She was approaching 30 and her biological clock was ticking. Marriage just seemed like the logical road to travel upon. Yet, something held Monique back. She had a longing too, but hers was for independence. *I'm not ready yet,* she convinced herself.

"So…I've been wanting to ask you something." Monique mentally prepared herself for this one. Dre was going to pop the question. She just knew it. Still, she replied, "Go ahead." "Are you pregnant?" He asked instead. "Am I…what?"

"Are. You. Pregnant?" he repeated.

"What would make you ask that?" Dre folded his hands together. "Well, I've been talking to some of my buddies from work and they were describing how their spouses acted when their spouses were pregnant; some of the character traits reminded me of you."

"I'm not your spouse, Dre."

Dre let out a deep breath. "I know, Mo. That aside, though, are you pregnant?" Monique shook her head. "We always use protection so there's no way that could've happened." "Well, there was that one time when we were both drunk on Valentine's Day and we didn't." Monique rolled her eyes. "I took an at-home test and it told me no." Dre pulled out his phone. "Okay but I was reading this article and it says that sometimes those are false negatives. Just know that if you are pregnant, I would be there completely and you could talk to me if…" "I'm *not,*" Monique clarified. "So this conversation is over."

Dre put his phone down. "What's got you in a mood?"

"I don't plan on getting married anytime soon and you've been hinting at it ever since you found out Nathalie was getting married." At the airport, Dre had mentioned his sister's wedding but Monique wanted to hear nothing of it. "Are you sure you don't want to get married?" "I'm sure," Monique told him. "Then, what are we doing here?"

"That's the same thing I'm wondering."

Dre asked, "When were you planning on telling me this?" "Whenever I felt ready. So that time was a few seconds ago."

"Whenever you felt ready, Monique? There are two of us in this relationship. We're supposed to communicate with each other." "I am communicating with you right now." Dre shook his head. "No. You only said something because I asked what was wrong. What if I hadn't asked?"

"Then you simply wouldn't know."

Dre was angered by this statement. "You know what? I lost my appetite." "You want to go back to the hotel room?" He waved his hand for the waiter. "Something like that."

As soon as they returned to the hotel, Dre went to the bar and Monique lay down to relax. Her feet were killing her and she had begun experiencing bouts of tiredness. *Am I pregnant?* As the thought sat, Monique realized she had attacked Dre without even listening to what he had to say. She called him to apologize but Dre didn't answer.

He returned around one in the morning, clearly drunk. "Where have you been?" "At the bar. I t-told you that."

"You're no good when you drink. You know that." He shrugged. "Baby, please don't do this right now. I have a headache. Can you just make some room on the bed for me?" Monique cringed. "You reek of alcohol."

"Well I *have* been drinking."

"I can't stand when you smell like that." Dre put his arm around her. "Come on, baby. Give me a kiss." Monique turned away from him. "I will when you're sober." Monique was madder that he hadn't been there to talk to her than she was about Dre's drinking. Still, this hurt Dre because it was coupled with Monique's words from the restaurant. *I'm only drinking because she won't commit to me,* he inwardly thought. *Now, she won't even look at me because I've been drinking.*

For most of the night, he racked his brain with fantasies of him and Monique walking down the aisle. *Too bad it's not gonna happen,* he convinced himself. *She's never gonna marry me.* By morning, Dre had made up his mind. "I think we should take some time off, Monique," he stated. Monique stopped dead in her tracks. "What are you talking about, Andre?"

"If we're not in this for marriage, what are we doing?"

"I never said I wouldn't marry you. I just said not now."

"If not now, when? You women claim that you don't want to wait around for a man but you expect a man to wait around for you?" Monique stood to face him. "First of all, cool it with the sexism. Second of all, I don't *expect* anything. You want to walk away? The door's wide open."

"So what…you're just giving up? After five years, this is how you treat me?"

Monique groaned because she was getting agitated. "How am I treating you, Andre?! You're the one who suggested we split apart." "If we're not in this for marriage, what are we doing here?" Monique sighed. "You already asked that."

"And I'm gonna ask it again."

"What's the rush on commitment?"

Dre sighed. "Mo, I want to start a family. Remember how I said I wanted two kids? I meant that. I want you to be my wife and the mother of my children."

Monique pushed her hair back. "I don't know what to say to that." "Say you'll marry me." She sighed. "I can't, Dre."

"Then, I guess that's it." Monique was taken aback. "So you're going to walk away from everything we have?" Dre nodded. "Yep. I'm done." She scoffed. "Bye, Andre. Once we get back, we'll go our separate ways." "I guess so," Dre stated half-heartedly.

Chapter I – *Dre couldn't understand why Monique was being so cruel. He loved her with every fiber of his being. Every breath he breathed, he did it for her. Monique, on the other hand, was focusing on her career – owning and operating Mo's Mix.*

2 MONTHS LATER

"I need results, people. We're supposed to be releasing a new product in two weeks, not two months. Chop, chop!!" Monique was finally back in her own element, free of Dre and as independent as she needed to be. It was truly relieving. "Ms. Ross?" She turned. "Yes?" "Your doctor's on line 2 for you." Monique nodded. "I'll take that in my office. Thanks, Dominique."

After returning from her trip, Monique began experiencing fatigue. So she had made an appointment with her doctor.

"Monique?" Dr. Seneca's voice sounded filled with excitement. "You're gonna be a mommy." The phone nearly slipped from Monique's fingertips. "I'm…I'm what?" "You're pregnant, Monique. You and Dre are gonna be parents. That's great news, right?"

Monique rubbed her head. "Not exactly. Dre and I are not together at the moment." "If you need anything done, I can--" "I'll call you back, Nancy," Monique said while hanging up. After that news, she needed a breather and there was one person she could always go to for that.

"Raven, sit down! I told you to stop running around the house!" Camille pushed her hair back and flung the door open. "Mrs.

Jones, I said I'll pay the rent when…" She paused. "Oh. Hey, Mo. Why didn't you call?"

"I thought dropping by would be better." Camille sighed. "Well, it's not. Trevor left his child with me once again and she keeps making a mess." "Why do you allow Trevor to do that," Monique inquired. "Why not just cut him off?" "When he gets back from his trip, he said he'll pay the rent. Right now, I need him for things like that because I don't have a job."

"You also don't have a child."

"But I will have a stepchild soon."

Camille pulled her hand out. Surely enough, there was a huge rock placed on her finger. "Oh, so he popped the question?" "Yes!" Camille exclaimed. "He makes me so happy."

Monique cut her eyes. "But, you met him at Walmart 6 months ago."

"Regardless, we're in love." At that, Monique shook her head. "You know what? I'm not here to lecture you. I came because I have news." Camille sat up straight. "Ooh, girl. I got news too but you go first." Monique just came out with it. "I'm pregnant." "By Dre?"

Monique stared blankly at Camille. "I haven't had sex since the break-up and you know I'm not the type to cheat." "Well, we can't all be saviors, huh?" Carelessly, Monique had forgotten about Camille's previous love affair with Donald, who had been cheating on his longtime girlfriend with Camille. "I'm sorry, Cam. I didn't mean it like that." Camille shrugged. "It is what it is. But, do you know that fool called me the other day?"

"Donald?" She nodded. "*Yes.*" "What did *he* want," Monique asked. "He wanted to see if we could catch up." "I hope you told him no."

"Actually, I'm having lunch with him in a few days."

"What?! You're engaged to Trevor." "It's not like I'm going on a date. It's just old lovers catching up."

"Is that how Donald spun it? He probably wants to ease his way back into your life."

Camille shrugged. "It is what it is, you know? And have you told Dre?" "I haven't spoken to him since we went our separate ways." "Are you planning on telling him?" Monique sighed. "I might. I might not. It is what it is, you know?"

Camille burst into laughter. "Look here. Don't you be using my words against me." Monique laughed too. "Aw, Cam. You know I'm just messing with you. I'll tell him…" "Good! You better."

"After I get the abortion," Monique finished.

"The…"

Monique wrinkled her face. "You didn't think I would keep his baby, did you? Dre and I are **done**. Besides, I have a career to focus on now."

Although Monique seemed convicted into her beliefs, this was merely an outward appearance. Inwardly, she was confused, hurting, and vulnerable. *I love Dre so much. I didn't want to hurt him but I can't marry him right now.* She thought about this as she visited Dr. Seneca. "You hung up the phone so quickly, Monique. Is everything alright?"

"Everything's fine," she lied. "But do you know how far along I am?" Dr. Seneca told her, "Well, you're about 6 weeks right now." *That's why my stomach has been poking out of my dresses.* "Okay…how much time do I have for the abortion?"

"For the abortion? Is that something that you want?" Monique sighed heavily. "Maybe. Can you give a rough estimate? I know there's supposed to be a cut-off date." "You have 2 more months; that's when you'll be 14 weeks pregnant." Dr. Seneca responded.

"2 months? You mean to tell me that I have 8 weeks to decide this?"

"That's precisely what I'm saying to you."

"Wow." Monique took it all in. *8 weeks can pass by very quickly.*

"Yep. So if you're serious about termination, you'll have to act soon."

"Duly noted."

With that on her plate, Monique drove home deep in thought. *I have to tell Dre…I just don't know how.*

"Hey, I think we should get Chinese food tonight. You're on it? Great." Caleb Paul turned to face Monique. "Hi, can I help you?" "Caleb, is that you?" "Do I…?" He paused for a long period of time. "You're Monique Ross!" She thought he'd remembered her until he added, "You're Andre's girlfriend and the genius behind Mo's Mix." Monique nodded. "Actually I'm only one of those now." Caleb let out a deep breath. "My apologies. Are you here to see Andre?" "Yes." Caleb pressed a button. "Dre, can you come to the front? Someone's here to see you."

Monique said, "But I'm surprised you only know me as Andre's girlfriend who started a business." Hearing that, Caleb got a closer look. "Should I know you as more?" "We both graduated from Nia University. I was in the class ahead of you." He gasped. "Wait, I do remember you. You're the one who used to run with Tara and Camille."

"Yep, that's me," she stated. "How are they?" Caleb inquired while he and Monique waited for Dre. "Tara's teaching now. I actually spoke to her class a while back and Camille's in between jobs at the moment."

"Hmmkay. And how are you?"

"I'm great. I started Mo's Mix but you knew that already."

Caleb nodded. "Of course I did." He pulled out a picture from his wallet. "My twin girls love it and Georgia always raves about it." "Georgia?" He nodded. "Yeah. She's my wife now." "Ah, a wife and a law firm. I see you're doing big things."

"Indeed I am," Caleb responded. Then, Dre finally came forward. "Sorry for making you wait, boss. I was just talking to Genna about…" He stopped once he saw Monique. "Mo, what are you doing here?" "Can we go to your office and talk?"

"Sure. Come right this way," he said.

The inside of Dre's office had changed since Monique had last seen it. There were more pieces of art and less novels about the state of the world. "Genna said that I was too dreary and cynical so she offered to re-decorate."

"Who's Genna?"

"My co-worker."

"Is that all she is?"

Dre smiled. "Oh, you're jealous. I get it, Mo. I'm jealous too." "Of who?" "Whoever has been feeding you. You look like you've been eating well." She took offense to this. "Are you tryna call me fat?!" He took her by her hips.

"Not at all. You look great. Your hips are so much wider and your breasts are so full. And your hair has grown back so much since..." He thought about it for a second. "Are you pregnant, Monique?"

"You keep asking me that, Andre."

"Alright and I'm going to continue asking until I get a straight answer out of you."

Instead of giving him the runaround, Monique answered, "Yes." "You are?" Monique snapped, "Isn't that what 'yes' means?"

"Ooh, those pregnancy hormones are really kicking in, huh" he joked. "Not funny, Dre." He kissed her cheek. "I'm sorry. Maybe I've missed you."

"Obviously not that much. You moved on to *Genna.*"

"First of all, Genna is my coworker. Secondly, it's only been two months. I can never replace the love that we shared within two months. I hope you haven't either." Dre cupped her face in his hands. "That baby in your belly is our baby, okay? Like I said two months ago, I'll do whatever it takes to raise our child the way he or she ought to be raised. I'm going to make you proud, Mo. You'll see."

She turned away. "No, Dre. I won't see. I'm not keeping it." "Wh-what? Why?" "I have a career to think about and a baby would just hold me back." His face dropped as his hands did too. "Wait. Isn't this a decision that we're supposed to make together?"

"The decision's been made. Just thought I'd let you know." He kissed her. "Would that change your mind? I love you, Monique." She pulled her face away. "I gotta go."

Once Monique got home, she slid on the wall shedding rivers of tears. *I keep saying that I'm giving this baby up when I don't actually mean it. I love Dre. I just can't marry him.*

As for Andre, he sat at his desk talking to Genna about a case but inwardly reflecting on the news Monique had shared with him. *I won't even get to raise my first child. Monique doesn't want to have a baby by me.*

In the middle of a sentence, he said, "Hey, can we continue this tomorrow?" Genna replied, "Sure, is there--"

"I'll see you later." Dre grabbed his things and rushed home so that only ones to see him break down were his dust bunnies. *I have to get Monique back.*

Truly, Dre was determined. He vowed to do whatever it took to win his way back into her heart. *What matters most to Mo?* In the midst of his thoughts, the paperboy slid a newspaper under Dre's door. Dre opened it and handed the boy $10. "Thank you." The boy nodded and went back to his bike.

Dre lifted the paper up and saw the headline: "Hair 'care' that isn't worth the fare." Underneath, there was an image of the new product Mo's Mix was supposedly planning to release. *How do they have pictures if it isn't even out yet,* Dre wondered. Adjacent to the first image, there was an image of a document from a science lab. The report was unrecognizable in the small print. Suddenly intrigued, Dre pried the paper open.

Hours later, he tossed the same paper on his boss' desk. "I think this is right up our alley." Georgia pulled the article closer and analyzed it. "I think you're right. Is your girlfriend asking for new representation?"

"Actually, Monique and I broke up but I would still like to help her."

Georgia placed her hands together. "Is she *asking* us to represent her?" "No. It was just a thought." She shook her head. "Well, keep your thoughts to yourself, Andre. Until Ms. Ross requests our representation, there's nothing we can do."

"I was just presenting the idea."

"I see. Why don't you speak to Ms. Ross about it first?" "I'll do that. Thanks boss." Georgia nodded and went back to what she was doing.

Monique was quite busy when she got the phone call. "Dre, look. I'm extremely busy right now so you better make this quick." "Well, I was reading…" "Hold on." Monique placed the phone down when her assistant came running in. "Yes, Dominique?" "Have you seen the paper? Twitter is blowing up about this." Dominque tossed the paper onto Monique's desk.

Monique glanced at the headline and groaned. "Andre, I'm going to have to call you back. There's a crisis right now." "Does it have anything to do with today's paper?" *He knows too?!* Monique internally griped. If she didn't get this under wraps, her company's reputation could take a big hit. "Yes, actually, it does. What are you calling me for?"

"I was wondering if you would like Paul and Friends to be your legal representation." Monique started reading the article and realizing the detriment. "We already have a lawyer, Andre." "But, I remember you saying you don't like his quote." Monique sighed. "I have to figure some things out right now. I'll call you back when I can." "Okay. I'll let you get back to work."

"Thanks. Love you." Monique was so used to saying this that she didn't even realize her words until she hung up. But, she let it slip from her mind; she had other issues to deal with. "Dominique, can you please report to my office?" Dominque rushed back. "Yes, Ms. Ross?" "Man the phone," Monique ordered. "If anyone calls, take a message for me. I have to speak with my lab workers ASAP."

Monique stormed down the stairs, angrier than ever. "Marcus, Roger, Anna, Nicole, Stacy, Kela, and Minnie. May I please have a word with all of you?" Kela stepped up first. "Well, Nicole and Stacy didn't show up today. Stacy's still on maternity leave, though." "Thank you for the notice, Kela. What about Nicole?"

"No one's heard from Nicole in days," Roger stated. "Then I have my first suspect," Monique proclaimed. After returning to her office, with 7 messages that required attention, she phoned Nicole six times before getting an answer.

"Hello?"

"Nicole? Where are you?"

Nicole coughed heavily. "I'm at home. I've been sick since Friday." Monique thought: *She's been "sick" since Friday; Roger said no one's heard from her in days. Maybe she's the mole.* "Okay, Nicole. Sorry to bother you." "No problem, boss." Even the way Nicole hung up quickly aroused Monique's suspicions. *What could she be up to?*

Before Monique could even get her thoughts straight, Donna busted in. "Burns may be pulling out." "What?" Donna sighed. "Amethius Burns just called and said due to the recent news, Burns may withdraw as a supplier."

"Thank you for that update, Donna. Can you phone Rosler and Datonsburg to see if they are still willing to work with us?"

"I can."

Monique nodded. "What's the status on the leak?" Donna surfed through her iPad. Monique scoffed. "You're still using that old gadget? I gave everyone in the office the newest version of the Jotter."

"I'm old school, Ms. Ross. You know that. But, anyways, April Spring says someone spoke to her privately this past weekend and that is where she gained the information. She will not disclose who the person was."

"Interesting. Very interesting." Monique rubbed her temples. "Well, find out as much information as you can about this April lady and the insider then report back to me ASAP." "You got it, boss." Donna quickly went back to her office. Dominique stood at the door. "Do you need me to do anything?"

Monique nodded. "Answer my calls while I'm gone. I'll be back." "Where are you going, boss?" "To handle some business."

Monique rapped almost twenty times on Nicole's apartment door. "Trevor, you told me you wouldn't be here until..." Nicole paused. "You don't look very sick," Monique noted. Nicole fake coughed twice. "Eh heh, eh heh. I am ill."

Monique shook her head. "If you weren't really sick, how come you couldn't come to work on Friday?" "I ran out of vacation days and there was something important I had to do."

"What was that? And how come you didn't come in today either?"

Nicole shifted uncomfortably. "How come you're asking so many questions?" "Someone leaked private information about our new product to April Spring. She's now claiming that our product can have adverse effects when used. Have you seen Spring's article?"

There was a paper wide open on Nicole's table so she had no choice but to nod. "So, I'm going to ask you this once, Nicole. Did you speak to April Spring?" Nicole lowered her eyes. "Yes, but…"

"No buts. Those were private trials only to be shared with myself and the scientists. Since then, we have improved the product but the consumers don't know that. All they will see is that at one point, people's hair was falling out. Do you know what that will do to sales?"

"She offered me $2,000! Do *you* know the type of conditions I'm living in?"

Monique sighed as she took in the rundown apartment. "I can see that. But, this is not the way you go about things when you're working for me. You're fired, Nicole. Effective immediately."

After that, Monique thought the problem was solved. She'd figured out who leaked the information and she'd taken care of it. However, when she got back to the office, there was more to the story. Dominique noted, "While you were gone, your phone was ringing off the hook with people begging to hear your side. This was following April's statements on Twitter."

Freedom of Speech is a real bitch, huh?

I would hate to be Monique right now…

Poor Nicole. Jobless due 2 injustice.

"Donna, get on that. Fix it." As Monique tried to enact her young spirit once more, a young spirit inside slowed her down. "You're kicking already?!" She held her stomach and sat on a nearby couch chair. "How am I going to run a business and have a baby," she thought to herself.

Inevitably, she ended up at Dre's condo. "Hey. I wasn't expecting company. If I was, I would've cleaned up and made you something…" "Don't try so hard, Dre. Your place is fine and I'm not hungry."

"Okay. So what brings you here?"

"I can't just stop by to say hey?"

"I mean, you can, but did you?" After dating for so long, Dre and Monique were privy to each other's moves. "To tell you the truth, I'm worried." "About?" Monique sat on the couch. "This baby. I feel like it'll slow me down at Mo's Mix."

"Then, take a break. Let someone else handle the business."

"Or I could have an abortion and move on with my life." Dre sat next to her. "Mo, it's not--" "Monique," she corrected. "We are not dating so please refer to me as Monique from now on." He sighed. "Mo, it's not that easy. When you--"

"Monique! My name is Monique." The baby responded to her yelling by kicking. Monique suddenly relaxed. "Oh my god. This hurts, Dre. How can something so precious hurt me this much?"

"That's the same thing I asked when you walked away."

"I walked away? But who initiated the break-up?"

"I did because you're so against marriage!"

Monique rubbed her temples. "I have goals, Dre." "And a life with me isn't one of them?" This question stumped her. "I never said that," she explained. "You didn't have to." Dre got up to answer his phone and Monique sat on the couch pondering his words. *I love Dre. But can I marry him?*

As Dre kept his back to her, Monique remembered the way she would always grasp it when they got intimate. She could envision faint traces of the red marks she left. Without realizing, Monique came behind Dre and kissed his neck. He ended his call and grabbed her waist. "Mo," he whispered – his breath caressing her cheekbones. "Dre," she moaned, calling out for her man. In seconds, they were on top of each other. Then, Monique came back to reality.

"No." She gently pushed Dre off. "That's what led to this madness in the first place." He kissed her bare belly. "Having a baby is not 'madness.' It's beautiful."

"Not when it stops your dreams." Dre held her belly; in a way, he was holding their child. "But, you get to create goals for this little guy or gal. And if it's a girl you can style her hair the way your mom used to style yours. If it's a boy, you get to watch him get his first haircut then learn how to tie a tie then--" Monique kissed Dre and they were back where they left off.

Once all their clothes had hit the floor, they lay on the couch naked – two human beings completely in love but separated by unaligned dreams. "Dre, I love you," Monique proclaimed. He kissed down her back and up her belly. He cupped her face in his hands. "I love you, Monique."

Monique didn't wish to escape the tenderness but she knew, deep down, that she had to. "Dre…" He held on to her tightly. "Don't leave just yet. Let me bask in the glory of your perfection."

"You're so poetic, Dre."

"Only for you."

For a moment, they forgot about the breakup as they were more concerned with life that was soon-to-be.

"You visited Dre and…" Camille was Monique's oldest friend so she always needed every last detail. "Let's just say things happened." "Don't tell me. Now you're having twins," Camille joked. "Why would I have twins, Cam?"

"Cause y'all did the nasty while you're already expecting."

"We didn't get that far but we were pretty intimate."

"Did he lick the cooch?"

"Waiter!" Monique had heard just about enough. She ushered the waiter over so that she could place her order. "Would you like the usual – apple martini with a lemon cake?"

Camille intervened, "She'll take an apple *juice* with a lemon cake but an apple martini for me please." Monique shook her head. "Give her alcoholic ass some water. She has no chill when she's drunk."

Camille cackled. "Mo, you're so silly. Don't you know that I never have any chill?" "Well, you can't argue facts." At the same time, the old friends burst into a fit a laughter. For a moment, they were 16 again. Monique and Camille had been in the same Biology class and, one day, they were both bored out of their minds. Camille had cracked a joke, Monique had laughed and a long-lasting bond had been bred.

"Do you remember Mr. Harriot?"

"Our sophomore Bio teacher?"

"Yes!!!"

Camille rolled her eyes. "Who doesn't remember that old geezer?" She slouched over in her chair. "Any of you ever been to a tundra? It's cold, really cold! I went to a tundra once...." Camille began snoring, executing a perfect impersonation of their old teacher. "Cam, you make me laugh."

"I know, Mo. You make me make you laugh."

"You make no sense."

"But I'll never change."

Again, the two burst into laughter then the waiter came. After their chatty meal and chatty ride home, Monique was in a great mood.

On the contrary, Dre's day could have been better. He had lost his case in court, been scolded by his boss, and was beginning to feel swallowed by the environment around him. As he searched for his stress ball, he discovered an old picture of Monique – one he'd put away to keep from depressing himself. On the back, it said: Mo's first trip to Disney Land. Dre recalled the day vividly and suddenly his mood shifted. He had a sudden urge to call Monique.

"Monique Ross' office. How may I help you?" "Put me through to Monique please." Dominque sighed. "One second."

When Monique heard who it was, she just rubbed her temples. "I'll take the call."

"What do you want, Andre?" She began.

"Nice to hear from you too."

"I'm busy. I don't have time to talk." Dre sighed disappointedly. "Alright. Well, I just wanted to hear your voice." "Bye Andre." Monique hung up, not realizing Dre was on the verge of a breakdown and he had called to hear her soothing words of encouragement.

Genna came knocking on Dre's office door. "Hey. You okay?" He worked to pull himself together. "I'm fine. Thanks for asking. What can I help you with?" She flashed two tickets. "There's a certain sold out concert tonight that I just so happen to have gotten tickets for."

"Are you asking me on a date, Miss Marx?" Genna shrugged. "I don't know. Am I?"

"I'll go," he answered impulsively. Upset by Monique's treatment, Dre made that choice.

Although her lunch date with Camille had gone well, Monique still had an ill feeling in her stomach. Deep down, she was extremely worried about her imminent press conference. *What will I say to the people? Will they even believe me? Will Mo's Mix go under?* Monique tried to contain herself but she knew she would have an anxiety attack sooner or later. Dominque came running in with water.

"Hey, boss. I saw you pacing the floor and I got worried."

"Thank you, Dominique. You're a lifesaver."

Dominique nodded and went to get Monique a dry towel. "If those reporters see you sweating, they'll know you're nervous then they will eat you alive. Stay strong, boss." "I will. Thank you." Monique took one deep breath and exited towards the conference room.

"Hello everyone. My name is Monique Ross and I am the founder and CEO of Mo's Mix. Recently, an article was published about Mo's Mix that was supposed to expose our 'dirty practices.' However, the information provided in the article dates back to last July – when the scientists here at Mo's Mix performed the *first* trial of our newest product. Since then, the product has progressively gotten better.

"Here at Mo's Mix, we have a dedication to integrity. We would not release a product that would intentionally harm our consumers so we do apologize for the misinformation. The issue has since been taken care of." Monique folded her hands. "Any questions?"

Almost every hand shot up. She selected a lady in a blue sweater. "Rae Sherman of NBC. Ms. Ross, what do you mean when you say that the issue has 'been taken care of'?"

"The scientist who released the information is no longer associated with Mo's Mix."

"What do you have to say to April Spring's comments then?"

Monique held her posture. "I have no response for that. Any other questions?" She selected a guy in green suspenders. "Hi.

I'm Carlos Lockwood of Trinity Magazine. You say that the information released is relative to the first trial. Will you be releasing information about the subsequent trials then?"

"I am sorry, Mr. Lockwood. I am not at liberty to do that."

"Why not?"

Monique had vowed not to entertain the asinine questions. She pointed towards a lady in a yellow beret. "Yes, ma'am. You in the back." Carlos snatched the mic from the woman. "Sorry, Ms. Ross. I didn't hear you answer. Why is it that you won't release information from the other trials so the public can see the validity in your statement?"

Monique sighed. "It is my hope that once consumers use our new product they will see that it has no adverse effects." "But, what makes you think they will trust you?"

This was a hard question and Monique could not quickly produce an answer. After a while, she stated, "When Mo's Mix first began, I told a story about my journey with natural hair, which latched on to the hearts of many. Nothing has changed since then. I do sincerely hope that my consumers will see that Mo's got their back because I do. I have vowed to always operate in my consumer's best interest."

Monique rose where she was. "I thank you all for your time but I'm afraid I must be going." She could feel a gurgling in her stomach and she didn't want the presses to know that she had a baby on the way. "Goodbye." Dominique quickly shut the conference door so that no reporters could pass through. "You were great up there, boss."

"Mhmm."

Monique could not open her mouth, for fear that vomit would come out. "Is everything alright?"

She held up her two fingers, which signaled Dominique to give Monique two minutes alone. In the bathroom, Monique barfed all her troubles into the stool. Then, for some reason, she called Andre. "Hey, Dre. I've been thinking and I don't want to do this alone. I know I seemed adamant about that abortion but I'm really just confused. I'm sorry about putting you off earlier. I just had this press conference and--" The voice mailbox tone came on.

Monique called back and left one more message. "I love you, Dre. Call me back once you get this."

Dre was enjoying his time with Genna and he began thinking of moving on from Monique. He and Genna went back to his apartment after the concert and they were drinking heavy. Although Dre was not exactly denying Genna's advances, he did tell her he would not sleep with her. After having been with Monique the night before, Dre felt it wasn't right. This disappointed Genna so she excused herself to the bathroom.

While Genna "sobered up," Dre finally turned his phone back on and noticed he had two missed calls from Monique. Upon listening to her voicemails, he suddenly had a change of heart. He could not leave his lady love behind. "Genna, I think I'm going to have to call you a cab." As Dre was speaking, the bathroom door flew open with Genna clad in only a bra. "What were you saying?"

Though it was tempting to entertain Genna, Dre stuck to his guns. "I'm not completely over Monique and I honestly think that she and I will end up back together. So, I don't want to string you along." Genna eased herself on top of Dre. "You won't be stringing me along. I'll help you forget Monique."

"She's…she's about to have my baby."

Genna finally ceased in her advances. "Oh." Dre pulled himself to the other side of the couch. "I know I should've told you this before I went out on a date--" Genna put her hand up. "I'll just be going." Truthfully, Dre felt bad because he had led Genna to believe she had a chance.

Analyzing his actions further, Dre realized that he wasn't thinking straight partly because he had lost his leading lady and partly because he was stressing about bringing a child into the world. *What will I teach my son? Will I be able to protect my daughter? Will Monique and I find other people before our child is born?*

These thoughts ran through Dre's mind and he worried himself. He worried himself so much that he began to drink and drink and drink some more. By early morning, Dre's state of mind contended that "drunk" was merely an understatement.

"You nailed that press conference. I wonder what April Spring will have to say about that one." Monique picked around at her salad. "My baby is becoming a businesswoman." Mr. Ross kissed his daughter's head. "I recorded you on my phone." Monique finally smiled. "Really, daddy?"

"Yes, really. I loved the way you handled yourself in front of those reporters. It's as if you could care less what they had to say. You have confidence in what you're doing with Mo's Mix. I like that. I sometimes even admire that." Monique smiled wider. "Thanks, dad. That makes me really happy."

"Of course, baby girl. You should've heard your mama. She was screaming, 'That's my baby, that's my baby!' It was so cute." "Where is mama, by the way?" Mr. Ross sighed. "She's still at the dry cleaner's. She works there day in and day out."

"I don't understand why you guys still work. I could take care of you."

"No, Mo. You earned your money. Let us earn ours." Monique knew her father was too prideful and her mother too pompous to take any money from their youngest child. "Where are James and Daniel?" At the sound of his name, James came in with his daughter in tow.

"Auntie Mo!" 3-year-old Arielle ran to greet her favorite, and only, aunt. "Hey, Ari. How are you?" Arielle grinned. "I'm great. How are you, auntie Mo?" Monique smiled. "I'm great too." Monique lifted Arielle and kissed her big brother on the cheek. "Hey, Jamie. What's new with you?"

"Nothing much. I'm still running grandpa's old auto shop. How about you?"

"Oh, you know, the same. Running a business too."

He grinned. "I heard my baby sister was on TV. Congrats, Mo." Monique nodded. "Thanks. Where's Daniel?" James shrugged, which could only mean one thing. Monique asked, "Is he back on the stuff?"

Before she could get a straight answer, Mrs. Ross returned. "My baby! Hey!" She kissed her daughter over and over. "Your hair's growing. What have you been using?"

"I don't think it's products that are making my hair grow."

Mrs. Ross looked down at Monique's belly. "You're not...?" Monique looked around at most of her immediate family. "I'm pregnant, guys." They were all ecstatic. Mr. Ross lifted Mrs. Ross in the air. Arielle skipped because she was going to be a cousin. James smiled.

That was one thing about Monique's family. In whatever she did, they were supportive. In whatever any one of their family members did, they were supportive. That was just a Ross tradition: support.

"How far along is it?" James asked.

"Last time I went to the doctor, I was 6 weeks so, right now, I'm probably at about 8 weeks."

"You still seeing that guy? Andre?" Monique looked down. "No, actually. We broke up a little while back but he is the father." James lifted her head up. "He's been supportive, though, right? Because, if not--" Monique put her hand on James' shoulder. "You have nothing to worry about with Andre, okay?" James nodded and they continued their walk.

"Where do you think Daniel could've gone?" James wondered.

"Auntie Pam's cabin, maybe?"

James snapped. "You're right. I'll drive over there." Auntie Pamela was the second mother to the Ross children. Whenever their parents worked late shifts, she would babysit and tell ghost stories. Although she never had any kids of her own, Auntie Pamela treated the Ross children like her children. So, when she died, it was devastating, especially for Daniel. He had known her the longest.

James and Monique approached the house slowly. They knew that if Daniel was having one of his moments, danger lay ahead. "Yes, Auntie. I miss you too." Inside, Daniel sat next to an old rocking chair. It was the one that Auntie Pam had taken her last breath in. From the corner, Monique and James watched in silent desperation.

They wanted to get their brother some help but knew he was past the point of recovery. Daniel sat by the rocking chair and cried. Monique and James came behind him. When Monique and James hugged Daniel, they could smell weed on him. But, they knew better than to lecture Daniel about his lifestyle.

"Hey, guys. You're just in time. Auntie Pam is about to make us all cookies. Aren't you, Auntie Pam?" Daniel stared at the empty rocking chair. "She's asking if you want chocolate chip or oatmeal...or oatmeal...or oatmeal raisin." Daniel burst into another fit of tears. Their late aunt had loved oatmeal raisin cookies.

"Daniel, you should come home. Auntie Pam needs her rest."

Daniel shook his head. "She's rested for too long. I want her to wake up." James said, "You think talking to her chair will bring her back?" Daniel cried, "It might! It's better than acting like nothing's wrong."

"We haven't forgotten Auntie Pam," Monique noted. "We've just accepted that although she's not in our lives, she lives in our hearts." Daniel touched Monique's stomach. "It sounds like she might live in your stomach." That was one thing about Daniel. It had been inexplicable since he was young but he was very intuitive when it came to pregnancy.

"I'm pregnant, Daniel." He smiled up at Monique. "I'm gonna be an Uncle. Again." She nodded. "You sure are." This made Daniel really happy and his siblings were finally able to pull him out of the abandoned cabin. Deep down, James and Monique knew Daniel would eventually find his way back but his presence right then was good enough, even if only momentary.

When Monique got ready to leave, Arielle wrapped herself around Monique's legs.

"Auntie Mo, when am I gonna see you again?"

Monique kissed her niece's head. "Soon, Arielle. I'll be back soon." She gave her family hugs and kisses then went on her way.

"It was good to see them, Dre. You don't understand how much I missed them." Dre scanned Monique. "No, I don't. Tell me more."

"Well, I missed James the most. I missed smelling his uniform. It always smells like car parts but that's what I love about it. That's *James'* scent. Then, his daughter Arielle is the greatest niece on the planet. Every time I see Laila, James' wife, I thank her for bringing such a beautiful baby girl into the world." Dre nodded. "That's lovely. Keep talking." Monique smiled. "You actually like hearing about my family?"

"I just love hearing your voice."

Monique went on and on and Dre just sat and listened. When he did that, Monique realized how deeply in love with her he was. And she felt the same. "Dre." "Yes, Mo?" She took his hand. "I am so sorry that I ever let anything come between us. I love you and I want you back. I want you in my life and in our child's life."

Dre kissed her head. "I love you too, Monique."

They kissed and it was full of passion – a sort of climactic passion. The food Monique was cooking got put on hold just so she could make love to her man. She whispered in his ear, "Say it. Say what I love to hear."

Dre grinned and chanted, "Oh, oh, oh. It's the Mo and Dre show." Monique smiled. "Say it again." Dre did. He sang the song as many times as Monique desired because he wanted to make her happy.

"You're looking well," Caleb said when he saw Dre. "You too, boss. Thanks." "You're back with Monique," Caleb suspected. "How'd you know?" "A man always knows."

Dre grinned and proceeded to his office. There, he sat the picture of him and Monique upright so anyone who entered would see the love of his life. Later on, Monique came to visit.

"Andre, I would just like to formally apologize for the other…" Genna paused when she noticed that Monique stood at Andre's desk. "Oh, I'm sorry. Have you seen Andre?" Monique nodded. "He said he'll be back shortly. Can I ask who you are?"

"My name is Genna."

Immediately, worry surfaced in Monique's eyes. "I'm Monique." Immediately, worry surfaced in Genna's eyes. The two women knew of each other but they had never actually met. "May I ask why you need to see Andre," Monique questioned.

"That's between me and Andre," Genna asserted. "Very well." Monique had never been one to pry. Andre would tell her, she internally decided. Upon his return, the tension heightened. "Hey, Genna. What can I help you with?"

"I wanted to discuss with you the *case* from this weekend." With that, Genna left. Monique stared at Dre. "What's she talking about, Dre? What case?" Dre quickly shuffled papers at his desk. "We...um...we went on a date this weekend, Mo. It was before you and I got back together."

"*This weekend?* When?" Monique folded her arms.

Dre sighed. "It was Saturday. You had put me off so I thought why not." "Did you plan on telling me about it? And what does she have to apologize for?"

"What are you talking about?"

Monique let out a deep breath. "She came in saying that she wanted to formally apologize for something." Dre panicked. He didn't know how to explain Genna's being at his house without making it sound like he had sex with her. But, he had vowed to keep honesty in his relationship. "Okay, she came over after the date. I told her I was not going to have sex with her but she still stripped and tried to have sex with me. I let her know that you were having my baby so..."

Dre stopped there because of Monique's face. "You told her I was pregnant? That wasn't your business to tell," she stated. "It was the only way to get Genna off." Monique scoffed. "Maybe you wouldn't have had to worry about that if she wasn't in your condo in the first place. Did that thought ever occur to you, Andre?"

The entire office was engaged in Monique and Dre's conversation. "Mo, can you please quiet down? You're causing a scene."

Monique rolled her eyes. "I can't believe you right now. You know what? I'm going to get lunch. When I come back, we will finish our conversation."

Almost as soon as Monique left, Genna popped back up. "So, what, is she your girlfriend again?" "Genna, I don't have time for this. I thank you for the concert tickets but we are co-workers so anything besides a work relationship is highly inappropriate. On top of that, I am back with Monique, which means that whatever we may have had is over."

Dre's words hurt Genna; it was obvious from her facial expression. Still, she straightened her back and walked out of his office with the little bit of pride she had left.

Monique tried hard to maintain her composure. She had taken an extended lunch to see Dre mainly about starting her case but also about reconnecting since they had lost two months. Yet, she was side-tracked when Genna stepped into his office. *Who is Genna anyway? Now that Dre and I are back together, will she be a threat to our relationship?* Because Monique was so preoccupied with her situation, she ran a red light and nearly hit an older woman. The older woman's daughter hopped in front of Monique's car as Monique slammed on the break.

"Watch where you're going!"

Because Mo's Mix was already hot in the presses, reporters were quick to snap pictures of the incident. Monique tried hard to hide her face. *This is not a good look for my company.* Minutes later, April Spring tweeted:

@SpringOfWisdom

Didn't anyone teach you to respect your elders?

@MoniqueRoss @MosMix #ThisDidntGoUnnoticed

Monique groaned and threw her phone onto the passenger seat. An officer came knocking on her window. "Ma'am?" She took a deep breath. "Yes?"

"May I please see your license and registration?" Monique quickly produced them. After taking down Monique's information, the officer issued her a ticket and said the victim's lawyer would be in contact with her to discuss a settlement. Monique was just gracious that she wasn't arrested. *Now* ***that*** *would've been a story for Spring.*

After the officer left, Monique got out to apologize to the daughter. "You were really brave for what you did. I'm sorry that I almost hit your mother." The lady stood. "Thank you for your apology. Luckily, you just bruised my ankle." "I'll pay any hospital fees if necessary," Monique promised. The lady nodded and helped her mother to a nearby van. "My attorney will be in touch."

Chapter II – *Monique and Dre worked through their differences once Dre reassured Monique that he wasn't going anywhere. On the contrary, the reputation of Mo's Mix still hangs in the fray.*

A FEW WEEKS AHEAD

"What do you mean you don't want that in the house?"

Monique sighed and pushed back her afro. "I *mean* that that statue is hideous and it will ruin the Feng shui."

Dre shook his head. "That's not what you said last week, though." "I changed my mind, Dre. Plus, we'll eventually have a baby running around. What if the statue falls and crushes our child?" Dre promised, "I'll keep it far away from the baby."

"So you mean in storage," Monique assumed. Dre groaned. "I agreed to let you have an entire den for your hair care products but you won't even allow me this slither of space for my statue?" "There are bigger things to worry about, Dre," Monique noted as she went to the phone. "Ross and Cassells Residence. How may I help you? Flowers? I didn't order any flowers." Dre quickly kissed her on the cheek and ran down the stairs.

He came back up with a large bouquet. "For you." Monique smiled. "What for?" "You're my lady. I don't need a reason." Monique put the bouquet down and kissed Dre. "How 'bout this? The statue can go in the house at a safer location."

"I would like that."

After sharing a few more kisses, Monique and Dre got back to planning what their house would look like. Dre slipped and said, "Our wedding picture would go right there." This led to a moment of silence. "Or am I still not allowed to touch that topic," he verbalized.

"Dre, this is what caused us problems last time."

"I know but we should at least talk about it. After all, we are having a baby together."

Monique rubbed her stomach. "Right now, I have a business to think about. We can discuss marriage once this crisis is over." Dre became infuriated. "Who's helping you with the crisis, though?! I am! I'm the one putting in extra hours just to work the case because someone is suing you!"

Monique didn't appreciate his yelling. "Yeah, but when was the last time you actually won a case?! I'm grateful for your help but I won't hold my breath on you getting Mo's Mix out of this hole."

Dre shook his head. "It's just those pregnancy hormones. You don't mean that." "What if I--" He slammed the door before Monique could finish what she was saying. She thought to herself: *What if I did mean it?*

Although she loved Dre, Monique knew what was what. He'd been in a "sophomore slump" throughout his second year at Paul and Friends and Monique, regrettably, hadn't taken notice to it until after she put him as the attorney for Mo's Mix. *Never mix business with pleasure,* Monique reminded herself. "Why not just drop him," Camille had asked. "That could cause a riff in our relationship," Monique had responded. Still, Camille had a point. Mo's Mix was at stake and Monique didn't know if she could count on Dre to help the business.

Dre ended up at his mother's house. Someone was suing Monique because the person claimed Mo's Mix messed their hair up. Then, two people had released testimonials arguing in favor of the plaintiff. Ironically, the two people did not come out with statements until after April Spring's article was published. So, Dre was on a mission. He sought to get one on one interviews with people whom he knew used Mo's Mix products faithfully. One of such people was his mother.

Though people could hardly tell, Mrs. Cassells was Ethiopian on her father's side and it showed in her hair. The first time Dre brought one of Monique's products to his mother, Mrs. Cassells was skeptical. She didn't believe it would work for her texture. Then, after a while, she started to see a positive result and she had begun using many more products from Mo's Mix.

Dre kept that in mind as he stepped inside his old house.

"Hi, mamma," he said as he kissed Mrs. Cassells' cheeks. "Ciao," Mrs. Cassells responded. "English, mamma," Dre begged. As she got older in age, Dre's mother had switched back to her native language. However, Dre – being born in the states – was only privy to minimal Italian. His father, who was fluent in Italian after being stationed in Italy during the war, had passed.

"You won't get through to her, Andre," Nathalie said. "She'll only speak in Italian." Dre's older sister handed their mother a bowl of soup. Mrs. Cassells accepted it graciously and stated, "Grazie." Nathalie nodded then looked back at her brother. "Why are you here? You seem worried, Andre."

"You remember my girlfriend Monique?"

"Sì."

Dre groaned. "Please speak English." Nathalie rolled her eyes. "Why don't you just learn Italian, huh? You ashamed of your *cultura*?"

"My *cultura* is not just Italian, though. It's also Jamaican and Mexican." Nathalie cringed. "Those belonged to papà. Mamma – she was Italiana; that's all."

"What about nonno," Dre asked. "He was *Etiope*, not *Italiano*." Nathalie asserted, "Nonna and mamma both called themselves Italiana. If they are Italian, so are we."

Dre shook his head. "So, because papà's gone you just forget about him?"

Manny Cassells, their father, used to beat Mrs. Cassells when she sassed him. Added to this, Mrs. Cassells said that her father used to beat her and her mother. "You don't remember what he did to mamma and what she said *nonno* did to her?" Nathalie challenged. Dre closed his eyes and attempted to block the painfully vivid memory. He wouldn't go to bat for his grandfather, because Dre had never met Mrs. Cassells' father, but Dre would go to bat for Manny Cassells, a scorned man who had to subdue his war demons. "Regardless, he was still our papà."

Dre's sister scoffed. "Yeah? Try telling that to your fratellos and sorellas." Dre scratched his head. "My what?" Nathalie shook her head. "Your brothers and sisters, dummy."

"Hey! I've told you about the name calling." She just shrugged and kneeled at her mama's side. Dre went to see his siblings. "Karen, Lauren, Miguel, Georgiana, David!"

Lauren ran and hugged her big brother. "Fratello! Ciao!" She kissed Dre on his cheeks. The other siblings followed suit.

Karen, who was always excited to see Dre, started rambling off in Italian. Once she saw that her brother was confused, she sighed. "Nathalie said you weren't going to learn our language." Dre noted, "Noi siamo Americano," which translated to "We are American."

Karen gasped. "I thought you didn't know Italian." "I only know a little," Dre began. "Cosi, io preferisco parlare in inglese." Nathalie came back as if she gravitated towards the first sign of her "native" language. She stared directly at Dre. "Infine," she said, meaning "Finally."

After establishing some general dialect with his mother, Dre had brushed up on the little Italian he knew and he was able to speak to Mrs. Cassells. Of course, Nathalie was there translating whenever Dre got stuck (which was quite often). A little while into the conversation, Dre brought up Mo's Mix. Mrs. Cassells, while confused at first, finally understood when Dre repeated "Capelli" a few times. This was the Italian word for "hair."

Mrs. Cassells beamed, "Buono! Buono! Buono!" Nathalie started to translate, but Dre stopped her. "I know what that one means," he said.

"Buono, buono," Dre repeated as he came back home. Monique came forward with remorse-filled eyes. "Babe, can I talk to you?" It had been hours, Dre realized. He guessed an apology was coming. "Sì." Monique stared at him. "Why are you speaking Spanish?"

"Not Spanish, Italian," Dre corrected. "But sì means yes in multiple languages and you have multiple cultures so I sometimes get confused." Dre kissed Monique's cheek. "Okay, let's try English. Yes, we can talk." Monique smiled. "That's better."

As Dre suspected, Monique did apologize and she also asked where he was at on the case. Although Monique originally had her doubts, she decided that her love for Dre superseded those doubts and she was willing to give him a chance. They sat down and Monique studied Dre's notes. While she couldn't speak Italian, she noticed one word that was repeated. "Buono? What does that mean?"

"It means we're getting somewhere."

Dre began showing Monique his plan, but she got a phone call from work. "Hold on a second, babe. It sounds good, though." She kissed Dre's cheek and went to her phone. "Hello? Wait, what? Slow down. One more time, Donna. Are you kidding me? Wow. Thanks for telling me." Monique hung up the phone and put her hand to her head. "What's wrong?"

"Someone else just came out saying my product tarnished their hair. I wonder how much Spring is paying these people for this."

Dre wondered, "Do you think you can find a motive? I mean, why would someone want to bring you down?" Monique went over the history of Mo's Mix in her head. The only time she'd made an enemy was when she supposedly put "Cocoa Puff" out of business, although the company was already plummeting when Monique entered the market.

"Who ran Cocoa Puff," she asked aloud. Then, she thought about something. "This is the digital age. I can just use the internet." Monique typed the "Cocoa Puff" into a search box then read, "The owner of Cocoa Puff – Malaysia Summers – stated that though the business was no more, she intended to re-emerge someday."

Dre looked over. "Do you think Summers and Spring have anything in common?" Monique pulled up April's twitter page. "I think they have a lot in common."

She compared the pictures. "Does this look like the same lady to you?" He scanned both the images. "I would say so." Monique nodded. "Then there's our motive. Because Cocoa Puff went down the drain, Spring is seeking to do the same with Mo's Mix."

"Where does Nicole come into this? Wasn't she the one who leaked the information?"

Monique scrolled down on the biography of Cocoa Puff. "That's what I was getting to. Nicole was a repertory player for Cocoa Puff. I guess I have to start running background checks."

"You don't already?"

Monique shook her head. "I never saw a need to. I didn't think some sleazy ex-entrepreneur would be coming after me."

Dre sighed. "It's the business world. You have to prepare for anything."

"Monique, where are you taking me?" She checked to make sure Daniel's blindfold was on all the way. "You'll see when we get there." He huffed. "I already told you. For my 35th birthday, I just want to chill at the bar." Monique, seeing that they'd reached their destination, snatched the blindfold off. "Who needs the bar when there's speed dating?"

Daniel stared blankly at her. "Speed dating? Really?"

"I figured you haven't dated in a while so it would be nice for you to test the waters." Daniel shook his head. "I hope they brought some men." Monique raised her eyebrow. "Men?" "Oh, yeah. You didn't know?"

"Since when were you into men, Daniel?"

"Since God made me that way. I came out of the closet while you were away at school."

Monique nodded. "*That's* why I stopped seeing you bring girls around and dad said you were out with your 'male friends'." Daniel nodded and scanned the room for a man who looked approachable. "Yep. I hope I find a nice guy who likes it rough." Monique put her hand up. "TMI."

"You straights tend to be more conservative."

Monique scoffed. "Us straights? Now you're labeling?" "Well, if it walks like a duck and quacks like a duck," Daniel murmured as he walked off. Monique just stood behind and smiled. She was happy that Daniel could crack jokes because she knew he was letting his personality out. She wanted Daniel to do more than cry over Auntie Pamela. "Mo? What are *you* doing here?" Someone asked, breaking Monique from her thoughts.

Camille walked in, clad in nothing but a skimpy black romper. "Hey, Cam. I'm helping my brother celebrate his 35th birthday. What are you doing here?" Camille flashed her ring-less finger. "Turns out, you were right. Never get engaged to someone you meet at Walmart. It took me going out to lunch with Donald to find out just how possessive Trevor is. He stalked Donald down and started sending him threats. I had to end things with him after that."

Monique, while she didn't approve of the way Camille was dressed, was happy that Camille was glowing. "You look good when you're by yourself, Camille. Can we just try a few more inches on the shorts next time?" Camille grabbed a drink and rolled her eyes. "We'll see." Monique laughed as her friend trotted to table after table. At the same time, her eldest brother lingered at one table. "You have an interesting story, Daniel. I like interesting things."

The guy rubbed Daniel's arm. At first, it seemed affectionate. Then, it seemed to be an early sign of possession. Monique walked over. "Hey, D. Who's this?" The guy stuck his polished hand out. "I go by Christina but you can call me Christian if it makes you feel better."

"If it...?" Christina continued, "I know how you women are when it comes to gay men. You think we're trying to imitate you. Truthfully, though, I could rock that outfit ten times better." Monique sighed. "I'm sure you could." Although she had qualms early on about Christina, Monique decided that Daniel could handle himself. "I'll leave you two alone."

By the end of the night, Daniel and Christina had a date scheduled and Camille was supposed to call a few men. Camille whispered, "I'm not calling any of them," while giggling, clearly drunk. Monique took her friend's arm. "Let me drive you home." "I'm fine," Camille said, "I'll just hail a cab like I did earlier."

"You don't have to."

Monique got an ominous vibe when pulling up to Camille's apartment. Something seemed off. "Did you leave your lights on?" She asked Camille. Camille looked up. "Huh? What'd you say?" Monique stopped the engine. "I said 'Come on.' Grab your purse and whatever else you brought with you."

Camille groaned. "Okay, mom." Monique took her friend by the hip. "Come on, drunkie. You know you're truly an alcoholic when you get buzzed after speed dating. They only had shot glasses and you didn't even go to enough tables to get drunk."

"I may have had a bottle of something before I left." Camille giggled as she spoke.

"You sure did. I can smell it on your breath."

Camille continued to giggle. When Monique unlocked the door, she noticed that it was off its hinges. She quickly sat Camille on the couch and scanned the area. "Hello? Who's here?" In seconds, Monique was covered in a foreign substance.

Chapter III – *After months of hard work and many tears, Monique had finally gotten her hair to a stable state. This was until she encountered Camille's surprise visitor.*

5 HOURS LATER

"What happened to her?"

"We don't know all the details but the EMT on site said that…"

After he heard, all Dre could do was stare at his lady. He was in so much shock. "Mo? Are you okay?" Monique opened her eyes for the first time since the incident. "Wh-where am I?" She held her head. "Why does the back of my head hurt so badly?"

Dre rubbed Monique's shoulder. "Someone broke into Camille's house. They poured a mix of ammonia, DHT, and other things onto your head and it burned your scalp. Also, your arms got burned a little. Luckily, none of the chemicals got into your bloodstream so the baby's okay."

"Who would do something like this, though," Dre inquired. Monique thought back to what Camille said at speed dating. "Camille was engaged to this guy, Trevor. She met him at Walmart but she went to have lunch with an old friend, Donald. Once Trevor found out, he got jealous and began stalking Donald. At that point, Camille broke things off so this may have been retaliation."

Dre shook his head. "The detectives said eyewitnesses saw a *woman* fleeing the crime scene and taking the evidence with her. They chased the woman down but then she made a sharp turn and they lost her."

Monique continued to massage her head. "Well, that was my best guess." She had a massive headache. "How bad is it?" Dre grabbed a mirror. "Take a look." Monique gasped when she first saw her head. She flashed back to depressing nights where she sat crying after she'd damaged her scalp months before. However, she had moved past that and grown her hair back. Now, Monique was back at square one.

"Dre, could you hold me?" He put the mirror down. "Of course. Come here." Dre kissed Monique's partially bald head. "You're still beautiful." She looked at him graciously. "Thanks, Dre."

"Always."

The workers gasped when Monique returned. She had requested that information regarding the incident remain confidential. So, none of the presses knew what happened, which meant none of the workers knew either. Monique pranced past with all of the confidence she could muster. *You can do this, Mo,* she told herself. Deep down, though, she felt herself crumbling to shreds. Monique had barely handled the social pressures before. She was not prepared to start then.

"Hi, boss. How was your weekend?" Monique gave a somewhat genuine smile. "It was fine. Thanks for asking. How was yours?" Dominique pulled out her Jotter. "Mine was great, actually. I dug up a lot of information on this April Spring lady. Apparently, she used to run Cocoa Puff – that atrocious business that preceded Mo's Mix. But, no one knows she ran Cocoa Puff because she changed her name. So I took a picture of Malaysia Summers from the internet and put it next to Spring. They were an exact match." Dominique pointed at the screen. "There's this app called Exacto that tells you if two pictures are the same person. The report came back and said 100%, meaning April Spring used to run Cocoa Puff." Monique folded her hands together. "Thank you for discovering that. Will you please email those results to andrecassells@paulnfriends.net?" Dominique scratched her head. "You mean your ex-boyfriend who apparently represents us now?"

Monique sighed. "Don't ask questions, Dominique. Just do as I say." Dominique nodded and went back to her own office. Monique glanced at herself in the mirror. *You can do this, Mo.* Donna came in next. "Bad news. A fifth person came out saying--" Monique put her hand up. "Just take care of it, Donna. I don't need you to tell me every time someone said my product messed them up. Just get Andre on the phone and fix it, okay?"

While Monique externally scolded Donna, she internally wondered: *how are you going to fix the crisis of your hair?*

"Oh, hey Monique. Are you starting a new trend?" Monique rolled her eyes at the desk girl. "Can I see Laila?" Felicia smacked her gum. "Laila don't work here no more. That bad ass lil daughter of hers was starting up too much trouble." "You mean my niece?" Felicia opened her mouth wide. "Wait. Laila yo sister?" "In law," Monique informed Felicia while exiting the shop.

The last thing Monique had wanted was to go near her old neighborhood. She knew what the kids would say. She even knew what the adults would say. So, Monique phoned Laila. "I'm not near my phone right now but if you leave a message, I'll surely get back to you. Laila." The voicemail tone came on and Monique cleared her throat. "Hey, Laila. I just... I need some hair advice. Please call me back as soon as you get this message. This is Monique."

Almost five seconds later, Laila returned the call. "Hey! I was just giving the little one a bath. What can I help you with?" Monique heard her niece in the background screaming, "MAMA!!" Laila groaned. "Coming, sweetie!" Then, she asked Monique, "Why don't you come over? If it's a hair emergency, it's better I deal with it in person, right?"

"Right."

Although Monique agreed, she was not thrilled to see Laila. She'd remembered when she was experimenting with her hair in high school and Laila was one of the ones who had teased her. Years later, much to Monique's surprise and dismay, James said that he'd "cuffed the Prom Queen." Six years after that, Arielle was brought into the picture. Boy, how the times have changed, Monique thought to herself. Although Laila was not necessarily Monique's first choice, Monique knew that Laila had a special touch when it came to hair.

She pulled up to James and Laila's apartment building and tried to move as quickly as possible. She didn't want anyone to see her. "Monique! Monique Ross!" She huffed when someone spotted her. Laurie, Monique's old classmate, came from the mail room. "Hey! How are you?" Monique made a conscious effort to turn her head so that Laurie would only see the front of it.

"I'm fine, actually. How are you?" Laurie smiled. "I'm great. I heard you started a business." "Mo's Mix, yeah. We create and manufacture hair care products targeted mainly towards African American men, women, and children; our slogan is 'natural locks rock'." Laurie looked at Monique's hair. "Let me see your hair. I mean, if you create hair care products, your hair would have to be great, right?"

"Actually…" Just in the nick of time, Laila called Monique and buzzed her in. For a second, Monique thought she had dodged a bullet. Then, she realized Laurie would see her hair when she ascended the stairs. Monique moved as quickly as possible. Still, she heard a shocked gasp emit from Laurie's lips. *Stay strong,* she told herself.

Laila quickly let Monique in and ran to help Arielle. Monique stood marveling at the décor of the apartment. *This does not fit the rundown building they live in,* she thought to herself. Laila, a savvy shopper, had found all sorts of trinkets at an affordable price. *She has to design my house,* Monique decided. Laila finally returned.

"Jesus, she's a handful. Get ready."

"Get ready?"

Laila looked at Monique's stomach. "James said you were…" Monique said, "Oh. Yeah. I am." Laila scratched her head. "Did you forget you were pregnant?"

"Maybe I want to."

"Oh, the pregnancy blues. I remember those. You'll forget them once your little monster is born."

Monique looked up at Laila. "My 'little monster'?" Laila showed Monique scars. "I won't sugarcoat it. Being a mom ain't always easy. I have a little person kicking me and biting me and scratching me and screaming at me 24/7. Then again," Laila looked at a nearby picture of Arielle. "I have little one who I can dress up, who I can teach, who I get to watch grow. The good offsets the bad."

Monique admitted, "It was a kind of spur of the moment pregnancy. We were a little thrown off by it." "We? James said you weren't with the father."

"James tells you a lot, huh?"

Laila nodded. "He's my husband; that's his job. When he's coming home from work and I know he's had a long day, I give him a nice foot massage and ask him everything that happened. It's how we communicate." Monique thought on Laila's words. *Is that what marriage is? It doesn't sound so bad.* Laila continued, "Sometimes, my sister offers to babysit Arielle because she loves to spend time with her niece. So, James and me get some alone time and we just kick back, relax, and relay whatever's happened in the week. It's so tranquil."

Monique nodded. "It sounds like you two are happy." Laila smiled. "We are. I cannot believe we're about to reach our ten-year anniversary." Monique asked, "Do you all have plans?" "Yes," Laila answered. "James is taking me to the beach where we met. He said it's one you all always went to as kids. One day I was sitting listening to him play guitar on the beach. The next, I was watching him fix cars. Before I knew it, we were married and we had Arielle."

"James plays guitar?"

Laila nodded. "You didn't know? He said he would've been a musician but your father stressed about him getting a," Laila began using air quotes, "more 'practical' job." Monique just sat and listened. There were things she did not know about her brother, she realized. Laila could see that Monique was getting uncomfortable. "Well, let's see your hair. Isn't that why you came here?"

Monique nodded and turned so that Laila could see the back. "Oh, that's not good but it's not completely unfixable. I have an idea. Just give me one second." Laila went to her room and Monique sat at a kitchen stool. This was when James came back. "James has returned," he pronounced. In seconds, Arielle ran from her room to the kitchen to the front door. "Daddy! Daddy! Daddy! I missed you *so* much." He picked her up and chuckled. "I missed you too, baby girl. Where's your mama?"

Arielle pointed to her parent's room. When she did this, Arielle and James both noticed Monique sitting at a kitchen stool. Monique turned the stool so they would only see her face. "Hey y'all." James kissed her head. "Sis, what animal mauled the back of your head?"

Monique sighed. Her brother was always candid. But, he saw that his joke was lost on his younger sister. "Hey, Ari, why don't you go back to watching cartoons while I talk to your aunt?"

"Okay!" Arielle kissed her dad and Monique then skipped back to her room. James asked, "What happened, sis?" Laila came back out at this point. "Tada!" She brought forth a wig. "This way, you won't have to deal with the social pressures." Monique stared blankly at Laila. "I'll pass."

Monique rose where she was. "I'll see you later, James." She kissed her big brother on the cheek then exited.

"A wig, Laila? All my sister's been through and you try to give her wig?"

Laila sighed. "What else could I have done? There's no easy remedy for that, James." "Did she tell you what happened," James wondered, realizing Monique had ignored his question. "Evasive as usual," Laila noted while putting the wig down.

"But, how was your day, sweetie? What kinds of cars did you fix today?"

Quickly, James and Laila got back to business as usual – as if Monique hadn't stopped by at all.

"She tried to give me a wig, Dre! Do you know how embarrassing that was?" Dre looked Monique in her eyes. "Hey. Be strong for me. Okay?" Monique broke down and cried. "I can't right now. I just can't. I'm about to have a baby and I have no idea how to be a mom; my hair is gone and my business is suffering. I don't know--"

Monique stopped when she felt Dre's embrace. "Hey, relax. We're in this together." She bawled into Dre's shoulder. "I know. It's all so overwhelming right now." He kissed her head. "I know. That's why I rented *Madea's Family Reunion* and I'm cooking up some spinach eggrolls just the way you like."

Monique sniffed the air. "I was wondering what smelled so good." Dre kissed her. "I know you're going through a lot right now and I thought it would be nice if I did this for you."

"Thank you, Dre." Monique kissed him back. "I really appreciate this." After she and Dre embraced for a few minutes, Monique resorted to the couch and popped in the movie. As it started up, Dre poured them each a glass of lemonade and placed the food in front of them. "I know we usually have wine but, until our child comes out, lemonade will have to do." Monique smiled. "Lemonade is fine."

It wasn't until after watching the movie that Monique realized she needed that laugh. "Dre, you're really awesome for this." He rubbed her shoulder. "I'm trying, baby. I just want to make you happy for the rest of your life." Monique rested her head on his shoulder. "Dre, I told you--" He kissed her. "I don't need an answer right now. I'm just letting you know that I'm here. Whenever you're ready, I'm ready."

Dre truly loved Monique. And Monique loved her some Andre.

"So when do I get to see some more grandbabies after this one?"

"Mom, can I have my first one without you hounding me for more?" Mrs. Ross gathered all the materials she needed. "I mean you just hit 27 so you're getting up there, Mo. I just think you should consider your family size now that you've started. Plus, Laila already promised me two more once Arielle turns 4." Monique sighed. "I'm not Laila."

Mrs. Ross glossed over the comment. "I hope that boy is trying to marry you." "Oh, he's trying alright," Monique stated. Mrs. Ross looked at her daughter sideways. "Then, what are you doing? Marry that boy!" "I will when I'm ready."

"When you're ready, he's gone be on to some pretty young thing and you gone be left raising his kids."

"Kid," Monique corrected. "Besides, Dre loves me."

"Is that what he said?" Mrs. Ross challenged.

"That's what he meant."

"Then why won't you marry him?" "I'm not ready," Monique reiterated. Mrs. Ross looked at her husband slumped over on the couch. "Sweetheart, marriage ain't about whether you ready or not. It's about finding someone who you love, and I mean truly love, and holding on to them for a lifetime." "There's more to it than that. You have the financial aspect, then the living together, then--" Mrs. Ross shook her head.

"Y'all already living together. I can smell him on your clothes every time you come over here. And what you mean financial? You both have good paying jobs." Mrs. Ross shook her head. "Hell, y'all already playing house. Might as well gone and get married. Got a baby on the way but you don't want no ring? Earl, do you hear this girl?"

Mr. Ross awoke from his slumber. "Wh-What?" "Our baby girl doesn't wanna get married right now. Even though she's pregnant." Mr. Ross looked at his daughter. "Is it because that boy don't wanna marry you? I could make him marry you if--" Mrs. Ross put her hand up. "Earl, please. You couldn't hurt a dead fly."

"Why don't you come on over and say that to my face?"

Mrs. Ross walked over to her husband and he kissed her. They started laughing. "See, Monique? Marriage ain't that bad. I chose to spend my life with this goofball." Mr. Ross got up. "Why don't you hush up and go make that bed warm for me?" He slapped his wife's butt.

Mrs. Ross smiled. "No can do. I'm helping Monique right now." She took her daughter's arm and they proceeded to the bathroom. "Now, what is it that you said happened?" Monique took the scarf from off of her head. "I can't really explain it…."

In an hour, Mrs. Ross whipped up a style she thought was do-able. When Monique saw it in the mirror, she almost wanted to scream. "Mom, I appreciate you trying but--" Mrs. Ross shook her head. "But you don't like it. Well, next time, do it yourself. How you got a whole line of hair care products and you can hardly do your own hair? Don't you have something that could fix this?"

Monique sighed. "We're working on a hair regrowth oil but my scientists haven't perfected it yet."

"What's that new product you just released," Mrs. Ross asked. "It's called 'No Stress.' It's geared towards those who have been relaxing their hair and decided they want to go natural."

Mrs. Ross nodded. "Why did my friend Gale say she heard about in the newspaper?" "In the first trial, we noticed that the pudding began progressively taking people's hair out more and more. We've given money to the test subjects since and they all say they were able to grow their back."

"So you have human test subjects? Why not use those wigs and dummies like the beauticians do?" Monique said, "We do use those but we also use human beings so we can see the results in real time. One of my old scientists released a confidential report about the first trial and now the test subjects are coming out and saying that it took their hair out."

Mrs. Ross let out a deep breath. "See, I told you that that business industry can be dirty but you didn't listen." "Mom, I make $17,000 a month, which equates to almost $200,000 a year off an idea I came up with in my dorm room. How could I ever give that up?"

"It's not always about the money, Mo. Your father and I could be living fancy if we took money from you, James, or Daniel. But, we don't. You wanna know why? We grew up during a time when people valued the work they did, not how much money they made off of it."

Mrs. Ross' words weighed heavy on Monique as she drove home. *Is my mom right? Do I only care about the money?* "Hey, Mo. I won my case and Caleb said--" "Not now, Dre." Monique was in a mood so she could care less about what Dre had to say. He came to the room anyway. "You don't care about the bonus I got? He said as an incentive for me to continue winning cases, he'll add $1,000 to the check I'm about to get, which would make it $6,000 instead of just $5,000."

Monique shook her head. "Is it only about money, Dre?"

He stared quizzically at her. "Is it...? No. I'm just saying that with the baby on the way and us trying to buy a house, it's nice that I'll have a little more to put aside. That's all. Baby, I put in 100 hours on this case and it paid off. Aren't you happy for me?" Monique realized she was letting her mother's words get to her. "Yes. I'm sorry. It's just something that my mother said that really stuck with me."

Dre came next to Monique. "Mo, you have to realize that she'll never approve of what you do. You wanna know why? She enjoys working at the cleaners since that's how she paid you all's way through college and that's how she met your father and that's how she was able to raise you and your siblings.

"Your mother enjoys her working class life because it keeps your family stable. She's only concerned with earning just enough to get by. As for you, you had an ingenious idea that caught traction and now you have a whole business behind that one idea. Being in the business world, your main goal is to make money. So, of course you're going to be focused on money, Mo. That's the heart of business."

Monique smiled. "I think you're about the smartest man I know, Dre. Thanks for that. Now, tell me more about your case." Dre smiled. "Well, first I spoke to the arresting officers and they said something didn't add up. So then I..." As Dre talked, Monique just listened intently.

"Hey, baby, you have an appointment with Nancy today at 12." Monique looked at her calendar. "Oh." Dre stared at her. "Oh? Why 'oh'? What's up?" Monique looked at the calendar again. "Today's the day, Dre."

"What day?"

"Today's the day I find out the sex of our child."

Dre paused. "Oh. This is all happening so fast." Monique nodded. "Yeah. Will you come? I can text you the address." Dre looked at his watch. "Um, I'll have to see. I have to get to the office early because Caleb is having a meeting. See you." He kissed Monique on the cheek and went quickly out the door. She just stood at the counter holding her stomach. *This is really happening.* Monique felt jittery the entire time she was in her office. Once 11:30 hit, she took a deep breath. *It's time to go.* After assigning tasks, Monique was on her way.

Dr. Seneca told her, "Hold still, Monique. This might be a little cold." Monique couldn't hold still. She was antsy. *Where is Dre?* She had called him 3 times but he hadn't picked up. Dr. Seneca rolled the sonogram machine across Monique's belly. "Oh, Monique. You are going to have a beautiful, healthy baby." Monique tried to contain herself but she was looking for Dre. Dr. Seneca said, "I need you to hold still so I can see this clearly." *Dre isn't coming,* Monique realized. After coming to that conclusion, Monique was as still as a body of water.

"I see legs, now I see feet. Let's have a closer look." Dr. Seneca moved closer to the screen. "Oh, it's a--" Dr. Seneca paused.

"Would you like to know now, Monique, or would you rather wait?" Monique somehow instantly fell in love with the image of her unborn child. "Now," she decided. Dr. Seneca stated, "Oh, let's see now. It looks like...you're having a little boy."

For some reason, this disappointed Monique. Dr. Seneca then said, "I'm only kidding. You're having a baby girl!" She printed the ultrasound and handed it to Monique. "You should keep that for the scrapbook." Monique nodded. "I'm going to keep this forever." *My baby girl.*

After reveling in the glory of her baby girl for a while, Monique called Dre. "Hello?" "Dre, where were you? I was waiting on you so we could go through this process together." Dre sighed. "I just got assigned to another case. I was meeting with a client. I'm sorry."

"You couldn't postpone the meeting?"

"If I did, I may have lost the client. You know how this business stuff works." Monique scoffed. "Yeah, I do but I know how this parenting stuff works, too, Dre. There are two of us so I expect you to be in the picture." He argued, "You weren't saying that when you wanted to have an abortion without speaking to me first."

"Are you seriously going to bring that up right now? I'm already angry with you."

"You have no right to be. I didn't miss the appointment on purpose."

Monique bellowed, "I needed you here, Dre, and you didn't show up." Dre groaned. "What was I supposed to do? Risk my job to come? Yeah, I get it. That's our child. But, long ago, I told myself that whenever I bring a child into this world they'll never have to worry about anything. I just want to make some extra money so our child can live comfortably." Monique yelled, "But, you're not listening, Dre! I needed you here and you didn't even bother showing up."

At his office, Dre tried to keep his composure. "I was meeting with a client, Mo. What was I supposed to do?" "Find a way," she said as she hung up. After that, Dre rubbed his temples. *Here marks the end to my happiness. Maybe I should've have encouraged the abortion.*

"Knock, knock." Genna came to his door. "Come in," Dre stated, lost in thought. "I heard you won the case." Hearing the voice, Dre looked up immediately. Genna was already locking the door. "Whoa, what are you doing?"

"I'm just coming to congratulate you."

"Can you please unlock that door?"

Genna started closing the blinds. "I don't think that will be necessary." At that point, Dre got up from his desk and unlocked his office door. "You need to leave." "That's not what you said before, Andre." He sighed. "Genna, it's over now."

"You told me you and her were over. You called me from the airport, remember?"

Dre remembered vividly. But, he knew he was hung over and he was just saying things. "Look, Genna, I may have said some things that led you on but I assure you that I am faithful. I will not cheat on Monique." "What if I just tell Monique how you came to my house the night before you all went on that trip? How you confided in me and we almost kissed? What if I tell her that," Genna challenged. "Then she really won't want to marry you."

"Get out," Dre demanded. He had heard just about enough from Genna.

"Monique Ross?" An officer stood at her door. "This is she," Monique replied. He brought forth papers. "You've been served.

The court will be hearing this case in 2 weeks. I suggest you lawyer up before then." The officer left the papers on Monique's desk then went on his way. Monique sighed and pried open the envelope. As she read through the document, relief brushed over Monique. It was for the accident, not for the scandal within Mo's Mix. Although Monique was not thrilled about having to go to court, she felt that the accident was the lesser of two headaches.

Donna slithered into Monique's office. "Was that about the case? What's going to happen to Mo's Mix?"

"Donna, please report back to your office."

Donna asked, "Am I going to be out of a job?" Monique, already frustrated, yelled, "NOW!" At that, Donna did as told. Monique began viewing the monthly report for Mo's Mix. She looked at the payroll despairingly. "Evan, please report to my office ASAP."

Evan, Mo's Mix's CFO, brought his journals with him. "Yes, Ms. Ross? Is there a problem?" "Why is Nicole Nicholson still on my payroll?" "Because you are legally obligated to send her one last paycheck. It says so in the contract." Evan pulled out his copy of the employee contract and pointed to the section he was referring to. Monique shook her head.

"Read underneath that section, where it says 'exceptions'."

Evan read, "In the instance that an employee chooses to leave Mo's Mix without prior notification, they shall NOT receive a final paycheck. In the instance that an employee intentionally harms another member of the Mo's Mix team, including vendors, they shall NOT receive a final paycheck. Harm includes verbal, physical, and mental abuse. In the instance that an employee intentionally slanders Mo's Mix, they shall NOT receive a final paycheck. In the instance that..."

Monique put her hand up. "Stop. Read that last line again for me." Evan did so. Monique stared directly at him. "If that was the case, why is Nicole Nicholson still on my payroll? I specifically told you that she was not to receive a final paycheck."

Evan pulled out his phone. "Yes, you did. However, you later sent an email stating otherwise." He showed Monique the email. Surely enough, it was sent from her official account. But, Monique knew for a fact she hadn't sent it. *There's a snake on the premises.* "Very well, Evan. I'm sorry for any confusion. Continue business as usual." Evan nodded and went back to his office.

Monique thought back to everyone who had been inside her office.

"Mo's Mix. How may I help you?" Dominque noticed the way Monique stormed towards her. "Um, I'm going to have to call you back. My boss needs to speak with me."

"Dominique, when you were in my office, did you happen to use my computer?"

Dominque shook her head. "No, ma'am. You did not give me permission to do so."

"Did you allow anyone else into my office during the time you were there?"

Dominque shook her head again. "No, ma'am. You didn't give me permission to do so." Monique noted, "You sound a little rehearsed there, Dominque. As if you were already prepared for this." Sweat beads began emitting from the young girl's forehead. "Oh, are you getting nervous? Why is that?" Dominque tried drinking water but she knew Monique was on to her.

She admitted, "Okay. I did get on your computer. But, it was only to see an email from my professor. I'd left my phone at home and my computer was in my office and I didn't want to leave your office unattended. I'm sorry. Please don't fire me."

Monique could hear the truth in Dominique's speech. "Relax. No one's firing you. Just don't do it again." Although Monique had gained that information, she knew Dominque wasn't the culprit. *Who else would have access to my office?* She had only given the code to her office and her computer to Dominique.

"Marley, are you busy right now?" Marley was the head of technology at Mo's Mix. Monique's next guess was that someone had broken into her office. He pointed to the technicians heavy at work. "No, not particularly. Ever since you gave me this tech team, I've been pretty lax." *Maybe a little too lax.*

"Marley, what do you know about breaking into offices?" Marley paused. "Uh-oh. Is there a problem?" "Just answer the question," Monique demanded. Marley told her, "To be quite honest, I'm a little old school. If there was anyone who knew something about that, it would be someone from the tech team."

When Marley said that, Monique could have sworn she saw a technician's eyes pop up. But, there were too many of them to tell which one it was. "Well, thank you, Marley. Get back to work." Monique knew that she couldn't fight a tech-head without another tech head.

"Daddy? Hey. Are you busy right now?" Mr. Ross let out a deep breath. "I just got done fixing Mr. Daley's computer for the third time. Why?" Monique covered her phone and whispered the problem that she had. Her dad said, "Well, why don't I come down to the office and have a look at it? I'll bring Daniel too."

"Thanks, daddy."

"No problem baby."

"Love you."

Mr. Ross said, "Love you too. We'll be there shortly, okay?"

After speaking to her father, Monique made her way to the security wing of Mo's Mix. Like every other wing, they were heavy at work. Agent Abby came forward. "Mrs. Ross, is there a problem?"

Monique scoffed. "There is. *Mrs.* Ross is my mother. I'm Ms. Ross." Agent Abby nodded. "Duly noted. *Ms.* Ross, how can I assist you?"

"You all monitor pretty much everything that goes on in the office, right?"

"Right."

"Can you send all the tapes from the last month to my email?"

Agent Abby went to her computer. "On it, boss. Sending videos in…oh." Monique stepped inside the office. "Why oh? What's going on?" "Someone from tech just erased the videos." Monique rubbed her head. "Can you track the IP address?"

Agent Abby worked her magic. "Got it. Here you go." She printed the information and handed it Monique. "Thanks, Abby." Agent Abby nodded. "Always."

Monique trekked back to the Tech Wing. *Someone from Tech is trying to screw me over.* Marley got up when he saw her. "Back so soon?" "Out of my way, Marley." Monique went desktop to desktop until she found the one she was looking for. "Aha!" Alas, there was no one sitting there. "Whose desk is this?"

Marley looked at his sheet. "That would be…Barry. Barry Houston." "Where is Barry Houston," Monique asked. "At home. His wife Stacy went into labor recently."

"*Wife?*"

Marley nodded. "You didn't know?" "No," Monique vocalized. "Was there someone on his computer today?" Marley nodded again. "Yeah, someone from upstairs. She just left." Monique wondered, "Who was it?"

"No clue. I only know what goes on down here, y'know?"

In fact, Monique *did* know and she resented the segregation within Mo's Mix. *Once this crisis is over, I gotta fix that,* she told herself.

"Well, can you at least describe her?" Marley sat down. "She was a curly haired sister. I mean, she had some serious curls. Never seen curls like that in my life. We was all wondering what she was doing down here but she was quiet, real quiet. So, I made my over to her like what ya doin, sister? That ain't yo computer. Turns out, she had hacked into the system and she was looking at all these surveillance videos and whatnot. She hit the delete button real quick. Then, she left."

Monique sighed. "Is that all you know? That she had curly hair?" Marley shrugged. "And she wearing a yellow dress, showing off her bosoms. That's all I know." When Marley said that, Monique had her second suspect.

"Donna, have you seen Diana today?" Donna shook her head. "Not for the last couple of hours." As long as Diana had worked for Mo's Mix, Monique got a vibe that something was off about her. Then, Monique had seen Diana wearing the dress that Marley described. And Monique knew that Diana's new weave would qualify as "serious" curls. "Okay. Thanks anyway." Donna nodded and went back to what she was doing. Monique went over to Lorenzo's office.

"Lorenzo, does Diana work with you?" He looked up. "No. She got switched to promotions last week." Monique raised her eyebrow. "By who?" "Who do you think?" Lorenzo narrowed his glance in on Donna. Ever since Monique had put Donna in charge of Communications, the employees all exhibited resentment.

"Very well."

Monique went back over to Donna, whom she realized was also wearing a yellow dress. "Are you sure you haven't seen Diana today?" Donna looked up. "No. Is there a problem?"

"Why'd you switch her to promotions without telling me?"

"I thought you'd be cool with it. You're cool with Evan running his sect of this company as he pleases. The same goes for Marley, Marcus, Hyde, Stanley, and George. But, when Donna does something, it's a problem. I'm starting to think you're a little bit sexist, Ms. Ross."

Monique blinked a few times to be sure she was hearing correctly. "Excuse me, Donna. Who are you taking that tone with?" Donna stood up. "You. I'm tired of you always riding my case about the things I do. How come you don't ride those men's cases?"

Monique rubbed her head. "Look, if there's a problem, you go to Yasmine and she will bring it to me and I'll review it."

"Why don't you tackle to problems directly instead of having some 'office therapist' do your dirty work?"

"Why don't you calm down and recognize who you're speaking to?"

Monique hated being an authoritarian but knew she had to when need be. Donna finally backed down. "I'm sorry, boss. I'll speak to Yasmine immediately." "That's what I thought." As Monique went back to her own office, she felt a little offended. *How dare she talk to me like that? I have to do something about this.*

"I keep telling you, Mo. You gotta put your foot down. Be a tyrant. Sometimes, it's the only way you get people to listen."

"Like how Pops got us to listen?"

Daniel shook his head. Mr. Ross looked up at Monique. "Why don't you just hand me that screwdriver right there?" Monique looked at her father. "Aren't you forgetting to say something?" Mr. Ross huffed, realizing his daughter wasn't one to take orders. "Please?" Monique obliged. "Here you go."

After Mr. Ross had successfully dismantled the alarm system, he told Monique, "It doesn't look tampered with. If anyone broke in, they probably had the code." This was frustrating for Monique. *Who would break into my office?* Then, she thought about Donna's behavior and Donna's very yellow dress and very "serious" curls. *Maybe she's upset because of how she feels I've treated her. But, why would she send an email that said send a check to Nicole? Something doesn't add up.*

"Well, thanks for your help, daddy. You too, Daniel. I really appreciate it." Mr. Ross kissed Monique's head and starting putting the system back together. Daniel gathered the tools from off the ground. "No problem, sweetie. Call me if you need anything else." She hugged her father. "I will."

Daniel put his arm around his sister. "This is a nice place you got here, Mo. Lil sis is coming up in the world."

Monique smiled. "I only learned from the best." Monique hoped that by saying this she could somehow enact Daniel's old entrepreneurial spirit – the one he had before their aunt died. "I'll catch you later." Daniel exited quickly with their father.

When Monique finally retired back in her office, she tried to list all possible motives for Donna but she could not think of any. *If it isn't Donna, then maybe it's Diana*, Monique internally noted, remembering what Marley had said. She called Diana.

"Hi, Ms. Ross. I'm out running errands for Rodney. How can I help you?"

"Have you been in the tech wing of the office at all today? Maybe around 2 hours ago?"

Diana shifted the phone. "Um, no. I've been out since 12:00 this afternoon. Why?"

Monique took note of Diana's uneasiness. "Just wondering. We'll speak when you return." "Okie dokey, boss." In the meantime, Monique called Evan back to her office. "Evan, I need you to put a stop payment on Nicole's check right now."

Evan folded his hands. "I'm sorry, Ms. Ross. I can't do that."

"Oh? Why not?"

"I just tell people who the money goes to and how much goes to each person. I don't actually handle the direct deposits."

Monique let out a deep breath. "That's Melodie, isn't it?" Evan nodded. Monique rubbed her temples and resented the fact that she wasn't on top of things. *Keep it together, Monique.* She told Evan, "You're dismissed." Then she called Melodie into her office. "Yes?" Monique motioned for Melodie to close the door. "Have you gone to bank yet?" She asked afterwards.

Melodie replied, "No." "I need you to do so immediately. I want you to put a stop payment on the check for Nicole Nicholson." Melodie stated, "That isn't possible. There's a direct link between your account and the employee accounts. So there's a scheduled drop off day to--" Monique huffed.

"Just get to the point, Melodie. Why can't you do it?"

Melodie said, "Well, today is Tuesday, which is the day that the bank withdraws money from your account so that it will be cleared by Friday, which is payday. On Thursday, I go to the bank and pick up the deposit statements."

Monique wondered, "What would happen if you attempted to put a stop payment on a deposit today?" "Well, there would be heavy fees from the bank because they require you to notify them of stop payments within 3 business days. Also, everyone in the office would have a hold on their check. I don't think you want to do that, boss."

Monique cut, "Don't tell me what I want to do, Melodie. How much would the fee be?"

Melodie pulled out her folder and a calculator. "One second...3.5% times the amount going out equals $13,470." Monique let out another deep breath. "Can we afford that?" Melodie flipped to another page of financial records. "Well, we're already under heavy scrutiny and this lawsuit could run us up..."

Monique snapped, "I didn't ask you to relay current events. I asked if we can afford it."

Melodie put her hands down on the table. "No, Ms. Ross. We can't. Even if we could, some people are working paycheck to paycheck. Holding their money could put them at huge disadvantage. Think about it: $6,000 bestowed to Ms. Nicholson or over $13,000 lost and about 160 people mad at you. The former doesn't sound too bad, now does it?"

Monique shook her head. "It isn't about what's good or bad, it's about the principle of the thing. Nicole does not deserve to get another paycheck from Mo's Mix. I'm going down to the bank."

"They're not going to listen."

Monique ushered Melodie out of her office. "Oh, they'll listen."

"I can take the next customer right here." Monique stepped up to the window. "Hi. I'm Keyan and I'll be your teller for today. What can I help you with?"

"Hi. My name is Monique Ross and I'm the owner of the business account for Mo's Mix." Keyan opened the door. "Step right this way, Ms. Ross." He led her to his desk. Monique explained, "I would like to put a stop payment on a direct deposit." Keyan asked, "May I please see some identification?" Monique gave him her driver's license and waited patiently. Keyan typed her name into the computer.

"I just pulled up your account information and I see that you're scheduled for a direct deposit this Friday. Because of that, I am unable to put a stop payment on the check without charging you a late fee."

"Today is Tuesday, though," Monique reasoned. "Something should be done."

"Ms. Ross, nothing can be done. Direct deposits are withdrawn at 9 AM three days prior to the scheduled direct deposit. I'm sorry."

Monique stayed where she was. "I have been a loyal customer to this bank for the past five years. I pay on time and I have never had to do something like this before. I just don't understand why-"

A woman who looked of a managerial nature came to where Monique was sitting. "Ms. Ross, as Keyan already said, there's nothing we can do – unless you feel like paying 13 K to the bank."

"It's my money. Why am I not allowed to say where it goes?"

The woman stared Monique down. "You are allowed. At least 3 business days prior. Since you didn't follow the rules, you have to pay a fee. Now, is there anything else?" The lady was clearly a lot older than Monique so Monique knew it wouldn't be an easy battle. "Nope. That will be all."

Monique went back to the office and Diana was waiting on her. "You said you wanted to speak with me." After such a long and grueling day, and with the extra weight in her stomach, Monique postponed the meeting, resolving to pick the issue back up after she made a phone call.

"Hello?" Daniel awoke from a long nap when he heard his phone ringing. "Hey, Daniel. Do you still have that connect at the bank?" He rubbed his eyes. "Um, yeah. His name is Keyan. Why?" Monique tapped her fingers on the table. "I might need a little favor." 30 minutes later, Monique was back at the bank. This time, Daniel was with her. Keyan, the teller from before, stopped once he saw who Monique brought.

"Daniel. It's been a while."

Daniel nodded. "Yeah, yeah, yeah. Enough with the small talk. My sister says you all been giving her a hard time." Keyan shook his head. "No we have not. Just simply following procedures. Why don't you two step inside?"

Keyan sat them down and logged into his computer. "Mr. Ross, there's nothing we can do. It says here that the money was already withdrawn from Monique's account. It's not standard procedure for us to do stop payments this close to the scheduled day of deposit."

Daniel folded his hands on the desk. "Is it standard procedure to do back door dealings with a local restaurant that's already in trouble with the feds?" Keyan gasped. "How did you--"

Daniel put his hand up. "I'm the one who's asking the questions here. You gonna do what my sister asked you or not?" Keyan hit a few buttons on his computer. "What was the name," he asked Monique.

"The account for Nicole Nicholson," she replied.

Keyan hit typed something in then said, "Done." At that, Daniel got up. "You have a nice day." Monique looked at her big brother in awe. She marveled at the way he had strong armed Keyan into giving them what they wanted. *All I needed was Daniel's commanding presence.*

"How do you even know that guy?" Daniel shrugged. "I met him at the gym and we hit it off. He told me he worked for a bank and I knew that would be good for the business. We had a short relationship, though. Aunt Pam died 2 weeks after I met him. So much for that one, huh?"

Monique offered, "He seems like a nice guy."

"He's a great guy. But, things change, Mo. I'm going out with Christina now and that's all I'm going to say on the subject."

With that said, Daniel got into his car and rode off. *Dismissive as usual,* Monique inwardly affirmed.

By the time Monique got home, she'd forgotten all about her fight with Dre. Then, she put her purse down and the sonogram stared up at her. *Oh yeah. That.* Dre walked in the door equally oblivious. "Hey, baby. How was your day?"

"Don't you 'hey baby' me. You missed the appointment earlier."

"I told you I was meeting with a client."

"If work is that important to you, then get to it. Don't let me distract you." Dre put his brief case down. "Baby, don't be like that." He held on to Monique's stomach and kissed her neck. "Don't you like it when I do this?" Monique did like it but her pride made her say, "No. Get off of me."

Monique pushed Dre away. He threw his suit jacket off and began loosening his tie. "What do you want me to say? Nothing I say is ever good enough for you when you're angry."

"I want you to say you're sorry," Monique yelled. Dre countered, "I did! And you didn't accept that. You just brushed right over it and proceeded to yell at me. Look, I'm sorry, baby. I'm sorry I wasn't there to see our child. I'm sorry that I hurt your feelings. I'm sorry that you felt abandoned. I'm sorry, Monique. Is that what you want?" She hugged Dre tightly. "That's exactly what I want."

Dre took in Monique's scent. "You seem like you had a rough day. Is everything okay, Mo?" Monique took a deep breath and let it all out – the events of her day. He sat back on the couch and listened as she took her heels off, threw her dress to the side and pulled on one of his old shirts while relaying the events of the day. Afterwards, Monique looked at the shirt. "This is much more comfortable than that stuffy dress."

"I can't say I don't like it."

Dre kissed Monique up and down her spine. "How was your day, Dre," she asked. He rubbed his neck. "The same as usual – boring." "Why don't you do something you enjoy? You always say it's boring at work and you don't seem too happy in your job."

"It's not about something that makes me happy anymore. It's about something that can pay bills. I mean, sure I wanted to be a chef but my father told me that wasn't a lucrative field. He said there was a greater need for lawyers. My mamma said if I wanted to be a chef so bad, why not start a family because I'd be cooking for hungry mouths every night. Their pessimism killed my dreams."

"I remember you telling me that. You had saved up so much for cooking school."

"But, I ended up spending that on law school. Now, here I am."

Monique kissed her man. "Well, you're my chef, Dre. And I'm loving every second of it." He smiled. "Thank you. That means a lot to me, Mo." "Always." After kissing Dre again, Monique went for the sonogram.

For a second, she stopped. "Wait. Do you want to know what our child will be?"

"Of course – so we can start planning what color we'll paint the bedroom."

Monique smiled. "Probably purples and pinks." Dre smiled too. "So it's gonna be a little girl?" "Yeah. Let's take a family picture." Dre raised his eyebrow. Monique pulled out her phone and held the sonogram between them. "We're a family now, Dre."

Dre couldn't stop staring at the photo Monique had taken. It's so beautiful, he told himself. Suddenly, he had an idea. "I'll be back," he told Monique. She turned over in her sleep. "What are you talking about? It's midnight." He kissed Monique. "I know. I'll be right back, baby. You're gonna love this." Monique shook her head. "Whatever you say, Dre. Just don't be loud when you return." Dre nodded and headed out the front door.

Monique rolled back over and proceeded sleeping. Yet, Dre's absence bothered her. She felt that she needed to know where he was. So, Monique called him. He didn't answer the first two times. The third time, he wondered, "Is everything okay?" "Where are you, Dre?"

"At the door," he noted while coming in. Dre showed Monique a picture frame he had pulled from the back of his truck. "I thought this would be a nice place to put the picture. Where did you think I went?"

Monique kissed him. "It doesn't matter. I love that idea. It's great, Dre." She kissed him again. "Goodnight." Dre sighed. "Goodnight, baby." In the back of his mind, he thought: *Mo must not trust me now. Is it because of Genna? It has to be.* That was the only logical explanation he could think of. He tapped Monique on her shoulder.

Monique shook her head, which meant that he needed to stop bothering her. She was serious about her sleep, especially because the baby gave her extreme tiredness. Realizing, Dre gave up and stuck to his own devices. Most of the night, he sat up feeling guilty for even going on a date with Genna, for even calling her when he felt that him and Monique were flying south, for betraying his woman.

Although Dre and Genna never engaged in a physical relationship, Dre suddenly felt like he had betrayed Monique. He turned over to look at her. "You're beautiful."

By morning, Monique awoke feeling refreshed as Dre finished a 2-hour nap. She studied her man. "You haven't slept at all." Dre said, "Incorrect. I crashed around 3." Monique looked at the clock. "It's 5:45, Dre. That isn't enough sleep to get you through the day." Dre arose to make some coffee. "It's gonna have to."

Monique pulled on her robe and went out to the kitchen. "Andre, talk to me. What's wrong?"

"Why did you ask where I was at last night?"

"Because I didn't know."

Dre looked down at his coffee. "Why did you need to know? Don't you trust me?" Monique sighed. "I do, Dre. I just had a moment. Is that the only thing that's bothering you?"

"I called Genna when we were at the airport," Dre admitted. "Okay. But we were broken up." Dre continued, "Before we caught the flight. And I also visited her the night before we left." Monique cut her eyes. "*That's* the phone call that you had to make and the errand you had to run?" Dre reasoned, "You were upsetting me. I was telling you about Nathalie's engagement and you just put me off – as if the idea of marriage was enough to make you gag."

Monique grabbed a glass and poured some orange juice. "Whatever, Dre. It's over now. Just don't let me find out you two did anything."

"You just said you trusted me."

"I *did*. Past tense," Monique noted when she went to take a shower. Though unusual, Dre came in behind her. "Dre, what are you doing?" He shut the door and proceeded to make love to his woman. Monique looked up at him afterwards. "What was that for?"

"To please you. You're my lady, Monique. I would never do anything to intentionally hurt you. I'm sorry that I entertained Genna and I'm sorry I didn't tell you about it." Monique kissed him. "I accept your apology." For a while, they embraced. Then, Dre's phone rang. He brushed Monique's head with his lips. "I should probably get that."

"Yeah."

After Dre left, Monique had a certain feeling in her body. She wanted more – not more pleasure but more of Dre. She wanted all of him. *Maybe we should get married.*

Later that night, Monique was on the side of the bed holding the phone to her ear when Dre walked in. "Are you...are you sure? Instantly? What's going to...No, I'm fine, mom. What's gonna happen to Etta? She'll be nothing without Junior. I can't believe this is happening. Oh lord." The phone dropped from Monique's hand as the tears came pouring. Dre sat by her side and held her. "Hello, Mrs. Ross? Yes, this is Andre. Monique is going to have to call you back. My condolences. You're welcome. Bye now. Bless you, too." Dre ended the call and held Monique. "It's okay, baby. You don't have to talk. Just let all your tears out." Although he had no exact idea of what was going on, Dre knew one thing: he needed to be there for his lady.

Chapter IV – *Monique's Uncle Junior, Auntie Pam's widowed husband, had parked his car on railroad tracks. Medics said he died instantly.*

DAYS LATER

"Monique, baby. You're looking good." Monique smiled and kissed her grandma. "You too, Grandma Etta." Monique's grandmother smiled and went over to her son. "Earl, your brother Junior was always a fighter. I could say that much. Even when Pam threatened to leave, he *fought.* He wanted to be sure she would stay. And she did. He was affected the most by her death, but that's a given." Etta glanced at her dead son's picture and said to Monique's father, "Earl, baby, you're my last one. Make Mama proud." Etta held her son's hand and they proceeded to the table.

The Ross Family was a large one. For starters, Etta had three husbands and 6 kids – 3 of whom had made their transition before they even had the chance to live. Anna, Earl's eldest sister, had disappeared and left her daughters in Etta's care. Moni and Lacy, Monique's twin cousins, had 3 and 4 kids, respectively. Then, Maci – Moni's eldest girl – had earned herself a spot on *16 & Pregnant* (metaphorically speaking, of course); her son's name was Bradley. On top of that, Neil, Etta's brother had Damien and Jesse – Monique's great uncles. Damien had Lele, Antonique, and Edward. Jesse had Arnie and Cheyenne. Cheyenne, who was Monique's age, was just getting off of bed rest after having her first son, Lyles.

The list just went on and on. Yvette, Arnette, Jill, and Patrick – Monique's other great aunts and uncle – had 2, 4, 2, and 3 kids, respectively. In addition, almost all of their children had children. All in all, The Ross' were a big family; they were gathering not only to mourn Junior's death but also to reunite. "The last time we got together like this, besides for Pam's funeral, was at the Ross Family reunion back in '05," Monique's father noted. Monique remembered '05 vividly. She had just turned 9 years old. Her 2nd or 3rd cousin Frederick (Monique wasn't too sure) knocked her off the swing set because he said it was "his" playground. Despite the fact that he had been going on 15, he had still felt the need to mark the territory.

Monique saw him again at the dinner. "Monique, hey." Now, she was 27 and Fred was 33 so that incident was water under the bridge. "Hey, Fred." "How's your eye," he joked, referring back to the family reunion.

"My eye is fine, actually. Thanks for your concern. How's the misses?"

Frederick sighed. "Missing in action." At this moment, Fred Jr. started running around pulling plates off the table and causing a ruckus. Most of the family deemed him the "trouble child" because his mother was addicted to drugs. "What happened with Nita," Monique asked. "She got busted. The whole drug operation was discovered so she got taken in. Then, the prison called me saying she had escaped but I haven't heard from her since."

"Ah."

Monique continued studying Fred Jr. *When I have Anysse, it can't be like this.* Monique gasped inwardly. *Did I just come up with a name for my baby girl?* Dre came back from getting Monique some water. "Hey. How are you feeling?"

"Dre, I just had an idea."

"Spill."

"Anysse. Do you like that name?"

Dre shrugged. "If you like it, I like it." Monique rolled her eyes. He laughed. "I'm kidding, baby. How 'bout Emelia? Or Etrese? Or Annabelle?" Monique replied, "Annabelle? Absolutely not, Dre. But, we'll see about Emelia or Etrese." Monique hung on to the first name. *Etrese, Emelia or Anysse? Decisions, decisions.*

"How come we weren't invited to the wedding," Jerry, Etta's first husband, asked. Monique folded her hands. "We're not married, granddad." "What you mean you not married? Earl told me you was pregnant."

"You pregnant but ain't married. That's some new-age shit."

"How you gone raise a child by just being someone's 'girlfriend'?"

"That child is gonna grow up wondering why his or her parents are different from the other kids' parents."

"You two should be ashamed of yourselves."

Monique had heard about enough. She scooted from the table and excused herself to the bathroom. Andre sat where he was. "What, you not gone go after her?" He turned to Jerry. "She doesn't like to be bothered when she's upset."

Earl nodded. "Pops, Andre's right about that. Mo likes dealing with things alone. She's very guarded. She doesn't want anyone to think her vulnerable. Being the baby of the family and growing up with two aggressive older brothers, she was privy to a lot of flak that taught her to be taut. She's tough, pops. You can't mess with Monique. No one can." Earl sighed as he analyzed his only daughter.

Mrs. Ross added, "Monique was close to Junior like Daniel was close to Pam. She's taking this really hard so could you all not get on her about marriage?" Yvette shook her head. "It just doesn't make any sense to me." She narrowed her glance in on Dre. "This was your idea, wasn't it? What, you afraid of commitment?"

"No, actually. I've talked to Monique about marriage but she's focused on her career right now."

"Back in my day, women didn't have careers. They had children. Their job was to take care of the home, cook the food, clean the clothes, and make sure everything was stable around the house. With two working parents, who's gone nurse that baby? Some stranger? Do you really want a stranger caring for *your* child?"

Yvette continued, "And if y'all ain't married now, are you ever gonna get married? You'll be busy discussing wedding plans and that child is gonna be neglected. Nowadays, y'all young folks got it backwards with this 'I'll have a baby *then* think about marriage'. In my day, marriage came first because marriage was the most important thing. I guess times do change, though." Suddenly, Dre felt vulnerable. Yvette's words contained so much truth that they taunted him for the rest of the night.

On the drive home, Dre was very quiet. Because they didn't want to bother Monique, no one had told her what Yvette said to Dre. She wondered, "What's up? You're awfully quiet." "Long day at work," he murmured. Dre pulled into the parking lot. Monique touched his shoulder. "It's more than that. What aren't you telling me, Andre?"

"So I'll take off work Saturday for the funeral and repast."

"Andre, don't shut me out." He came around to open Monique's door. "Mo, it's been a long day. Let's just go inside and wind down." Monique sighed. "Andre." He looked at her. "Yes?" "What's wrong? What's upsetting you?" As much as Dre wanted to hide it, he saw the pleading in Monique's eyes. "Let's talk about this inside."

They sat face to face on the couch, feet crossed Indian style. "Monique, I know I said I wouldn't pressure you but your aunt brought up a good point. While we're doing all this debating about marriage, who will be taking care of our daughter? We'll be trying to figure out who we are as people while our daughter is trying to figure out where she'll get breast milk from; who'll rock her to sleep; who'll change her diapers; who'll take her to get check-ups and shots. Mo, I think we are making a big mistake by not getting married. I understand that you don't have to be married to care for a child but we love each other dearly and I believe you're just scared.

"Honestly, I'm scared too. But, we know each other, Mo. We live together. We support each other financially, emotionally, and spiritually. What's *really* stopping us from getting married?"

"Me," Monique vocalized. "I'll marry you, Dre."

"And I know you've said that..." Dre took a long pause. "Did you just say what I think you said?" "Yes, Dre. I've been thinking about it too and you're right. We should get married." "Really?" Dre got on one knee for verification. "Monique Ross, will you marry me?" Monique smiled. "Yes, Andre Cassells. I will." Monique knew her words made Dre happy but the idea of marriage, at that point, made Monique equally as happy.

"I'm so happy for you!!" Camille hugged her friend tightly. "My baby's finally getting married! Ooh, I'm so proud. How did Dre react when you said yes?" Monique smiled and recollected the moment. "He played it off but I know him well enough to understand that he was ecstatic." Camille nodded. "I'm sure he was." Then, she pulled her hair up. "Thanks again for helping me move into this new apartment. I appreciate it."

"Of course. I'll do anything to keep you safe, Camille. You're like the sister I never had." Camille smiled and started tearing up. "Aw, come here, Mo." The friends shared an embrace that only best friends could share. They squeezed each other tightly. James came up the stairs clapping. "How cute." He and Camille had not been on the same page since high school. "James, refrain from your commentary. Please."

He sighed. "That wasn't sarcasm, Camille. I thought the moment was actually nice. It's nice that Monique can still withstand you after all these years." "I could say the same for you. The only difference is that Mo never had a choice to have you in her life." James held his chest. "Ooh. That *almost* hurt."

"Tell that to the salt dripping off your shoulder."

"It must be coming from your mouth 'cause you stay salty."

"You of all people should know since you stay on my case."

Monique stepped in between them. "This has gone on for years. Can you two at least *act* like you like each other?" "Camille is great at acting. After all, she played the role of submissive so well." This angered Camille. "I could say the same for Laila, your little *wife*!" This angered James. "You leave Laila out of this." Camille began pulling off her earrings. "Why don't you make me?!" Monique grabbed Camille's shoulder.

"Camille, stop it. You cannot fight a man. I don't care how tough you think you are. He is still a man, which means that he is naturally stronger than you. Please calm down." Once Monique was sure her words had registered with Camille, she turned to James. "James, you have a daughter and a wife so there's no reason for you to still be getting into petty arguments with Camille. Besides, you shouldn't be stepping to a woman like that. I have never known you to be an abuser and I won't let you start now. I'm gonna need you to calm down, too. Both of you...just..."

As Monique lectured them on calming down, she felt an ironic unrest in her stomach. *What is going on?* It lasted for a period of three seconds then died down. She thought back to the literature Dr. Seneca had provided. "The kicks will feel unprecedented," one brochure said. "But, there's no need to freak out. It's just your baby letting you know that he or she is on the way."

Camille and James both rushed to Monique's side. "Are you alright?" She held her stomach. "I'm fine. I think the baby just kicked." Camille sighed. "It's probably because you yelled at us. When you get emotional, the baby feels it too." Monique wondered, "How do you know that?"

James commented. "I guess after the 8th abortion you learn something."

"Fuck you, James. I've only had 3."

He clapped. "That's *so* much better." "Do you know how many Laila's had?" "None," James stated assuredly. Camille chuckled. "Oh. You obviously don't about her college days then." Monique looked up at them. "Camille, you're probably right about the stress. Can you both just chill out for now?"

They nodded and focused on the task at hand. Because Monique was already putting a lot of stress on herself, she decided she would watch the van while Camille and James hauled in the boxes. After a while, they actually began talking, as the friends they once were. Monique realized that the two had put aside their differences because they didn't want to stress her out. To Monique, this was a sign that both Camille and James truly cared about her.

"So…" Camille looked around her new apartment. "Everything's done. Thank you both. I really appreciated this." Monique and James nodded. "Any time." Before they left, James hugged Camille then exited. "What was that for?" Monique asked. James let out a deep breath. "You remember how Camille and I used to be good friends?"

Monique reflected. "Oh yeah. What ever happened between you two?" James admitted, "I found out that she was sleeping with Donald and I knew he was bad for her. I told Camille that but she didn't want to listen. So I said that if she was going to degrade herself like that, I wanted nothing to do with her. At the time, I thought it would be a wakeup call for Camille. But, sadly, it only drove a wedge in our friendship."

"Wow. I didn't know that."

As with finding out that James played guitar, Monique realized there was still much to learn about her older brother. James continued, "So, what made Camille finally leave Donald alone? I heard it was when you all were at Nia." Monique nodded. "It was. He had been hitting her for a while but, this one time, he put her in the hospital. After that, she told him never to speak to her again. They've patched up their relationship since but Camille will never forget that."

"Understandable." James sighed. Monique held her aching belly. "Can you drive? My stomach is killing me right now." "Are you sure you want to go to work?" Monique sat up straight. "Positive. There's business to be handled." After hassling Diana, Monique's lead had failed. Although the employee seemed sketchy, Monique hadn't been able to find a strong enough motive explaining why Diana would sabotage Mo's Mix.

"Marley, can you come to my office?" Because he and his team had seen the perpetrator, Marley was Monique's only hope. "Yes, boss?" He said when he came upstairs. Monique nodded towards the door. "Could you please close that?" Marley did as told and sat down in front of Monique's desk. "Is there something I can help you with?" Monique pulled out a sheet of paper. "Actually, yes. These are employee photos I took last month. Can you identify the woman who came into Tech on Tuesday?"

Marley analyzed the sheet. "This one." His finger landed directly on Donna's face. "Okay. You're dismissed." Monique looked closely at the photo of Donna. Donna had a very memorable face so it was highly unlikely that Marley would mix her up with someone else. Then, Monique thought about the way Marley had quickly identified Donna without hesitation. *I may just have my culprit.*

Monique walked over to Dominique. "Get Donna Roberts in my office right now." "She's in a meeting," Dominque said as she nodded towards a nearby conference room. Monique stepped in. "This month, I was hoping--" "Donna, could you come here for a second?" Monique interrupted. Donna folded her hands. "Ms.

Ross, I'm in the middle of a meeting." Monique looked towards one of Donna's subordinates. "Kyle can cover you. Right, Kyle?" He nodded. "Yes, ma'am." Donna sighed and handed Kyle the clicker. "Ms. Ross, what is this about?" Monique walked towards her office.

"Come in and shut the door."

Donna did so. "What's going on, Ms. Ross? Why did you call me in here?"

"Where were you on Tuesday around 3:45?" Donna thought about it. "I was on lunch. I had to finish up some extra work so I took my lunch at 3 instead of 2. Then, I came right back and continued working." "Did you stop in the Tech wing at all?"

"I went to say hi to a friend but that's about it. Why do you ask?"

"Someone from that department informed me that you went onto one of the computers." "Who said that," Donna wondered. Monique shook her head. "It doesn't matter. I just need to know that it's not true." "Well, it's not," Donna blatantly lied, realizing she'd been caught. She *had* been the one on the computer deleting surveillance videos so, internally, she freaked out. Not only was Donna worried about being fired but she was also worried that the person who instructed her to delete the videos would be angry.

"Are you sure about that, Donna? You're sweating." Donna maintained her composure. "Well, it is rather hot in here so that's how I would expect my body to react." Monique resented the smugness in Donna's tone. "Who do you think you're talking to, Donna? I am your boss so I suggest you lose the attitude. This is the *second* time you've been verbally aggressive towards me. Do I need to write you up?"

Donna loosened her body. "No, Ms. Ross. I do apologize for my tone and I will do better at working on my attitude." Monique nodded. "So, back to what I was saying, are you sure you did not get on one of the computers in the tech wing on Tuesday?" "As I said, I only stopped in there briefly. I didn't stay long because I didn't have any assignments down there."

"You're sure you didn't have anything you needed to *delete*?"

"Ms. Ross, what is this about?"

"Just asking questions, Donna. Trying to figure some things out."

Donna challenged, "These questions seem rather specific." "Maybe you feel that way because you're guilty." Donna could not argue with that one. She was guilty. But, she could not tell that to Monique. "Or because people tend to investigate when they suspect something." "Are you suggesting that I'm investigating right now?" "You are interrogating me," Donna noted. "Only because I had an eye-witness account and the same person identified you in a line-up." "Who?" Monique shook her head. "That's unimportant. Are you sticking with your statement? That you did nothing wrong?" Donna nodded.

Monique sighed. "Well, if I find out otherwise, you're fired. Effective immediately." Donna stood in front of Monique – astonished. She had not thought about how her actions could affect her job.

"Is there something else I can help you with, Donna?"

"No, Ms. Ross."

"Then, why are you still here?"

Once Donna left, Monique checked the payrolls again, verifying that Nicole was not on there. Much to her dismay, she saw

Nicole Nicholson where it had been before. She called Evan into her office.

"Yes, Ms. Ross?"

"Why has Nicole not been deleted from the payroll?"

"Well, she was still paid for this period. On Friday, she will be removed because that is the start of the next pay period." Monique shook her head. "Evan, I emailed you saying that I talked to the bank and there was a stop payment put on Nicole's deposit. You should have received that email Tuesday evening." "I received no such email, Ms. Ross." Monique rubbed her head. *That doesn't make sense.* Evan had been the one to confirm Nicole's payment and now he apparently hadn't received the email Monique sent him. "Evan, where were you on Tuesday around 3:45?"

"I was in my office," he stated half-truthfully. "How long do you stay after work?" "Maybe 2 hours. Why?" Monique took some notes. "I'll be asking the questions. How well did you know Nicole Nicholson?" "Well, I didn't. I guess she was a co-worker but I never really had any conversations with her."

Monique tapped her pen. "What about Donna Roberts? You know her?" Evan shrugged. "I mean, she used to work under me. Then, she got moved to communications so that's all I have to say about it."

"Do you speak to Donna on an intimate level at all?" Monique had seen some of the interactions between Donna and Evan. Evan replied, "No. That violates our work code."

Monique nodded. Evan had done his reading. He knew exactly what to say and exactly when to say it. If he was the culprit, he was almost too smart to be caught. "Good answer but why do I have a sneaky feeling you're only saying that to eliminate my suspicions?" Evan folded his hands. "I don't know what would arouse your suspicions in the first place, Ms. Ross." At this, Monique let out a deep breath.

"Well, I won't take up any more of your time. You have a good rest of your day, Evan."

He nodded and left. *There's a snake on the premises.* Something was amiss within Mo's Mix, Monique realized. Nicole's actions had been the stepping stone to an even greater issue.

"How do you rewind?"

"You hit that orange button right there."

"What about fast forward?"

"Green." Agent Abby pointed towards it. "Pause?" "Blue." "How do you print images?" Agent Abby hit a square button. "After you pause the video, you can hit this button to print the image that you see on the screen." Monique nodded. "Great. Thank you. Try to work around me while I watch these tapes. I have an investigation to perform." The security team bobbed their heads and continued to work.

For 3 ½ hours, all Monique saw were people walking on the streets or cars coming to and from the parking lot. And just when she felt her eyelids getting heavy, something happened. Monique pounded the blue button and rammed the square button simultaneously. She threw the image in her purse then continued to watch. "You dirty little liars," she said to herself.

Once Monique had gotten back to her office, she had pieced the whole story together – at least what she thought was the whole story. Evan and Donna had some sort of intimate relationship, which was completely inappropriate considering he had a wife and it *did* violate work code. Nonetheless, Nicole found out about it because she saw Donna and Evan kissing in Evan's car. Monique figured Nicole had blackmailed them. "Check and mate." Monique lined the pictures up chronologically as she figured everything out.

"Hey, boss?" She jumped when Dominique came to her door. "Um...yes?" Dominique pointed to the security checkpoint, where a flamboyant man stood proudly. "April Spring's manager is here to see you." *This can't be good.* "Send him in," Monique said. She quickly placed her pictures into a nearby drawer. "Donovan Green. Pleased to meet you." He stuck his hand out. "Monique Ross but I can't say the same." They shook hands and Donovan came to sit down.

"So...you're probably wondering why I'm here."

"Actually, yes. This is quite the surprise."

"Well...there's no easy way to say this but...April's thinking of filing a lawsuit against Mo's Mix." Monique's eyeballs widened. "For?" Donovan gasped. "Oh, you haven't seen?" He pulled out a Jotter. "Well, let me show you." Donovan opened a picture of an old Cocoa Puff product. "This is the product that April designed." It was called "No Stress," which was the same name that Monique had given her product.

He flipped to Monique's pudding. "This is the product that you sold." "April never marketed No Stress so how can she--" Donovan put his hand up. "I'm getting there." He pulled out papers that said Malaysia Summers (a.k.a April Spring) owned the name "No Stress" in all its uses as a hair care product. "So, unless you change the name of your little pudding within 30 days, April will sue." Monique groaned. *This is more stress than I need right now.* "Alright. Is that all?" Donovan held his chest as if offended.

"Are you kicking me out, Ms. Ross?"

"Mr. Green, I have an extremely busy schedule so if you're not here to talk business, I have nothing else to say to you except have a nice day." Monique used her hand to usher over her security guards and they led Donovan out.

"Baby, I was coming home from work and I saw the most adorable flower pot. It had little hands on it, as if it was made by a child. I thought it would be great for our daughter's room. Would you like to see?" Monique looked over at Dre. "Sure." He could sense that something was off. "Baby, is everything alright?" She pushed her afro back. "Sure." This told Dre what he needed to know. "Are you still trying to find out who sent Nicole that final paycheck?"

"I'm trying to find the snake," Monique noted. "If I don't figure out who's sabotaging my business, Mo's Mix might go under and if we go under then..." She paused. "Then, I don't know, Dre." He came and sat next to her. "It's not healthy to worry, baby. Just relax. Trust that God will get you through this."

"I'll bet my Uncle Junior trusted in God and look what happened to him. First, God took Auntie Pam then He took Junior." Dre rubbed Monique's thigh. "Perhaps God has a greater plan for them." "What plan?"

"That they'll be together. That your uncle won't suffer anymore. That your auntie won't feel any more pain. I can't exactly explain it but God always has a plan."

"That doesn't make me feel better, Dre!" Monique yelled. She went and slammed the bedroom door. Ever since her aunt's death, everything seemed to come crashing down around her. It was then that Monique and Dre had begun growing apart, which led to their break-up. It was then that Daniel checked out of the world and allowed his business to go under. It was then that Uncle Junior started doing drugs again. Everything seemed to lead back to Auntie Pam's death.

"Monique, can I come in?"

"Go away!"

Dre came in anyways. "I can't do that. I know you need love right now." He hugged Monique. "You'll see God's plan in time. I promise you." As hard as Monique tried to deny Dre's words, she could not deny His word. She let tears fall while Dre spoke. "He loves you. He watches over you. He has a plan. I promise, Monique." She cried into Dre's shoulder. The more Monique did so, the more relieved she began to feel.

She looked up towards the sky. "Thank You," she told Him.

"How do you feel now?" Monique awoke on the bed in pajamas. Dre had a tray on the nearby desk. "Fine, I guess," she responded. "You started dozing off so I placed you on the bed and changed your clothes for you. This is dinner," Dre stated as he handed Monique the delicious smelling food. "Thank you. I appreciate this." He kissed her head. "I know. Since you're dealing with a lot right now, I made lasagna because I know you love it."

Monique sat up straight. "You got that right."

Dre left so he could show Monique what he'd bought in addition to the flower pot. She was about to attack the meal when she realized he hadn't given her a fork. "Dre, could you…" He came into the room with a fork but this was not just any fork. It was one with an engagement ring on the end. "Let's make it official, Mo. I want the world to know that we're getting married."

Monique cried tears of joy. "That is so sweet, Andre. I don't...I don't know what to say." She took a deep breath and added, "Except yes." Dre got on one knee and slid the ring onto her finger. "I love you, baby. Forever and always." Monique hugged him tightly. "I love you, too. Until infinity." While Monique ate, all she could do was stare at the ring. *We're really doing this, huh?* Once she was done eating, Dre showed her a newspaper clipping.

"There's a 4-bedroom house on Broadway Boulevard. I think it would be really nice for us. It's close to the subway and bus stations so we wouldn't have to always drive to work. Then, there's a college nearby so we would probably be able to find a local babysitter if necessary. Plus, the down payment is within our budget and I have a friend at the bank who said he would help us with getting a loan. On top of these, Nathalie's friend Morgan is a real estate agent. I could..." Dre paused because he had lost Monique. "How does that sound so far?"

Monique looked at the picture of the house. "Why don't we just look at the house first before we start talking about loans and bus stations and colleges and real estate agents? It's a lot for one sitting, Andre." He sighed. "Yeah, you're right. I was just saying this could be an option." She rubbed her head. "It could. I've had a long day, though. Can we just talk about this later?" Monique began laying down. "My feet hurt and I'm so tired." He let out a deep breath. "Sure. I'll let you sleep." "It's already after 10. You're not coming to bed too?"

"I have work that I need to do. Night, baby."

"What's wrong," she asked.

Dre pulled out his brief case and started towards the living room. "Nothing. Get some sleep. I'll see you in the morning." Monique sighed. "See you." She knew something was amiss with Dre but she couldn't pinpoint what it was. *He'll tell me when he feels comfortable,* Monique decided. As she began going back to sleep, her text message tone went off. At first, Monique thought to ignore it. Then, it went off again. And again. On the fourth message, Monique figured something was wrong.

Dominique: Boss, you need to get over to Mo's Mix right now.

Dominique: Some serious shit just went down.

Dominique: Excuse my language.

Dominique: We need you here.

Dre pulled up slowly to the crime scene, unaware of what was happening. "Did they say what went wrong?" Monique shook her head. "No. Dominique just told me I had to get here ASAP." Once they got out the car, Monique immediately smelled smoke. "What's going on," she asked the officer. "Ma'am, this is a crime scene. I'm going to need you to step back." She pulled out her ID. "I own this business. What's going on?" The officer used a flashlight to look at the ID. "Oh. My apologies, Ms. Ross. Right this way." Dre attempted to go after her. The officer held up one hand.

"Are you an employee at Mo's Mix?"

"No."

"Husband?"

Dre sighed. "Not yet." The officer shook his head. "Well, you can't come back here. Only employees and spouses are allowed in this area." Monique flashed Dre a look to say she was sorry then proceeded to assess the damage. "Some kids were smoking in the back and they carelessly threw their cigarettes away. It looks as if the fire began in the basement then worked its way up to the second floor. Once it reached the chemical wing, smoke detectors went off and firefighters were able to stop it. But, there was one casualty."

Monique gasped. "Injury or…" She didn't want to say the other word. The officer motioned towards a motionless Agent Abby. She was not dead but the look on her face said she wanted to be. "What happened?" Agent Abby looked towards her badly damaged thigh. "They didn't want to get caught." "Who, the kids?"

"No, the…" As Agent Abby was speaking, she experienced a coughing fit. The medics kindly asked Monique to step away. *What is going on?* Monique went back over by Dre. "This is too much. This is just too much." She began crying again so he held her. "C'mere. Calm down, baby. I got you. Just relax." Monique took a deep breath and called Dominique. "Hello?"

"Where are you?"

"I'm on the east side of the building giving a statement to the officers."

Monique went over there. "Dominique, what happened?" Dominique said, "I was getting ready to leave and, as I headed towards the parking lot, I smelled smoke. I thought it was just someone smoking even though they're not supposed to but when I got closer to the ground floor, it smelled stronger than just a cigarette. So, I used the fire exit and I called 911."

"Do you know who else was in there?"

Dominique shrugged. "Just some people from Finance."

"Who from Finance," Monique wondered.

"That guy who's the CFO, Melodie, and Clark. Oh, Marley and Agent Abby were here too. He said he was closing the tech wing after cleaning all the computers and he smelled the smoke as well. He went to save Agent Abby because he heard her calling for help." Dominique pointed towards Marley with a mask on his face. "He can probably tell you more about it."

"Thank you," Monique said as she made her way towards Marley. "Ms. Ross, I can't work here anymore," he exclaimed. "You got people setting buildings on fire and shit! I just can't stay here!"

"Marley, calm…"

"Calm down? Is that what you're gonna say? Agent Abby is over there traumatized. This is not okay, Ms. Ross! I quit!" He threw the mask away from him then went to his car. Monique just held her chest – preparing for the anxiety attack. As Monique started feeling short of breath, the baby started kicking heavily and her body began shutting down.

"Monique, breathe. Just breathe!" She awoke in a hospital room with her legs pried open. "You're almost there. Just breathe." Monique did as told and she pushed out a beautiful baby girl. Then, the baby's yawn led to choking, which led to blood spewing from the small child's mouth. Monique reached out for her baby but the doctors said it was too late. They ruled it infanticide. "Monique, you killed your child," the voice in her head said. "You knew how stressful your life was. You put that on an innocent baby. How could you?!"

Monique's body popped up and she was back at her old home. "Andre? Andre!" Her body was still palpitating so Mrs. Ross came running in with water. "Hey, hey. Calm down. Andre is out talking to the officers and discussing the next moves for Mo's Mix. He brought you here because he knew you needed family." Mrs. Ross looked at the ring on Monique's finger. "I see you finally came to your senses." Monique sat up and drank the water. "Mom, not now."

Mrs. Ross sighed. "I was only trying to lighten the mood. What happened?" Once her mother asked this, Monique emitted a river of tears and spilled her guts to her first best friend. "Oh, baby. I know. You have bills to pay, a child on the way, and your business seems to be falling apart. That's a lot to take on, huh?" Monique nodded. "It is." Mrs. Ross rubbed her daughter's shoulder. "Why don't you take one of those off your plate?"

"Are you suggesting that I have an abortion?"

Mrs. Ross scoffed. "Of course not! The thought of taking an innocent child's life just appalls me. I meant that you should take some time away from the business and let somebody else handle it." "Who else knows business like me?" Mrs. Ross looked towards a picture of Daniel. "Who inspired you to get into business in the first place?"

"But, mama, he doesn't even want to get back into it. He lost his fight."

"Trust me, baby. He'll do anything to help you out because you're his only sister." Monique thought about it. Her mom was right. "Now, back to what you said before. Why would I *ever* suggest you have an abortion? What kind of inhumane person does that?" In this moment, the southern conservative was coming out of Mrs. Ross.

"Sometimes, people feel that that's the only way out," Monique noted, reflecting on the many abortions Camille had. Mrs. Ross shook her head. "They never thought about adoption?" "What about in the instance of rape?" Monique challenged.

Mrs. Ross shook her head again. "That's not the case with you. You made a choice to lay down with Andre and you knew what could come out of it. So, now you have to deal with this decision as an adult. If you choose to have an abortion just so you can run your business, then I hope you know a way to clear your conscience. I never raised you to be selfish. You probably picked that up from college."

"Selfish, mama? Isn't it selfish to bring a child in this world who you don't know how to raise? Better yet, isn't selfish to bring three of them then force them to struggle and to always have to fight?"

"Is this a general or specific question, Monique?"

"I don't know, mama. Why don't you ask the invisible scars I have?"

Mrs. Ross huffed. "You turned out fine." "Yeah, but it was never easy. I always had to fight." "But, you don't have to fight anymore. You have a fiancé with a good job. You have a business and you have a family that loves you. That's a lot more than I had. So, why would you not want to have this child?"

"What if I'm not ready to lose my ambition? Raising a child is a sacrifice and I don't know if I can give up my business."

"Then let some other family raise the child you carried for nine months. I wonder how Dre will feel about that."

Monique argued, "It's not Dre's body, though." "When his sperm connected to your eggs, your bodies became one. You are equally responsible for this child." "Says who?"

"DNA," Mrs. Ross finished with.

"We need to talk." When Monique saw Dre again, this was the first thing she had to say. "About?" Monique held her belly. "I went to Dr. Seneca last week and she told me I was 10 weeks pregnant. That means that I can still have an abortion because the legal cut-off date is 14 weeks. So…" Dre stopped in his tracks. "You still want to have an abortion?"

"Dre, this baby is taking a lot out of me. I don't know if I can handle it anymore."

"That's why you have me. We'll do it together."

"I don't know if *I* want to do it anymore, though, Dre. I'm tired. I'm worried. I'm irritable. Bottom line, I'm not happy. And if I'm not happy, then our daughter's not happy. I don't think it's fair to myself or the child to have to go through this; whatever I feel, she feels. I can't do this anymore." Monique pulled out her phone. "I'm calling Dr. Seneca. I'm…" Dre took her hand. "Baby, let's talk about this. Before you do anything, let's just talk about this."

Monique took a deep breath. "Okay." Just as she was about to begin speaking, she got a call from Daniel. "Hello?" "Hey," he said. "I talked to mom and, after much debate, I decided I would come help you out with Mo's Mix. This is not to say that I'll take over the business but I'll do any heavy work you need for the next few months. I want you to relax, okay?"

Monique replied, "Okay. Thank you. Can you be at the office at 7 tomorrow morning for clean-up?" "5:45? Got it." Monique chuckled. "Alright. Thank you, Daniel. This means a lot." "Anything for my baby sis." Once Daniel said this, Monique came to her senses. Although she was scared of becoming a terrible mother and putting her child through struggles, Monique realized that Mrs. Ross had always done her best to make a way for her children. *Mama's right. I am strong.*

"Baby, I just had an intense moment and I got scared that I was going to mess up."

Dre told her, "That's normal. You can read all the books in the world on parenting and get all the advice but, ultimately, you won't know anything until you actually become a parent. And then you go from there. No parent is perfect but, as long as we do our best, I'm sure our daughter will realize that we care for her."

Dre's saying "our daughter" gave Monique a renewed sense of self. *Our daughter. Our family.*

Monique and Daniel walked up to a horde of angry employees. "Ms. Ross, am I out of a job?"

"What's going to happen to my family?"

"I have kids to feed."

"I live paycheck to paycheck."

"Who did this?!"

Monique began to crack under pressure so Daniel held her to steady her. "I'm here, Mo. Your big brother's got ya." They proceeded forward as Monique stood to face the disgruntled workers.

"Last night, there was an accident at Mo's Mix and I'm sad to say that Agent Abby is currently in critical condition. However, doctors believe that she will make a full recovery. I'm not sure I can say the same for Mo's Mix. Until further notice, the chemistry, security and tech wings will be under repairs so they will be shut down. In that time, I can provide checks to those with sick days. Once those sick days are up, though, I will not be able to pay employees. Mo's Mix will take a big hit paying for these damages and I'm sure you all understand that. I am sorry for any inconveniences. Can everyone please meet me in conference room A? Thanks in advance for your cooperation and, again, I am sorry to all those who will be affected by this."

Monique stepped down from the podium and she could sense universal disappointment. She felt as if her employees wondered how she let a crisis of that magnitude happen. *I think I've lost their trust.*

"As some of you may have already realized, I am expecting a child soon. Also, I am preparing to purchase my first house. These things so, I have decided to scale back my time at Mo's Mix. In the meantime, my brother Daniel will be assisting me. Daniel has an MBA in Finance and Economics so he is highly qualified to help me. In addition, he ran his own business called Dan's Plan, which was a web-based service dedicated to helping people lose weight. Among its products were shakes, workout videos, weightlifting equipment and fitness plans designed by certified dieticians. Unfortunately, Dan's Plan experienced bankruptcy so Daniel decided to dissolve the business. Even still, Daniel has made a modest living as a personal accountant and business advisor for friends and family."

Monique looked towards Daniel. "Employees, please greet my brother Daniel Ross." The employees remained deadpan as Daniel stood. Monique sighed and continued. "Also, I've brought in an old friend of mine, Sheila Flores. She works as a grief counselor for businesses. So, she'll be here to talk to those who work in departments that are temporarily closed. Sheila is qualified because she too was a disgruntled employee. Her old boss, John Summers, was stealing from his company and this resulted in widespread layoffs. During her experience with being unemployed, Sheila wrote a novel titled *It's Not Over*. I want you all to remember that: it's *not* over. I truly am sorry this happened and I will do my best to repay everyone. But, please keep up hope these next few months. Thank you for taking the time to hear me out. You all are dismissed."

As the employees with assignments went to their stations, the others remained in their seats. "Where are we supposed to go," one belted. Sheila sat Indian style on the stage. "Nowhere. I would like to talk to you all here." Monique took a deep breath and thought about when she had met Sheila. "You know, it sucks. You spend all these years in school trying to build a career. Then, you have one only to realize your boss is a corrupt ass individual." Sheila had groaned. "But, what brings you here?"

Monique had looked down at her malnourished belly. "I haven't eaten in 3 weeks. My parents can't support me anymore and my boyfriend is in law school. So, I'm just trying to get food stamps to survive." Monique vividly remembered bursting into tears. "Look at me complaining. At least I'm earning a final check." Sheila had held Monique. "Hey, it's going to be okay. Just keep up hope." Monique hoped that she had given her employees the same reassurance. Monique hoped she herself could remain positive. *My business might be failing.*

"Ms. Ross, it's easy to lose faith when things like this happen. I mean, an entire floor of your business has just been demolished. But, not to worry. We have assessed the damages and we see that some causes were not within your control. Therefore, we have decided to cut you a check for $5,000." Monique wanted to bash the lady's head in right then and there. She had never been a fighter except when it came to what was fair. "$5,000?! The damages were worth at least 10,000!!!"

The lady opened her file. "Please calm down, Ms. Ross. The insurance does not cover all damages. We only cover what we believe wasn't within your control." "What's that supposed to mean?" Monique asked, trying to calm herself. The lady pointed to a report. "This says that the fire might have been caused by a cigarette but there were chemicals involved – the same chemicals you have in some of your labs. So, how do we know you didn't set your own building on fire just to earn a quick buck? Nonetheless, we here at Arthur Muller are compassionate; we are giving you the benefit of the doubt because we understand that Mo's Mix is a reputable business. To cover damages, we will give you $5,000."

Monique pulled out her phone to show the lady images of Mo's Mix. "You see this? An *entire* floor was obliterated. Not to mention the expensive equipment and materials that were completely incinerated. Then, people's lives were at stake. One of my employees is currently in critical condition. So what the fuck am I going to do with $5,000?! That's chump change!"

The lady seemed to be angered by Monique's tone. "We could give you nothing and tell you, 'C'est la vie.' How does *that* sound?" Daniel held Monique's shoulder. "Step down, Mo. You're not gonna win this one."

"But, Daniel, I know--" He shook his head. "Just take the $5,000. It's better that than nothing." The lady nodded. "Listen to him. There ain't nothing like a strong man." Monique could hear hunger in the lady's tone. The insurance lady liked the sight of Daniel. "Funny – his boyfriend says the same thing." Upon saying this, Monique stormed out and the astonished insurance lady held the check in her hand. "She was just saying that, right? You're not really…" Daniel took the check. "Nope. I'm gay and proud of it." He walked out.

"$5,000?! What am I supposed to do with $5,000?" Daniel shrugged. "Improvise. What would Madame Dublier do?" Madame Dublier was a character from a book that Mrs. Ross always read to her children. Although Daniel and James admired Madame, Monique saw much of herself inside the character. Monique laughed aloud. "Hey, hey! I'll make a way!" Daniel added, "'Cause I am Madame Dublier." This was Madame Dublier's signature saying just before she solved all the problems. *Mommy, do you think I'll ever be like Madame Dublier?* Mrs. Ross had smiled saying, "Of course, sweetie. Now go get some sleep." Monique had smiled too and begun skipping off to her room.

"So I have a date with Christina tonight." Daniel said, bringing Monique back to the present. He tapped his fingers on the dashboard. "I don't know about him though."

"What's wrong?"

"I just met him a few weeks back and he's already asking to come over and he wants a title and he wants us to start synchronizing our outfits." "Oh, I see. You don't like commitment." Daniel shook his head. "Commitment doesn't like me." Monique wondered, "Is there any other reason you don't know about Christina?"

"Something doesn't seem right with him," Daniel admitted. "I feel like he walks around with this chip on his shoulder and it's probably because we're gay. My thing is, though, if you accept who you are then no one else's opinion should matter. I mean, I understand that there are people out there who hate me for who I am or don't approve of who I am but *I* love me and *I* approve of who I am. And I need a partner who feels the same way, honestly. That's another reason I'm sort of wary of Christina. I'm not sure if he fully accepts himself."

Monique sighed. She was seeing a part of Daniel she had never seen before. All the years that she had known him as straight, he kept to himself and he never talked about what went on inside of him. *Maybe it was because he was hiding from himself. Now that he has openly admitted to being gay, he's seemed to have found himself.* "Well, what are you going to do?" Daniel pulled out his phone. "I'm going to call him. I'm going to break things off. It's the only reasonable solution." As Daniel made his phone call, Monique's phone started going off. She couldn't answer it because she was driving.

"Daniel, can you check my phone?" He picked it up and balanced his own phone on his ear. "Hey, Christina. You're probably at work right now but we need to talk. Text me when you get this message. Bye." Daniel hung up and peered at Monique's phone. "It's Camille. She called you three times. You want me to call back?" Knowing Camille, three calls meant it was serious. "Yeah. This could be big." Daniel slid his finger across Camille's name.

"Mo? Hey. You need to--"

"It's Daniel," he said. Camille sighed. "Where's Mo? I need her." "She's driving right now. What's up?" "Tell her to get over to my place immediately. I might know something that can help her out." Daniel looked over at Monique. "Camille says she wants you to come over."

"But, I have to get back to--"

"She says it's important." Monique sighed and turned the corner. "On my way."

"What do you mean he was here?"

"Somehow he found me," Camille cried. "I swear I didn't tell him where I was." Monique hugged her friend. "Calm down, Camille. Just calm down. Have you called the police?" Camille nodded. "Yes. Right after he came. I'm putting out a restraining order but that's not why I called you."

"What else is up?"

Camille sat on the couch. "I think Trevor may have something to do with what happened at Mo's Mix a few nights ago. He said, 'Let your friend know that there's more where that came from.' First your hair and now this. I'm worried, Mo." Monique let out a deep breath and had a flashback.

Nicole said: "Trevor, you told me you wouldn't be here until..."

Monique's next question was, "Who is Trevor's baby mama?" "Some girl named Nicole," Camille replied. "Why?"

"Is her last name Nicholson?" "I don't know. Why are you asking me all these questions?" Monique pulled out her phone. "Excuse me for a second." She dialed Dominique's number. "Hey, Dominique. Are you busy?" Dominique had just returned from lunch. "Not exactly. What do you need, boss?"

"Did you know Nicole Nicholson?"

"I helped her schedule an interview. She asked me to watch her daughter while she did the interview and I was like—"

"Did she tell you the child's name?" Monique interrupted. "Raven," Dominque confirmed. Monique pushed her afro back. "Okay. Thanks Dominique. Back to work, please." After this, Monique grabbed her purse. "Cam, I gotta go. Daniel can stay here with you just in case Trevor comes back." Daniel scoffed. "Oh, because I didn't have anything to do."

"Your job is making royalties from Dan's Plan."

Daniel shrugged. "But I'm also supposed to be meeting Christina." "You said you'd help me out, remember? Help me out by staying with Camille. I have an errand to run." "But, who's at Mo's Mix?" He asked. Monique sighed. "Good question." "You already know there's a snake on the premises and you would leave your business..." Monique put her hand up. "I got this. I got this."

"You owe me one," Veronica told Monique. Veronica was Monique's old friend who had graduated #1 in her class at St. John's. From a young age, Veronica had been exposed to the world of business since her father had been one of the city's most successful stock brokers. Then, Veronica became one herself. Now, she was in partial retirement as she searched for another venture. "Will you pay me for business sitting?" "I'll take you out to lunch so we can catch up and you can order that expensive shrimp you love so much," Monique responded. Veronica chuckled. "Good enough."

Since Mo's Mix was in the hands of Monique's good friend and Camille was in the hands of Daniel, Monique felt confident that she could run her errand. Unlike the first time, she banged on Nicole's door. The little girl from Camille's apartment answered. "My mommy's not home," the child said in an innocent voice. "Then, who's watching you?"

"Um..."

Obviously, Nicole had coached the girl on what to say so Raven didn't have a response. Nicole began walking forward. "Rae, just shut..." Nicole froze when she saw Monique. "Long time no see, Ms. Ross." Monique barged inside. "How are you, Nicole? How have you been?" Nicole shifted uncomfortably. "I've been fine. Can I ask why you're here?"

"I just wanted to visit an old employee and perhaps patch up the tension. I've never been one to end a work or personal relationship distastefully."

"Then, why were you gunning so hard to put a stop payment on my last check?"

Monique laughed. "Well, Nicole, that was just business. Based upon your breach of the contract you signed, you did not qualify for a final check." Monique thought about something. "How did you know I was attempting a stop payment?"

"The bank called me," Nicole lied. "Are you sure it wasn't Evan? Or perhaps Donna?" Nicole shook her head. "Who? Do I know these two people?" "The security cameras say so," Monique stated. "The ones that were destroyed in the fire?" With every word, Nicole began to seem guiltier. "Convenient, wasn't it?"

"For whom?" Nicole challenged.

Monique chuckled. "Whomever would be affected by the content of the videos, of course." "Your tone suggests that you think I might be one of these people," Nicole said. "The photos don't lie."

"What photos," Nicole wondered, suddenly caught off guard. Happy that she finally had the upper hand, Monique smiled. "That's confidential information. You have a nice day, Nicole." Nicole nodded. "I hope your head feels better. I heard you took a pretty nasty blow a while back."

"She did it," Monique exclaimed. "She did all of it! Nicole is a goddam criminal." Dre asked Monique, "What happened to taking a break from Mo's Mix?" "I can't, baby. There's too much at stake." Dre sighed into the phone. "Like the life of our child?" This sent a shockwave into Monique. "What's that supposed to mean?"

"My brother died because my mom put a too much stress on herself and she drank her way into a miscarriage. That's the last thing I would want to happen for us." Monique took a deep breath. Dre had told her about this in confidence and he had cried to her because he hadn't been able to meet his brother.

"You're right, Andre. But, this business is also my baby and I can't let anything happen to her."

Dre understood. "I know. Just scale it back a little. Daniel's helping you, right?" Monique pulled back into Camille's parking lot. "Yes. I'm actually getting ready to give him some assignments right now." "Then you'll go home and take a nap?" Monique sighed. "Then I'll go home and take a nap."

"Thank you, Monique. I have a meeting with a client so I'll see you later, alright?"

"Alright. Bye, baby."

"Bye. Love you, Mo."

Monique smiled inside and out. "Love you too, Dre."

When she walked up the stairs, Monique smelled smoke coming from Camille's apartment. She immediately thought the worse. "So it wasn't enough to set my business on fire, huh?" She began banging on the door. Daniel opened it up and stared quizzically at his younger sister. "Mo, what you talking about?" As soon as Monique walked in, she realized that Camille and Daniel had been smoking weed.

"Cam, I thought you quit." Camille took the blunt from Daniel. "Bad habits die hard." Monique rolled her eyes. "What part of 'I have asthma and I'm pregnant' don't you all understand?!" She slammed the door and went out to her car. Daniel came running down. "Why you getting mad? Camille and I were just letting off some steam."

"Okay, but you're about to be working on my business with me, Daniel. Nothing is gonna get done if you're gonna be fucking high all the time. Plus, I can't do anything if my fucking business partner is in JAIL!" Daniel took a whiff of fresh air in an attempt to sober himself. "Sis, calm down. I won't do it anymore. I promise." "That's the same thing you told Auntie Pam," Monique cut. She knew this would hurt Daniel. "Don't bring Auntie Pam into this."

"You promised, Daniel. When she died, you said you'd stop."

"Don't bring Auntie Pam into this," he repeated. He had been getting better but Monique's comments were reminding Daniel that the pain was still there. "What would she say if she saw you now? She'd be disappointed to see--" Daniel kicked the side of Monique's car. "I'm out of here. Don't ask me for no more fucking favors." He pulled out another blunt and continued smoking as he stalked off. Monique leaned her head on her steering wheel. *So much for him helping me.*

"What did you say to him?" Mrs. Ross peered at Daniel, who sat sulking in a corner. Monique fixed her sunglasses on her face. "The truth," Monique responded vaguely. At this, Mrs. Ross grabbed Monique's arm. "You talk to me, little girl. Your father and I have been trying so hard to help Daniel heal and we thought we saw progress. Now, it looks as if he's regressing. I hope this ain't your fault."

"People don't heal from trauma," Monique noted. "Daniel can cope but he'll never heal. You have to get over it, mama. You've been trying so hard to make Daniel someone he's not. No wonder he pretended to be straight all those years. It was because *you* could never fathom having a gay son." Mrs. Ross slapped her daughter. "Just because your uncle died doesn't mean you act out of turn."

"Deaths are births to ugly truths," Monique stated aphoristically. Then, she proceeded to take her seat in the first pew. Mr. Ross came next to his daughter. "I know you're hurting, Monique, but you can't take that out on the people around you. You're angry that you and your uncle never patched things up before his…before his…" Mr. Ross couldn't find the strength to speak the words. He couldn't understand why his brother would go so soon. So violently. Monique took off her sunglasses and held her father's face. "It's okay to cry, daddy. Why do you think I had those sunglasses on?"

Mr. Ross kissed her head and let his daughter's tears fall onto his pants. Just the same, Monique allowed her father's tears to fall onto her dress. "I love you, baby." "I love you too, daddy." They shared a rather intimate moment – one they hadn't shared in a while. Once the moment was done, Monique went to see her uncle one last time. "Uncle Junior, for the longest you and I were on the same page. It was as if our thoughts were in sync. Then, you hurt Auntie Pam and I found it hard to ever forgive you. Now, I wish I hadn't been so selfish. If Auntie Pam could forgive you, why couldn't I? I love you, Uncle Junior." Monique blew a kiss to her late uncle. "Bye now."

Andre was Monique's rock during a cold storm. He held her throughout the funeral as she cried profusely while their daughter responded accordingly. Monique lay on his arm at the burial and throughout the repast. When Monique and Andre came into the repast, Yvette noticed the ring. "Nice to know that I talked some sense into y'all." Monique quickly tucked her hand away. "Can we not do this right now? We're here to celebrate the life of Uncle Junior, not comment on mine." Yvette looked around as if she wanted to figure out who Monique was talking to. "I'm sorry. Was that directed towards me?" Monique sighed. "Yes it was. I was pretty clear about that."

Yvette narrowed her glance in on Monique. "You will not speak to me any kind of way, little girl." Monique replied, "Or what?" "Or what? See, that's the problem with you young kids. You always want to challenge somebody. 'Or what'?" Yvette shook her head and walked off. "I won't even waste my breath on you," she murmured. Dre rubbed Monique's arms. "Why are you so angry?"

Monique sat down at the nearest table. "Because, Dre. I didn't get to speak to my uncle one last time. We hadn't talked since Auntie Pam's funeral, which was a year ago...." Monique paused. "A year ago today. Auntie Pam died a year ago today." She said it aloud so the entire family could hear. They all looked at her and nodded in recognition. "It's not fair," Monique cried. Dre continued to rub her shoulders. "I know it's not. But, you can't be mad at yourself. You didn't know this would happen. Just think: now your uncle is in a better place. He's free of pain." Monique rubbed her belly as the tears began reforming. "Yeah, but I'm not."

At this point, Dre knew that nothing he was saying would register with Monique. "I'm here," he told her. "I know this is a rough time so just remember that I'm here, okay?" Monique smiled. She liked that Dre didn't try to rationalize her pain. *This is one of the reasons that I love him,* she thought to herself.

After the repast, Dre made a visit to his family. He had been seeing Monique's family for a whole month and he started to miss his own. "Andre!!" His mother exclaimed. Though she hardly got up, she was excited to see her eldest son. "Come sta?" Dre grinned. "Bene, mamma. Come sta?" From a far corner, Nathalie looked on to her brother and mother speaking in Italian. "Mi sento fantastica," Mrs. Cassells beamed. She rocked her arms as if there was a child in between them. "Bambino?" Mrs. Cassells asked. This was the Italian word for "baby." Dre stared quizzically. He hadn't told his mom about the baby but she already knew.

Then, he looked back to Nathalie. "You told her already? I said I wanted to surprise her." Nathalie shrugged. "Oh well." "You're always running your *bocca*!" Dre yelled. "Silenzio for once!" Nathalie scoffed. "Sei arrabbiato?" She knew this would stump Andre up, as his Italian was harshly limited. Nathalie stepped closer. "Sei arrabbiato?" He remained silent.

"Tu sei arrabbiato," she decided while walking off. Dre just rubbed his head. His mother held her son. "You are angry?" This caused Dre to look up.

Mrs. Cassells told him, "I'm just translating what Nathalie said. Don't expect me to speak English for long." "Mamma, I miss your English," he cried. "Impara l'italiano," she replied. This was a phrase that Andre was used to hearing growing up. He had gotten many things from his father, including stubbornness. So, any time his mother would say "impara l'italiano," he would let it go it go in one ear and shoot straight out the other. However, since Mr. Cassells' death, Mrs. Cassells hardly spoke in English anymore. That day, Dre vowed that he would "impara l'italiano," or learn Italian, for his mamma's sake.

Since silence had ensued, Mrs. Cassells went back to rocking her arms. "Bambino?" Dre nodded. "Sì." "Chi è la mamma?" Mrs. Cassells wondered.

"Monique," Dre answered. "I was hoping you'd say that." Mrs. Cassells held on to her cross. "There's no rush, but are you two ever going to get married?" Dre nodded again. "That's actually why I came to see you. Last week, Monique and I decided we would get married."

"Is it because she found out she was having a baby?" Mrs. Cassells questioned in a disapproving tone. Although she was elated to be a grandmother, she was not at all thrilled about the idea of a baby out of wedlock. "No, mamma. We decided it was something we both wanted."

"Well, that's good for you all. Give Monique my blessing and tell her that her product still works like a charm." Dre kissed his mamma's head. "Will do. I gotta get back home because I have to finish up some work but it was nice seeing you."

Mrs. Cassells kissed his cheek. "Oh, you too, sweetie. Ciao!" "Ciao!"

Monique kissed Dre as soon as he got in the house. She had no particular reason for doing so. She just wanted to do something nice for him. In addition to showering him in affection, she had cooked his favorite meal: sautéed lamb. "Monique, you didn't have to do this." She kissed her man again. "Of course I did. You're my love, Andre. I want to make you feel good." He took another whiff of Monique's cooking. "You've succeeded." Monique smiled and set the table. "Mangiamo!"

Dre stared at her quizzically. "Is that Italian you're speaking?" Monique giggled then switched to French. "Mangeons!" Dre laughed. "Oui!" One of the things he loved about Monique was that she had adapted to his multicultural background by learning minimal French, Italian, Spanish and Amharic (the official language of Ethiopia). Amharic had been the hardest to learn but Monique took on the challenge. She even knew how to write in Amharic at a basic level.

"Je t'adore."

Monique shook her head. "Non. Je *t'aime*."

Dre chuckled. "Même chose."

Monique giggled again and started cutting her lamb. Happily, she and her soon-to-be enjoyed a nice meal of lamb and lemonade. Afterwards, she rubbed Dre's back as he read over his case. Then, they switched. Dre rubbed Monique's feet while she wrote up a schedule for the next work day. "Dre?" Monique asked. He kissed her petite foot. "Yes, baby?"

"We're really having a baby. Like we're really doing this." Dre let go of Monique's foot and rubbed her shoulder. "Yes, we are. Are you having second thoughts?" Monique peered down at the beautiful ring on her finger. "Maybe. I don't know." Dre sat next to Monique. "What's going on in that beautiful mind?"

"You know when you have that moment that you realize you've really grown up?" Dre nodded. Monique told him, "I'm having one of those right now. It's crazy." As she spoke, Monique's eyes fell to the old guest bedroom. It had been converted into a room for their daughter. "In six months, she'll be here, Dre." He kissed Monique's belly. "Six interesting months lie ahead."

Monique held her belly. "You can say that again. I can't believe I'm really going to have someone looking up to me and expecting so much out of me. I don't know if I'll be able to handle it." Dre turned to Monique. "What does that mean?"

"I don't know, Dre. I'm having second thoughts about this whole working mom thing again. Maybe my great aunt was right. We can't work *and* take care of our child." "Okay, so you'll take some time off then bounce back, right?" Monique scoffed. "Why does it have to be me? What if I wanted to work?"

Dre asked, "Don't you need recovery time?"

"I do but why should I have to miss that much work?"

"So your body can heal itself after nine grueling months."

Monique wondered, "What if you took a leave of absence?" Dre shook his head. "Caleb would never allow it." "I'm sorry. Since when did Caleb come into the conversation of you raising our child?"

"Since he is my boss."

Monique rolled her eyes. "And? This is a milestone in your life and he's gotta respect that." "That's not fair to ask of him, Monique." This angered Monique. "But it's *fair* for me to be a stay at home mom when I have a business to run?!" Dre rubbed Monique's stomach. "Baby, calm down." She snatched her body away. "No! You're being unfair, Dre! Actually, you're being a little sexist. Am I just supposed to give up my business?"

"Am I supposed to sacrifice my job?!" Dre countered.

"Why are we even having this baby in the first place?!" Monique yelled. Then, she had an epiphany. "It's because it was an accident. We didn't plan any of this, Dre. I just got pregnant and we felt obligated to raise the child. Oh my god – I'm turning into my mom." Monique held her head so it wouldn't start spinning. "We have no idea what we're doing, Andre. We can't raise a child." Dre had been wanting a family for a long time. He just never had the courage to tell Monique.

"It's too late to think about that now, Monique. We have to make the best of our situation." Monique glanced at her cell phone. "Or I could call Dr. Seneca and arrange to end all of this." Dre's eyes got wide. "Wait, shouldn't we talk about this?" "What more is there to talk about, Dre? We're not ready to raise a child." Dre put his hand on top of Monique's phone. "We should think this through."

Monique had all but made up her mind. "Move your hand, Andre." He kept it where it was. "I can't do that." "Please move your hand." Dre slid the phone away from Monique. "I'll move it if you promise you won't schedule an abortion." "I can't promise that."

"Then I can't give you your phone."

Monique was quickly losing patience. "Give me my phone, Dre!" She hollered. He kept his hand where it was. "I told you my condition." "It's not your body so it's not your decision!"

"You weren't saying that a few minutes ago. You called her *our* baby. So, shouldn't I have a say?" "You *don't* have a say, Dre. If I want to have an abortion, I will. That's the end of the conversation." Monique aggressively pulled Dre's hand up from on top of her phone. "Now, if you'll excuse me, I have a phone call to make." Upset, Dre tried to grab the phone. In the process, they both watched the device fall to the floor and crack.

"What did you do?!" Monique ran to pick up the shattered device. "Really, Dre? You just broke my phone." He said, "I didn't mean to. You were just talking crazy and I had to do something to stop you." "So you broke my phone?!" Monique had a sudden urge to throw the device at him. "If you're *so* invested in this child, how come you couldn't take a leave of absence from work?"

"I'm already on thin ice with Caleb, since I've been struggling with cases. I just don't want to test it."

"No. You're selfish. That's it," Monique decided. "That's it? So that's the only reason I want to work? Because I'm selfish? Are you even aware how ridiculous you sound?"

"Are *you* even aware that I'm angry and saying things like that will just make me angrier?"

Dre ignored Monique's statement. "If there's anyone being selfish, it's you. That child never did anything to you. Why should she have to suffer? You have no idea who our daughter will turn out to be."

"She'll probably be miserable if her parents can't even raise her right."

"How do you know that, Mo? Parenting is a learning journey."

Monique shook her head. "I can't do this right now. Just leave me the hell alone for the night." Dre grabbed her waist. "Let's talk." Monique pushed him away. "I meant what I said." She went into the room and locked the door. Dre simply bowed his head and sighed. *Just when I thought it was getting easier.*

"An abortion? That's intense, man." Dre took another swig of beer. "I'm saying. I've been telling her not to but it's not my body so it's apparently not my decision." The more he thought about how Monique had treated him, the more Dre drank. His buddy Knox finally stopped him after about round 13. "Aye, man. Don't you have work in the morning?" Dre looked at his watch. It said 12:13 AM. "Shit," he said to himself. "I do." Slowly, Dre rose from the chair and reached for his keys. Knox grabbed them. "I'm driving."

"But how are you gonna get home?"

"The same way I got here – I'll call a cab," Knox responded. Dre nodded and followed Knox to the truck, drunker than he had intended. As Dre walked, the street lights wobbled from side to side. "Do the street lights always shake like that?" Knox chuckled. "Man, you drunk as shit. Monique is gone have a cow." While they drove, Dre and Knox caught up. It had been a while since they saw each other so there was much to talk about.

Hearing that Knox was only in town for a few days, Dre jumped at the opportunity to have a couple of beers with an old friend. Knox hauled Dre up the stairs and told Monique, "He's all yours." Monique groaned and pointed to the couch. "Lay him there and I'll deal with him in the morning."

"Yes, ma'am," Knox replied. Monique rolled her eyes and began walking off. Knox stated, "Hey, congrats on the baby. I'll bet you'll be a great mother to your dead infant." Although he was less drunk than Dre, Knox was a little tipsy himself. Already irritated, Monique pointed to the front door. "You can leave right now, Knox. You were always just Dre's friend."

"I'm just saying. You should be ashamed of yourself for even *thinking* about killing an innocent child, let along going through with it."

"How 'bout you get pregnant and try to make a better decision? Oh wait. You can't get pregnant. Therefore, you will never understand why I'm doing this." Knox shook his head. "Dre told me all about you. Personally, I prefer him single."

"And I prefer him sober but you don't hear me complaining." Monique pointed to the door again. "Now leave before you start something you can't finish." "Like you and motherhood?"

This infuriated Monique. "GET THE FUCK OUT MY HOUSE!" Dre awoke to Monique's roar. Everything was still wobbling but he was conscious enough to know that something was wrong. "B-baby, what's going on?"

"Dre, get your friend."

Knox pointed at Monique. "Dre, control your bitch. She should know not to raise her voice at a man like that." Dre stood. "First of all, Knox you need to apologize right now for being disrespectful and sexist. Second of all, you need to leave our house and don't come back till you know how to act."

"I wouldn't even be here if yo ass hadn't been drinking so much."

Dre sighed. "That's true." He turned to Monique. "Baby, I'm sorry for bringing this man around you. I know you don't really like him." Monique shook her head. "Just get him out." Knox scoffed. "You gone let her order you around like that, Dre? You better tell her that she's way out of line." Dre, realizing Knox was past the point of apologizing, started ushering his friend out. "The only one out of line here is you. Good luck getting home."

Quickly, Dre snatched his keys and slammed the door in Knox' face. Monique crossed her arms. "There should be a spare blanket in the linen closet. You can use that tonight." She slammed and locked the bedroom door. Knowing he had really upset her, Dre took his spot on the couch. *I'd probably be an awful father anyways.* He thought this over and over until he fell asleep.

Monique was no stranger to Bloody Mary's. She had mastered them when Dre was pursuing his law degree and his outlet had been drinking. At one point, though, it had gotten out of hand and Monique had begged Dre to stop. She even told him about her family's history of drinking and how it was linked to domestic abuse. Dre promised he would limit his drinking after that but old habits clearly died hard. As Monique prepared Dre's Bloody Mary, she remembered his promise. *I will never lose control again.*

Dre had never physically put his hands on Monique but his drunk yelling always felt like he was slapping her. When Dre's Hennessy laden spit had flown on Monique's face the night before, she realized how much she detested his drinking. She even had half a mind to pour the Bloody Mary onto Dre. But, Monique took the high road and just slid the drink down to him. "Is that what I think it is? Mo, you're a lifesaver." She let out a big sigh. "Not according to Knox." "Hey, don't let him get to you."

Monique shook her head. "But you brought him here in the first place. If you hadn't gone out to get drunk, that never would've happened." Dre rubbed his throbbing head. "So now this is somehow my fault?" Monique shook her head. "I'm going to get dressed. It's too early for this, Dre." Once Monique left, Dre's demons began to taunt him.

You promised her you'd stop drinking. It wouldn't be the first time you broke a promise. Suddenly, Dre had a flashback to his mother crying as police officers hauled him away. "You promised you wouldn't lash out anymore!" Nathalie yelled. Dre's drunken spout had gotten him into a street fight with Nathalie's awful ex-husband Roberto. Although the man had threatened Dre's family, the officers had no knowledge of that. Knowing Roberto would get off after putting their entire family in danger, Dre paid Roberto a visit. The night ended with Dre in jail and Roberto in intensive care.

"I just don't understand, Andre," Monique noted. "Do you enjoy hurting the people around you, Andre? Not only did you promise me you'd stop, but you promised Nathalie and your entire family. How do you think they would feel about this?"

"Probably the same way they'd feel about your abortion," Dre spat. Monique paused where she was. "What did you just say to me?" Dre grabbed his keys. "I'll see you later." He left out of the door, too upset to think about anything except getting far, far away. Monique rolled her eyes and finished putting her earrings on. *I'll deal with him later.* She had a busy day ahead of her so there was no time to coddle Dre and his addiction. First, she had to go get a new phone. Then, she had to speak with Dr. Seneca. After that, she planned on apologizing to Daniel. And before the end of the day, Monique would check on Mo's Mix.

Once she had gotten her phone, Monique made a call to James. "Ross Repairs. How can I help you?" "Hey. It's me." James shifted the phone in his hand. "Oh. Hey sis. How are you?" "I'm well. And you?" James wiped sweat. "I'm surviving."

"What does that mean?"

"It means that I'm trying not to let Uncle Junior's death affect my life too much. It's hard, though."

Monique sighed. "Who you telling?" James asked, "Is everything alright? How's the baby?" "The baby's…fine. I just need some advice." "Shoot."

"I want to have an abortion, James. Andre and I talked, better yet argued, about it last night and I'm not sure if we're ready for this whole parenting thing."

"But, didn't you guys start looking at houses and get engaged?"

Monique sighed again. "Yes." "So obviously you all are mature enough to handle a child. If you want my advice, here it is: keep the baby. I understand that you're scared it'll be too much but you could have everything together and it will still be hard. Parenthood is not an easy task. It's still rewarding, though, because you get to mold a miniature version of yourself and your partner. Just give it some thought, sis. That's my advice to you." Monique allowed James' words to sink in. *He's right.* "Thank you, James. I appreciate that."

"No problem, little sis. Is there anything else I can help you with?"

"Have you seen Daniel?"

James said, "No. Mama said he's probably at Aunt Pam's cabin." Monique let out a deep breath. "Okay. I'll go over there to check on him." "Cool. Let me know that everything's okay with him." "Will do," Monique said. Then, she heard customers in the background. "I'm gonna let you go, Jamie. See you later."

James smiled. "You are the *only* one who can call me that. But, see you later, Mo." Monique hung up and booked it towards her Aunt's abandoned cabin.

"Danny? You in here?" Monique heard faint sounds from the living room so she went towards them. Much to her dismay, she didn't find Daniel. The wind was just blowing in from a window. Every time Daniel came to the cabin, he went to one room and sat in one chair. *If he's not there, where is he?* Monique phoned her older brother. He didn't pick up. The only time Daniel turned his phone off was at work.

So, Monique dialed the number to Mo's Mix. "Mo's Mix. You're on with Daniel. How can I help you?" Monique gasped and hung up. She rushed over to her business. "Daniel, you're here," she exclaimed. He put a finger up to let Monique know he was on the phone. "Yes, I got that. You have a lovely day, sir." Daniel hung up.

"I just spoke with the attorney of the woman from that accident. He said that because you've sent a check to Ingrid and her family, they have decided to say the dispute was settled outside of court." "How'd you pull that one off," Monique wondered. "I didn't send them any…" Daniel showed her his checkbook. "Consider it an investment into your business." Monique smiled. "Thank you so much, Daniel. I thought you were mad at me."

He said, "I was. But then I realized you were only trying to help. So, I got out of my feelings and I came here because I made you a promise that I was going to help get Mo's Mix back on its feet." Monique nodded. "I appreciate you doing this." "That's what I'm here for, little sis." She kissed his cheek then went to check on each department to see how they were doing. When Monique got to Finance, she noticed a certain unnerving atmosphere. Something definitely was amiss. "Everyone, we must be on our p's and q's. We wouldn't want Ms. Ross finding out that…" Evan stopped when he saw Monique. "Ms. Ross. How are you?" He looked at her stomach. "How's the baby?"

Monique put her hand up. "Cut the crap, Evan. Why don't finish saying what you were going to say?" He turned back to his department. "Very well. Team, we were just planning a surprise baby shower for Ms. Ross, weren't we?" The finance department nodded in unison, as if I they had been instructed to do so. "Well, get back to it. Don't let me ruin the surprise." Monique walked off, skeptical but determined to keep it to herself. When she got back to her office, she asked Daniel, "Have you noticed anything fishy lately?"

"Other than the fact that you increased the payout for department heads? No." Monique widened her eyeballs. "I did what?!" Daniel turned the computer to her. "This is from your domain. You increased the payout for department heads last night. Is there any reason in particular that you did that?" Monique studied the computer. "I didn't do that." "Well, someone did using your computer." Monique scratched her head. "That doesn't make any sense. No one but me has access to that room."

"What room?"

"There's a room on this floor that I go to whenever I give people promotions or raises. I have a computer where I do everything at. But, I'm the only one who knows the code." Daniel looked at the screen again. "Do you think someone broke in?"

"I have no reason to think otherwise."

Since Agent Abby knew vital information about the fire, Monique was hoping Abby could pinpoint a culprit. Monique called Dominique into her office. "Yes, boss?" "What hospital is Agent Abby currently at?" Dominique pulled up the information. "I can send you the address."

"Oh, would you, Dominque?" Monique hugged her trusted assistant then trekked towards the hospital.

"Abigail Newhouse, please."

"Are you family?"

"I'm her boss."

"Visiting hours don't begin until 1." Monique looked at her watch. It was only 10 o'clock. "Surely, you can make an exception." The lady shook her head. "Surely, you can wait like the rest of them." The nurse pointed to the hordes of visitors who had not been permitted inside. Monique pulled out a $50 bill. "Did I say boss? I meant sister." The nurse quickly snatched the money and opened the doors. "Ms. Newhouse is in room 2B." Monique smiled and proceeded inside. *A little bribery never hurt anyone.*

Once Monique got to the room, she immediately felt remorse. *This is my fault.* Agent Abby's leg had been burned badly in the fire along with the large bruise on the back of her neck. She was wrapped in bandages and a man cried at her side. Agent Abby was awake but clearly in a lot of pain. "Hey, Agent Abby. How are you?" Agent Abby worked to sit up. "I'm fine, Ms. Ross. Just a little bruised."

"Can you explain to me what happened?"

The guy hopped up. "You selfish bitch! My sister's been through a lot and you have the audacity to ask for a story?!" "Excuse you. I'm trying to make sure justice is served so I'll need you to refrain from the disrespect."

"I'll need you to leave. How are you even here? Only family's 'supposed to be back here. What'd you do, lie?" He didn't wait for a response. "It's just like you sleazy business people. You're not here about justice. You're just here for your own self-interest." Monique glanced at the sketchpad on a nearby chair. *Artsy liberal, I suppose.* "I'm here to get an understanding of what happened. That's all. Yes, I did lie to get back here but it's only because I need to see Agent Abby."

"What if Abigail don't wanna see you?"

Monique turned. "Is that true?" Agent Abby nodded. "I just…I need some time off. I promise I'll tell you the story once I'm out of here." Monique sighed. "Very well. Bye Agent Abby and her belligerent brother." The guy pointed to the door. "Leave!" Agent Abby pulled his hand down. "Samuel, relax. Just please relax."

As Monique made it towards the front of the hospital, she noticed that there were police officers posted. *What's going on?* She hoped her bribery didn't get her into trouble. "Are you Monique Ross?" One officer asked. Monique nodded. "Yes. Why?" He nodded towards the front desk. "Abigail Newhouse is in this hospital and her brother Samuel Lee has asked that you stay 100 ft. away from her at all times." Monique scoffed. "He put a restraining order out on me?"

"He says it will be active until the case is settled because, as of now, you are liable to be treated as a suspect."

"Why would I burn my own business?"

The officer shrugged. "Don't know. I just need you to leave this hospital." Monique pulled her purse up onto her shoulder. "I was planning to." When she stepped outside, paparazzi people started snapping pictures. "Monique, is it true that you put one of your employees in critical condition?"

"Is it true that you don't pay your workers what they deserve?"

"Ms. Ross, did you set your own building on fire?"

"Are you only out for profit?"

"Do you really care about your workers?"

Monique pushed her way through the crowd and made it back to her car. There, she waited a while. Once she felt it was safe, Monique drove towards Dr. Seneca's office. Although she was clear of paparazzi, Monique had other dangers to worry about. She parked in front of Dr. Seneca's building and someone slammed into her car.

"Watch where you're parking," Monique yelled. A woman got out and charged at Monique. "Watch who the fuck you mess with! This is for Nicole." The woman started beating Monique with a purse. Monique made sure to hold her stomach. Once the lady seemed to get tired, Monique kicked the woman with a heel. "If Nicole keeps sending threats my way, she will go to jail. You understand that?" The woman shrugged. "And? She's been before." She grabbed her purse and drove off. Monique rubbed her head. *I really gotta start doing background checks.*

As Monique sat in Dr. Seneca's office, the doctor checked her stomach for scars. "That's a pretty nasty fall you took there. Tell me it wasn't on purpose." Monique scoffed. "Why would I fall on purpose?" "You'd be surprised at the lengths some women go to when they get pregnant with a surprise baby."

"Dr. Seneca, are you insinuating that I'd try to give myself a miscarriage?"

Dr. Seneca shook her head. "No, Monique. I'm simply asking. Why all the hostility?" Monique rubbed her head. "People have been down my throat about this abortion as if it's their body." "Is Andre one of them?" Monique sat up straight. "How'd you know that?" "He made a drunken phone call to me last night expressing his grief. He tried to convince me not to let you go through with it." Monique couldn't believe that Andre had been so sneaky. She thought they had a better sense of communication. "Wow. He didn't tell me that." "As I said, he was drunk. He probably doesn't remember now," Dr. Seneca reasoned.

She handed Monique a pamphlet. "Here are some things you should know before you go through with it." Dr. Seneca sighed.

"Typically, we try to do the abortion at 14 weeks, so it's now or never, Monique. You're already approaching week 14. If you decide you want to keep the baby, you can't go back. That's something you should think about." Monique held the pamphlet tightly. "Can I just have a moment to myself?" Dr. Seneca nodded. "You may. I'll be waiting outside so you can come get me when you're ready to make a decision."

As Dr. Seneca left, Monique thumbed through the pamphlet. The more she read, the more she started to lean towards one decision. Once she came to her decision, Monique wanted to cry. Before summoning Dr. Seneca, Monique called Andre. Surprisingly, he answered. "I'm doing it, Dre. I'm really doing it." On the other end of the phone, he burst into tears. On the one hand, he had no job so he was happy that Monique wouldn't be having a baby. On the other, he had been elated to be a father. "Okay," Dre said. Monique told him, "I love you." "I love you too," he responded. Filled with grief, Dre was beginning to lose it. "I-I'll call you back, Mo." "Bye."

Monique hung up and marched towards Dr. Seneca. She told the doctor her decision. Dr. Seneca sighed. "I had a feeling you'd say that." They scheduled another appointment for a week from then in preparation of what was to come.

Chapter V – *Minutes after the decision, Monique receives a call from the hospital saying that Agent Abby began to experience internal bleeding and asked that Samuel give Monique Agent Abby's regards. These were Agent Abby's last words.*

1 WEEK LATER

"Abigail Newhouse was a beloved secret service agent who retired and went to work as a security officer for Mo's Mix. Unfortunately…" Monique began blocking out the pastor's words. She still couldn't believe that Agent Abby was dead. From the back of the room, Monique made sure to keep her sunglasses up. She knew Samuel would have a cow if he saw her. But, when Monique saw Samuel, he didn't seem angry. He just seemed sad. He was experiencing extreme sadness. "This is my fault," she said to herself at the funeral and at the repast.

"They say one life ends when new life begins," Agent Abby's mother noted while staring at Monique's belly. "And who might you be?" Monique couldn't bear to tell this woman her identity, especially with Samuel staring like he recognized her. "I'll just be going." In Monique's little black dress and high heels, she didn't get very far very fast. "Where do you think you're going?" Samuel asked.

"I came to pay my respect to your family but I should leave."

He grabbed Monique's arm. "There's blood on your hands now. You know that, don't you?" Monique yanked her arm away. "Don't touch me." She quickly went to her car. Once Monique arrived home, she began crying. One of her best employees was dead and Monique felt responsible. Also, she felt guilty about the hell she'd put Dre through about the baby and having an abortion. "That's finally over," Monique said as she held her belly.

She didn't know how Dre would react to the news. Then again, she didn't know where Dre was even at so she had a few words for him, too. As Monique prepared her rant, he walked back in after being gone for almost a week. "Dre, where the fuck have you been?!"

He held Monique close and kissed her passionately. "I was soul searching but I realized I need to be here with you. No matter what happens, I need to be by your side because I love you and I'm going to make you my wife. I'm sorry, Mo. Please forgive me." Monique could see pain in his eyes. She took him into her loving her arms. "Oh, Dre. Is this about the abortion?" Dre sighed. "That plays into it but it's more than that." "I have something to tell you," Monique admitted, realizing she hadn't been clear over the phone. "I do too."

"When I said I'm 'doing it', I meant that I'm keeping the baby – *our* baby." Monique held her belly. "I'm thinking of naming her Emelia. But that's not all. I was looking at the house you told me about and I actually really liked it. I've been to that neighborhood and…" Monique paused, realizing she had lost Dre. He took her hand because he knew he had to tell her the news. "Baby, I just quit my job." At the same time, the couple stared at each other in disbelief.

MO'S MIX: *Queen-dom*

Introduction – *Passion is a combination of skill and determination. This second novel challenged my skills as a writer because I had to keep with the pace and the context of the first Mo's Mix. In order to do that, I needed a little determination.*

ACKNOWLEDGEMENTS

This second book was actually a lot harder than the first. In fact, the novel is nowhere near complete as I am writing this foreword. One aspect that has changed is that when I was writing "Mo's Mix," I didn't have anything to compare it to. So, essentially, "Mo's Mix" could be anything it wanted to be. With "Queen-dom," I am bound to the context of the first.

However, that's what makes writing this novel interesting. How can I combine my own creativity with the same flare as the first? For "Queen-dom," I would just like to thank all those who bought "Mo's Mix" as soon as it dropped. My mother Adrienne, my best friend Kayla, and my sister Justice all three supported a story they had absolutely no idea about. Then, after they read it, they each provided accolades that restored my confidence. At times, I wondered if I was doing something meaningful by publishing "Mo's Mix" and thanks to my mom, my best friend, and my sister, I was able to see that I was.

Also, I would like to thank God. You will always be my personal advisor and confidant. Any skills I have are attributes which You have bestowed upon me. Thank You. Finally, I would like to dedicate this novel to my father, Ronald V. Plummer. You may not be with me in body but you are with me in spirit and in mind. This is all for you, dad. Rest easy.

Author: Javanna Plummer

Illustrator: Pierce Cruz

Chapter VI *–Mo's Mix is a black haircare business that knocked out rival business Cocoa Puff, which was started by Malaysia Summers (pseudonym: April Spring). Years later, April was feeling vindictive and began a revenge plot, which led to the death of Abigail Newhouse.*

5 MONTHS LATER

Earl Ross stared from Andre to Monique and back. "How many checks did it take you to pay for that ring," Mr. Ross queried. "Or did you borrow from your mama? She got white in her so she must come from money, huh?" Monique touched her father's hand. "Daddy, be nice."

Mr. Ross did not apologize for his temperament. He just pointed out, "The man usually asks for a woman's hand in marriage *before* proposing." Monique motioned towards her belly. "As you can see by this, Andre and I have decided against conventional standards of marriage and family."

Andre nodded and said, "Mr. Ross, I have loved Monique since the very first days she and I spent together. I knew that she was smart, ambitious, loyal, strong, courageous and – most of all – more beautiful than I could've ever imagined. Your daughter has my mind, body, and soul and I will always love, cherish, and protect her and your grandchild the way women ought to be loved, cherished and protected."

Earl looked Andre in the eye. "I hear you, son. I like that even though my wife and I challenge you, you never back down because you love my daughter enough to deal with her difficult parents. Courage is important in us men – as well as providing for our women, which I know for a fact you're doing.

"Besides having financial stability, I want Monique to be with someone who loves her dearly and I can tell she's happy with you just by that goofy grin she's always wearing whenever y'all come around. Mo is my youngest child and my only daughter so that means I have to protect her. But, you're a good man, Andre. You're the first man who could meet Monique's many requirements and, to me, that's a sign that you will be a great husband and father. So, you two have my blessing."

Charletta Ross nodded. "Mine too." Then she looked at Andre. "I'm not gone give you a long speech like Earl but I will tell you this: a good man with a good job is all I've ever wanted for my baby girl." Monique rolled her eyes. "Mama, please."

"Baby, I'm serious. Men with good character and financial stability are hard to come by. You got yourself a good one." Monique looked at her man. "Trust me, ma. I know." A little while later, Andre shook hands with Monique's parents and all seemed to be sound in terms of Monique and Andre's engagement. Alas, there was a different vibe at the Cassells household.

Bella Cassells, Andre's mother, looked Monique up and down. "Bambino," Bella murmured in Italian. "Bambino!" Bella could not wrap her head around the fact that Andre and Monique had conceived a "bambino" out of wedlock yet they were parading their "sin" around like it wasn't a manifestation of blasphemy (in Bella's eyes). Andre let out a deep breath. "Mamma, you promised to speak English around Monique."

Bella put her hands on her hips. "Okay. Who do you think you are, Andre? Do you really want to turn into your papà?" Although Bella had only 8 kids, Andre had 11 siblings. Andre put his hand on the back of his neck. "Does everything always have to go back to papà? Aren't you supposed to respect the dead?"

"Do *you* respect that awful man? He was a liar, a cheater, and an abuser."

"He was also my father so I acknowledge his place in my life."

Bella glanced at Monique's stomach while speaking to Andre. "Don't turn into Manny." Andre let out a deep breath. "I won't, mamma. Promise. But do Monique and I have your blessing?"

"I hope you're as good a *mamma* as you are a businesswoman," Bella directed at Monique. Monique raised her eyebrow. "What does that mean?"

"Know when to put work first and when to put my grandchild first," Bella hissed. Without further ado, Bella walked off. Throughout the day, Bella's words sat with Monique. "She despises me, Andre. Why else would she always hold me in contempt?" Andre put Monique's suitcase on the conveyor belt then rubbed her shoulder. "Bella Cassells is an ethnocentric Italian straight out of Florence. It'll be a cold day in Hell before she accepts anyone with non-Italian blood."

"She's not even fully Italian herself, though. Plus, she married a Jamaican Mexican and had 8 of his kids."

Andre shook his head. "Doesn't make sense, does it? I think my mamma was in love with the idea of my father so much that she never saw him for who he truly was until he was unleashing his war demons on her face.

Andre sighed. "When my dad died, my mom took her anger out on us." Andre put his own suitcase on the conveyor belt as he thought about the time he had gone to jail. *There is no reason for you to act like a heathen, Andre. You only have half of Manny's black genes.* "But, never mind that. Let's worry about our trip." Monique looked at the pamphlet for Jamaica, where she and Andre were headed. "I'm down with that." Hand in hand, she and Andre marched towards customs.

"That is absolutely unacceptable. I don't care that you have to take a test; I assigned you this task *last* week so I expect you to have it completed and...what's that? Dominique, stop complaining. I understand that you're stressed out because of midterms but..." Monique took a breath because she saw Andre coming back from the bathroom. "Calm down, alright? Calm yourself and do as I asked. Bye." Quickly, Monique hung up and stuffed her phone into her purse.

"Who was that?"

"Wrong number."

Andre thought about how long he'd been gone. "You spent 10 minutes talking to a wrong number?" Monique sighed, seeing as she had been caught. "Guilty as charged." Andre exhaled while he sat down. "Baby, we're on vacation. Leave work at home." Monique looked around Le Papillion, a restaurant attached to a posh hotel in the south of Jamaica. Manny Cassells had taken Andre there once and this was when Andre's love for cooking had blossomed. So, being back meant a lot to Andre.

"You know how I am with work," Monique mentioned.

"I do, baby, but can you please enjoy the view? We're out of the country, for Christ-sakes." Monique looked out at the ocean. From where she and Andre were seated, they had a picturesque view of the Atlantic. Monique touched Andre's hand. "Let's rent a boat and sail away to Never-never land."

Andre grinned. "Now you're talking. But, how's my beautiful fiancée feeling this lovely evening?" Monique stared down at her bulging belly. "Pregnant. I'm feeling very, very pregnant." Andre glanced at the belly where his daughter sat. "I can't wait to meet her." Monique grinned wide. "You and me both."

"Speaking of which, we still haven't come up with a middle name."

"I meant to ask you about that. I was thinking--" Monique's phone cut her off midsentence. She didn't want to answer in the midst of the conversation, but seeing that it was Daniel, Monique knew it was important. "Daniel, talk to me." Andre huffed and studied his menu while Monique put work first – as always. Once Monique was off the phone, the mood had died. "I'll take a beer and some chips," Andre told the waiter in Jamaican.

"I'll have the Chicken salad with a light ranch dressing and a lemonade." Andre translated Monique's order then the waiter was off. As they were eating, Monique picked up on Andre's discontent.

"Why do you look like someone just told you your favorite team lost?"

Andre sighed. "My unhappiness stems from something deeper than just a team losing, Mo. It comes from the fact that you're still putting work before me. You need to realize that when you accepted my marriage proposal and decided to have my child, there is a certain responsibility that comes with those. I don't appreciate--" Monique put her hand up to cut Dre off before he spoke too recklessly. "Whoa; who are you talking to like that?"

Andre let out a deep breath. "Sorry if I'm coming off cross but I'm just **tired** of feeling like I only have *some* of your attention. At times, I fear that Emelia is going to be treated as more of a hobby than a priority and I don't want that, Mo. I want our little girl to feel love from both of her parents. Now, I do understand that you have obligations to Mo's Mix but you're going to have to have to find a better way to balance those obligations with your responsibilities at home."

Monique said, "I am doing the best that I can, Andre." "By taking a work call in the middle of our meal? That's rude."

"So is quitting your job without warning me first."

"I got another job a week later."

"Which you eventually got fired from."

Andre sighed. "I thought we said we weren't going to talk about it." "We need to. Why did you get fired?" "It should be clear by now," Dre answered. "Law just isn't my passion. And I know that because when you're passionate about something, it shows in everything that you do. With passion, it's…." Dre stopped because he was gaining some new perspective on his fiancée.

"It's…your whole life. Mo's Mix is your baby. So, you're going to do everything in your power to protect it." Monique looked Andre in the eye. "What are you saying?" Andre took Monique's hand. "I'm saying that although we won't always see to eye-to-eye and although it might get difficult, all those obstacles are worth it because I can't lose you, Monique. I love you."

Monique smiled. "And I love you, Andre."

The rest of the trip went as planned. Monique and Andre toured some of Ochos Rios – the hometown of Manny Cassells – before taking a cruise of Jamaica's capital. In Kingston, the couple checked out the Bob Marley museum, gazed at the Blue Mountains, and watched a performance at the National Dance Theater Company of Jamaica. Then, it was time to go home.

"How was that for a birthday celebration?"

"I'll tell you this: it *might* make me consider giving Emelia a sibling."

Dre raised his eyebrow. "Is that an innuendo, Ms. Ross?" Monique smirked. "Soon to be Mrs. Andre Cassells." Dre smiled. "Don't make me blush." Monique came in front of him and put her arms around his neck. "You know I don't have to be at the studio until 8…"

Knowing where Monique was going with that, Andre grabbed her hips and started leading her to the bedroom. "That's all the time I need." After the couple's passionate lovemaking, it was time for Monique to tell the world about Mo's Mix while Andre would actively seek employment. When Monique was showering, Andre was pulling a suit from his suitcase. An hour later, they were both fully dressed and ready to go. "Break a leg today, Dre." "You first." The couple kissed goodbye and went to perform their respective tasks.

She said, *"Trying to be a girl's girl*

In a man's world

Is almost like a death wish.

So, I want you to remember this:

People are only capable of what you allow.

Baby girl, this is my vow.

So that you won't go through

The same struggles as I.

Sometimes you'll smile

Sometimes you'll cry

Just know that Mama Mo's

Got your back

Until the day I die."

The hosts of Power 101 clapped. "That was so beautiful," Alisa Janis complimented. "I'm sure your baby girl is smiling." Monique held her belly as she grinned. "I'm sure she is too." Alisa looked at notecards she had prepared. "Power 101 fans, Alisa's Jukebox is on and jumping. I'm feeling good today. How 'bout y'all?"

Alisa went to her next notecard. "If you just tuned in, you're probably wondering whose voice that was. This woman goes by the name of Monique Ross and her business is Mo's Mix. If you don't know what Mo's Mix is, shame on you."

Alisa looked at a third notecard. "Here's the skinny: M-dub is a black-owned haircare business that supports the growth and development of African-American hair. Mo's Mix hopes that by promoting black hair, black women will feel more confident in rocking the locks they were born with."

Alisa went to her fourth card. "Monique was featured in *Spotlight* magazine as 'the wake-up call for black women.' These provocative words allude to the fact that Monique is a fairly young black woman who's the CEO of a booming, black business. Plus, Ms. Mo deems herself a 'proud girl's girl.' I wonder how many of my female fans can relate to her on that – probably none judging by the way most of y'all go about."

Alisa's co-hosts laughed and she continued, "But, to kick off the show, I'll be asking Monique some questions written by me and my co-hosts. Then, I'll also be taking some questions from our online blog. Let's chat with Monique Ross, the wake-up call for black women."

Once she felt she'd given sufficient time for this thought to sit, Alisa said, "First question was submitted by Tina from good ole' *Nawlins*, Louisiana." The other hosts stared blankly as Alisa attempted to have a southern drawl. Alisa just sighed and read, "Tina wonders: What inspired you to start Mo's Mix, Ms. Ross?"

"It all goes back to my journey with natural hair. I grew tired of products that only somewhat satisfied my texture so I thought 'Hey, why don't I make my own?' Thus, I built a brand." Alisa nodded. "From Janet in Michigan: What can you tell fans about this 'brand' you've built?"

"Mo's Mix has the core values of respect, integrity, dedication, and hard work. These core values are reflective of some of my own personal values. I chose them because I feel that respect, integrity, dedication, and hard work are at the forefront of success."

Alisa nodded and responded, "I have to agree with you on that, Ms. Ross, especially the part about respect. Woman to woman, I'm sure you understand the need to command respect when it comes to these sexist men." Alisa cleared her throat and nodded towards Doug Jackson and Stefan Lucas, who both laughed off Alisa's subtle shade. Eager to ease the tension brewing, Sasha Nunez pulled out a third question. "From Donovan in Ohio." Sasha began. "How long have you been running Mo's Mix and were there any deterrents along the way?"

Monique took a deep breath. "It's been 6 years now and, as with starting any company, exposure is of the utmost importance. During the first year, no one really knew about Mo's Mix. I spent 12 months selling products out of my boyfriend's apartment so the business was really underground at first. But, once I acquired an office space, sales dramatically increased and I was able to jump-start my career."

Doug wondered, "Are you still with the boyfriend?" Monique showed Doug her ring. "We're actually engaged." "A beautiful, intelligent, successful black woman is a turn on to me. Your fiancé is lucky to have you." Monique blushed and stared down at her ring. "I'm sure he knows that."

Doug knew he was making Monique uncomfortable, but he continued, "If you weren't engaged *and* pregnant, I would've had to holla at you real quick." Doug was clearly overstepping, so Stefan chimed, "You'd have better luck hollering at a dead woman 'cause you are **clearly** out of Ms. Ross's league." The hosts of Power 101 laughed and the atmosphere quickly went from awkward to normal.

One by one, Alisa and her co-hosts moved down a list of questions. "Here's one from me." Alisa eventually stated as she prepared to ask Monique a question about her braids. Though Monique had many hair fumbles in the past, her pregnancy had proved positive for her scalp. Inevitably, though, naysayers like Alisa assumed Monique had to be wearing extensions. "What kind of hair is that?" Alisa asked; she lived and breathed controversy.

"Excuse me," Monique casually replied. "What kind of hair did the stylist use?" Alisa repeated. "I'm sure Power 101 fans want to know." "This is my hair," Monique informed Alisa. Alisa raised her eyebrow. "But it's so long. You **sure** it's all yours?"

Monique nodded. "Yes, but if my word's not good enough for you, you can look closely and notice how it's emerging from my scalp." The co-hosts snickered at Monique's sarcasm. Alisa let out a deep breath. "No need to be snide, Ms. Ross. I'm just surprised is all." Alisa couldn't wrap her head around the idea that that was *all* Monique's hair unless Monique had something besides black in her. "Are you mixed?"

Monique laughed a little. "I am, actually. I'm half black on my mom's side and half black on my dad's side." Alisa stared blankly. "But that just means you're black." Monique smiled. "Exactly." Alisa's co-hosts laughed aloud at Monique's condescendence.

As for Alisa, she just cleared her throat. "Well, glad we established that. But, I would like to conclude this little Q&A and thank Ms. Ross for coming out. As a final word, I encourage you all to get in-the-know about Ms. Mo and tell everyone about Mo's Mix. Next, we will go to Doug with the news. What's the latest, Doug?" Doug began reading his news report while Monique took her microphone off and left the showroom. Immediately after, Alisa yanked her mic off and followed Monique out.

"I don't appreciate the way you tried to embarrass me on my own show," Alisa asserted. Bree wedged herself between

Monique and Alisa. "First of all, Ms. Janis, you need to realize that you are speaking to the CEO of Mo's Mix. If you didn't already know, Ms. Ross holds a considerable amount of power here in Willowsville so it might do you some good to watch your tone. Otherwise, this little rinky-dink show of yours **will** get shut down. Is that understood?"

Alisa rolled her eyes. "I was just asking questions to give my fans some insight about Ms. Ross. She didn't have to catch an attitude."

"Ms. Ross was simply answering your silly little question. Perhaps you didn't like her answer because it revealed your own ignorance but, at the end of the day, you embarrassed *yourself* by making a tactless assumption. You have a nice rest of your morning, Ms. Janis." Monique needed to say nothing after that so she just left the building. Meanwhile, the daft radio host stood with her mouth hanging open.

"Well done in there. I'll have to thank Mr. Ross for finding you." Bree shrugged. "I'm just doing my job." Since it was Bree's first day, Monique was filled with questions. "Where did you work last?" "I had a position in marketing at my Alma mater but, due to budget cuts, I was laid off."

"Oh. How long were you there?"

"6 years. They hired me straight out of school." Monique raised her eyebrow. "You're…28?" Bree nodded. "Yes and, according to this calendar that Mr. Ross emailed me, so are you. Happy birthday, Ms. Ross." Monique grinned. "Thank you."

When Monique opened the door, Andre was wearing his "Kiss the Chef" apron and dancing at the stove. "Hey, Mo."

Monique kissed Andre. "Hey, Chef Dre. You hear the show?" Andre smiled as he recalled Monique's witty responses. "Yes. I always knew my baby was sharp." Monique shook her head. "That woman was mad disrespectful so I had to put her in her place. But tell me why after the show she had the audacity to say I embarrassed her. Bree, my new PR, stepped right in Alisa's face and told Alisa that she embarrassed *herself* by asking me those stupid ass questions."

Andre laughed. "What did Alisa have to say to that?" "She had no response, as expected." Andre nodded and put the chicken onto a plate. "Voila!" Monique sniffed the air. "Well, it *smells* delicious. What is it?"

"The entrée is chicken that was marinated in my secret sauce for 16 hours. For sides, I've prepared red beans and rice, greens, and some corn bread." Andre took note of Monique's disapproving face so he added, "And I know that grease is harmful to our daughter, so I decided bake the chicken. Plus, the greens have my special low-fat flavoring and I didn't put any butter on the corn bread. I promise you it is all healthy."

Andre made Monique a full plate and placed it down on the table. "I didn't know if my uncle would let us use his timeshare so, in the instance that he didn't, this was going to be my gift." Dre pulled out Monique's chair and positioned a gold box in front of her. "Now, I just get to spoil my baby. Happy birthday, Monique."

Georgiana, Andre's little sister, had snapped a picture of Monique holding her pregnant belly. Andre, who was in awe of the photo as soon as he saw it, decided he would frame it and write "Emelia" in cursive print on the side of Monique's stomach. Monique smiled at the image. "Dre, this is beautiful." Andre sat down with his plate. "I already know where I want to put it when we move into the house."

Monique rolled her eyes. "We haven't even been approved for the loan. Don't speak too soon."

"I guess I'm an optimist," Andre lamented. This was a loaded comment, he realized. Andre was not only staying optimistic about getting the house but also about pursuing his cooking dream, which Monique had demanded he put on hold until Emelia was *at least* two. "So, I got the job and they want me to start tomorrow," Andre continued. Monique raised her eyebrow. "At Roger Muller?"

Dre nodded. "Yep. Someone from Nia gave me a 'stellar' recommendation apparently." "That's good, right?" Monique wondered, picking up on Dre's unenthusiastic tone. Andre shrugged. "Relatively speaking, I suppose so. I'm glad that I'll be making money to support our family but we both know where I *really* want to be." Monique looked Andre in the eye. "Remember what we agreed upon?"

"Once Emelia is born, we will revisit the idea of cooking school as a plan for the *distant* future, right?" Monique put her hand atop his. "You know where I stand on this and why." Andre sighed. "I do but I don't like being put off."

"Oh my God; it's my birthday. Please don't start this conversation right now," Monique pled. Andre kissed her hand. "I'm sorry if I'm killing the vibe but I just think about a time when you left your parents' house because they told you to just go work with Daniel since his company was more 'established.' They didn't think you could make it on your own. At that time, who believed in you, Monique? Who took you into his cramped studio apartment and shared his raggedy bed with you?"

Since Monique was quiet, Andre said, "It was *me*. **I** did because I always knew you would be prosperous. Morrisa and I even went out and told people about the products you were making in order to help you achieve your goals. A year later, you got the office space and you were able to build Mo's Mix from the ground up.

Andre took a deep breath. "Yet, when I come to you with *my* passion, I get shot down. I don't think that's completely fair." Monique exhaled because she clearly couldn't use her birthday as an excuse to avoid the conversation. "Back then we had *nothing*, Andre. So, we had nothing to lose."

Andre shook his head. "I disagree. Back then, we had each other; we will always have each other." "What about Emelia?" Monique challenged. "If this dream fails, you and I are back in those slums and is that *really* where you want to raise our daughter?"

Andre argued, "These are just hypotheticals. None of this might even happen."

"You have to always prepare for the worst," Monique stated. Andre replied, "Worst case scenario: you end up surrounded by the people you're running from." Monique cut her eyes. "What's that supposed to mean?" "It means your whole life has been about escaping that dark place in your heart. I see despair in your eyes anytime we visit Vieille Ville."

Monique sighed. "My life got better when I moved to Nouville, Dre. Whenever I'm back in Vieille Ville, I'm reflecting on the times when people from the state were threatening to take Daniel, James, and me away if our parents kept sending us to school with holes in our clothes and no food in our bellies. Luckily, Daniel got a job when he was 14 and that helped my parents out a lot.

"Still, we sometimes had to split one pack of ramen noodles between the five of us or, when we didn't have cable, we performed skits to pass the time. Then, in college, I was *always* working because that was the only way I could afford school. All I'm saying is that I can't go back to those days, Dre."

Andre saw that Monique had begun reminiscing on drearier days so he rubbed her arm. "I get it, Mo. I really do. But, you and I both have careers now so we don't have to worry about where our next meals are coming from or who we'll have to beg for money." "Exactly. I want to ensure that Emelia never has to endure the same pain we had to endure. That's one of the reasons I'm on the fences about you going to cooking school."

Andre sighed. "Let me tell you a story about my older sister Nathalie. She is mentally deteriorating in her desk job. When we were younger, she said by the time she reached her 30s she wanted to be somewhere in corporate making six figures from a corner office. Sadly, our dad died right before Nathalie was supposed to go to college so she halted her dreams to help our mamma cope. Now, every time I look Nathalie in the eye, I see despair because she's not where she wants to be, Mo. I would hate ending up like that."

Monique listened to Andre's argument. *I'm following my dreams. Why shouldn't he follow his?* After giving this idea some thought, Monique finally said, "Okay." "Okay?" "I'll ask some of the investors at Mo's Mix if they know of any financial aid for culinary arts institutions. How does that sound?"

Andre smiled. "That sounds like you're finally on board with this." He kissed Monique's hand again. "Which is why I love you, my Queen." Monique smiled wide. "You flatter me with your praises and your gifts but your presence is the only present I'll ever need, my King." She looked down at her belly. "Emelia, you know you're about to be an heir to one of the greatest empires to ever exist. Your mother is a valiant Queen with a strong King by her side."

Andre gazed at Monique. "Who'd be nothing without the woman who lights the spark in his bonfire heart."

Chapter VII – *Though she should have been at home resting, Monique spent the latter part of her pregnancy working as if she were still in the former.*

A LITTLE WHILE LATER

Daniel stared quizzically at Monique when she walked past his office. "Did we forget where our comb was this morning," he directed towards her. Monique rolled her eyes while stepping inside. "My braids were getting old so I thought I'd try something different." "If you're trying to scare people, I'd say you succeeded." Monique rolled her eyes. "Don't be mad because my luscious locks are more marvelous than your neglected naps. You need to get those soldiers in line, Daniel." She shook her hair in his face. Daniel moved back. "I'm sorry – I didn't hear a thing you said. That pet on your head was distracting me."

Monique walked towards Daniel's door as her hair bounced. "It's only as distracting as you allow it to be." In her own office, Monique sat down slowly because her feet were hurting. Dominique stepped inside. "Ms. Ross, I…" Dominique paused and stared at Monique's new do. "Where is Ms. Ross and what have you done with her?" Monique laughed. "Cute, Dominique. But what is it?"

Dominique said, "There's a marketing meeting in forty-five minutes to pitch product names but, in an hour, you are supposed to be speaking to the press about why you took No Stress off the shelves, when you will be re-releasing it, and what happened with Abigail Newhouse."

Monique raised her eyebrow. "I thought we agreed to keep Ms. Newhouse's death private."

"That's kind of hard when her brother just did an interview with *Spotlight*." Monique sighed. *I'm too pregnant for this kind of thing.* "Okay so here's how this is going to go: you get your hands on that article for me, tell Mr. Lawrence that I will have Mr. Ross oversee the marketing meeting and inform Bree that I will be ready for the press conference." Dominique raised her eyebrow. "Is Mr. Ross the official COO yet? I remember that you said all meetings were to be overseen by you or the COO – if we ever got one."

Monique stared Dominique down. "Dominique, I am the CEO of this company so if I say Mr. Ross oversees the meeting, he oversees the meeting. Do you have a problem with that?" Dominique shook her head. "I don't, but Dennis Quaver emailed me stating that the board would like to further assess Mr. Ross's credentials before making anything official."

Monique folded her hands. "Mr. Quaver and I have had several conferences about this, though. What's changed?"

Dominique looked at the notes she had taken. "After a meeting this morning, our board of directors collectively feels that 'because of familial ties' you weren't impartial to Mr. Ross when you gave your recommendation. Therefore, the board would like to perform an 'independent review' then come to a final decision."

Monique stated, "Mr. Ross's resume should have already been faxed to Dennis Quaver for review. Along with that, you were to contact Mr. Ross's previous employers so that they could speak to the board on Mr. Ross's behalf, which I asked you to do when I was in Jamaica. Have you done either of these tasks?"

"I have not."

"Why haven't you?"

Because Dominique didn't have a legitimate answer, Monique motioned her hand towards the door. "Get to it." Before

Dominique could leave, Monique added, "And, for the record, the issue of Mr. Ross's status in this company would not have even been an issue had you done as I asked, Dominique. Isn't that your job?"

Dominique nodded. "It is."

"At least you know. That will be all."

Feeling slightly embarrassed, Dominique scurried back to her office while Monique pulled her hair into a bun. Then, Monique took notecards from her purse and read, "As you may have already heard, Mo's Mix removed 'No Stress' from the shelves. You are perhaps wondering why this is so. Following the release of the product, a party whose identity shall remain anonymous filed a lawsuit against Mo's Mix.

"Said party held intellectual property rights to the name 'No Stress'. Although thorough research was done regarding this matter, the rights to 'No Stress' were left private, which is why the mix-up occurred. However, Mo's Mix will be changing our product name to avoid future conflict. At this time, that is all the information that will be disclosed about 'No Stress'. Thank you."

Monique sighed since she had gotten that out of the way. Next, she wrote a farewell to Agent Abby. "In addition, Mo's Mix has been asked to speak about Abigail Newhouse, someone who we hope is resting peacefully. A while ago, there was a fire at Mo's Mix and the injuries Ms. Newhouse sustained in this fire led to her death. Investigation into the fire is still ongoing and..." Monique paused because images of Abigail in the hospital were invading Monique's psyche. "Ms. Ross, they're ready for you."

When Bree entered, Monique came back to reality. Because of her violent recollections, Monique thought that the press conference was just a bad idea. So, she handed Bree the notecards. "Tell the presses that I had other business to tend to and I could not speak." Bree took the cards. "Alright. Anything else?"

"Just read everything you see on the cards. On the last one, I wrote some common questions with pre-prepared answers. Follow the answers I wrote and, if they try to weasel any other information out of you, explain that you are not at liberty to disclose that." Bree nodded and went towards the press conference room. Monique tried blocking the thought of Abigail Newhouse. *If you let it affect you, you are allowing it to affect the business as well. Mo's Mix is you. You are Mo's Mix.* Monique said these mantras as she was walking.

Dominique came running up. "Sorry to bombard you, Ms. Ross, but Attorney Marx is here to see you."

Andre had been Mo's Mix's courtroom attorney before deciding to step down from Mo's Mix after he quit Paul-n-Friends. So, in Andre's absence, Monique ordered Daniel to get a new attorney ASAP. Low and behold, Andre's former co-worker and brief fling Genna Marx had wowed Daniel. Although Monique had hired Genna, Monique didn't care for Genna's presence.

Dominique explained, "Attorney Genna Marx works for Paul-n-Friends, the same firm--" Monique put her hand up. "I know who she is." Genna walked up with a smirk that started to bother Monique. *What's she so happy about? Her place at Mo's Mix is about as temporary as her place in Andre's life.* Before Monique could laugh at this internal commentary, Genna was front and center. "Ms. Ross. Long time no see." Monique sighed. "Not long enough. What are you doing here?"

"I got an email from Mr. Ross stating that I was hired. Did Mr. Ross not inform you?"

Monique exhaled. "He informed me perfectly well but that doesn't answer my question. What *business* do you have being here?" "It's about the case. Maybe we should take this in your office?" Monique looked over at her employees congregating in the nearby conference room. "I'm actually busy at the moment so either talk right here or handle it with my assistant."

Genna sighed. "Very well. The jury is likely going to rule in favor of Tasia Matthews, the woman who filed that personal injury lawsuit against Mo's Mix. Because you failed to show up three consecutive times, an admission of guilt will be presumed and you will then owe Ms. Matthews $500."

Monique rolled her eyes. "Why should I have to pay her anything when she--" "That's not all." Genna interrupted. "This has segued into a class action lawsuit, which means you'll owe Tanaja Sanders, Asa Sanders, Mollita Jackson, Tito Carlisle, Graham North, and Marvin Younge $500 too. In total, that's--" "Ridiculous," Monique interrupted right back. "I was never told of any court dates."

"Ms. Matthews's attorney says that he emailed Andre the information. I take it that means you and Andre don't communicate very well?"

Monique scoffed. "Andre quit Paul-n-Friends so he had no access to that email account." "Then I guess it's on *you* for not hiring me sooner."

"There are things more important at Mo's Mix than some low grade attorney desperately seeking a man who doesn't even want her. But, in the interest of this case, we needed an attorney and you were the best available. Even still, your stay here is temporary, Attorney Marx. Please don't forget that."

Genna smiled and decided if Monique wanted to take it there, it could be taken there. "You say I'm the **best available**. Is that because Andre told you I was good? He of all people would know just how *persuasive* I can be and I don't just mean in the courtroom." Monique shook her head in disgust. "That will be all, Attorney Marx." "What are you going to do about the case?"

"We can discuss this further at a later date because, right now, I have a meeting to attend. I'll have my assistant set something up and she'll email you the details. Until then, I don't want you stepping foot into this building."

"What if it's urgent?"

Monique chuckled. "There are these gadgets called cell phones made for communication. I take it you know how to use one." Monique waved her hand to have an intern to escort Genna out of the building. Then, Monique stepped over to Dominique's office. "Call our in-house attorney and ask him to get in touch with Ms. Matthews's attorney. Then, have someone in HR put out an ad for a new courtroom attorney."

"What about Attorney Marx?"

"What about her?"

"How about 'Stress-Free'?'" One creative analyst suggested. "It conveys the same message as No Stress."

A second creative analyst scrunched her face. "Yeah, but it's so bland. 'No Stress' was a counter argument to the fact that perms *relax* the hair; it affirmed that although our product is figuratively doing the opposite of relaxing, it would not cause stress, which is the literal opposite of relaxing. In other words, there would be *no stress*. That's what jumped at people. Stress-Free does convey that same meaning but it's not as exciting."

Monique listened intently as Patricia Samuels, née Paul, spoke. "Your analysis of the name was so spot-on I would've thought you came up with it yourself. Who are you?" "Patricia Samuels." Monique gazed at her. "Patricia Samuels – we just hired you but you look so familiar."

"I went to Nia before transferring over to Jones Christian College."

"Oh, you're Patty Paul, but you're married now. Nice to see you again."

Patricia nodded. "You as well. So, Ms. Ross, what's your take on the new product name?" "I agree that Stress-Free is kind of bland but I like that it embodies what we were trying to say with No Stress. No Stress was catchy and simple. Someone give me something catchy and simple. Quick!" An intern named Brian Gatsby stepped up. "I got it!" Everyone turned because he was just supposed to be typing the meeting's minutes, not adding input. "If I may speak," Brian quickly retracted. Monique looked at him. "You may. Lottie, take over for Brian." A second intern took Brian's place at the laptop while Brian spoke.

"People also use pressing combs to straighten their hair, right?"

Monique nodded. "Right…" She wasn't entirely following Brian's statement so he explained, "Since 'press' rhymes with 'stress,' the new name could be 'No Press? No Stress'. This name could lend itself to the fact that people believe wearing their hair natural is more stressful on account of social pressures to fit Euro-centric standards of beauty. By saying 'No Press? No Stress,' Mo's Mix is essentially challenging those beauty standards."

Though the creative analysts, marketing specialists, and senior marketing execs didn't seem at all impressed by the intern's boastful manner, Monique decided, "I like it. Carry on with the pitch."

Brian went to the white board and wrote: **No Press? No Stress. Quani. Walmart.** Then he stated, "Here's the scenario: Quani is at the store searching for some new haircare products because her old ones aren't working. Quani is searching for products geared towards natural styles. When Quani goes to the section where our product sits, she sees: Oil Sheens, Curl Puddings, and texturizers among other basic products with unexciting names. Then Quani sees 'No Press? No Stress.' This sticks with Quani firstly because it rhymes and secondly because it has double meaning. Thus, Quani buys our product and tells her friends about it."

"What if Quani's one of a kind," someone challenged. "How will your name have market appeal for the **entire** market – not just for one person?" Seeing that they were trying to break the intern, junior marketing executive Marlon Thomas interjected, "If you look at the girls who go natural, they are artsy people trying to get in touch with their spirit. Since Brian's name is poetic, it will stick out to the artist in them. My boyfriend's a sucker for a good poem and he will buy something based on the sole criterion of poetic flare."

Monique nodded because she too liked the product name. "I support it. Good story, by the way." She directed at Brian as she took a picture of the white board. Monique was carefully documenting his progress as an intern to see if he would be a good fit for Mo's Mix. "Any more opinions?" Monique asked next.

Once a vote was taken and majority ruled in favor of Brian's creative name, Monique stated, "Someone go make a mock-up label to see if the words fit. Someone else go check to see how that artwork is coming. Come to me before the end of the work day with results. Meeting dismissed." Antonio Lawrence, Senior Marketing Executive and President of Communications, felt slighted by the way Monique had completely seized a meeting *he* had called. Antonio caught up to Monique as everyone was leaving. "Excuse me, Ms. Ross?"

"Yes?"

"You are my superior and I completely respect your opinion but I'm not on board with the whole 'No Press? No Stress.' name. I think it might be over people's heads." Monique put her hand on her hips. "You're entitled to that opinion but we took a vote and majority of the marketers liked the name. So, if you think you have better name, set up another meeting and do a pitch." Antonio grew silent so Monique sighed. "But, that's not necessary because you *can't* think of a better name. You just don't like the idea of an **intern** overshadowing you at **your** meeting because you're the President of Communications, right?"

Antonio didn't like Monique's dismissal. "If we're doling out criticism, you might want to think twice before letting said *intern* give you the name that will be put on products nationwide."

Monique smiled, sensing Antonio's superiority complex. "I take ideas from all arenas, Mr. Lawrence, because a job title is by no means an indication of one's skillset."

Antonio decided to ignore Monique's slight shade. "Fair point, but as President of Communications, I feel that I should have the final say." "Have you decided to become selectively ignorant to the fact that I am the CEO **and** founder of Mo's Mix? My decisions will *always* hold precedence over yours."

Antonio shook his head. "Another fair point, but I still feel that you came in and monopolized *my* meeting." Monique let out a deep breath. "Let me make something clear, Mr. Lawrence: what little authority you hold inside Mo's Mix is only relative to your department. Since I hold all the true power and I like 'No Press? No Stress,' we're going to use that name. Is that okay with you?"

Antonio resented Monique's smugness. "No but, as you've made clear, my opinion is inferior to your own." He sighed. "This just reminds me of when our team was divided about the name 'No Stress.' Yet, you still signed off on it without a second thought." Monique put her hands on her hips. "Donna told me you *all* loved the name." Antonio laughed. "We both know Donna's a liar, now don't we? Isn't that why she was booted out?"

"She was fired for inappropriate relations with a co-worker."

Antonio said, "That's not what Maisha from HR said. Apparently, Donna was involved in the fire and you're using 'internal dating' as a cover for that. Are you trying to conceal the fact that you screwed up, Ms. Ross?" Monique had heard enough from Antonio. "I don't know who wronged you today, Mr. Lawrence, but I will *not* stand for this blatant disrespect. Step down in the next 2 seconds or kiss employment goodbye."

Antonio changed his demeanor. "My apologies, Ms. Ross." Monique then said, "I suggest you go see Yasmine to get that attitude in check. There are people higher up than you who lost jobs over that." Antonio raised his eyebrow. "I'm a department head. There's no one higher up than me."

"You're the President of *communications*, Mr. Lawrence." Monique clarified. "The ladder of this company goes C-suite, lead scientist, head of technology, head of security, *then* you then all other employees. In other words, you're nothing but two notches above an intern. Remember that." Monique walked off so that her words could really settle in.

There was a note on her desk when she returned to her office. *Dr. Seneca's secretary called. Twice.* Monique sighed. "Dominique, what time was my appointment?" "A half-hour ago, Ms. Ross."

"While I was in the meeting, right?"

Dominique nodded. "Right. Should I call her back?" "Please do and send her my apologies." Dominique dialed Dr. Seneca's number while Monique held her belly. "Emelia, get ready for a roller coaster."

"This is my belated birthday gift to you."

Monique raised her eyebrow. "You're taking me to the strip club?" Camille rolled her eyes. "No. I'm just here to pick up a check so I can give you my real gift."

"A check? Camille, you're a…"

"Bartender," Camille quickly explained. "I have a little more class than stripping, Mo." Monique linked arms with her friend. "Thank God." As Monique and Camille walked into a back room, the owner of the club looked Monique up and down. "You look familiar but maybe that's because I've seen you in my dreams."

Monique scoffed. "Is that your way of flirting?"

"Depends. Is it working?"

She rolled her eyes. "I'm engaged." "Engaged and pregnant? Sounds to me like a shotgun wedding." "It's not," Monique fired.

"Ooh, defensive. You know, people always get defensive when they hit with the truth." "It's *not* a shotgun wedding." Monique repeated in a sterner tone. "And if I have to say that again, I will make sure this club gets audited. I'll bet the IRS would *love* to know why you only pay your employees in cash." The club owner let out a deep breath. "It was a careless assumption. I apologize." He handed Camille an envelope. "See you at work on Sunday, Camille."

"Yep." Camille and Monique quickly exited.

"Why'd you get so bothered in there?" Camille and Mo walked arm in arm down the street. "Maybe I'm tired of people asking me if this is a shotgun wedding. Dre and I are getting married because it's something that we both want, not because I'm trying avoid the label 'baby mama'."

"You know what would silence those naysayers? Jump the broom while you're still pregnant."

"You mean elope?"

Camille nodded. "Yep. You have so much going on with the baby and the business and the house so I don't really see a large ceremony in your future." Monique admitted, "Dre called me the 'antithesis of romance' when I said I wouldn't mind tying the knot at City Hall." "Do it then," Camille suggested. "Shut these haters up." "Are you just saying that or do you mean it?"

Camille laughed. "You know I'm just talking, Mo. I fully believe in ceremonies." This was an allusion to the fact that Camille was secretly planning a wedding for Monique, but Monique didn't know it yet. So, Monique just said, "Which is why you almost walked down the aisle with Trevor, a deadbeat who worked with you at Walmart."

Camille rolled her eyes. "That was 27 year old dazed and confused Camille. Now, I'm 28 year old *single* Camille who is damn sure ready to mingle." "What happened to Darrell? I liked Darrell."

"Darrell also liked Darrell – a little too much if you ask me. Can you believe that he would take longer than me in the bathroom whenever we went out?"

Monique shook her head. "Please don't tell me that's why you broke up with him." Camille said, "It's not. I woke up one time and saw him in my purse. For weeks, I thought I had just been dropping money but this fool was stealing it." Monique scrunched her face. "Ooh, I don't deal with thieves. I'm glad you dropped him."

Camille sighed. "Me too. I told him to keep whatever money he had and use it for the bus to take his black behind away on." Monique started laughing. "Cam, did you really say that?" "Yes. He deserved it."

"You're just as bad as some of these guys then."

"James did used to say I was one of the boys."

Monique thought back to a time when James and Camille had been close friends. "Oh yeah, he did. Why'd you two grow apart again?" Eager to avoid the question, Camille responded, "Here's your car." They got inside and Monique asked, "Did something happen between you and James?" Camille started the ignition. "Off we go."

Since Camille clearly didn't want to talk about it, Monique decided to let the conversation go. "Where are we headed, Cam?" "You'll see." 30 minutes later, Monique and Camille were riding bumper cars, playing mini golf, and dodging paint balls. Afterwards, Monique sat on a bench. "We are children at heart," She noted. Camille smiled. "Yes, but you have to admit that was fun." While Monique and Camille chatted, James pulled up in his escalade.

His daughter Arielle was going to a birthday party at the same amusement park. Monique looked over. "James? Ari?" Arielle ran to Monique. "Hi, Auntie Mo." Monique hugged her niece. "Hey." Arielle touched Monique's stomach. "My cousin's getting big, huh?" Monique grinned. "She is." "So it's a girl?!"

Monique nodded. "Yes."

"Yay! We can play dollhouse together when she gets old enough."

"She's really excited about being a cousin." Monique pointed out. James laughed at Arielle's excitement. "A sister too, actually." Monique raised her eyebrow. "Oh?" James nodded. "Yep. Laila told me last week."

"Girl or boy?"

"Boy."

"I suppose his name will be James too," Camille commented. James let out a deep breath. "Maybe. What are you two doing here?" "Celebrating Monique's birthday."

"Oh. Cool." The atmosphere had grown immensely awkward on account of the underlying tension between Camille and James. Knowing the two needed a moment alone, Monique said, "Ari, why don't you introduce me to your friend?" Monique went off with Arielle while James and Camille just stared at each other.

Eventually, James said, "You don't have to make this difficult." "I don't know what you're talking about." James rubbed Camille's elbow. "I'm sorry I didn't call you back but it's just that Laila's been on to--"

Camille put her hand up. "It's always the same with you: heartbreak." James took Camille by the hips. "It doesn't have to be. You overcomplicate things when you overthink."

Camille rolled her eyes and pulled herself away from James. "You oversimplify things when you ignore the gravity of very serious situations." James sighed – knowing exactly where the conversation had ventured. "You could've kept the child if you wanted to."

Camille reminded him, "You said either Jalen disappeared or you did."

"Okay, but that was years ago. Why are you still on that?"

Camille groaned. "This is exactly what I'm talking about, James. You're undermining the significance of bringing a child into this world. I will *never* stop thinking about my baby. I gave him away thinking that it was the opportunity cost for being with you but – as it turns out – that was wrong. Yet, while I was wallowing in my own personal defeat, you were off getting married and having another child. Now, you're giving Laila a *second* baby?" Camille finally took a deep breath. "If I didn't know any better, I'd say you actually love her."

"She's my wife, so that's kind of an understood thing," James spat sarcastically. Camille rolled her eyes. "You always have something smart to say." "It's the truth, though." Camille stared

James in the face. "Oh, really? Look me in my eyes and tell me you love her."

James turned away from Camille's discerning eyes. "That's stupid; of course I do." "Look me in my eyes and say it then." James grew uncharacteristically silent. Camille scoffed. "You can't even say it, can you?" "You can't let bygones be bygones."

"I wanted my baby," Camille admitted. "But I wanted you more. Yet, I *still* ended up losing both of you." "You have me," James informed her.

"When? When I drunk dial your phone, we have sex and you're gone before morning?"

"You know how I feel about you, Camille. Just promise me you'll keep quiet," James begged. Camille didn't respond so he grabbed her arm. "Promise," James pled. Camille started flashing back to her abusive relationship. "Let me go." "I will once you promise that you won't say anything." Unintentionally, James tightened his grip. As a result, Camille's body tensed up. He released her arm then. "I'm sorry. I didn't mean to grab you like that."

Camille snatched her reddening arm away. "You know I don't play that." James looked her in the eye. "I know. I'm sorry. Just promise me you'll play it cool." Camille rolled her eyes again. "Whatever. Congrats on the baby." Monique was getting closer to them so Camille went to the car. "Everything good?" Monique asked when she walked up.

James nodded. "Yep." He hurried off to where Arielle was. Meanwhile, Monique stood wondering what ever happened between her brother and her best friend.

Later on, Andre came home feeling uneasy. He had been in a heated courtroom debate and, upon hearing that Andre would likely lose the case, Andre's boss said his piece. So, Andre was in an unpleasant mood. But, as soon as Dre saw Mo, all that anxiety went away. He kissed her multiple times. Monique grinned after the 5th one. "I missed you too, baby." Andre laughed and snuggled next to her on the couch. "Mo?" Monique turned into him. "Yes, Dre?" Andre held Monique's belly. "There's a person in there."

Monique giggled. "It's perplexing, right?"

"It is. I mean, I was there for the births of my younger siblings and my sisters' kids but, now that it's my child, it feels different. The other times, I could just play with the babies and leave the responsibilities to someone else. I don't get to have that barrier with Emelia. This time around, the responsibility is all mine. If we're being honest, I'm scared that our kids will end up hating me."

Monique looked up. "Kids – like plural?" Andre nodded. "Yeah. We're giving Emelia siblings, right?" Monique sat up straight. "Once she turns 6 maybe." "6? That's a big age gap."

"Dre, I'm barely balancing one baby with my business. What will I look like with 2 or 3?"

"Or 4," Andre added.

"*Four*? You want *four* kids?" "I just want all my children to have a brother and a sister." Monique lay her head back and started imagining how misshapen her body could become after pushing out four children. "I might as well say bye-bye body." Andre rubbed Monique's stomach gently. "I know it's a lot to think about but we should consider our family size now that we've started."

"I say 3 is enough."

"3 kids?"

Monique shook her head. "3 **people** – as in you, me, and
Emelia." Andre wrapped his arms around Monique's shoulders.
"So you don't want any more after her?" Monique told him, "No.
At least not right now." Andre sighed. "When have I heard that
line before? Oh when I brought up the idea of marriage. Right."
Monique turned back towards Dre. "Don't tell me you're getting
upset."

Andre shrugged. "I guess a part of me thought you had changed.
Alas, you're the still the same business-minded Mo who puts her
career before anything else in her life." Monique scoffed. "That's
not true. I've never put my career before you." "Then how come
we aren't planning a wedding right this second?" "I told you I
didn't want a big ceremony," Monique reiterated.

"But, every woman wants a big ceremony. Right?" Monique
said, "Excuse the discredit to Chaka but I'm *not* every woman.
I'm like that person who pours the milk then the cereal –
unconventional."

"You got that right," Dre murmured. Monique didn't appreciate
his snide tone. "Besides, who'll be taking care of four kids if
you're working at a law firm and I'm at Mo's Mix?" "We can
start planning and figure that out." Monique sighed. "I don't
want to plan something that might not happen."

Andre got up from the couch and walked to the kitchen. "Okay."
"I know that 'okay,' Andre, and it means that it's definitely not
okay." He loosened his tie and began pulling food from the
refrigerator. Monique stared blankly at him. "You're going to
walk away because you didn't like where the conversation was
going?"

"I'm going to walk away because I haven't eaten since lunch and
my belly is screaming out for mercy. Am I allowed to do that,
your majesty?"

Monique raised her eyebrow. "What do you mean are you *allowed*?" Andre told her, "In your world, you are the sun, Monique – meaning everything must revolve around you. In this Queen-dom, you reside as the ruler and the rest of us are mere jesters to your throne. So, your majesty, I am petitioning to eat the leftovers that I prepared yesterday. Does her royal highness grant me the privilege to do so?"

"Andre, you know I hate your sarcastic tangents. Please stop."

"You know what *I* hate? My job. But if I quit, I will upset her majesty and be forced to sleep in the dungeon otherwise known as the living room."

Monique rolled her eyes. "Now you're just being annoying." Dre groaned. "No, 'annoying' describes every last one of my goddam co-workers. They sit and gripe about their problems as if they actually have *real* problems. There are children getting killed in drive-bys or living in food desserts yet my co-workers want to complain because their wives ask for family time, or because their kids want expensive cars or because whatever team they were betting on lost."

Dre shook his head. "They don't have *real* problems, Monique. And I have to listen to them whining all. Day. Long."

Andre sighed. "It doesn't get any better with my clients. Let me tell you something about these clients: the business owners I represent are some of the most entitled Homo sapiens you'll ever encounter. I just can't stand..." Andre paused because he was getting angry. "I want out, Mo."

Andre rubbed his face. "I want out so badly. I can*not* work with these people anymore. If I don't quit or get fired, you'll find my body on the side of the highway somewhere because I just gave up on life."

Monique stood with her hands on her hips. "Andre, don't talk about death right now." "I know that's a grim way to look at the situation but I'm so unhappy, Monique." Monique began recalling all the deaths that were plaguing her and she couldn't bear the thought of adding Andre to that list. "I know but *please* don't talk about death, Andre. Especially not your own. I just--" Andre came over because he realized he had been too dramatic. He pulled Monique into his chest as she cried. "I know you're still grieving. I'm sorry."

Monique wept into his shoulder and Andre rubbed her back. "It's all going to be okay. Junior, Pamela, and Abigail are all up in Heaven looking down and smiling on you; they're probably hoping that you'll realize they're where they are meant to be."

"Are you saying that they were destined to die, Dre?!" Andre rocked Monique side to side. "Everyone dies, baby. Some just leave this world sooner than others because He has a greater plan for them." Realizing Andre had a point, Monique cried out in truth. Dre held her to steady her. "Death just paves the way for new life, which is why God gave us Emelia and He gave Laila her baby. He's essentially replacing your aunt and uncle."

"What about Abigail?"

"Her replacement will come in time," Dre assured Mo.

"The pink one!" Camille exclaimed. Before she could run over to it, Daniel pulled her back. "This is Monique we're talking about – not you." Camille rolled her eyes. "Well, what would Mo like?" Daniel set his eyes on a black and gold crib that just screamed Monique, to him at least. "That one." Camille looked at the price tag. "This thing's almost $600. I wasn't trying to go over 100."

"You are so cheap."

"I'm a bartender. What other choice do I have?"

"Why don't you get a better job?" Daniel wondered. "You have a Bachelor's degree, Camille."

Camille sighed. "True but I slept with some of my old bosses and I hear that most of their wives left them because she couldn't put it down like me. So, I doubt they'll be viable references." As Daniel laughed, Camille admitted, "On a more serious note, though, I honestly don't know any old employers or professors who'd actually vouch for me." Daniel decided to keep the conversation light. "You slept with married men?" Camille nodded. "Yep. I was fresh out of college and ready to make my mark on the world."

"I see, I see. Luckily for you, the first move I made when I left school was investing my money. I'll now be using some of the dividends earned to subsidize my second niece's nursery." Camille rolled her eyes. "So many unnecessarily used words in one sentence." "But I bet you know what every last one means." Camille smirked because she did. Though she tended to downplay it, Daniel knew Camille was smarter than she put out.

James came over. "Why you going all out for Mo's baby? You told me you got Ari's crib from a hobo." Daniel chuckled. "I only said that because Laila did not appreciate its avant-garde aesthetic." "That thang was ugly. I thought it really did come from a hobo." Daniel rolled his eyes. "I'll have you know I paid $500 for that."

"You forreal?"

"Well, I used a coupon, but the tag price was 5."

James shook his head. "That dude at the thrift store only gave me 50 for it." "You got ripped off." "I thought it was trash," James noted. "One man's trash is another man's treasure," Camille mumbled. James looked over. "You say something?" Camille glanced at the list in her hand. "So what else are we getting?" Daniel, who knew there was unresolved tension between Camille and James, took the list from her hand. "You two should talk."

Daniel started scanning the store for the next item while Camille leaned on the crib.

"What are you even doing here?" She asked James.

"Daniel wanted me to help him get some baby stuff for Mo." "Daniel asked *me* to help him get some baby stuff for Mo." Daniel, who had planned this, walked off smirking. Camille shook her head. "I don't even know what he wants us to talk about. There's nothing left to say."

James looked Camille in the eye. "I know a part of you resents me for what I did to you but I had a lot of pressure on me. Remember I was only 21."

"Exactly, James. *Only* 21. You had no business getting married."

"I bet you wish it would've been to you, huh?"

"So I could end up getting cheated on and lied to? No thanks."

James played with one of Camille's curls. "I'd be faithful to you." James moved his hand to her arm. "For what it's worth, I wish we could've raised our son." Ironically, two little boys came playing hide and seek around the cribs. The woman with them yelled, "Skyler, Rodney, get back over here!" The boys continued playing and Skyler bumped into Camille. "Sorry!"

Skyler ran around Camille so that his friend wouldn't be able to tag him. Camille stared at Skyler because something about him seemed familiar to her. Watching the two boys play made Camille wonder what her son would have been like. Camille studied Skyler and Rodney intently while she thought about Jalen. After a while, James moved his hand up and down her arm. "You still here?"

Camille came back to reality. "Yep." "What you thinking about?" Daniel returned before Camille had to answer. "So I've gotten everything off the list and, since you two aren't threatening to kill each other, can I presume you're amicable again?" Camille gently pulled her arm away. "Something like that." After paying for the items, Daniel and a sales clerk walked over to the crib.

"How is Ms. Ross, by the way," the clerk asked as Daniel was typing in Monique's address. "How'd you…" Daniel looked up and saw Evan Armoire, the guy who had been working to destroy Mo's Mix while also sleeping with his equally deceptive co-worker (Donna Roberts). Bearing this in mind, Daniel answered, "From CFO to sales clerk. You've practically upgraded, huh?"

Evan sighed. "Considering that you black balled me, this is the only place I *could* work at. But, kicking me out isn't going to stop what's coming to you, Mr. Ross." Daniel wondered, "Oh, what's coming to me?" "A storm," Evan informed him.

"I thought we were already weathering a storm." "It's not over," Evan whispered. Once Monique's address was put in, the order was complete. Evan put on a fake smile while taking the company Jotter back. "Thank you for shopping with us and have a nice day. Come again soon."

Monique was reading an article and relaxing when Daniel called her. "Mo, there's news." "Business or gossip?"

"I want to say business but you know as well as I do that the two are beginning to intertwine."

Monique sighed. "Sadly, you're right. Spill." "I just ran into Evan Armoire." Monique gasped. "What? Where?" Daniel shook his head. "Doesn't matter. He said that the storm isn't over." "Is that a metaphor for what's to come?"

"Indeed it is, sister. It might do you some good to invest in an umbrella."

Monique exhaled. "Duly noted. So how do we stop him and whoever might be working with him?" Daniel, who was coming towards his penthouse, looked at a newspaper stand. "It might start with taking a look at Samuel's *Spotlight* interview. Apparently, he wants to 'make sure the truth comes out'." "Read it then get back to me."

Daniel scoffed. "That sounds like something you should be saying to your assistant."

"Then call Dominique and tell her to read it."

"Why can't *you* call Dominique," Daniel questioned. Monique said, "I'm on the phone right now and it would be rude to just hang up."

Daniel laughed and hung up anyway. Since he was taking care of that, Monique hoped to continue relaxing. She was supposed to appear in court later that day with Genna to defend Mo's Mix; if the other side knew how much Monique detested Genna, Monique feared they might have used it as ammunition. *Just pretend she **didn't** try to steal your fiancé,* Monique reminded herself.

By the time Monique got to court, she was convinced that she and Genna were almost acquaintances – at least that's how Monique hoped it would appear. Genna nodded when she saw Monique. "Ms. Ross." "Attorney Marx." They went into the tiny court room and pulled out contracts and nondisclosure agreements that completely invalidated everything the other side was trying to claim. In the end, the class action lawsuit had failed and Monique didn't have to pay a dime.

In the same courtroom, Andre also won his case, but he was not as happy about it. Afterwards, the client confessed, "Originally, I had my doubts about you but obviously they were wrong. Thank you so much." Andre nodded. "You're welcome." He called Monique to talk about the "good" news but Monique's line was busy because she was calling him to talk about the great news.

Andre sighed. "Must be on a work call," he thought. "Must be in court," Monique decided. As they hung up their phones and got ready to leave the court room, Monique and Andre locked eyes. Monique walked over and wrapped her arms around Andre. "Baby, guess what? We won!" Andre smiled while holding Monique's hips. "That's great news."

"And how did your case go?" Monique wondered.

"I won."

Monique rubbed his shoulder. "That's my man." Andre sighed. "Yeah, but you know how I feel about this stuff." Monique nodded. "I do. Want to talk about it at home?" "Or…we can talk about it over lunch. Tell your driver he can go back to Mo's Mix because your fiancé is taking you out to celebrate your win in court today." Monique laughed. "Do I have to say all of that?" While Monique and Andre started discussing lunch plans, Genna walked over. "Sorry to interrupt this lovely moment but can I borrow your girlfriend for a second, Andre?"

Monique made her ring very visible. "You know good and well that I'm his *fiancée* but why do you need to 'borrow' me?" Genna revealed, "Samuel Lee has been doing some investigating of his own and the chemicals used in that fire can be found in your labs, *Ms*. Ross."

"Meaning?"

"You're about to be on trial for murder, *Ms*. Ross."

Knowing that she had ruined a good moment, Genna walked off wearing a smile. Monique took Andre's hand. "Can I take a raincheck on lunch?"

While Laila gave Arielle a bath, James went through some of his old photo searching for pictures of him and Camille. There were only a few so James cherished each one dearly. When he finally found one, James had an immediate flashback to the way that he and Camille had been lying on his bed and her hair had fallen onto his face. Suddenly struck with a warm memory, James sniffed the picture to see if he could recall the scent of Camille's curls.

"What are you doing?" Laila returned from putting Arielle in bed. James quickly grabbed a picture of Arielle and let the other one fall to the floor.

"Looking at our baby girl," James lied. "Is she really 4 already?" He used his foot to casually slide the other picture under the bed.

Laila sat down next to James and began talking about how Arielle was growing up so fast but, the entire time, James couldn't get that image of Camille out of his head. So, inevitably, he wound up at her apartment. As far as Laila knew, James was going to the shop.

"What do you want?" Camille began.

"Can I come in?"

"No."

"Why, you busy?" Camille motioned towards her work outfit. "Pretty much." James studied Camille's "Teasers" t-shirt and the way it hit her chest perfectly. Then, he glanced at her nicely chiseled legs in her skintight work pants. "You work at Teasers?" James asked to stop himself from fantasizing too much.

"Isn't that what my shirt says?"

James threw his hands up. "Excuse me for trying to make conversation." "James, I need to get to work and you're--" James kissed Camille in a way he knew she couldn't resist. She was willing at first but then Camille stepped back. "You have a daughter and a pregnant wife." "But, I need you."

Camille scoffed. "When *I* needed *you*, you needed convenience so Laila was the better option. You made the bed, now lie in it." Camille pushed James out of her doorway as she left the apartment. "I have to get to work." "Call me." "No." James rubbed her chin with his thumb. "Please?"

"No. I don't need Laila coming after me."

"Forget Laila. Worry about us."

Camille laughed aloud. "James, there is no 'us'. There is a you and there is a me. At the moment, I'm choosing to put *me* first and everything else second. Now, for the *third* time, I gotta go to work. Goodbye." Camille left the building while James lingered in the hallway thinking about his next moves. Since he didn't want to be home and all of James's friends were either with their wives or mistresses, James decided he would visit Teasers. First, he needed some money.

"Unless you're here to tell me that Mo went into labor and your car broke down, I don't understand why you're on my doorstep."

James let out a deep breath. "Danny, I need money." "Do I look like the bank? This is the 3rd time this month." James said, "All my money is tied up in bills right now but I need some quick cash." Daniel sighed. "Is it the bar or the strip this time?"

"Strip. I just found out Camille works at Teasers."

Daniel raised his eyebrow. "Why does that concern you?" James got silent and Daniel then understood. "You *still* barking up that tree, huh? You'll sleep with her, confide in her, impregnate her, and pretend that you actually cherish her but you'll never marry her. No wonder she's always ready to tear your head off."

Indignantly, James replied, "I won't marry her because I have a family to protect but of course you don't understand the concept of marriage or families since you'll never even be able to have your own ch…" James stopped himself before going further. Daniel told him, "Don't hold back. I already know you what you were going to say. But, at the end of the day, at least there's no chance of me impregnating my *many* partners."

James rolled his eyes. "That's because you bend over for men and there's no way two men can…actually, scratch that. You're not men. There's no way two *women* can have a baby."

Daniel shook his head. "You see the problem with you 'Christians' is that you vehemently believe homosexuals are the devil's doing. But it's the same type of 'Christian' who is coming to me for money so he can go cheat on his pregnant wife with his baby mama. I wonder how God would feel about this, James."

James let out a deep breath. "You're blasphemous so you're the last one who should be questioning *my* religion. But can I have some money or not?"

Daniel shook his head. "Not. And, for the record, I do the bending over." Daniel slammed his door as horrific images of Daniel's sexual escapades with men settled in James's head. James shuddered at the thought of his brother's trysts. Then, he went to see if Monique could help him out.

"He's suggesting that it's premeditated? How could it be premeditated?! Samuel thinks they *planned* to kill Abigail?! That would mean that I was really oblivious. Was I really that oblivious, Dominique?" Monique waited for an answer while Andre rubbed his temples. He was frustrated because Monique was still talking to Dominique as if they hadn't been having the same conversation for over an hour. Really, Andre just wanted Mo to sit down with him so they could discuss his unhappiness but she was too preoccupied with work to care about that sort of thing.

Andre pulled out a beer and flipped the TV on to the cooking channel. He made sure to turn the volume up so he could drown out Monique. Hearing the noise, Monique put her hand on her phone's speaker. "Dre, could you turn that down? You see I'm on the phone." Dre sighed and did as requested. "Anything you want, your majesty," he mumbled. Andre drank beer after beer while attempting to numb the pain that was taxing on his brain. After the third beer, Andre heard the doorbell ring but he didn't answer because he thought it was Daniel, which would mean it was more work and more reason for Monique to ignore Andre.

James kept buzzing but Andre refused to move an inch. Monique came from the bedroom with her hand on the phone speaker again. "Dre, you gonna answer that or just laze on the couch watching TV?" Andre looked dead at Monique. "Mo, I had a long day. Can you not do this right now?"

Monique rolled her eyes. "Dre, I'm pregnant – enough said. Now, answer the door." "Ordering me around like I'm your servant. Those pregnancy hormones are in full effect, huh?" Not wanting to argue, Monique decided she was going to go back to the bedroom and continue talking to Dominique. Andre sighed again. "I can't win for losing." He finally opened the door and realized it had been James standing there, not Daniel. "Oh, my bad." Andre said. "You looked like Daniel from over there and--"

James cut his eyes. "Don't ever say that again." "You're brothers so you two look alike," Andre mentioned.

"That doesn't mean you have to point it out." Andre threw his hands up. "Again, my bad. What's up?" James looked around. "Where's my sister?"

"On a call," Andre told him. Seconds later, James heard Monique yelling and knew she was in business mode – meaning she was not to be bothered. "Do you know when she'll be off the phone?"

"No time soon. Do you need something?"

"Money."

"How much and for what?"

At first, James was hesitant about confiding in Andre. Then, James thought that as a man Andre would understand James's desire. Alas, Andre heard what the money was for and he shook his head before James could even say the amount. "I can't support your infidelity. Mo would kill me if she found out." "Which is why Mo don't have to know."

Andre said, "I don't lie to Monique." "Yet," James challenged. "You don't lie to her yet." Andre shook his head. "I don't lie to her *at all* so I can't give you the money." James scoffed. "Why, 'cause you a lil punk who does whatever my baby sister tells you to? A real man would march into that room and order her to get off that phone so she could make him some damn dinner. A real man wouldn't let her work while she's 8 months pregnant. A real man--"

Andre stepped forward while cutting James off. "A *real* man doesn't leave his pregnant wife and 4 year old daughter in the middle of the night just to see some half-naked, insecure females who never had love from any *real* man. So, they opted to degrade themselves since, all their lives, they were dealing with **little boys** like you – cowards who use infidelity to disguise themselves as 'real' men. To me, y'all are *real* messed up."

Andre's sister Lauren had stripped when she was trying to pay for med school and Andre shuddered at the thought of some horny men touching on his sister's body. Not realizing Andre's viewpoint, James scoffed again. "You sound like more of a faggot than Daniel now."

"You shouldn't be talking about your brother like that."

"My brother's a faggot – just like yours."

At his breaking point, Andre informed James, "You have officially overstayed your welcome. Get out of my house." "Am I making you uncomfortable?" Andre opened the door. "I don't think that was a question." James shook his head. "I never thought Monique was a lesbian, but *clearly* she's marrying a woman." Andre, who had no tolerance for misogyny, took James's shirt and shoved him into a nearby wall. "You know what?!" Monique saw what was going on and rushed over.

"Andre, what are you doing?!"

Andre quickly let James go. "He was getting disrespectful." "I don't care. You have *no* right to put your hands on my brother like that." Andre, realizing that he had lost his temper, told Monique, "I know. I'm sorry." James laughed at this. "See, I was right. You're Monique's fucking bitch!" Angrily, Andre turned around and punched James one good time. So, finally, James left the condo. Monique shut the door behind him.

"Andre…"

Andre grabbed his three empty beer bottles. "You're mad; I know. But, he was way out of line." Monique glanced at the bottles. "Have you been drinking again?" "Yes, but that's not why I did that. James said things that could make a sober man turn volatile." Monique raised her eyebrow. "Such as?"

"I don't want to talk about it."

Monique sighed. "You don't want to talk about it. Of course." Andre poured himself a glass of water. "I know I lost it, Mo. I'm really sorry." Monique crossed her arms. "Why are you so angry? Lately, you've been more aggressive than usual."

Since this was the conversation he'd been longing to have, Andre admitted, "I'm stressed about work and worried about raising Emelia right and wondering if we'll be able to get this house and reflecting on the fact that it was a misogynist like James who used to beat my sister then left her to raise his two children."

Monique exhaled. "I didn't realize how much you were keeping inside. I'm sorry that I haven't been more alert to what you were dealing with." She came over and took Andre in her arms. "But, I'm here now, okay?" Andre kissed Monique. "I know."

Monique rubbed his shoulders. "I love you Andre, but as my fiancé and the father of my child, I need you to always be in control of your emotions. Otherwise, you could end up back in jail and it might not just be for a day."

Andre rested his head on Monique's shoulders as he reflected on the day he had found out Nathalie's ex-husband was beating her and the kids. "I blacked out when I found he was hitting Siena and Sebastian too. They were babies at the time, Mo. You can't hurt your babies." Andre put his hand on Monique's stomach. "I'll kill a man if he ever touches our Emelia."

Monique sighed. "I will too but those are our paternal and maternal instincts, Dre. If you allow yourself to become too reaction-driven, you'll forget that an eye for an eye makes the whole world blind."

"What other choice did I have, Mo? We'd gone to the police on several occasions but, due to Nathalie's reluctance to testify, they were going to let Roberto walk. And if he would've walked, he would've been roaming the streets still terrorizing my sister."

Monique sighed. "So the next best option was beating him so badly he could've ended up in a coma?"

"I didn't mean for that to happen."

Monique said, "Exactly, Dre. You lost control." While thinking back to the altercation, Andre replied, "In that moment, we were two animals in the wild. I was on the hunt for an abhorrent creature and, as soon as I laid eyes on him, natural instinct told me to attack." Monique looked Andre in the eyes. "You got out of that one by the skin of your neck." Andre took a deep breath. "I would say that applies to both me and Roberto."

Monique and Andre were having this crucial conversation as James was getting money from his father. Mr. Ross reasoned that "men are gonna do what men wanna do." With 50 singles and a $50 bill in his pocket, James did exactly what he wanted to do. From her post, Camille noticed that one man was hands-on with every girl who approached him. When Camille looked closely, she saw that it was James. *Is he serious? He does not give up.* Camille started thinking of what she would say to James the next time she saw him and thus became more focused on him than she was on her job. "'Scuse me, bartender? I asked for a drink like a half-hour ago and you still haven't made it for me."

Camille rolled her eyes and walked over. "Dude, it's been 10 minutes. Don't get your tidy whiteys in a twist." The guy laughed. "I wear boxers, actually." "Could've fooled me," Camille murmured while studying James and the fifth girl of the night. *If he can do this to Laila, what makes you think he won't do it to you too?* The guy at the bar took notice of the way Camille kept glancing over at James. "You're looking like you seen your husband here." Camille immediately put on her poker face. "Definitely not that. What can I get for you?" "Another shot of brown."

"Coming right up."

While Camille made Trevor his drink, she continued to peek at James from the corner of her eye. So, finally, Trevor turned in the direction of Camille's eyes. "Who we looking at?" Camille grinned as she placed the cup down. "No one. I'm just amazed at how many men in that crowd are wearing rings." Trevor shrugged. "Pleasure is something we men treasure."

"Is that supposed to be poetic?"

Trevor touched Camille's arm. "Maybe." Camille saw a hunger in his eyes and it sort of bothered her. "Let me know if you need anything else," she told him while taking his tip and walking away. Camille went to tend to another man who had his hand up. Once Camille got closer, she saw that it was James. "Hey."

Camille rolled her eyes. "What are you doing here?" "Same thing as everyone else."

"There are 2 other strip clubs in the city. Why'd you come to this one?"

"I guess I thought there was something *special* about it." Camille rolled her eyes again. "I'm tired of these games, James. I want you to take me seriously." "I do." Before Camille could respond, Trevor was waving her over. "I'll be right back."

Trevor looked Camille up and down when she returned. "You miss me?"

"Did I...?" Camille paused and then she realized it was her ex-fiancé. "How did I not recognize you before?" "I cut off my dreads," he revealed. Camille nodded. "You did, didn't you?" Trevor said, "I miss *you*, Camille."

Camille sighed. "Trevor, you know why we're not together."

"Because of a little baby? That's petty."

Camille told him, "It wasn't the child; it was her mother. Nicole used to work for my friend, which I thought was weird. It was like I was part of some bigger scheme." "What the hell you talking about? No one was scheming." This was a lie, actually. Trevor had only proposed to Camille because Nicole wanted him to weed out as much information as possible. The plan was working until Trevor got jealous of Camille having lunch with an ex then stalked the ex. This led to Camille calling off their engagement.

Camille shook her head. "And, besides that, you're mentally unstable." "Your daddy's a psycho and ya mammy's a racist so you *might* be confusing me with yourself, girlie." Camille scoffed. "There's absolutely no reason for you to be disrespectful. I wasn't comfortable in the relationship anymore and that is why I ended it. Move the fuck on." Camille rolled her eyes and went in the opposite direction. James, who could tell that something was wrong, came by her. "What did that guy say to you?"

"Doesn't matter. What would you like?"

"An explanation. Did that guy say something offensive to you, Cam?"

"If you're not ordering anything, I'm gonna have to ask you to clear the bar for people who *are* ordering."

James sighed. "Fine then. Can we meet up after your shift?" "James, go home. Your wife's waiting on you." "But--" "For your own sake," Camille added. Since he had run out of cash, James decided to heed Camille's advice.

As soon as he stepped into the bedroom, Laila asked, "Where have you been?" "At the shop. I told you that." "You don't smell like the shop." Laila pointed out. James said, "Sometimes, when I'm fixing the cars, I smoke because it helps me to focus."

Laila folded her arms. "Do you drink too?" James crawled into bed. "Yes. Being cross-faded clears my head when I'm trying to start up those busted old engines." "What about that perfume smell," Laila wondered. James said, "Air fresheners. I put them in after I finish so the customer will have a nice scent when they get their car back."

"Why does this all sound so rehearsed?"

James kissed his wife. "Don't make a big deal out of it. I was at the shop, okay?" "Okay." Though she was letting the issue go, Laila couldn't forget the picture she had found under their bed when searching for Arielle's teddy bear. *Why was James looking at a photo of him and Camille?*

On one side of the bed, Laila waited for James's snores so that she could check his phone. On the other side of the bed, James asked himself if an unhappy marriage was worth keeping his daughter happy. Neither party had peace of mind at the end of the night.

Over in The Core (Downtown Willowsville), Camille was waiting for the bus and Trevor approached her again. "Can I help you?" She asked. He came closer and Camille saw a knife in his hand. She jumped back.

"I said I wanted to give you a baby, right?"

Camille started mentally mapping out getaway options as she stepped away from Trevor, a drunken fiend. "I want my child to have that good hair like you got," he continued. Camille continued stepping back. "That's not happening." Camille ran as fast as she could in the opposite direction. Too drunk to follow her, Trevor wobbled to his car and passed out in the driver's seat. By the time Camille caught her breath, she realized she was missing something.

Phoneless and lost, Camille stopped in front of the Thornberry Academy of Culinary Arts. Juwan Thornberry was closing up for the day and he saw Camille checking her pulse when he came outside.

"Are you okay?" He asked her.

"No." Camille looked behind her to if Trevor was there. "There was this guy... he pointed a knife towards my stomach and…" Camille caught her breath. "And I ran and I dropped my phone somewhere but I'm not going back that way so…" Camille continued panting so Juwan unlocked his phone. "You can use mine." Camille nodded and took it from his hand. "Thank you so much."

She called Daniel for a ride then sat on the curb. "Would you like some water?" Juwan wondered. "Yes, please." Juwan grabbed a bottle from his trunk and sat on the curb with Camille. "I guess I should ask you your name."

"Camille Harrison. You?"

"Juwan Thornberry."

Camille looked at the sign for the school. "You own this?" "Nah. My dad does, but he promises he'll pass it down to me." "And you'll carry on a Thornberry legacy, right?" Juwan raised his eyebrow. "How'd you know?"

"You're typical – an entitled rich boy who inherits whatever his father or grandfather owns." Juwan held his chest playfully, so Camille added, "But, I'll give you this. You're the first white boy I met named Juwan."

Juwan laughed. "I get that a lot but I'm actually black on my father's side." Camille raised her eyebrow. "Why is this the first I'm hearing of a black-owned cooking school in Willowsville? That should've made the headlines by now." Juwan laughed again. "I like a woman with a sense of humor."

"Then you'd love me," Camille mentioned. Juwan smirked. "Duly noted." "So if you don't own this place, what **do** you do?"

"Head chef. I could cook for you sometime."

Camille raised her eyebrow. "That's a bold statement considering we just met." Juwan chuckled. "That was very forward of me. How about I take you out to dinner instead?" Camille smiled. "That sounds a *lot* more reasonable."

At this point, Daniel pulled up. So the conversation was cut short. "Thanks for the water." Juwan nodded and pulled out a business card. "Anytime. Here's my card if you ever feel like taking me up on that offer." Camille blushed. "Duly noted." She got into the car feeling good about herself.

A little further down the block, Trevor was snoozing in his car when his baby mama and her friend came knocking at the window. "Where is Camille?!" April hollered. Trevor wiped his eyes. "Man, I don't know. She ran off when she saw the knife." "See, that's her black side kicking in," Nicole commented. April rolled her eyes. "Did you at least get information out of her?"

"No," Trevor answered.

April groaned. "You are so freaking useless. I knew sending you in would be a mistake. You never fail to..." Nicole put her hand on April's shoulder. "Aye, shut up and look over there." April turned. "What am I looking at?" "Blackmail," Nicole sung as she picked up Camille's phone. April smiled. "And this is why I call you my better half." Nicole grinned. "Partners in crime."

Then, April turned to Trevor. "Once again, you have failed me. You know what that means, right?" Trevor's eyes got wide, knowing his termination was imminent. "Please don't cut me off. I need this money for back child support." Nicole scoffed. "You surely do."

April rolled her eyes. "Nicole, please no baby mama drama today. Trevor, get out of the car." "But this is my car."

"Which was saved from the repo men because of my money so technically I own a portion of this car. Now, get out." Trevor huffed and unbuckled his seatbelt. Once he was out, April hopped into the driver's seat and Nicole went back to the car that she and April had arrived in. Seconds later, they each drove off – leaving Trevor stranded in front of Teasers.

Chapter VIII – *After retrieving Camille's phone, April feels that she is ready to begin doing more damage. On a lighter note, however, Monique is about to welcome her baby girl into world.*

1 WEEK LATER

"It's time." Andre said as he looked at himself in the mirror. "I'm really doing this." He stepped outside and the guests smiled; Dre's entrance signaled the beginning of the ceremony. After Andre's brothers, his groomsmen, came down the aisle, Arielle skipped down the aisle throwing flowers to and fro. Then, Camille, Monique's cousin Amber, and Andre's sister Georgiana floated in their gorgeous bridesmaids' gowns made by Charletta Ross.

When Monique walked down the aisle escorted by her dad, she couldn't stop smiling. The few guests who Andre had invited stood as Monique marched towards her soon-to-be. It had been a surprise wedding (Mrs. Ross and Camille had been planning it for months), but that was the beauty of it. In her mother's vintage couture wedding gown (the only couture Mrs. Ross even owned), Monique made her way to her future husband.

Andre couldn't stop cheesing either. A part of him couldn't believe that the wedding was really happening. Mr. Ross put one hand on Andre's shoulder before handing Monique off. "You're a good man, Andre. Stay that way." "I will, sir. Promise." Andre and Mr. Ross shook hands then Mr. Ross kissed Monique's head. "Baby, you ready for this?" Monique wiped the tear streaming from her eye. "Daddy, I really don't know."

Mr. Ross laughed. "That means you're definitely ready." He hugged his daughter then handed her to her soon-to-be. Monique and Andre decided to make poetry of their vows.

Andre, to Monique:

Sometimes you just know

You don't want to take it slow

Because you cannot deny the delightful feeling you get inside

Each time your eyes meet those of your love.

Monique, baby, you're my gift from above.

An angel in the flesh, in that gorgeous white dress.

The mother of my child.

The one who makes me smile.

The love of my life

Whom I shall soon call my wife.

I love you, Mo.

I have loved you from the start.

You already know that's till death do us part.

Monique, to Andre:

What can I say about my Andre?

Funny and loving.

Caring and kind.

I am so glad to call you mine.

Now, I'm no poet but...

I love you like a fat kid loves cake.

I love you like a bad kid loves to break.

I love you like peanut butter loves jelly

And they both love the bread.

Instead of stating all the ways

I love my Andre

I'll say this:

His love is eternal

His love is true.

Baby, I cannot wait to say "I do"

Because I do love you.

"I now pronounce you man and wife." The guests smiled as Monique and Andre shared their ceremonial kiss.

At the banquet hall, Andre took his wife in his arms so that they could do the honorary couple's dance. Slowly, they rocked side to side and looked each other in the eyes. *This is the start to forever,* Monique thought to herself. *This is the day that the Lord hath made,* Andre inwardly affirmed. At the conclusion of their dance, Andre kissed Monique passionately. "I love you, Mo." Monique held Andre in her arms. "I love *you,* Dre." Mo and Dre shared a few more loving exchanges then Andre gave the floor to his sisters and Camille.

"My sisters and Camille all have a surprise for you." As opposed to a traditional reception, Camille and Andre's sisters had decided to plan a baby shower/reception since Monique was still pregnant. The event, which had been decorated by Andre's sisters, had a sesame street theme since that was Monique's favorite show as a little girl.

So, in addition to making a 3 tier black and gold wedding cake with the letters "M" and "A" in cursive writing at the top, Mrs. Ross made a batch of cupcakes in the shapes of sesame street characters. But, before they got to Sesame Street, Monique and Andre walked over to the black and gold cake and stood for pictures as they fed each other a slice. Then, Monique and Andre moseyed over to the desert table to greet the guests who were in awe of Mrs. Ross's 3-D replicas.

"I call Oscar the grouch," Camille decided. "Is that because you are a grouch," James joked. Camille rolled her eyes. "Don't start with me."

Laila, who was trying to protect Arielle's brand new dress with a napkin, watched Camille and James's interaction closely. Ever since she had found that picture, Laila was on her guard. Camille, who felt Laila's beady eyeballs, moved closer to Monique and further from James. "So, Mo, how you feeling?"

"Like this child went from the size of a pea to the size of a bloated watermelon all in under a year." Laila walked over with Arielle. "I remember that feeling. Arielle was a big baby." Arielle looked up. "What'd you say about me?" "I said you were a *ginormous* baby."

Arielle raised her eyebrow. "Ginormous? What does that mean?"

"Really, really big," Camille explained. Laila cackled to herself. "That's a shocker." "What is?" Camille wondered.

"Given your background, it honestly surprises me that a word like ginormous even exists in your vernacular."

"You think because I grew up in foster care I'm automatically supposed to intellectually inferior?"

Laila took a deep breath. "You're taking this way out of context. By the way, that means--" "I *know* what it means, Laila. And, since we're making judgments, it's you who should have a limited 'vernacular'. You came from money yet your biggest accomplishment in life was lying on your back for a man who doesn't even love you while you bear his children and do weaves for clients who see you as a means to an end. By the way, all this means is that you're submissive and broke, which makes you about the same as me. Only difference is I'm not submissive." Laila, suddenly embarrassed, grabbed Arielle's hand and walked off. Camille rolled her eyes and grabbed a fork. "Artificially intelligent, pretentious bitch."

Monique put her hand atop Camille's. "Whoa, Cam. Those are fighting words." Camille rolled her eyes again. "That heifer is always judging folks like she's the crème of the crop. But I guess she has to overcompensate since she's a college dropout. I had my trials and tribulations but I still got my degree." "We both did," Monique asserted. "We each came from nothing and we still made something of ourselves." "Uh, that's a stretch," James commented. "Camille's working in a strip club."

Camille crooked her neck to stare James in the eye. "For your information, that strip club keeps my lights on, clothes on my back, and food in my belly. Unlike you, I'm not able to spend the rest of my days relaxing in my grandfather's auto-shop while my other siblings are actually working for their money."

James said, "First of all, no one's 'relaxing.' The shop went bankrupt twice and it was my job to pull it out of that rut. Second of all, you might've been better off inheriting from your grandpa. Your momma's family controls 25% of Willowsville, after all."

Camille stepped in James's face. "For your information, they disowned her when she had four children by three different black men. Then, she disowned those kids to get back into her family's good graces. Basically, she chose money over motherhood. So, *don't* comment on what you don't know." Since James and Laila had both irked Camille's nerves, Camille went to the corner to eat her cake in private. Monique stared blankly at her brother. "Did you have to do that?"

"I don't appreciate the way she called my wife out of her name."

"Your wife disrespected her."

"Oh, so now you're taking sides?" Andre, who didn't like James's defensiveness, stepped over. "Don't speak to my wife like that." "One: she's been your wife for like an hour. Calm down. Two: she's my goddam sister. I'll speak to her however I feel like speaking to her."

"She's your sister second but a woman first and women deserve respect."

"Women deserve men, not wannabe men who get mad over everything like a female."

Monique raised her eyebrow. "Like a female? That sexist, James." "You know what? Y'all are both irritating right now." James went to eat with Laila and Arielle and Monique just sighed. "Today is supposed to celebrate our union and the life of Emelia – not become some melodramatic display of unresolved tensions." Andre rubbed Monique's shoulders. "You're right. Today is about us."

Due to Andre's persistence and his sisters' careful planning, everything went according to the schedule. By the end of the night, Monique was happy again. As everyone started going their separate ways, Camille looked at her phone to see how much time she had before work. Seeing that she only had an hour, Camille asked Monique, "Do you think you could drop me off at home? I'd take the bus but I'm already running late."

"You know I would but we have to pack the truck with all these gifts and space is going to be tight." Camille looked at the large pile of baby gifts and wedding gifts that Monique and Andre had received. "Okay. I'll ask Daniel."

Daniel glanced up from his phone when Camille approached him. "I have a date so, whatever you're about to ask me, the answer is no." Camille put on her puppy dog eyes. "Please?" He sighed. "What services do you require?" "Transportation." Daniel rolled his eyes. "Since when was I your chauffeur?"

"Since you decided to entertain my craziness."

Daniel laughed. "Fine. Where to?" "My apartment then Teasers." "You gonna pay me?" Camille opened her wallet. "I have a bus pass with $5 on it. You want that?" Daniel shook his head. "You know I don't do public transportation."

"Taking it would save you tons of money."

"I can't be caught dead on the bus. It might ruin my credibility within my circle of friends." Camille raised her eyebrows. "You actually have *other* friends? I thought I was the only person who could tolerate your overzealousness." Daniel rolled his eyes again. "Don't push your luck, white girl."

"Only half."

"Until you start dancing."

Camille grinned. "Hush up." Daniel put his hand on Camille's shoulder. "But, because I like you, we will work on those moves together." Camille and Daniel laughed while going to his car. Behind Daniel's car, James was parked. James held the door open for Laila but still looked back at Camille when he saw familiar curls in his peripheral. Not wanting to incriminate himself, James quickly turned away.

Laila scoffed. "What was that?" "What was what?" "That look. You gave Camille some look." "I didn't give her any look. You're seeing things."

"Oh, I'm just 'seeing things,' right?"

James sighed. "Laila, I'm not interested in Camille, okay?" Though James was saying this to cover his tracks, he knew his words would hurt Camille. While walking past, Camille was careful not to make eye contact but she had never been one to hold her tongue. "Wow," she commented.

Laila glanced at Camille. "You got something to say?" Camille shook her head. "Nope. Just talking to myself." "As you would expect from a crazy person," Laila dismissed. This caused Camille to pause in her walking. "Mind repeating that a little louder?"

"As you would expect from a crazy person," Laila enunciated. "You said it about yourself; why can't I say it too?"

Camille put her hands on her hips. "First of all, that was a joke. Second of all, why were you all in my mouth? Third of all, why are you even worried about me? You got James; be happy."

Laila stepped out of the car. "I *got* James? Since when were we in competition for him, Camille?" Camille, realizing she had said too much, took a deep breath. "I'm just talking." Camille got ready to walk off but Laila grabbed her arm. "You got something to tell me about my husband?"

"Laila, you already know I don't like you so I'm asking you nicely to take your hand off of me."

Laila squeezed Camille's arm. "I don't play that secretive stuff. You got something to say then say it." Camille yanked her arm away and stepped in Laila's face. "Keep your hands to yourself unless you want to start round 3. I promise not to go easy on you this time." Laila looked Camille dead in the eye. "Keep your comments to yourself then, hoe."

Camille gave off the coldest stare she could produce because she was sensitive about being called that word – given the number of times she had heard it. "You better check yourself before I have to do it for you. You are entering dangerous territory," Camille warned.

"You're a hoe, Camille. Once you accept that, your life will be so much easier."

"You're a subservient, passive woman who's been getting cheated on and lied to since the beginning!!! Your husband--" James finally stepped in between them, seeing that Arielle had awoken from her nap. He didn't want his daughter to bear witness to the drama. "Lai, let's go."

Laila took a deep breath and started getting in the car. Camille, who was riled up, decided she was tired of keeping her feelings in. "You know what, Laila? I *do* have something to tell you about your husband: the truth."

Laila raised her eyebrow. "What 'truth'?"

James looked dead at Camille. "Don't do this." "I have to." As Camille got ready to reveal all, she heard her phone buzzing. Just minutes before, Monique had received a text message from Camille's old phone. Once Monique saw the attachment, she texted Camille's new number.

Monique: We need to talk. ASAP.

Camille: What's going on?

Monique: [Media Attachment]

Camille held her face when she saw what April had revealed. "Oh my god." Daniel looked over. "What is...oh snap." James, who didn't like the looks on either of their faces, was about to go over and see for himself. But, Spring had not been discreet in her blow-up. She had sent the information to everyone in Camille's contacts, which included James. James heard his phone buzz but Laila snatched it from his hand. "I'm tired of you hiding things from me, James. I want to know…"

Laila was by far the most shocked by the reveal.

"GET OUT!!!!" She hollered. "Just get out!!!" James took Laila into his arms. "Calm down, baby. Let's just talk--" Laila slapped James. "What's there to 'talk' about? You hid a baby from me for ten years, James! 10 years! We've been married for 10 years, so this makes me feel like our entire marriage is a lie."

Although Laila was distraught, she wasn't the only one who hadn't known. Camille started, "I'm sorry, Mo. I should've told you." Monique took a deep breath. "I knew you two had history but I never thought it was this deep. Does this mean you only had two abortions?"

Camille sighed. "Yes."

"And is this why you missed so much class senior year that you had to graduate out of summer school?"

"Yes."

"And is this--" "Please stop with the questions," Camille begged. "I feel awful enough as it is." Monique rubbed Camille's arms. "I know, Cam. I'm just…shocked. I thought I was your best friend." Camille looked Monique in the eye. "You *are* Mo, but, because he's your brother, I was put in an awkward position so your mom asked me not to say anything."

"My *mom* knows?"

Camille nodded. "Yes. She was the one driving me to meet with the adoptive family." "Did Daniel know too?" Camille nodded again. "Yeah." Monique rubbed her temples. "How could everyone keep this from me?"

"Daniel said it wasn't his business, your parents were too embarrassed to say anything, and James didn't want to disrupt his and Laila's household."

Monique shook her head. "Well, it's surely disrupted now." Daniel walked in while that thought sat. "Camille, you gotta go. There's confidential business to discuss." Camille let out a deep breath. "Okay. Talk you later, Mo." "Bye, Cam." Once Camille left, Daniel slammed a paper onto Monique's desk. "What is this?"

"This is a court order from Samuel Lee's attorney asking to see the tapes from the fire." Daniel explained.

"Have Bree give him the tapes from my back-up camera. Problem solved."

Daniel shook his head. "Problem not solved. If Lee sees those, he will know that two of your employees were involved in all of this and that will decimate the reputation of Mo's Mix. You can't have the world thinking that you hire *arsonists*, Monique." "So what do you suggest I do?"

"Tell him that your cameras were destroyed in the fire, which isn't a complete lie."

"What happens if someone sees that I have back-up cameras?"

"Have a custodian move them to an unseen location."

Monique shook her head. "If I do that, it will look like I'm tampering with evidence in an attempt to cover my tracks. I did not kill Abigail Newhouse and I don't want anyone thinking that I had any involvement."

"You were at home with Dre when it all went down. You have an alibi," Daniel noted. Monique said, "Someone might claim that I ordered Evan and Donna to carry out the fire in some ludicrous insurance scandal. If that claim leaks to the presses, they will run with it." "So you'll just give him the tapes?"

"I will give him the tapes," Monique confirmed. Daniel exhaled and continued, "I'm supposed to be going to a meeting with the board of directors in 25 minutes. Why?" "They want to further review your credentials."

"What, they don't think I'm qualified?"

Monique sighed. "They just think my recommendation was biased because you're my older brother. The meeting is to ensure you're what's best for Mo's Mix." "But, you know I have what it takes. Can't you overrule the meeting?"

"Daniel, just go."

"You're letting these men walk all over you, Mo. You're relinquishing control," Daniel sang.

Monique scoffed. "I'm not, actually. Relinquishing control would be trying to stop the meeting and causing unnecessary drama." Daniel shook his head. "They wouldn't treat you like this if you were a man. But, because you're a woman, the male-dominated board feels that you can't make decisions on your own."

Monique inwardly analyzed what Daniel was saying. "I didn't even think of it like that."

"But, if this is what you want, I'll go to the meeting." Daniel started leaving but Monique put her hand up. "Hold tight for a second." She called Dominique into her office. "Email Dennis Quaver and inform him that it's asinine to question what has already been established so the meeting is cancelled."

Dominique said, "I would but Mr. Quaver's already in the main conference room."

"Why so early? The meeting wasn't scheduled to start until another 20 minutes from now."

"Since he's the board's chairman, he decided to arrive earlier so he could check things out around here."

Monique sighed. "Send him into my office."

"Ms. Ross."

Monique showed her ring. "*Mrs*. Ross-Cassells." "Oh. Congratulations." "Thanks." Quaver shut the door and sat down. "So, why did you call me in here?"

Monique pointed out, "Daniel Ross's qualifications have been faxed and his references say they've spoken to you. In addition, you sent an email stating that you were filing the paperwork to make Mr. Ross an official COO. These things considered, what's the purpose of this meeting that the board is calling?" Mr. Quaver nodded. "I see where you're going with this. The board did feel that Mr. Ross was qualified but a recent speculation has caused us to question why exactly you put your brother in charge."

"What speculation?"

Quaver cleared his throat. "Excuse me if I'm spreading a rumor but a fellow board member says that he saw Mr. Ross leaving a *gay* bar, which led board members to wonder if you want to put Mr. Ross in charge in some effort to ride the wave of this pro-gay era. Now, this is all speculation; we don't actually believe someone as qualified as Mr. Ross would choose to live his life in sin. So, we want to speak with Mr. Ross privately and squash these rumors."

"Why is his supposed sexuality relevant to him representing my company?" Monique wondered. Quaver noted, "Some board members, including myself, are deeply religious and don't believe in *that* type of lifestyle. So, if Mr. Ross were *that*, we would recant our decision to make him COO."

Monique folded her hands so that she could really hear what Quaver was saying. "Let me get this straight: you don't want Mr. Ross to represent Mo's Mix because of his *supposed* sexuality? Is that or is that not discrimination, Mr. Quaver?" Quaver was silent so Monique continued, "And, should you 'recant your decision' based on a rumor, it would appear as if you are intolerant towards members of the LBGT community, which would upset those same people who frequent your stores and faithfully purchase your products. So, if I were you, Mr. Quaver, I would tell my board to keep its homophobia a little more private."

Quaver grinned. "If you were me, *Mrs.* Ross-Cassells, you would not want your company to turn into some human rights organization propelling 'equality for all' by putting a black woman and a possibly homosexual man in charge. The problem with pining for too much equality is that in all your humanitarianism, you begin to forget that you are a for-profit business, not a non-profit organization. But, obviously, you're not me, Mrs. Ross-Cassells. So you don't have the intellect to think this way. Have a wonderful day now." Quaver got up and went over to the conference room while Monique came to one conclusion: *he cannot be Board's chairman anymore.*

In a moment's time, Monique thought of a way to shake up the leadership of her board of directors. For a while, Monique had been sitting on this one idea and, after her encounter with Quaver, she decided to run with it. Hagen Sullivan, the board's vice chair, had caught Monique's eye because Hagen created a grassroots music label that worked from the underground to the mainstream and produced a diverse group of talent.

Many of the singers and rappers who had signed with *Sull*-ful Records had gone platinum at least twice. Monique admired Hagen for these accomplishments. Though Hagen was favored by the (few) women on the board, her firm womanist views clashed with the sexist views of her male counterparts, which hindered Hagen from ever winning presidency.

To eradicate this sexism and demote Dennis Quaver, Monique decided, "This year, Mo's Mix will have its very first all-inclusive board election. As you know, a new chairperson is to be chosen in the next few weeks and, typically, the chairperson is selected based on recommendations from the most senior members of this board. However, I feel that all board members should have a say. Therefore, we will be having an *all-inclusive* election, meaning that *everyone* on this board will vote on a chairperson. I will be exercising my 50% to ensure that this election becomes democratic.

Quaver looked up. "I mean no disrespect, Mrs. Ross-Cassells, but let me make some things really clear. First of all, this board also controls 50% of this company so we can easily trump your decision. Furthermore, there were arsonists amidst your employees, meaning you hired criminals.

"One would think that as CEO *and* founder of this company, you would be more mindful of who you hired. But, you were not. So, at any given moment, you could be replaced by someone who is actually competent enough to run this business. With that being said, the board election should remain as it always has been."

Monique stepped forward. "I mean no disrespect, Mr. Quaver, but Hagen Sullivan, Regina Cartwright, and Lonnie Mathers have all felt that sexism stifled them from their desired board positions. Therefore, they will use their collective 15% to further ensure that this election becomes fair. Furthermore, a group of your company's former stock brokers was just hauled off to prison for insider trading. One would think that as CEO, founder, and chairman of the investor's board, you *might* have been a little more alert.

"I've concluded that you are, in fact, smart enough to detect something like that happening but you allowed it because you were in on the entire scheme. So, at any given moment, the board of directors can replace you with someone a little less felonious. With that being said, Mr. Quaver, I suggest you refrain from your disrespect unless you want this instance to be added to the *overwhelming* evidence that has been already been presented in that slander suit you're facing."

Quaver took note of Monique's firm tone. "My apologies, Mrs. Ross-Cassells." Quaver then looked at Daniel, who had just walked in. "And may I presume that you're Daniel Ross?" "I am," Daniel answered. He sat in front of the board. "Let's get this meeting started, shall we?" Though Daniel didn't like the way the board had strong-armed Monique, he knew that she wanted as little drama as possible so he just played along.

"He's a misogynistic racist who deserves to rot in hell but, sadly, he didn't let this be known until after he was brought into the company. So, if I cross him now, I could get booted out of my own business." Monique took a breath. "Other than that, my day was *flawless*." The yoga instructor stared blankly at Monique. "I guess that's what I get for asking."

Monique sighed. "I'm grumbling, I know. I've just been feeling testy."

"Is it because your baby's almost here?"

Monique nodded. "Yes. She could come any minute now." Andre massaged her shoulders. "Which is why you have me." The instructor smiled at the exchange. "You two make a lovely couple." "Thank you." While the instructor went off to talk to the other couples, Monique practiced the exercises she had been taught. Andre, who was there helping her, put his hand on Monique's thigh. At the feel of Dre's fingers, Monique thought back to moments when their intimacy made time stand still.

She rubbed his fingertips and Dre could feel the heat rising in Monique's body. So, as soon as they got home, Andre carried Monique to the bed and started kissing on her neck then her shoulder blade then her elbow then her fingertips then her stomach then her belly button then between her breasts then her lips. "I love you so much, Mo."

Monique grinned. "I love you, too, Andre."

He stroked her stomach. "How much longer we got?" Monique looked at the calendar on her phone. "If Emelia comes out on time, we have 3 more weeks. But, the other day, Dr. Seneca said our daughter may make her appearance sooner than that." "What if she's an Easter baby? That would be something, wouldn't it?" Dre asked.

"Mama Char would then think that Emelia is God's gift to the world." "Well, she's God's gift to us," Dre mentioned. Monique smiled at her unborn child. "She sure is." While Mo and Dre chatted about their excitement for parenthood, a courier came to the door. "Package for the Ross-Cassells residence," he said when Andre opened it. "What is it?" Andre wondered. The courier pointed to a box for a crib and a bag of the other items Daniel, Camille, James had bought.

"These are from Daniel Ross, James Ross, and Camille Harrison. It says I'm supposed to get a signature from either Andre Cassells or Monique Ross-Cassells."

"I'm Andre Cassells," Andre stated as he signed the sheet. When she heard Andre sliding the crib inside, Monique hobbled from the bedroom. "From Daniel, Cam, and James?"

"Yep."

"I'll have to tell them thank you."

Andre nodded and looked at the crib. "I just wish I knew how to put one of these together." "There are instructions, baby." "I almost broke Nathalie's crib for Siena, which is why I got banned from going anywhere near Sebastian's crib," Andre confessed. "Oh lord. I'll call James."

Andre made certain face when he heard that. Monique put her hands on her hips. "Dre, this is for the crib. Whatever happened between you and James can be put aside."

"Why don't I call Georgie and Miguel? They put together Siena and Sebastian's cribs."

Monique said, "Okay, but I'm still confused as to what went down between you two." "I told you: he was way too disrespectful." "What did he say," Monique wondered.

"It doesn't matter. I'll go call my siblings." Andre pulled out his phone and Monique gazed at the picture of the crib. *I love it,* she thought. Daniel had done well. In the same manner, he had also done well with the board of directors.

"How would one of these board members have even seen me leaving the gay bar if they weren't there themselves?" The board was silent, especially Dennis Quaver. Realizing, Daniel narrowed his gaze in on Dennis. "Come to think of it, I *do* recall seeing someone from this board at the bar that night. It was--"

"Enough," Quaver interrupted. "We will continue with making you COO as long as you vow to keep your homosexuality under wraps."

Daniel chortled. "Because hiding who you are works better for business, doesn't it?" Since Daniel clearly knew something that the rest of the board didn't, Quaver ended the meeting. "That will be all." Daniel was happy because he got what he wanted while remaining true to himself.

But, this victory would be short lived. Malcolm Khan glided into Mo's Mix walking as if he owned the place. He went up to Dominique. "Can you tell me where Daniel Ross is?" "Are you Attorney Khan?" "I sure am."

Dominique stood to walk with Malcolm. "Right this way." As soon as Daniel locked eyes with Malcolm, Daniel's entire body froze.

"What are *you* doing here?"

Dominique came on the side of Malcolm. "This is Malcolm Khan from Rutberger's Law Firm, the second largest law firm next to Roger Muller and the second most prestigious next to Walker Brothers. Attorney Khan is interested in being a courtroom attorney for Mo's Mix." Daniel quickly got into his business mindset. "So I'm assuming Mrs. Ross-Cassells reopened the position. Is it because Attorney Riley or Attorney Marx quit?"

"Neither quit, but Mrs. Ross-Cassells ordered me to find another court room attorney."

Daniel sighed and told Malcolm, "Follow me."

"Nice space," Malcolm complimented.

"Thanks."

"Proud of you."

"Thanks."

"I know it's been years since we last talked but--" "I'm not sure what Mrs. Ross-Cassells told that daft assistant, but Mo's Mix already has its attorneys. I brought you into this office to save you some embarrassment but, unfortunately, we are not looking for any new legal representation at the moment."

Malcolm sighed. "I didn't realize there was a limit on how many attorneys one business could have." Daniel replied, "There isn't. Mo's Mix just happens *not* to be seeking a new attorney right now." "Then, why did your boss order her assistant to find another courtroom attorney?"

"I'm sure there was some sort of miscommunication between the child and Mrs. Ross-Cassells. Nonetheless, Mo's Mix is *not* seeking any new counsel so I'm lost as to why you're still standing here, Attorney Khan. You can escort yourself out."

"Why are you giving me the cold shoulder, Danny?"

"Attorney Khan, we are not friends so I ask that you refer to me as Mr. Ross. And, to answer your asinine question, busy schedules don't allow much time to for warmth."

"I guess I'll catch you later then, *Danny*."

Daniel huffed. "We don't run in the same circle so I highly doubt that, Attorney *Khan-man*."

Malcolm had done questionable things to attain his position and Daniel knew this. So, Daniel brought up the nickname Malcolm's classmates had given him in law school. Malcolm shook his head. "You know, if anyone should be mad, it's me. You cut off contact for six years. Now, I finally find you and you treat me like I'm worth as much as that pen you're using to tune me out."

Daniel stopped writing an agenda for his next meeting and folded his hands. "Attorney Khan, this is a place of business. What you see as 'tuning you out' is me fulfilling my duties to this company. But, of course, you're too egotistical to consider any option that doesn't make you appear as the victim. This considered, please take your melodrama and that tacky suit elsewhere." Malcolm scoffed. "I'll have you know I paid a lot of money for this suit." "*You* bought that? I thought it might've been a gift from some low-grade boyfriend."

Malcolm raised his eyebrow. "What makes you think he would be low-grade?"

"Anyone besides me is."

"Now who's egotistical?"

Daniel shrugged. "And this is why we never would've worked; we're too much alike." "Great minds think alike, Mr. Ross."

"Saying that gives the assumption that both our minds are great but we both know that's not true," Daniel duly noted. "This is all a defense mechanism," Malcolm decided. "This process of trying to tear me down ties back to the superiority complex I've come to realize you possess. In the six years we've been apart, I've had a lot of time to think and overthink about our situation. I first suspected you suffered from a superior complex when, the very first day we met, I asked you if…"

Daniel cut his eyes so Malcolm stopped. "You know that bothers me." Daniel iterated.

"I do, Danny. But, I was a psych minor. I can't help but analyze and overanalyze, especially when it comes to you." Daniel vowed not to let Malcolm try to trick Daniel into talking about the relationship. "And I was a finance major, which is why I understand that time is money. Right now, you're wasting both of those. So why don't you do us both a favor and leave? The door's wipe open, after all." "Maybe it's open because you're inviting me back in."

"Don't think so." Daniel snapped and Dominique was in his office. "Yes, Mr. Ross?" "Escort Attorney Khan out for me." "Right this way," Dominique said. Malcolm sighed. "I'll be back." With that, Malcolm left the office and Daniel put his hand on his head. *I don't need this right now.*

Malcolm was the love of Daniel's life, but Daniel tried hard to forget that. *I really don't need this right now.* To distract himself, he went to visit Monique and find out why she was trying to get rid of Genna.

Daniel arrived at an inconvenient time, though. Georgiana and Miguel were there putting the crib together, Monique was trying to forget the pain in her swollen feet, Andre was arguing with his sister about going to cooking school and Nathalie's kids were playing hide and seek with Arielle. When she heard the doorbell, Monique hobbled over.

Daniel glanced inside at the chaos. "What's going on here?"

Monique put her hand on her head. "Andre's siblings are putting together the crib but neither one can drive so Nathalie had to bring them and she brought her two kids with her, which was right after Laila begged me to watch Arielle. And now I have a headache." Daniel stepped into the cramped condo. "Maybe I should go?"

"You're here now so what's going on?"

"It's about Genna."

"Please tell me she quit on us," Monique joked.

"I don't understand what the issue is. Sure, she tried to seduce Andre, but that's old news. She's been helping us." "I'm about integrity," Monique asserted. "So, a woman who knew Andre was engaged and *still* tried sleeping with him has no place in my business."

"Then why'd you agree to bring her onto the case?"

"Genna was the best available. But I've made it clear that her stay is only temporary."

Daniel sighed. "I get that you're upset by the past but look at you and Andre now. You're married with a kid. You shouldn't be worried about a Genna." "I'm not but I feel like she's only working at Mo's Mix to get close to Andre again."

"So, if we just boot her out, who will we bring in?"

"Malcolm Khan."

Daniel scrunched his face. "Negative. He's a blast from my past." Monique shook her head. "You tell me to let things go but look at you." "The conflict between Malcolm and I is different than you and Genna's."

"The difference being that you were the one who wronged him?"

Daniel sighed. "It was a misguided arrangement – the relationship, that is." Monique said, "Malcolm's good, like really good. He works for Rutbergers. Andre couldn't even get a job at Rutbergers. But, because you're my brother and I love you so very much, I will consider other options. Is that okay?"

Daniel put his arm around Monique's shoulder. "That's perfectly fine. How's my niece doing?" Monique groaned. "She's restless. She's been kicking nonstop." "Can I touch her?" Daniel asked. "Sure." He put his hand on Monique's stomach. As soon as Daniel felt Emelia, he had a flashback to when he and Malcom talked about kids. Quickly, Daniel moved his hand. "Um, I should go."

"You okay?"

"Fine, but I should go."

Daniel had to leave quickly before he got too caught up with thoughts of Malcolm. But, Arielle caught Daniel's leg as he was heading out. She wrapped her tiny body around him. "Hi, Uncle Daniel." Daniel peeled Arielle off of him. "Bye, Arielle."

For the next half-hour, the chaos continued. Then, Andre and Nathalie stopped arguing because they both were hungry. Monique, Georgiana, Miguel, and the children decided to sit down and grab something too. Andre made the kids peanut butter and jelly sandwiches and sent them to the couch. Then, he warmed some leftover lamb on the stove and put it onto plates for the adults.

"This is good, Andre," Georgiana commented. She licked her fingers as she was eating her lamb. "Really good. Did you use nonna's marinade?" "I did. How did you know?"

"I'd know that taste anywhere."

After everyone had eaten, Georgiana and Miguel finished the crib then they wheeled it into Emelia's nursery. Georgiana glanced at the picture on the wall. "You put my picture up!" She exclaimed. Monique grinned as she came in after them. "Of course. It was beautiful."

"Thank you."

In the living room, Miguel plopped next to his brother. "Little Miguel is almost a college man, huh?" Andre said. Miguel chuckled. "Yep and you're going to have to stop referring to me as 'little' Miguel. I'm 18 years old." Andre laughed. "I know. It's just that when *I* was graduating high school, you were graduating kindergarten. Time has really flown."

Miguel nodded. "It has."

"Are you excited about Prom?"

Miguel sighed. "Yes and no." "Why 'no'?" "I want to bring a guy but mamma wants me to be 'traditional'." Andre scoffed. "It's your prom so you should get to make the choice." Georgiana, who had gotten excited when she heard the word "prom," said, "Guess what, Andre?" "Don't tell me you're going on Prom too."

"I am! My boyfriend Jamir asked me."

"And mamma approved that?"

"Yes. I'm going to Prom as a sophomore," Georgiana sung.

"What's a prom," Arielle wondered. "It's when girls dress up in pretty clothes and get their hair and make-up done and do their nails and get to take bunch of pretty pictures and ride in limos," Siena replied.

"What's a limo," Arielle asked next. "It's like a big, big car. It's like two cars attached to each other and there are different colors. Some are white, some are black, and some are even silver. Some are longer than others too." Nathalie raised her eyebrow. "Have you been watching that Prom channel even though I told you not to?"

Siena smirked, having been caught. Since the crib was done, Nathalie stood. "I will deal with you later, Siena. Georgie and Miggy, are you two ready to go?" Georgiana nodded then talked about how excited she was about Prom. Miguel, who had been getting an earful ever since the minute Georgiana was asked, rolled his eyes on the way to the car. Noticing, Andre laughed while shutting the door.

"She seems excited."

"Trust me, she is."

Andre looked at Arielle. "Could you hand me those plates, please?" "Yes." Arielle gave him the three plates from the peanut butter and jelly sandwiches. After Andre placed them in the sink, he handed Arielle some crayons and a coloring sheet. "You can do that until your mom gets here." Monique took note of Andre's careful nature. *And he's excited about being a dad.*

After putting all the dishes away, Andre wrapped Monique in his arms. "What's going in the beautiful mind?" Monique leaned into Andre. "I was just watching you interact with Arielle. It gives me good vibes about how you'll be with Emelia."

"Really?"

"Yeah. Like I said, she's about to have the best daddy on the planet." Andre smiled. "You flatter me, Mo." "I try, Dre."

Camille, who was getting ready for work, started to wear her hair in a ponytail. Then, a scar from years before mocked Camille so she let her locks hang down. "Why don't you pull that mane up," a co-worker asked Camille later on. "I'd rather wear it down."

"What, so you can feel better than everyone because you got that long, wavy hair?"

"No, because I'm more comfortable with it down."

The bartender rolled her eyes. "Just like a mixed girl." Camille sighed because it seemed like a no-win conversation. Instead of responding, she went to check in with Rob, who looked Camille up and down when she stepped into his office. "Camille, right?"

"Yeah."

"You came in late for your last few shifts."

Camille sometimes got so hung over she forgot she was supposed to be at the club – until she would look at her clock. "I know. I'm sorry." "This is unacceptable. Deja has to cover for you because your ass is God knows where doing God knows what."

"You can't use God and a cuss word in the same sentence. That's blasphemous."

Rob scoffed. "Shut the hell up and put this on." He threw lingerie at Camille. "You're skinny enough for it, right?" Camille stared blankly at Rob. "Why are you giving me this?" "We filled that bartender spot after the third time you came in late. Instead of just firing you, I'm prepared to offer you another position. I've seen the way some of these men look at you."

"I'm not a stripper," Camille asserted.

"You will be if you want a job."

Inwardly, Camille reflected on what Laila had said. *You're a hoe, Camille. Once you accept that, your life will be so much easier.* At times, Camille believed those words to be true. And, since she was on the verge of being evicted, she knew she needed fast money. "Fine." "You *actually* gone do it?" Rob cackled. "You really is a hoe then. I almost had hope for you."

Camille sighed and took the lingerie from off the floor. In the bathroom mirror, she saw herself in a new light. *This is the beginning of the end,* Camille thought. By the end of the night, she felt icky because not only had Camille prostituted herself for a quick buck but she hadn't even made that much cash. "You got a body, but you ain't got rhythm," Marquis, the new bartender, told Camille.

"What?"

"The only reason you made those few dollars was 'cause men were staring at your booty but you need more rhythm if you're trying to make some *real* cash."

"And let me guess: you're going to teach me rhythm?"

Marquis shrugged. "I could if you want me to." Camille smiled a little bit. "I'll get back to you on that." She pulled on her jacket and caught the bus home. There, James waited by her door. "What are you doing here?"

"What did you have on that phone?" James countered.

Camille let out a deep breath. "Doesn't matter." "How did that lady find out about the adoption, Camille?" "I don't know." James hollered, "You do, though! It's something you're not telling me." Camille put her hand on her head. "James, I just got off of work. Please don't do this with me right now."

James glanced at Camille's get-up. "Since when were you a stripper?" "Since today. Move." James allowed Camille to open her door but came in after her. "You should go home," she told him. James unzipped her jacket. "Should I really?" When Camille felt James's hands on her back, she remembered the good times with him. In moments, James and Camille were using intimacy to push away their problems.

When Camille awoke, she half expected James to be gone. But, he wasn't. He was in the kitchen making breakfast. Camille leaned on her bedroom door. "You're still here?"

"Yeah. Laila kind of kicked me out."

"Well, you lied to her about a child. That's big, James." James kissed Camille. "I know but her kicking me out is all the more reason for me to come see you." Camille wanted to stay and immerse herself in James but her phone was ringing in the bedroom. "I'll be right back." Seeing who it was, Camille stayed in the bedroom to take the call and spoke in a hushed tone.

James, still wondering how April Spring knew about the adoption, tried listening to Camille's conversation. But, Camille was off the phone before he could hear anything. "Who was that?"

"Work," Camille answered quickly.

"Do you always whisper when 'work' calls you?"

Camille put her hands on her hips. "James Ross, are you getting jealous?" James shook his head. "Definitely not that. Skeptical, maybe. I just want to know how that April Spring lady knew about the adoption." Camille shrugged. "Beats me. Don't you have to be at the shop?" "Yeah, but I want an explanation first. Who were you talking to?"

"You're not my man so I'm not obligated to tell you anything."

James sighed. "And this is the point where I leave." Camille rolled her eyes. "Shut the door on your way out." James grabbed her from behind. "I was just playing. Don't go getting soft on me." Camille pulled herself away.

"You do always leave unexpectedly, though." James sighed. "I have other obligations." "You right. Go be responsible then."

James kissed Camille again. "Not yet. Right now, I want to lose myself inside you. I just want to forget everything." Camille pulled away again. "Well, *I* want to remember – to recall a time when I let another family have our baby because I thought that meant I got to keep you."

"Camille, **why** do you keep bringing this up? It's old news."

"It's not old news," Camille hollered. "I loved Jalen!!!"

"You made your choice!"

"I chose *you*!" she screamed. When James was silent, Camille continued, "But you didn't choose me. So now *I'm* choosing me and guess what that means, James? It means I'm gonna get Jalen back." James raised his eyebrow. "What you talking about?"

"That phone call was actually an attorney who's been helping me with the case."

"How can you even afford an attorney?"

"Don't worry about it."

James sighed. "What's the point of this?" "I want my son." "If you get him, please tell me you're not gonna come asking me for child support." "Suppose I do. What then?" Camille challenged.

"Then I'll say that I gave up my rights as a parent so, technically, I'm not his father."

Camille scoffed. "Get out." "What?" "Get out. I cannot believe you just told me that." James kissed her neck. "Camille, you don't mean that." "Get out," she repeated. "You don't mean that." The more James kissed her neck, the more Camille began to think she hadn't meant it, but she had.

"What goes with Emelia?"

"Bedelia," Dre joked. Monique rolled her eyes. "That might've been funnier if the spellings were the same." "I'm a chef, not a comedian. I'll keep my day job." "You're a *lawyer*, Andre," Monique enunciated.

"Lawyer by occupation, chef by passion."

Monique sighed. "I have a confession to make. Dre, you've been bringing in the most money since the fire and, if you go to cooking school now, we probably won't be able to get the house unless you find a job that pays as much as the law firm. But, with your classes and our baby, I know that will be a lot to ask of you." Dre rubbed Monique's hand. "Why didn't you just say something sooner?"

"You know I hate feeling weak. I'm basically begging you to stay at your dreadful job because my oversight was inadequate and I allowed arsonists to come into my business and…" Monique took a deep breath because everything was coming full circle. "I need to sit down." On the couch, Monique thought again about Abigail Newhouse. "I should've done more, Dre. I should've been able to stop what happened. I shouldn't have been at Abigail's funeral. She should not be dead." Andre came next to Monique. "I know, Mo." A little tear fell from Monique's eye.

"How did I let people like that infiltrate *my* Queen-dom?"

Andre rubbed Monique's shoulder. "Nobody's perfect, okay? Mistakes happen. The important thing is that you and Daniel are getting M-dub back on its feet, right?" Monique nodded. "We are, but I just hate that Abigail had to die. Daniel told me that I was blindsided because of my pregnancy and the deaths of Auntie Pamela and Uncle Junior."

"He makes a good point but you're naturally resilient, Mo. I'm sure you were on your guard," Andre offered. Monique shook her head. "I don't think so. This time last year, if I wasn't somewhere barfing into a stool or running off to Dr. Seneca's, I was trying to stop myself from crying over my dead relatives.

"Those cretins saw my vulnerability and used it to their advantage. They capitalized on my weakness and--" Andre put his finger to Monique's lips. "Baby, relax. It's not healthy to worry so much." "I can't help it, Andre. I just feel like I'm not doing my job as the CEO of Mo's Mix."

Andre assured her, "You are, though. You made a mistake but it doesn't mean you're failing."

Monique nodded. "Thanks, baby. That helps." "To ease your mind, let's get back to talking about middle names. I like Bella." "I like Char."

Andre laughed. "We both want to incorporate our mother's names, huh?"

"What if we mushed them together," Monique suggested.

Andre raised his eyebrow. "*Bella-Char*? That sounds like a name that would disqualify someone from a pool of job applicants." Monique said, "One: it's not going to be Emelia's first name. Two: I don't even like you joking about that because I feel like I was passed over for many jobs based on my name. 'Monique' had my blackness written all over it."

"You don't think 'Andre' did too? One time, this teacher said I should've just changed it to Andrew to avoid stereotyping from potential employers." Monique exhaled. "It's sad, you know. As black parents, we want to be creative but, in the same regard, we don't want our children to be overlooked for jobs in the future just because of a name."

"Well, look at you. Passed over for small positions and now you've achieved one of the highest: CEO – a CEO named Mo. That's a slap in the face to those bigots." "*Ooh*, don't get me started on bigots. Let me tell you about Dennis Quaver, this guy who's…" As Monique and Andre chatted up a storm, Daniel was on a mission to stop the one that April Spring had brewed.

"Here's that address you requested, Mr. Ross." Daniel took the card from Dominique's hand. "Thank you very much." "May I ask why you needed it?"

"You may not. See you tomorrow, assistant."

Bree was leaving for the day and she heard this conversation. *What is Mr. Ross up to,* she wondered. Unaware that Bree was trailing him, Daniel got into his town car and drove towards April Spring's 2 story Apiqua mansion. April had her hand on her hip as she opened the door. "May I help you?" "May I come inside," Daniel asked. April stepped to the side and allowed Daniel to come in.

"What's this about?"

"Those adoption papers you put onto your twitter page."

"Free speech, right?"

Daniel shook his head. "It's libelous." "Sue me then." Daniel looked around April's lavish home. "I'm sure you can afford it. Your daddy pay for this?" April scoffed. "I have my own money, you know."

"From what – selling extensions to idiot white girls who actually think you're of one them or exploiting innocent business people who've done you no wrong?"

April rolled her eyes. "I have no idea what you're talking about." "To my first point, hearsay tells me that your dad was seeing one of his black employees and out came you. To my second, you need to get over whatever imaginary beef you think exists between you and my sister." April ignored the latter and focused on the former. "Who told you that about my father?" Daniel was determined to stress the latter, though. "Unimportant. How'd you get your hands on those papers?"

"Unimportant," April countered. "What's imperative is that you protect yourself from what's coming." Daniel informed April, "No, what's *imperative* is that you stop whatever game you're playing."

"I won't stop until I get what I want."

"And I won't stop until you and all your bottle blonde descendants know not to mess with a Ross." April laughed aloud. "It was a Ross who crossed me first."

"How so?"

"That's on a need-to-know basis, Mr. Ross, and you don't need to know. What you need to do is leave." Daniel, who had already gotten what he came for, let out a deep breath. "It's not like I wanted to stay long anyway." In the car, he looked at the phone that April had picked up from the ground. "Bottle blonde bimbo," Daniel murmured. He thought that by getting the device back, April had no more ammunition.

Alas, April was two steps ahead of Daniel. Her half-brother Devin had already transferred all the files onto a computer so Daniel had not really stopped what was coming. Bree, who was down the block, went up to April's door after Daniel drove off. "Mr. Ross, I don't know what else you want me to…" April paused when she saw it wasn't Daniel.

"Bree, right?" Bree raised her eyebrow. "How do you know me?" "I've done my research. Why are you here?"

"What were you and Mr. Ross talking about?" April put her hand on her hip. "Wouldn't you like to know?"

"Answer the question."

"Just as soon as you answer me this: how'd you find me?"

"I followed Mr. Ross," Bree confessed. April grinned. "Sneaky, sneaky, Ms. Perry. I'm surprised you're on the *other* side – given what happened to you in college."

Bree sighed. "That was years ago. I'm over it." "You're over it but you're working for the woman who wronged you? If I didn't know any better, I'd say you have a revenge plot of your own."

Bree exhaled and thought about losing the love of her life. "I'm not admitting to anything." April wrote a number down on a napkin. "You're not fooling anyone, except for Monique, of course. That accident changed your entire face, didn't it?"

Bree was silent so April continued, "I know all about what happened, Breanna. I also know those doctor bills and your student loans are just eating away at your pockets." "They are."

"Join the winner's circle then. You'll be able to pay off your debts and work with people who equally detest that awful woman and her disgusting family. Doesn't that sound nice?" Bree stared at April's offer scribbled onto the napkin. "I'll get back to you on that," she replied while leaving.

"She will destroy any and all alliances," Andre started. "Camille is one of your closest allies, which makes her an easy target for April. But, in order to corrupt you and Camille's friendship, April must first destroy your image of Camille. It's a war tactic dad used to talk about. To vanquish the enemy, you start with corrupting the enemy's liaisons." Monique couldn't stop staring at the picture of Camille at the strip club that an anonymous number (April, of course) had sent. Monique shook her head. "This can't be true, can it?" Andre rubbed Monique's arm. "Most likely not. Camille's just a bartender."

"As far as I know."

But, in a week, Camille had become "Cherry Pop," a club sensation whose striking red hair made the men go wild. On a Friday night, Marquis approached Camille while she pulled her wig off. "I see my lessons paid off," he said. Camille giggled. "They have. Are you up for another teaching session tonight?" Marquis smirked. "You took the words right out of my mouth." Hours later, he and Camille were getting high in his apartment. Marquis believed that the mind was free when one was high, thereby making the body free as well.

He stared at Camille as she sucked in the smoke. "I never woulda thought you smoked." "I quit for a while but, deep down, I knew it wasn't permanent." Camille passed the blunt to Marquis. "Your theory was right, though. I've been smoking before every shift and it's been paying off."

Marquis touched Camille's thigh as he took the blunt. "Now, we both know it's not only the weed that's been giving you rhythm." "Oh? What else then?" Marquis moved his hand up Camille's thigh. "It's also the way your body loosens when it's being touched."

"I didn't realize it was doing that."

Marquis came closer. "You know, when you smoke, your senses are heightened." "That's bs," Camille decided. Marquis rubbed on her shoulder with his fingertips. "Is it really, though?" He pulled Camille's bra strap down and kissed on her neck. Camille giggled but moved her head away. "I said we were just smoking together."

Marquis sighed and sat on the arm of the love seat next to her. "Why you holding out? I don't bite." "I'm getting older so I want more than sex. If you really like me, you'll respect that." "If you wanted more than sex, you wouldn't be a stripper."

"I'm only stripping because it keeps the bills paid."

"That's a lie. You like dancing on that stage and having the spotlight hit you. You like being the center of attention." Marquis took a puff then handed the blunt back to Camille. "I'll make you my center of attention." "But, will you make me your wife?"

Marquis laughed because he assumed Camille was joking. Camille, who felt too embarrassed to admit she had been serious, laughed too. "It must be my high kicking in. Now I'm talking crazy." Camille took one last puff and put the blunt out. Marquis started to roll another one but Camille shook her head. "It's getting late. I'ma go home."

"I could drive you."

"I'm fine taking the bus."

"It's almost 2 AM. You know these streets dangerous after dark."

Camille shrugged. "They're pretty dangerous in the daytime too." Marquis grabbed his keys. "I will drive you. My treat." "You don't have to." He took Camille's hand. "I know." As soon as Marquis pulled up to Camille's building, he stared at her. "You fine. You know that?" Camille blushed and started getting out but Marquis pulled her to him and kissed her.

Camille, who felt an immediate attraction, did something she had promised to stop doing. "You can come upstairs." In an hour, Marquis was passed out and Camille was wondering if she was just a creature of habit.

Daniel was heading into his building and he saw Malcolm waiting. "What are you doing here?" Malcolm stood in Daniel's face. "We both know what I'm doing here." "How did you find me?"

"You haven't moved in 6 years."

"It isn't like you to forget my address."

Malcolm kissed Daniel. "Stop deflecting and invite me up."
Daniel pulled away. "I can't do that." "Why?" Daniel reminded
Malcolm, "We broke up for a reason."

"Yeah, a reason you won't tell me."

"I *did* tell you, Malcolm. We were in two separate places."
Malcolm looked Daniel in the eye. "No, I'm talking about the
real reason." Daniel, who didn't feel comfortable discussing it,
started going inside. Malcolm said, "I think I know what it was:
you were afraid of how the world would receive you. You posed
as this self-assured SOB but, when that confidence was tested,
you cowered. Why? Because you *were* a coward, Daniel. You
were scared. You were in denial. You were--"

"Put up against a wall," Daniel fired back. "I felt like I had no
other choice." "You **always** have a choice. You *chose* to live in
fear." Daniel shook his head. "You don't even understand."

"What don't I understand? Tell me."

"It doesn't matter. It's over and done with now."

Malcolm gripped Daniel's hand. "It's not, though. I'm still in
love with you and I'm willing to try again if you are." An image
of a shotgun flashed in Daniel's head so he pulled his hand away.
"Malcolm, it's over." "I know you miss me. I can see it in your
eyes."

"That isn't true."

"Say it then," Malcolm pleaded. "Say you don't miss me and you
don't love me and I will walk away." Daniel, who had prepped
for this day, took a deep breath. "I *don't* miss you and I *don't*
love you. I actually never did. Au revoir, Malcolm." Malcolm
kept his composure. "Hasta la vista, Danny."

After Malcolm left, Daniel went upstairs to pour himself
something to drink. As Daniel did so, the same image of a
shotgun flashed in Daniel's head again. Daniel's hand began

shaking from anxiety. As the glass fell to the floor, Daniel remembered the sound of glass breaking as a bullet came through his car window. Feeling sick with grief, Daniel threw his entire bottle of alcohol towards the ground and watched it break as his heart did too.

Meanwhile, Andre had done some grocery shopping. While bringing the bags into the house, he noticed Monique trying to lift up a 24-pack of water. "Baby, you don't need to do that." Andre started taking the water from her. Monique scoffed. "I'm pregnant, Dre, not helpless."

"Mo, you're steadily approaching your due date. You should relax." Monique turned her body away from Andre. "I got it." Andre sighed and watched Monique hobble to the counter with the water. *She's an independent woman.* Inevitably, though, one of the bottles of water fell from the pack and busted open. Monique gasped. "My water broke." Andre, who thought it was a joke, grinned and came over. "Very funny, Mo. I said I would help you with…" As he was walking over, Dre realized that Monique actually hadn't been kidding. "I'll call Dr. Seneca."

Chapter IX – *While awaiting the arrival of Emelia, tensions run high. But, once baby Emelia B. Cassells is born, a calming shockwave is sent into the world and Monique is ready to ride this wave as she enters motherhood.*

5 HOURS LATER

James gazed at Camille while recalling the first time they had been in the hospital together. "Stop staring at me." "No." He touched her thigh. "I've missed you." Camille looked into the window at Monique. "We're supposed to be here supporting Mo."

"I know but being in a hospital with you brings back memories."

"Of what? Me crying as that other family took our son away?"

James groped Camille's thigh. "No. Of the way you held him and you said he looked like me. I don't forget that." Camille moved to the side. "Please stop touching me." "I miss you and you won't take my calls." Camille took a deep breath. "I meant what I said about getting Jalen back. Since you want no part of him, you and I seeing each other will just be tense from now on."

"Is that your drawn out way of saying you got a man? I'll understand if you do."

Camille sighed. "I don't."

"Then who gave you that hickey?" Camille pulled her hair down to cover it. "Don't worry about it." James leaned on the window. "I wish it would've been me." Camille groaned. "James, you are *not* doing this right now. How many times do I have to tell you it's over?"

"You can say that as many times as you want but it's never over with us, Camille. I'm your weakness and you're my strength."

Camille rolled her eyes. "Don't get poetic." "But you like it when I do." "James, stop. I'm serious." James moved his hand from Camille's thigh to her waist. "You're not wearing underwear. Can I assume that's because you had someone over last night?" Camille moved to the side again. "Don't worry about it."

James moved his hand up Camille's back. "No bra either. Were you rushing out because you got the call that Mo was in the hospital?" Since Camille didn't answer, James chuckled. "You *were*, Camille, meaning he stayed the night. Was the sex that good? Was he better than me?"

Before Camille could answer, Laila walked up with her arms crossed. "What do you think you're doing? I step away for 10 minutes and *this* is what I come back to?" Camille moved away from James. "Laila, it's not what it looks like."

"It's actually exactly what it looks like. And it needs to stop."

Arielle skipped over. "What needs to stop?" "Go in there with your auntie," Laila ordered. Arielle skipped into the room while Laila put her hands on her hips. "Camille, I know you were a child of the system so you might not understand the concept of family but let me put this into terms that even someone like you can grasp." Laila put on her condescending voice. "James…and I…are married…and we have **two** kids. So. The past. Is. *over*. Was that simple enough for you?"

Camille rolled her eyes. "I love how you're attacking me like I'm the only sinner here. James cheated on you before you all even got married, which means that your supposed union doesn't even exist. In case you haven't already realized, James is *not* in love with you, Laila. I may have been a 'child of the system' but at least I have some common sense."

Camille stepped into the room while Laila shot James a look. "You told me that we weren't together when you slept with her, James. Was that a lie too?" James opened the room door. "Today is supposed to be about Mo. Let's not make it about us, okay?" Laila shook her head in disgust. *What kind of man did I marry,* she asked herself.

In the room, Monique saw the unhappy looks upon Camille and Laila's faces. She wondered, "Is everything alright?"

"Fine," they both lied.

Monique nodded. "If you say so. Has anyone seen Andre?" He had gone to get Monique some pasta so she could carb-up before the birth but he hadn't been back since. In the cafeteria, Andre spotted Lester Thornberry, the founder of Thornberry Academy of Culinary Arts. Lester also owned Touchdown, a 5-star restaurant with locations scattered across Willowsville. For a while, Andre had been keeping tabs on Lester and now Andre was seeing Lester in the flesh. "What can I get for you?" Lester asked.

"Pasta."

"Pasta," Lester yelled to the back. "You don't strike me as a pasta man, though." "What does a pasta man look like?" Lester glanced around the cafeteria then pointed to a big man who was spilling pizza on his shirt. "Him. That guy is definitely a pasta man."

Lester told Andre, "I could see you eating a nice greasy sirloin burger stuffed with mozzarella cheese and jalapeno peppers then topped with Applewood smoked bacon and caramelized onions. This would be ordered with a side of large waffle fries and a tall beer." Andre raised his eyebrow. "That's so specific." "Maybe I'm just hungry but you remind me of a football player and I know you athletes eat well."

"I'm not an athlete anymore but it's not a meal without a meat. Good observation." Lester said, "I'm almost never wrong, except when it comes to my son. He changes his food palate every other day."

Andre laughed. "How old is he?" "30 with the mannerisms of a child. I just pray he finds a good woman soon because--" A man who looked exactly like Lester stepped up. "One pasta." Lester handed the pasta to Andre after charging Andre's card. "You a chef?"

"Not exactly. Why?"

"I said 'palate' and you knew what I meant. Why don't you talk to Juwan?" Andre and Juwan struck up conversation while Lester continued taking orders. Meanwhile, Monique wondered where Andre was with her pasta. Camille, who was eager to be away from Laila's death stares, offered to find Andre. When Camille walked into the cafeteria, she saw Andre and Juwan laughing together. Camille put her hands on her hips. "Andre Cassells, your wife is waiting on her food."

Juwan's eyes lit up when he saw Camille again. "Hey stranger." Camille smiled softly. "Hey." Andre, sensing some chemistry, shook Juwan's hand and headed back to the room. Juwan said, "It's Camille, isn't it?"

"Yep. And you're Juwan."

He grinned. "And she actually remembered." Camille raised her eyebrow. "What's that supposed to mean?" "It means that I must've left an impression on you if you remembered my name."

"Or...you left a business card."

Juwan chuckled. "There's that too. I was hoping you'd use it but you didn't." "Maybe I was waiting on fate to bring us back together." "Well, it sure worked in your favor then." Since more customers were coming, Camille waved at Juwan. "Nice seeing you again."

"The pleasure is all mine."

Camille blushed. "I'll...I'll let you get back to work."

Camille went back to the room smiling. "Was there a pot of gold in the cafeteria," Mrs. Ross joked. Camille sighed and sat down. "No. It's just...I saw a nice man I met the other day and we had a moment."

"You meet a lot of *nice* men, don't you?" Laila sneered.

Camille rolled her eyes. "I'm not even going to entertain that with a response." Monique looked up from her pasta. "So...how's everyone's day been?" This was her attempt to make small talk. It had been five hours and Mo wanted to do anything besides think about her painful contractions. An hour later, it was time to welcome baby Emelia into the world. As Emelia's head started coming out, Andre stayed close to Monique – assuring her that he would be by her side through it all.

During the last 20 minutes, Andre whispered calming mantras in Monique's ear so that she wouldn't be too focused on the baby coming out of her. When Emelia finally arrived, everyone was silenced. No one could believe that, after nine grueling months and 6 ½ hours of hard labor, Emelia could make her presence pretty casually. Once Emelia was wrapped in a blanket, Monique held her daughter closely. "Hi, baby."

Emelia held onto Monique's thumb while Monique spoke. Andre took a mental picture of the moment while his sister Georgiana took an actual picture. Then, he held his daughter for the first time. "Hey, baby girl. You excited to see me? I'm excited to see you." The mere sight of Emelia made Andre shed a tear. "She's so beautiful." Arielle, who had been outside with Laila during the birth, ran to see her cousin.

"What's her name?"

"Emelia Bella-Char Cassells."

Mrs. Ross put her hands on her hips. "Bella-Char? If that's not ghetto, I'm not sure what is." "It's supposed to combine your nickname with Andre's mom's name." Mrs. Ross shook her head. "I'm just happy it's not her first name. Now, can I hold my grandbaby?"

"I'm your grandbaby too," Arielle mentioned. Mrs. Ross smiled. "Yes, but I've been holding you for five years. Can't someone else get a turn?" Arielle stuck her lip out playfully. "Fine." Mrs. Ross laughed and took Emelia into her arms. "My god, you're gorgeous. I'll bet you get that from your mommy because she gets that from me."

Mrs. Ross rocked Emelia in her arms. "It's so nice to finally meet you."

While everyone took turns gawking over Emelia, Monique dozed off. When Monique opened her eyes again, Emelia was napping in a nearby crib that Camille was watching. "Since you're Mo's child, that means I get to be your god mommy and your auntie. You excited about that? I know I am." Camille softly stroked Emelia's hair. "I'll spoil you like you're my daughter."

At that, Monique cleared her throat. Camille looked back and laughed. "I'm sorry, Mo, but I might have to steal your child from you. I'm in love with this precious angel already." Monique positioned her body to sit up straight. "You know what? Me too. I have someone to watch over, love, and protect from now on."

Camille sighed. "It's nice, right? Having a baby?"

"You'll have another one, Cam."

"With whom?"

"That guy from the cafeteria?"

Camille rolled her eyes. "I just met the man. Why would I even be thinking about having his babies?" Monique shrugged. "You never know." Camille continued to glance at Emelia. "When I do

have another child, I hope he or she's as beautiful as Emelia."
Monique smiled. "I hope so too."

"Home sweet home," Monique whispered as she stepped into
condo with the carrier. Andre, who had picked up the bill, looked
on with worried eyes. "Our deductible is 1,000?!" He started
looking over the list of expenses. "That's just ridiculous. You
were only there a day." Monique placed Emelia in the crib. "We
can use our savings to pay it. It's fine, Dre." Andre let out a deep
breath. "I guess."

Monique, who was still tired, yawned and stretched. Andre came
over and rubbed her shoulders. "Hey, get some sleep. I know you
need it." Monique kissed Andre and went to lay down. As she
took her shoes off and slowly crawled into the bed, Monique's
phone started ringing. She groaned. *Just when I thought I could
take a break.* Although her eyes were barely open, Monique still
answered. "Hello?"

"Hey. It's Bree. I hate to bother you on your maternity leave but
it's important."

Monique tried blinking so that her eyes wouldn't be so droopy.
"What's going on?" "I sent those tapes to Samuel Lee's attorney
like you asked and now Samuel has released the names of the
people who were involved in the fire and told the presses that
you hired arsonists to set your building ablaze in an insurance
scandal because you were pregnant and needed some extra cash
for your child."

Monique sighed. "Schedule a press conference and assert that
these accusations are **completely** false." "How should I address
the fact that you hired these people?" "Note that everyone makes
mistakes?"

Bree said, "I don't know how the press will receive that, Mrs.
Ross-Cassells. They're already hounding you about that product

release. If you use a cliché 'we all make mistakes' mantra to tackle something that needs to be addressed in depth, then they might try to say you are losing control of your business and suggest someone else be in charge."

Monique rubbed her tired eyes. "Does Mr. Ross have any ideas?" Bree sighed. "He's been cooped up in his office all day. I don't think he wants to be bothered." Monique, who had noticed Daniel's quietness at the hospital too, told Bree, "Have him call me." "Will do." Bree hung up the phone and started towards Daniel's office.

"You will not get away with this, April...Malaysia...whoever you are. I am determined to--" "Mr. Ross?" Bree unknowingly interrupted. Daniel clapped so that the main lights in his office would come on.

"Yes, Ms. Perry?"

"Is everything okay?"

"If you came in here just to ask me that, you are wasting your time." Bree let out a deep breath. "Mrs. Ross-Cassells would like you to call her."

"Okay. Is that all?" Bree nodded. "Yes, Mr. Ross." "Then you can leave." As soon as Bree exited, Daniel shut his blinds. He had not been able to erase the image of a shotgun from his head. *Go away,* Daniel inwardly yelled. All Daniel could see was the gun that belonged to Maliq Khan, Malcolm's father. Daniel continued pushing the thoughts away until he had finally cleared his head. Then, he called Monique. But, by this time, she was fast asleep.

Andre heard Monique's phone ringing so he came over and answered it. "Hello?" "Where's Mo?"

"Asleep. Can I help you with anything?"

"Not unless you can magically become my sister in the next five seconds."

Andre chuckled. "Don't think so but what do you need?" "There's confidential business to be discussed only with Monique." "Understandable. But, as a word of advice, your attorneys should look into that business that used to be in the building where Mo's Mix is. It was called Misha's Beauty School and it was run by Misha Jones AKA April's biological mommy. Apparently, Misha quit Summerland Corporation because she was uncomfortable working with John after something happened between them."

Andre pulled up the article on his Jotter. "Misha supposedly made a nice lump-sum of cash after telling a journalist at *Spotlight* what John did to her. It says this money allowed Misha to pay for her school. Mysteriously, though, the school was burned to the ground 3 hours after it opened. Misha was pregnant at the time and she went into labor from the anxiety the fire caused.

"On top of that, Misha suddenly disappeared after giving birth and the dates on this article concur with the time that John took in a child from an 'extramarital affair'. I can email you this article if you would like. Or would you rather wait until Mo wakes up so she can send it to you instead?"

Daniel scoffed. "I doubted you. My bad." "You forget that I used to work for Mo's Mix." "Yeah, before you quit because it was 'too much pressure'."

"You try working for your wife," Andre uttered.

"I will never take a wife," Daniel reminded Andre. "Or have you chosen to forget that I enjoy the pleasure of men?" Andre exhaled. "I'm sorry. I didn't mean it like that. I just meant--"

"Don't back track. I've accepted that homophobia is ever-present in black men."

Andre said, "I'm not homophobic. My brother's gay." Daniel laughed. "Having a gay sibling doesn't change one's homophobia. If anything, it brings it out of you. Look at James."

"I'm not James," Andre assured Daniel. "I'm sorry if I offended you." Daniel took a deep breath. "Thank you for apologizing. That definitely means you're not James." Andre laughed and told Daniel, "I'm sending the article right now. Let me know if you need anything else."

"I will. Thank you."

Andre hung up the phone and sent Daniel the link. Then, Andre went into Emelia's nursery because he had heard her waking up. "Hey, baby." When Emelia looked up at Andre, he could see that she wanted to be held. So, Andre picked up his baby girl and sat with her in a rocking chair.

Andre kissed Emelia's head and held her close to him. "This is really happening. I'm really a father." He looked his daughter in the eye. "No matter what, I will always protect you, baby E. Nothing and no one will ever be able to harm my baby girl."

While watching Camille sleep, James looked at the scar on her head; it made him think back to the time he had abandoned Camille, only to find out years later that James's abandonment led her into to the arms of an abuser. James touched Camille's scar. "Hey," he greeted when she woke up. Camille lay on James's shoulder. "Hey." "How come you always hide your scar?"

"Because people ask too many questions."

"True, but don't you think that by hiding it you're allowing Donald to still have that power over you?" "Huh. I never thought about it like that." James pushed Camille's hair back so that her entire face could be shown. "I like you better this way." Camille stared at herself in the mirror. *It's time for something new.*

As Camille thought about this, she realized that James – like the scar – was a representation of her past. "James, you need to go." "What?"

"I can't do this with you anymore."

James raised his eyebrow. "You were doing 'this' just fine an hour ago. Why are you all of a sudden changing your mind?"

"It's time for me to grow up." James stroked the hairs on Camille's arms. "Camille, I don't want to lose you." "Sometimes, you have to lose people before you realize what they're worth to you." Camille removed herself from James's clutches. "You're married and you need to leave." James sighed and sat up. "If this is really what you want." "It is," Camille clarified.

After showering and doing some self-evaluation, Camille decided that she was going to take Juwan up on his offer. "I was thrilled that you called," he said when he saw her coming downstairs in a dress that hit her curves in all the right ways.

Camille grinned. "You left an impact on me." Juwan took Camille's arm. "I'm flattered to hear you say that." They went bowling and then to dinner at Touchdown. As Juwan walked Camille back to her apartment, he kissed her cheek. "I'm sorry if that was forward of me but I couldn't help myself. You're beautiful." Camille touched her cheek. "It was perfect."

While Camille was trying to begin again, Daniel was actively plotting his counter-revenge. Dominique came his door. "I know Mrs. Ross-Cassells isn't here but, no, I cannot point you in the direction of a tampon if that's what you're wondering." Dominique raised her eyebrow. "Where is that even coming from?"

"That red mark on your dress is actually part of the design? I thought maybe you had an accident."

"Mr. Ross, I am 19 years old. I don't have 'accidents' anymore." "What, because birth control regulates your menstruation to every couple of months?" Dominique cleared her throat. "You have a visitor."

"Does this person have a name?"

"Malcolm Khan is here. Again."

"Tell him I'm unavailable." "But you *are* available." Daniel sighed. "It's not your job to question authority. Just tell him what I just told you." Malcolm stormed into the office. "You can go," he directed at Dominique. Knowing that Malcolm and Daniel had extreme sexual tension, Dominique left them to that as she went away quietly.

"Daniel, you need me."

"First of all, I didn't say--" Malcolm slammed a photo of Genna meeting with April Spring onto Daniel's desk. "You need me. That woman is not on your side." Daniel shook his head. "Mo was right. It's all about integrity."

"This means I'm hired, right?"

"Negative. It simply means that the position is open and you will be placed into a pool of candidates."

"So, in other words, I'm hired."

"It's nothing definitive," Daniel explained. "I feel like it is," Malcolm countered. Malcolm left the picture on Daniel's desk and exited. As for Daniel, he called Shaney Watson, the director of human resources. "Mrs. Watson, put out an advertisement for courtroom attorneys." "Attorney Marx is out?"

Daniel stared at the picture. "You are correct." Next, he snapped for Dominique to come into the office. "You know, Mrs. Ross-

Cassells actually calls me by my name when she needs something," Dominique verbalized.

"Well, as you can tell by my voice, I am *not* Mrs. Ross-Cassells."

"Do you even know my name?"

"Assistant #7."

Dominique shook her head. "What can I help you with?" "Tell Genna Marx to get her ass down here immediately." "Should I use those exact words?" "If you so desire," Daniel answered. Dominique started to leave but she couldn't shake the fact that Daniel had been snapping at her like she was an animal. "One more thing – Mrs. Ross-Cassells is all about respect. That's why she takes the time to learn all employees' names. You don't seem to hold the same values, Mr. Ross."

"I respect my equals. You are a college sophomore – i.e. a peon to me."

"I'm a senior," Dominique corrected. "Mrs. Ross-Cassells also learns her employees' back stories, which is why she knows that I began college at 16 and I'll be out before I'm 20. But, as you've already pointed out, you're *not* Mrs. Ross-Cassells."

"I don't like your attitude," Daniel noted.

"I don't like yours."

Daniel shrugged. "My disdain takes precedence over yours because I sign your paychecks." "Actually, you won't be signing anything until you're officially made COO."

Daniel folded his hands. Instead of schooling the child, he decided to remind her, "We both know that it's happening, whether you like it or not."

Dominique wondered, "How's that going to work, though? You and Mrs. Ross-Cassells operate on two completely different ideologies: you take a Malcolm X approach and she's more akin to Dr. King." "Different views but the same goal at the end of the day," Daniel pointed out.

"True, but Mrs. Ross-Cassells seems so liberal and I just don't get that vibe from you."

"I'm more liberal than you realize, Dominique."

Dominique took note of the fact that Daniel actually used her name. "I thought I was 'assistant #7'." Daniel shrugged. "Obviously, I'm not as transparent as you might've assumed."

While Dominique and Daniel were drawing enemy lines, Emelia was drawing a bow from a basket in the grocery store. Monique looked down at her baby. "What you got there?" When Monique saw the bow, she was in awe. *It's perfect.* Days later, Monique put this Easter bow onto Emelia's head. "Tada!" Andre gazed at his daughter. "She is so precious. Let's get a picture." He stood behind Monique and positioned the phone in front of them. After their photoshoot, Monique looked at the clock to see if it was feeding time yet.

Emelia was sucking on her glove so Monique gently pulled it out of Emelia's mouth. "I think you're hungry." Monique placed a bib on Emelia then fed the baby. Andre watched in awe. "I just want to capture every moment. This is too cute." Monique smiled. "She is too cute. I'm in love, Dre."

Once Emelia stopped sucking, Monique placed the infant into the carrier. "Be prepared," she warned Andre. "My grandma said she wanted to invite the *whole* family to Easter this year. You remember the last time you were with the Ross clan." Andre thought back to the funeral and repast for Uncle Junior. "Oh, I remember. Is Yvette going to be there?"

"You know she is. Wherever Etta goes, Yvette surely follows."

As Monique had supposed, much of her dad's family was there when she arrived at her grandmother's house in The Creek (the quietest part of Willowsville). Since the Ross Easter was being held at Etta's house that year, it was pertinent that every Ross family member show up (including extended family members like Camille). "And this is Andre, my husband," Monique declared as she talked to a woman who Monique could recognize by face but couldn't pinpoint their familial relationship.

"Who was that," Andre asked afterwards.

"No clue. But she just gave us $200 for Emelia."

"Is it Easter or Christmas," Andre joked.

Before dinner, most of the time was dedicated to Emelia, since everyone was eager to see the baby. Then, at dinner, the conversation switched from Emelia to the slew of Southern style food on the table. "Char, you cooked all this?" Mrs. Ross nodded. "Sure did. My mama made sure I understood that the best way to a man's heart is through his stomach."

Yvette looked at Mr. Ross. "Earl must really be enjoying your cooking. He put on some weight since I last seen him." Mr. Ross patted his belly. "Maybe I'm pregnant. You never know." Laila, who was still pregnant, tried to ignore the subtle shade. Arielle announced, "My mama's having a baby." Everyone looked at Laila.

"How far along?"

"5 months."

"I guess that'll be the next baby we see, unless Earl is 9 months along and he's just now showing."

The Ross's started laughing as they ate their food. Etta looked over at an empty seat. "Where's that little mixed girl who's always with y'all? What's her name, Catherine?" James raised his eyebrow. "You mean *Camille*, grandma?" Etta said, "Yeah. That's her. Where she at?" James shrugged. "Maybe she just didn't want to come this year."

As if she had heard her name, Camille showed up a short time later. She had been running late because there were 3 people in front of her at the hair salon. The guests turned as Camille stepped in behind Etta. "You cut your hair," Etta noticed. "I actually *just* did. That's why I was running late. But here I am."

"Better late than never, right?" Etta replied.

Then, the Ross's got back to their eating once more. Although Camille wasn't technically a part of the family, they had accepted her because that was the way the Ross' were. Arielle, who sat across from Camille, looked at a blemish on Camille's head. "What's that?" Arielle pointed to the scar. Laila pulled her daughter's hand down. "Ari, it's not polite to point or stare."

"But it's *so* big. Where did it come from?"

"An accident," Camille replied.

"Like a car accident?"

"Sure."

Etta, who was always skeptical, said, "I was in a car accident once and I didn't get no scar like that. That had to have came from something else." Yvette turned to Etta. "What, like somebody hit her?" Etta shrugged. "Could be."

"It doesn't matter," Camille told them. "I've moved on." Yvette shook her head. "You can't have moved on if you won't even talk about it. Obviously it must still affect you. The only way to release pain is to face it. Where that scar come from, girl?" Per tradition, other members of the Ross family started adding their two cents.

"You ain't gotta be afraid of us."

"You scared to open up because we black?"

"You think we gone *judge* you?"

"I don't know what the other side told you but we *not* the villains."

Camille, who didn't like how everyone was jumping down her throat, slammed her utensils on the table. "Yes, I was a victim of domestic abuse but do you *really* want to know how I got this scar? My ex found out that I had an abortion and he realized I had done it because I was through with him. So he slapped me, I fell back into his closet door, and my head got cut. *That's* the story." Yvette, who didn't like the way Camille had caught an attitude, decided she had to school a youngster. "Perhaps that scar was God's punishment for you having an abortion."

Camille, appalled by Yvette's dismissal, excused herself to the bathroom. James started to defend Camille, but he knew that was the last thing she would want. *We have to establish boundaries.* Monique, not feeling so cautious with her words, asked Yvette, "Is that really all you took from that – that she had an abortion?"

"If you willingly rip a child of God from your womb, you are doing the devil's work. She should've never been shacking it up with Ike if she wasn't trying to become Tina."

"So you would raise the child of an abuser even though it would serve as a constant reminder of your pain?"

"If that's what God wanted."

Monique let out a deep breath. "Wow. Just wow." Since everyone had finished their food, they started on games and music. As the children ran around the house searching for Easter eggs, Monique nursed Emelia and watched. *That'll be you in a few years.*

Hours later, Camille went to a second, more sensual Easter celebration. Teasers had a special Easter deal so many men came out for the show. "Tonight, we have a special surprise for you all. With it being Easter, I proudly present to you Bobby's Bunnies." Camille and all the rest of the strippers working that night stepped out in sleazy bunny costumes – each one unique to the girl. Camille's was red, since she was Cherry Pop. Trixie, a second girl, had handcuffs hanging from her costume since she was into "tricks" – i.e. the name Trixie. Star had glittery stars on her costume because she had a star tattoo on her left breast. Finally, Tease had a costume that exposed most of her body but not all because she was a "tease." Since the name of the club was Teasers, Tease was the name given to the headline act.

As Tease went into the audience, the guys threw money her way before she even started dancing. Tease laughed and started off the set that she and the other girls had practiced. She bent over to the floor and touched her toes as Trixie swung around the pole, Star hopped onto the bar and Camille sat inside a cage seductively licking a cherry lollipop. In all, the night went well for "Bobby's Bunnies." They each walked away with enough to pay about 3 months' rent.

When Camille was taking her wig off, she noticed that one guy was staring at her like he wanted to devour her. Feeling uncomfortable, Camille hurried towards the bathroom to change. But, the guy was faster than her. He blocked the door. "I seen you dance a couple times yet I never seen you leave with any of these guys."

"This is just a job," Camille told the man.

"It doesn't have to be," He responded while grabbing her thigh. "Why don't you come with me?" Camille stepped back. "I'll pass." The man would not let go of her thigh. "I think you're real pretty." "That's nice. Now could you let me go?" He tightened his grip and started pulling Camille to him.

"I got a real nice car and I'll cook for you in the morning."

Camille shook her head. "I said no thank you. Will you please let go?" Because the guy didn't loosen his grip, Marquis came over. "If she don't want to come with you, she don't have to." Marquis was bigger than the first guy so the first guy let Camille go and disappeared. Marquis looked Camille up and down. "You're welcome."

"I didn't need your help."

"You kinda did," Marquis mentioned. "What I get in return for saving you?" Camille raised her eyebrow. "Excuse me?" "I helped you out. You owe me." Marquis came closer. "Plus, you act like you don't know nobody after that night we had."

Camille took a deep breath. "That night was a one-time thing." "It doesn't have to be." Camille told him, "It does." Marquis stared Camille in the eye. "What if I don't agree with that?" Camille moved away. "Then you just gone be one unhappy camper." She started going towards another bathroom but Marquis grabbed her arm. Camille flashed back to when her ex had done the same thing and said, "Let me go."

Marquis was determined to get what he wanted, so he started pulling Camille into the bathroom. Knowing what followed, Camille grabbed the first bottle she saw and smashed Marquis over the head with it. He fell backwards and the club owner ran out in an angry rage. "What is wrong with you?!"

"I told him to let me go and he didn't."

"That was a $165 bottle of alcohol?!"

Camille cut her eyes. "He could've *raped* me. You could at least show some compassion." Roberto shook his head vigorously. "You hoes kill me. Dressed like that, what do you expect? Respect?" Roberto let that thought sit then said, "I should've fired you when I had the chance but I thought I would be nice and let you strip."

Camille scoffed. "*Nice*? How would asking me to degrade myself ever constitute as nice?"

"You *chose* to accept my offer. I didn't hold a gun to your head."

Camille nodded. "You know what? You're right. I can leave whenever I choose. So that's exactly what I'm about to do: leave." "You quitting on me?" Camille threw the wig at Rob. "I'll dry clean the costume and have it sent to you."

"Keep it. It's probably disease infested now anyways."

Camille rolled her eyes and left the club with the little bit of dignity she still possessed. She thought about taking the bus, but Camille knew there would be other creatures trying to take advantage of her. So, Camille walked to a well-lit area and called Monique. While Camille waited, she made sure to keep her jacket closed and avoid eye-contact with anyone.

2 MONTHS LATER

"I haven't heard from you in weeks. Is everything alright?" Camille was still reeling in the incident at Teasers so she had kept her distance from Juwan. But, they ran into each other when Camille was going to an interview at Lincoln Insurance. She was finally going to start utilizing her Bachelor's degree. "Everything's fine. I've just been busy."

Juwan nodded. "Understandable. It's nice to see you, though."

"Likewise."

"Whenever you have some free time, you should stop by the school. I'd love to show you what I do for a living." Camille liked Juwan's confidence. She said, "I definitely will." They parted and Camille went to her interview. Afterwards, Camille decided she would visit Juwan just because she was feeling good.

Juwan was in the kitchen by himself when Camille came. "Knock, knock." He smiled when he saw her. "Well, that was fast." Camille shrugged. "I went to run an errand and realized I had time to kill so I thought I'd drop by." Camille looked around the kitchen. "Is it usually this empty?"

"Nope. It's just that my father's doing informational sessions all day so classes were canceled."

Camille nodded and looked at the bowl in Juwan's hand. "What's on the menu for today?" Juwan put the bowl down and motioned towards the food in front of him. "I'm making a brunch of frittatas, crepes, and homemade biscuits."

Camille noted, "My friend's husband made a frittata for me once and I've been hooked ever since."

Juwan wondered, "Want to try mine?" "Sure." Juwan put a piece of a frittata onto a fork and fed Camille. As soon as she bit into it, all the frittata's flavors slapped Camille's tongue. "This is really good. Job well done." Juwan smiled. "You're just full of compliments. Would you like to try one of my crepes too?"

"Definitely." Like the frittata, the flavors of Juwan's crepe were pleasing to Camille's taste buds. "You know the best way to a woman's heart is through her stomach, too," Camille commented. Juwan stepped closer. "Oh, is that right?"

Camille's heart started beating fast as she gazed at the luscious lips that were merely inches away from her own. Juwan licked his bottom lip as he stared at Camille's nicely fitted sundress. Camille tried to suppress her libido but she caught sight of Juwan's beautiful brown biceps that were trying to escape from his form fitting black t-shirt. This made Camille get hot inside. Similarly, the sight of Camille's butt was enough to drive Juwan wild. Overcome with desire, Juwan kissed Camille and pushed her back into a nearby stove.

"Mr. Thornberry, you--" His secretary stopped when she saw what was going on. Juwan and Camille quickly composed themselves. "Mr. Thornberry, you have a visitor." "I should probably go." Camille pulled her purse on her arm and planned for a hasty exit. But, Camille paused in her tracks when she saw who Juwan's visitor was. "Andre?"

"There are three phases to becoming a part of the academy. Phase one is assessment of your culinary skills. In the first round of phase one, you have three recipes and you will have to cook them all within 45 minutes..."

After explaining this phase, Lester clicked his remote and there was another list of rules. "Phase two will test your knowledge of food. In order to be a master chef, one must not only prepare food but one must also *understand* food. Phase two will contain a series of written tests that increase in difficulty as you matriculate through each round and these tests will consist of..."

Lester explained phase two and clicked to one final set of rules. "Finally, phase three contains only one round and, in this round, each candidate will receive an ill-prepared dish. In 45 minutes, the candidates must fix their dishes and make them edible without changing the original content of the dish. This will be judged on preparation, presentation, and taste. From this phase, 1 candidate will be admitted into the Academy. But, if you don't make it, there is a new session every 3 weeks. You'll just have to pay the $500 audition fee every time. Any questions?"

Lester only took a few hands before telling everyone to go on his website if they had any more inquiries. As he was leaving the auditorium, Lester saw Andre again. "Where do I know you from?" "Nouville Children's Hospital." Lester nodded. "Ah, that's right. Are you coming to audition?"

"I just might."

"You'd better act fast. Slots are filling up quickly." Lester pulled out his Jotter. "Right now, there are only 15 left. If you don't register soon, you'll have to wait 3 weeks before getting another chance to audition."

"Do you have to pay when you register?"

"Of course. This is not a charity," Lester duly noted. Then, he walked off to talk to another potential student. Andre stayed where he was and assessed the costs of following his dreams. From Juwan, Andre had found out that tuition was somewhere around $20,000 excluding the costs of books and kitchen supplies. As he reeled it all in, Andre let out a deep breath. *This is going to cost us a fortune.*

Emelia awoke crying for the third time that hour. *What is it now,* Monique wondered. She paused in her reading to go tend to Emelia. "Aw, what's wrong? You hungry?" Monique offered a bottle but Emelia turned away. "You need your diaper changed?" Monique felt underneath Emelia but it was still dry. "You want entertainment?" Monique made a silly face and Emelia started grinning.

"Aw, that's what you want." Monique smiled down at her daughter. Emelia smiled for a second then cried. At first, Monique didn't understand what was going on. Then, she noticed that it was feeding time. "See, I knew you were hungry." Monique gently lifted Emelia up and breastfed the baby. Monique started to placed Emelia back down before realizing she never wanted to let go of her child.

"You're two months old and I still feel like I just met you yesterday." As Monique was speaking, Daniel came to the door. Monique held Emelia in one arm and went to open it. "Tell me this is a personal house visit." Daniel sighed. "I wish I could. It's business."

Monique groaned. "This better be good. You know I'm still on maternity leave." Daniel said, "The board election was today." He pulled out his Jotter. "I had your assistant record each person's speech so that you wouldn't miss out."

"Email those to me, please."

Daniel hit a button. "And… done. How's my niece?" Monique grinned down at Emelia. "She's well. I still can't believe it's been two months already." "Before you know it, she'll be crawling around here." Monique shook her head. "Don't even remind me. It's so cramped that I worry *everything* might fall on Emelia."

"Aren't you and Andre supposed to be getting a house?"

Monique nodded. "Yes but we were put on a waiting list and the bank won't loan us the money until we have been approved for a house. The problem is that we set our eyes on these houses *last* year – when M-dub's revenue was at its highest point yet. Right now, revenue is at a low."

"Could it have something to do with the fact you haven't re-released that product?"

Monique sighed. "We said late June/early July, right?" "July is steadily approaching. Do you even have a set date?" Monique shook her head. "No. I've been calling the lab but they keep telling me another few weeks."

"What's wrong?"

"Whoever runs the lab is apparently a tyrant and his workers are striking against him. Because they won't work, we don't have anything to send out to stores."

"Why not partner with another lab?"

Monique sighed. "Either too expensive or they don't want to work with us. At this point, we might have to push back the release date yet again." Monique pushed her hair back. "This is why I created my own lab – so that I wouldn't have to deal with shit like this."

"Well, our labs are still under renovations."

"It's been almost a year. I don't understand what's taking so long."

Daniel pulled up an email. "The man in charge said that every type of flooring they've tried to install has sunken in. His workers have been searching for a material that holds but work is slow because some people signed on to the project for 6 months and, now that it's taking a year, they have other projects they're doing." "What other projects? Mo's Mix should be their primary focus."

"You know people love to operate on their own agendas."

Monique rolled her eyes. "It's chaos, Daniel. Complete chaos. I'm sure April is loving this." "Probably so. She hasn't tweeted at us in weeks – likely because the damage of her previous tweets is still in effect." Emelia started crying so Monique bounced her baby up and down. When Daniel saw the way Monique held her baby, he put his Jotter away. "But, you know what? You're still on maternity leave. I'll handle this business stuff."

Monique smiled. "Thank you." Daniel patted Monique's shoulder and left. Once Emelia had fallen asleep, Monique allowed the baby to rest on her chest while she watched the videos from the board elections.

Prior to his first audition, Andre wanted to brush up on his knowledge of cooking. He had some time before his next meeting so Andre pulled out a book. 15 minutes later, a knock came on Andre's door. "It's open."

Chauncey Arthur said, "Andre, let's have a chat." Andre quickly put the book under some papers when he saw that Arthur had stepped in. "Yes, Mr. Arthur?" Andre's boss shut the door. "I just received word from Adam Yates that you lost your case in court the other day, which would make that the 3rd straight one you've lost."

"That's true, but I've won more cases than I've lost."

"Duly noted, but you're losing high-profile cases, which results in a profit loss. This business has investors to pay so just know that when you're losing, Bob Morrison from Rother's Publishing is late on his mortgage payments, Anna Storms from *Spotlight* can't afford her cancer treatments, and David Gordon from Gordo Foods can't send his daughter to med school. Knowing that, do you feel good about yourself, Andre?"

Mr. Arthur sat on the ledge of Andre's desk. "Don't answer that. You're black *and* Mexican so I'm sure you've realized how inferior you are. But, here at Roger Muller, there is a certain image you have to keep up. If you're losing consecutively, people are going to think you're a *loser*, Andre. We want people to know that Roger Muller produces only winners."

Mr. Arthur scooted close to Andre. "When you go home to your wife, what do you tell her? That you *lost* again? Don't you want to be the breadwinner in the household or do you just like being the man behind the woman?"

Mr. Arthur didn't allow a response. "Don't you have any pride in yourself? I thought black people were supposed to be all about that kind of thing." He chuckled to himself. "Wait, what am I saying? You're barely even black. When you look at your history, which side do you connect to: power and status, new slaves who keep my people wealthy, or border jumpers who make our lawns look good?"

"No race is superior to another, Mr. Arthur," Andre pointed out as he tried to ignore Arthur's ignorant and racist comments. *I need this job for the baby,* Dre reminded himself.

Mr. Arthur laughed. "I guess that's what you have to tell yourself to forget that you're an inferior breed, Andre. You're a goddam mutt." Andre stared dead at Mr. Arthur. **"Don't** call me that."

"I call as I see it," Arthur asserted. "You're a mutt who doesn't know his place in the world and *that's* why you keep losing these cases. How do you expect to convince the jury of your client's innocence when you can't even convince yourself of your heritage?" Mr. Arthur shook his head. "You have no heritage."

At this point, Andre stood. *No job is worth sacrificing my dignity.* "You have no backbone, you spineless schemer. The only reason you steadily win cases is because you bribe parties from the opposing side for information. You hurt people to get ahead because, for someone of your stature, money is about the only thing that will save your sorry soul."

Andre was finally telling Mr. Arthur feelings that had been bottled up for months and Andre wasn't going to stop until Arthur fully understood what he had gotten himself into. Andre continued, "If you had any pride in *your*self, you wouldn't have become a servant to these investors who are only out for profit and using a whole lot of pathos to make you feel inferior.

"In my opinion, you have *zero* self-respect. Then again, to have some self-respect, you would actually have to have a **self** to begin with. You sold your soul for profit so long ago you can't even locate it anymore." Andre took a deep breath. "I'm sorry for people like you, Arthur, but, at the same time, I realize you are a cruel, heartless bunch who deserves to rot in the Hell you have created for yourselves.

Andre finished, "No matter what you say, though, I *do* know my heritages." Hearing this, Arthur started laughing again – a cover to hide his embarrassment. "This was all a test to see how well you could argue. I wanted you to defend your heritage and you did. Job well done, *mutt*."

Andre stared Arthur dead in the face one final time. "I quit."

"Kaitlin Mosby."

Nicole looked up from what she was doing. "Do I know her?" "No, but you need to," April noted. "She's our next move." "I thought we already did our damage by having Devin convince his co-workers to go on strike." April folded her arms. "Yes, but we need *more*. Monique needs to be on her knees begging me to ease up."

Nicole stared blankly at April. "April, what's the point of all this?"

"I told you: revenge."

"Revenge for what? "

April shook her head. "My mother and I almost lost our lives inside that building so the least my father could've done was respect the short lived legacy of Misha's Beauty School. But, *no*, he had one of his cronies buy the building and they sold it to that wretched woman who operates the business that destroyed my beloved Cocoa Puff."

"Your 'beloved' Cocoa Puff was an attempt to spite your father; you only created a black haircare business to remind him that he raped and impregnated one of his employees." April rolled her eyes. "Those were only allegations."

"If so, why did your uncles feel the need to torch Misha's Beauty School, forcing your mom into a psychotic breakdown? Admit it, April. Your father is scheming Swede trying to escape fate."

April hated hearing Nicole speak so negatively of Mr. Summers and April prepared to slap Nicole. But, Nicole caught April's hand mid-air. "You crossed the line now. I'm bowing out." "There is no out, Nicole." April stated as she snatched her hand away. "Leave and I will destroy you."

Nicole put her hands on her hips. "You try so hard to distinguish yourself from your father, but we both know it was you who said 'pull the plug' when Abigail was in the hospital. She could've survived that fire but you didn't want her to expose your dirty deeds."

"Keep talking and you'll end up with a fate like hers," April warned.

Nicole laughed. "If you even *think* about killing me, I will do one of two things: a) drag you to Hell right with me or b) haunt you for the rest of your being. When you're sleeping, I'll come into your room and whisper into your ears that your father is a notorious white collar criminal who will eventually have his day – in Hell."

Angrily, April shoved Nicole. "Leave my father out of this!" Nicole shoved April right back. "See you on the other side, blondie – that is if you ever get out." "What?" Unbeknownst to April, Nicole had been recording the entire conversation. As a result, Nicole's case would be thrown out and April would be taken in for questioning.

"Dumb blonde," Nicole murmured when the police hauled April away.

"Attorney Kaitlin Mosby is here to see you."

Daniel was eager to find someone – anyone – better than Malcolm. Daniel had decided to give Malcolm a fair shot and Malcolm had blown all his competition out of the water. Before Daniel made anything official, though, he scheduled one last interview. "Send her in," he told Dominique. Daniel didn't want Malcolm thinking it was easy to get back into Daniel's life. Thus, Dominique stumbled upon Kaitlin Mosby. The attorney walked in wearing a big smile. "Hi! I'm Kaitlin Mosby and I'm here to speak with you about your courtroom attorney position."

Daniel hated how peppy Kaitlin was, but he decided to hear her out. "Please sit." He pulled out his list of questions. "What sparked your interest in Mo's Mix?"

Kaitlin replied, "For a long time, it was hard to find products that would satisfy my hair texture. Then, I stumbled upon yours. This was a year ago and I've been faithfully using Mo's Mix products ever since. Now, my hair is healthy and I've been able to try tons of new styles."

Daniel raised his eyebrow. "So you're a fan of the business, I presume?" Kaitlin nodded. "I am. I feel that my affinity towards your brand will motivate me to have a stronger defense in court."

"You sure you won't be too star struck?" Kaitlin, who could tell Daniel was being sarcastic, sighed. "I'm sure, Mr. Ross." Daniel nodded. "Okay. Where do you work currently?" "At the Walker Brothers firm."

Daniel's eyes got wide. "The one run by Anderson Walker?"

"Yes. You're familiar with it?"

"I am. It's one of the best law firms in Willowsville, if not *the* best."

Kaitlin raised her eyebrow. "You seem a little *star struck*, Mr. Ross." Daniel, who saw that Kaitlin was countering his previous sarcasm, grinned. "I like that you weren't afraid to challenge me. That shows me that you're confident and confidence wins cases." Daniel tapped his fingers on his desk. "Pretend I'm Justice Ross for a minute and convince me that something in this office does not belong."

Kaitlin looked at a silver pen on Daniel's desk. "That pen. It parades itself as something valuable because it has a fancy silver coating but, on the inside, I'll bet it barely has any ink. By allowing it to have a place in your office, you are essentially suggesting that you enjoy things that are outwardly attractive yet inwardly subpar. This would ruin the value of your space because everything else in here appears to be of high quality both inside and out.

"For example, you have your degrees on the wall. They look nice because they tell world that you know what you're doing. However, your success exhibits an application of the principles which earned you those degrees – further validating that you know what you're doing. Therefore, your degrees are both attractive and are very much accurate. That pen, sadly, does not convey this same quality because nine times out of ten, it doesn't even write anymore. Thus, it destroys the appeal of this high-quality office." Kaitlin picked up the pen and tried to write her name, only to discover it was out of ink. "I rest my case."

Daniel hung on to her every last word. "You're in."

Camille was coming home after another failed interview. *We see your qualifications, Ms. Harrison, but we've spoken to some of your references and umm...* As Camille blocked the moment from her head, she saw a rent notice taped to her door. Camille groaned. "I don't even know how I'm going to pay this." Camille yanked the note off.

Inside the apartment, Camille threw her things on the counter but couldn't shake the feeling that something was off about her apartment. Camille couldn't pinpoint an exact cause, but she just didn't feel safe. *Don't tell me Trevor broke in again.* Camille looked around to see if anyone was there but no one was. For a minute, Camille reckoned that she must've been paranoid because of Trevor's attempted assault and Marquis' attempted rape. Just when Camille was calming down, Devin Summers came to the door. "Hi."

Camille shot her head around. "Who are you?" Devin stepped inside. Camille put her hand up. "Whoa, did I say you could come in?"

"It might do you some good not to cross me, Camille."

"Why is that?"

"Because I don't fight fair. I will take Monique and her affiliates out by any and all means."

Camille raised her eyebrow. "How do you know Monique? How did you even know my name?" Devin held a flash drive. "This contains every piece of information from that phone of yours. Now, you can work with me and have this information destroyed or you can be plowed down in the destruction of Mo's Mix. The choice is yours, Camille."

Camille folded her arms. "I would never betray Mo. Not for anything." "But what about Jalen," Devin challenged. "Don't you miss him? Don't you hate that regret you feel in the pit of your stomach every time you bypass a boy who's Jalen's age?" Camille *had* felt all these emotions but, still, she shook her head. "I'm a strong believer in karma."

Devin nodded. "As am I. In this life, what goes around must come back around. You lost your actual baby, Monique can lose her metaphorical one and everyone's happy. At the end of the day, she and Andre's relationship will forever be stifled by Mo's Mix. So, if Monique really valued her man, she would bow out quietly.

"Of course, that would upset the Willowsville black community because Monique is a black woman running a black business; she is virtually in a class of her own. If Monique walks away, Willowsville's black women will have nothing left for them – *especially* not the ones who come from Vieille Ville like you, Camille.

"Thus, Monique has a heavy burden. But, if I were you, I would tell her to quit while she's ahead. She won't like what we have in store for her."

Camille put her hands on her hips. "Which is?" "That storm Evan was talking about? It's *not* over." With that, Devin left and Camille called Monique to warn Mo of the imminent threat. But, Monique was too busy gazing at Emelia to answer. Dre, who had just gotten in from another failed interview, came behind

Monique. "Baby." Monique put her hands atop Andre's. "You feeling alright?"

Andre shook his head. "No. I think I keep purposely tanking these interviews because what I really want to do is follow my dreams. But, I know they'll cost us a fortune and it just depresses me." While carefully studying Emelia, Monique wondered, "How much will it be?"

Andre pushed his head into Monique's shoulder. "At the informational, Lester said there's a $500 non-refundable audition fee. Then, if I actually make it into the Academy, I'm required to pay a $350 kitchen fee each semester and my books are going to run us up about $8-900 and my utensils will be another $200. And I haven't even gotten to the tuition, which is $25,800 a semester. So, in total, it's too much damn money."

Monique offered, "One of Mo's Mix's investors told me about a grant he's implementing now that he's the CEO of Techie. Landon George always had a passion for cooking before deciding that he had a stronger affinity for business. Even still, George wants to help those people who still want to pursue a cooking career. So, Techie is offering a $25,000 grant to an aspiring cooking student who wows Mr. George with a meal. Throughout a period of 3 weeks, applicants will visit George's house and cook for him. The applicant with the most outstanding meal is then awarded the grant. If you were to get that, it would help us out a lot, Dre."

"Is it renewable?" Andre asked.

"Yes. The grant covers up to 2 years at your culinary arts institution and has to be renewed based on academic standing. I think you should apply for it." Andre nodded. "I will but I have one request."

"Shoot."

"Please don't intervene. I want to feel like I earned this my own way." Monique promised, "I won't step in." She grabbed her Jotter. "Here's the link to apply." In the living room, Andre began filling out the application. Meanwhile, Monique peered over Emelia's crib. "Hi, sleepy head. You hungry?" Emelia stared at Monique for a few seconds then started crying. Monique took the infant into her arms. "You must be hungry." In a nearby rocking chair, Monique sat and fed her daughter. As she nursed Emelia and watched Andre from the corner of her eye, Monique had one thought: *Life is good right now.*

"Mr. Mercy will speak to you now," the assistant stated. Daniel nodded and stepped into Adrian Mercy's office. Mercy was the "tyrant" whose workers were striking against him. Because Daniel needed the Mo's Mix product to be released, he visited Mercy Labs in their Vieille Ville location. Mercy recognized Daniel. "Daniel Ross of Dan's Plan."

"Sure am."

"My wife and I loved that workout program that used to come on Channel 13. We were sad to see you go."

"All good things must come to an end."

"Very true. To what do I owe this visit?"

Daniel pulled out papers. "Currently, I am the actin COO of Mo's Mix and this lab provides products for Mo's Mix. I'm here to find out why we haven't received any shipments of samples." Mercy got up from his desk and looked out towards his nearly empty workspace. "Almost every one of my workers went on strike because I cut their wages from 50 cents an hour to only 25 cents."

Daniel raised his eyebrow. "I thought minimum wage was a *little* bit higher than that."

Mercy chuckled. "Answering sarcasm with sarcasm. I like you already."

Daniel grinned. "Good to know. But let's be serious for a moment: why are your workers striking?" "Inflation just drove up the costs of supplies so I cut their wages in order to avoid cutting other wages."

"Basically, you took money from the proletariat to ensure that the bourgeoisie remain the bourgeoisie." "When you say it like that, you make me sound unethical."

Daniel shrugged. "I tell it like it is, Mr. Mercy. In my humble opinion, you're a greedy businessman who has a lifestyle he needs to uphold. I understand that. But, I also have a lifestyle *I* need to uphold, which is centered on products manufactured in your labs. So, I need you to march out there, threaten those people with loss of jobs and get the train running in here. If not, I will take testimonials from each one of your disgruntled employees and see to it that this company's bureaucrats step into the shoes of the semiskilled laborers – even if only momentary."

Daniel gave a half-smile and left the building. On the outside, he ran into protestors. "Mercy shows no mercy," they chanted over and over. Daniel wanted to ignore them but one lady caught his eye. She touched Daniel's arm when she saw him looking her way. "I constantly had to take days off because two of my kids are diabetic and I'm always running to the hospital for them. Then, I live in a rough area and I sometimes come late to work because I'm afraid of leaving my kids in the house alone.

"Yet, Mercy threatened to fire me if I missed another day of work. Mercy shows no mercy," the woman cried as she rejoined the crowd.

A man with a Spanish accent said, "I requested time off to go visit my dying tío in México. Mercy told me that I could take the time off, but I wouldn't have a job when I got back. I ended up missing the funeral because I couldn't lose my job. I got too many mouths to feed. Mercy shows no mercy," he chanted with his fellow coworkers.

One by one, each worker voiced their individual complaints but there was one common denominator: a tyrant named Adrian Mercy. Daniel had first thought it was a typical case of worker's wanting better wages, but the protestors' stories made it clear that other, more severe forms of maltreatment were going on. Apparently, 3 of Mercy's workers had filed complaints of sexual harassment against him but Mercy's lawyers silenced the allegations. Then, Mercy was a notable racist, referring to his black employees as "black boy" or "black girl" and once calling a Hispanic employee a "border jumper who got lucky."

In all, it was clear that Mercy was a vindictive, bigoted man who needed to be stopped. Daniel went up to the woman who had first caught his eye. "How long have you been working here?" "Too long for him to be treating me like this."

"Have you ever thought of applying elsewhere?"

"I have but word on the street is that if you leave Mercy, he makes sure you don't find a better job for *at least* a year."

Daniel shook his head. Because Mo's Mix needed their products, and it was clear that the employees were fed up, he decided to make a risky move. "I know of a place that will hire you," he told the woman. "Where?" She wondered.

"Mo's Mix."

Daniel decided that he was going to hire Mercy's disgruntled employees right under Mercy. "And if you try stopping me,"

Daniel uttered. "I will take every last claim that they have and use them to bring you down. The difference between me and your *former* employees is that I'm actually smart enough to win against you in court."

Mercy exhaled. "I've actually already hired new people. I was just giving these guys a week to voice their frustrations because I figured it would be the only time they got featured on the news in a non-gang related incident." Daniel took offense to this. "That's a little prejudiced, don't you think?"

Mercy gasped. "Oh, I thought you were just passing as black to appease affirmative action."

Daniel shook his head. "You thought wrong. Now, I have more ammunition to destroy you." "The battle won't be easily won," Mercy declared. "That's what you think." With that, Daniel finally left the lab and called Dominique.

"Mr. Ross, I'm not on the clock right now and I have an Econ class that I'm already late for," Dominique noted as she rushed towards the classroom. "Skip that and go to the address I'm about to text you. I own the floor of a building downtown and it's about to be converted into a make-shift lab. I need you to make sure it is spotless by 5:00 tonight."

"What about a key," Dominique wondered.

"You came from the hood. You should know how to pick a lock."

Dominique scoffed. "That's a harsh assumption. Do *you* know how to pick a lock?" "I do, actually," Daniel answered. "But I'm going over there now. They key will be underneath the sign on the door. When you leave, take the key with you."

Daniel hung up and instructed the driver to go over to his old office. When Daniel got there, he saw the sign that used to make him light up.

Dan's Plan

Partners – Daniel Ross, Malcolm Khan, and Avery Foster

Daniel made a mental note to have the sign removed eventually but, for the time being, he gently placed the key beneath it and quickly left the building.

On the other side of town, Monique wanted to yank her hair out. Emelia had been crying nonstop for 30 minutes. Her foot was hurting but she couldn't express this so she just cried. Monique studied Emelia and saw that there was a scratch on the child's foot. "Aw, baby got a booboo." Monique put Emelia down to have free hands while searching for a Band-Aid but Emelia's cries got louder once her mother was gone. "Baby, I'll be right back. I just need to find you a Band-Aid."

Monique searched high and low but there were no Band-Aids in sight. *Where did Andre put that first aid kit?* While Monique looked for it, Emelia's cries only got worse. Yet, when Monique actually found a Band-Aid, Emelia was fast asleep – tired from all that crying. "How bout that?" As Monique watched her daughter, one thing came to mind: *Welcome to motherhood.*

A half hour later, Monique stood looking towards a scale on the floor. *The moment of truth.* Slowly, Monique stepped onto the scale. In her youth, Monique had been on the heavier side but she shed these pounds as she reached adulthood; this was prior to the pregnancy. At that moment, Monique was 30 pounds more than she desired to be. She tried to hold back tears while staring at the haunting number.

"Baby, I'm home," Dre announced. He was excited to tell Monique about his new job – especially because it wasn't at a law office but paid like it was a fledgling firm. "Baby?" Andre went into the bedroom when he didn't see Monique in the living room. "Mo…?" He stepped into Emelia's nursery next.

"Monique?" Since Monique wasn't in there either, Dre finally came into the bathroom. "Oh, here you are. I have some news." Monique sat on the ledge of the bathtub and continued to stare at the scale. "Me too."

Dre sat next to her. "What's wrong?" Monique kept her eyes glued on the scale. Andre, who realized what was bothering Monique, pulled her into his shoulder. "You're beautiful, okay?" "Will I still be beautiful when I break the floor because it can't hold all my blubber?"

Andre kissed Monique's head and sang, "I'll love you when your hair turns grey, I'll still want you if you gain a little weight. The way I feel for you will always be the same…"

Since it was their song, Dre waited on Monique to finish. "Just as long as your love don't change," she belted. Andre laughed and told Monique his good news. He had gotten a position as a site counselor at the local community center. Evenings during the work week and on Saturday afternoons, Andre and two other counselors would do a mentoring program for at risk youths called: "Generation Gap: A word from your elders."

"The pay is $4,000 a month," Andre stated excitedly.

"How did you even stumble upon this?" Monique wondered.

"Nathalie works for TVA and they sponsor Generation Gap. Since this is a predominantly black community, they were looking for three black people who have faced obstacles yet overcame them. The end-goal is to get the black youths off the streets.

"In the interview, I talked about how my mamma struggled to find jobs because of the language barrier. Then, I told them that when my father was alive, his army pay got us by but, with 9 mouths to feed, we were living paycheck to paycheck inside this city's low-end.

"I also mentioned that my family had to become a close-knit because those streets aren't kind to our kind. I finished up by talking about the street fights I used to get into and how that guy tried to recruit me into his gang but I told him no. The site manager and the leader of the program feel that my 'touching' story can really resonate with these youths so they hired me."

Monique smiled. "That's good. You seem so happy about it." "Trust me, baby. I am. Anywhere besides that awful firm would make me happy."

"Even working at a fast-food joint?"

"Even there," Dre said. "With unskilled labor, you know what you're getting yourself into. At these specialty jobs, you expect they'll at least treat you with some decency. But, higher on the corporate ladder, it's the *same* type of people; they just have more money." Dre leaned back onto the shower as his thoughts came full-circle. "Like Kanye said, the people highest up got the lowest self-esteem and the prettiest people do the ugliest things. Wealth is seen as 'pretty' because of its relation to power and prestige. Once you look past the wealth, though, you'll see that this world is full of similar people wearing different clothes."

As Dre began his analysis on the implications of wealth, Camille thought about her lack of wealth. She was still unemployed and she was late on her rent. "You know money is not the *only* form of payment I accept," Martin, the building manager, noted.

Camille scoffed. "You're disgusting."

Martin shrugged. "And you're broke but who's judging?" "Not you obviously," Camille mumbled sarcastically. He leaned on Camille's door. "So...let me guess: you don't have my money?"

Camille shook her head. "Nope." Martin stared at Camille's chest, which was peeking out of her tank top. "I usually let you pass but I don't know about this time." Camille closed her sweater. "I paid you half up front like you asked. The rest is not due till the 5th. I'll have it then, okay?"

"If not, expect to see an eviction notice."

"It's not like I haven't before."

"Before, they were warnings. This time, I'm serious."

Camille rolled her eyes and slammed the door. *What am I going to do?* Camille had so many bills from loan sharks and Sallie Mae that she didn't even answer her phone if the number wasn't familiar. *Maybe I should just go back to stripping,* Camille thought. Teasers wasn't the only club in the city, after all. Then again, Camille knew she would probably encounter the same type of men she had barely dodged at Teasers anywhere she went. So, she decided against stripping.

While Camille thought about her financial options, or lack thereof, a knock came at her door. It was James. "What do you want?" He pulled an envelope from his back pocket. "A little birdie told me you seemed to be in need."

Camille sighed. "Daniel and his big mouth."

"It was my mom, actually. I hear she visited you before Easter."

Camille sighed and took the envelope. "Yeah, she did. How much is this?" "$5,000. That should hold you over for a while, right?" "If by 'a while' you mean a month." James stepped inside. "Well next month I'll come back with 5,000 more." He started to kiss Camille but she turned away. "You're making me feel like a prostitute."

James cupped her face. "But you know you're worth more than that to me." Camille tossed the envelope on the counter. "Do I, James? Do I really?" "If you want me to prove it to you, I will." "How are you going to prove it?" Camille asked.

James kissed her. "By telling you what you deserve to hear."

"What's that?"

"I love you," James confessed. He wrapped his arms around Camille. "And I'm giving you this money because I want to take care of you, not because I think of you as a prostitute." When Camille felt James's embrace and heard his kind words, she fell apart inside. She forgot that she was, technically, with Juwan. "I love you too, James," Camille said.

James balanced his head on Camille's and held her. "I love you," he repeated for emphasis. Then he lay his head on Camille's shoulder. "And I need you right now."

"What's wrong?"

"Laila's been having anxiety, which she blames me for. So, she took Ari down to Orlando and they haven't been back in a week." James held Camille tightly. "I haven't done right by either of you and that bothers me. Cam, I'm barely holding it together. I just…I need you."

James slid his hands under Camille's tank top. "I long for this – the feel of you." He stuffed his head into her curls. "I think about your laugh all the time." Slowly, James worked his way up Camille's back. She wrapped her arms around his neck as he clasped her shoulders. "I'm sorry I ever took you for granted." Together, Camille and James's bodies swayed with the music that played in their heads.

"Daniel Ross, you are a genius." Monique pushed Emelia's stroller into the office space that had become a lab. Daniel drafted the construction workers who would no longer be fixing the science wing to reconstruct the space. Then, Daniel had Dominique phone all the names of people Daniel had recruited from Mercy Labs – Vieille Ville.

Monique wondered, "How did you even find workers so soon?" She looked at the samples of "No Press? No Stress" lined up on tables. "Let's just say I went to the Mercy Labs and did some field recruiting."

"You capitalized on the fact that those people were striking and offered better conditions?"

"More or less."

Monique shook her head. "Mom always said you were the devious one." "Which came in handy because now we have something to tell the press. At this rate, the workers will be done by the Fourth. I say we release the products on Independence Day and say that we are celebrating black liberation, since 'No Press? No Stress' supports the transition from relaxed hair to natural hair."

Monique nodded. "I like it. What about you, Emelia? You like that idea?" Emelia looked up at the sound of her name. Daniel glanced in at her. "Hi, baby E." Emelia wasn't yet used to Daniel and she started crying. Monique picked Emelia up and patted the infant's back. "That's your uncle, baby."

Daniel shrugged. "I guess she doesn't know me yet." Monique bounced Emelia up and down. "She will." While holding Emelia, Monique took a tour of the lab that used to be the headquarters for Dan's Plan. "It looks good, Daniel." "You can thank your assistant for that."

"Dominique organized all of this?"

"Under my instruction, of course. Since she had to miss a few classes to make the arrangements, I decided to call this 'field experience' so that her professors won't think she's skipping lessons to lollygag."

Monique said, "It seems that you two are getting on pretty well."

Daniel shook his head. "I only tolerate her because she's your assistant but, personally, I would prefer a male. They give you less attitude."

"Yeah, because men internalize everything." Monique started. "Take Dre for example. I asked him to wash the dishes last night. He says, 'Later, I'm writing a speech.' 2 hours later, I'm like, 'Dre, did you wash the dishes?' He says he's *still* writing his speech. After another hour, I asked him a third time and he got so irritated that he brought up the fact that I always do the dishes behind him so there's really no point of him washing them. If I hadn't nagged him, I would've never known that bugged him."

Daniel sighed. "You two really are married. An argument about *dishes*? Come on now." "It probably wouldn't have been an argument if he would've said something a long time ago. But, hey, he's a man so I should expect that, right?" "As long as you expect women to take at least 45 minutes to shower, an hour on make-up, two hours on hair, another 30 to look at themselves in the mirror and talk about how flawless they are then a final 10 minutes to claim they woke up like that."

Monique rolled her eyes. "Now you're just exaggerating." Daniel shook his head. "I don't think I am. But, what's Dre writing a speech for anyways?"

"He got a job at Nouville Community Center as a site counselor and all the counselors are going to be speaking at the center's kickoff program. The people in charge really took to Dre's backstory about growing up in the projects and how he had to fend for himself and his siblings."

Daniel chortled. "But Andre was what they would call 'foreign.' Didn't people love him?" Monique scoffed. "Don't believe the hype. Given Andre's milk chocolate complexion, how do you think the other side perceives him?"

Daniel nodded. "I see where you're going with this. I always thought Dre was just black. So when you said he had all that other stuff in him, I almost didn't believe you."

While putting Emelia back into the stroller, Monique explained, "As far as Andre is concerned, he is just black. But, his siblings are another story. Nathalie, David, and Karen swear up and down they're so Italian.

"On the other end, Miguel uses his name and the little Mexican blood he has to pose as purely Spanish. Then, Georgiana and Lauren don't take a side; they just tell people that they're melting pots. As for Dre, he says he always told people he was black; he didn't even include the other races and his mom hated that."

"Why?"

"Because she wanted Dre to embrace his Italian blood."

"Isn't she half Ethiopian, though?"

Monique said, "Only in her hair. Everything else about Mrs. Cassells is strictly Italian." Daniel glanced at his niece. "And what about the little one? How shall I classify her?" "She will be raised as a black child." "Her hair will definitely say so. You know those naps are going to start forming at 6 months," Daniel mentioned.

Monique put her hands on her hips. "As they should." "Oh, that's right. I can't talk about 'naps' around someone with natural hair." "No, you can't, because it's offensive. I ought to take out a lawsuit against you for even using the term 'nap' around me. It's a defamation to my hair's character."

Daniel chuckled. "Yet, you talked about my 'neglected naps'. But, speaking of hair, when do you plan on getting yours done again? Those braids are well past their time."

"I will redo them when I have some free time."

"I hope that's soon because your *naps* are looking like they want to escape confinement."

Monique scoffed. "Excuse me for having fabulous *coils* that don't wish to be tamed." Daniel looked at Emelia. "Do you hear how conceited your mommy is? I pray you don't turn out like that." Emelia glanced at Daniel because he was unfamiliar to her. But, when he smiled, she did too.

"And I saw Mickey Mouse and he was *so* big and I got to hug him. Mommy has a picture of it. Show Uncle Daniel the picture, mommy." Laila laughed and pulled out her phone. To calm her nerves, Laila had decided to visit her family in Orlando. During the trip, Arielle had begged to go back to Disney World so they did. "You look good," Daniel complimented. "I can see you've both gotten tans."

Laila nodded. "Thanks. We spent the entire trip soaking up the sun."

"How did James like it?" Daniel wondered. "I remember he complained the whole time Ari first went to Disney World." "James didn't go," Laila confessed. "It was a mommy and me trip," Arielle added while Laila showed Daniel the images she had taken.

Daniel looked at pictures and asked, "Does this have anything to do with a certain curly haired family friend?" Laila rolled her eyes. "It's not even about her. It's about the fact that James keeps lying to me. Plus, he unlinked our bank accounts so I don't know when he's taking money out."

Daniel shook his head. "Shameful." Then, he looked at the bags Laila had brought with her. "To what do I owe this visit?" "I'll be at the shop all day but Marlene doesn't like kids running around."

"And you brought Arielle to Mo's Mix because…?"

"Because she's your niece," Laila reminded Daniel.

"True, but this is not a daycare service." "I'll pay you $50." Daniel clapped his hands. "Deal. The office closes at 5."

"James can pick her up."

Laila gave Daniel his money then left. Daniel sat on his desk and just stared at Arielle. "What do you like to do," he asked her. Arielle took out her notebook. "I like to draw." She started pulling out messy crayons that threatened to stain Daniel's lush white carpeting. He stopped Arielle before she could unpack. "Wait, wait, wait. You can't do that in here."

"Why?"

"You'll stain the floor."

"So, where am I supposed to go?"

Daniel snapped and Dominique begrudgingly walked into his office. "Mr. Ross, I already told you about snapping at me. I am not an animal." Daniel looked at Dominique to see if she understood who she was talking to. "And I am your boss, not your friend. So, I suggest you stop speaking to me so colloquially."

Dominique took a deep breath. "I apologize, Mr. Ross. I just feel that as your employee I should be treated with respect."

"And I feel that you are wasting your time coming to me with that asinine request. Everyone in this office is treated with the utmost respect."

"You snap at me like a dog," Dominique hollered. Daniel stared dead at her. "Lower your voice when speaking to me." "What if I don't?" Dominique challenged. Daniel stood up and towered over Dominique. "Do you really want to test that, Dominique?"

Dominique, who knew she needed the money, exhaled. "I lost my temper, Mr. Ross. I'm sorry."

"You'd better be. Now take this child out of my sight."

"Babysitting is not in my job description."

"Neither is questioning a superior. Go!"

Dominique sighed and walked towards Arielle. "Come with me, please." Arielle grabbed her belongings and followed Dominique out. Dominique wondered, "What's your name?" "Arielle. I would ask yours but I know it's Dominique."

"You were listening in there?"

Arielle nodded. "Mhmm. Are you two married?" Dominique raised her eyebrow. "No...Why?" "My mommy and daddy yell at each other like that and they're married." Dominique shook her head. "Mr. Ross and I are definitely not your parents."

"Do you even have a husband?"

"Nope."

"Boyfriend?"

"Don't worry about it." Dominique answered. "Why not?" Arielle questioned. Dominique went into her office. "Here I am. Set your stuff down in the corner because that's where you'll be sitting." While Dominique got to work, Arielle began drawing. She drew based on things, people, or events that inspired her. At that particular moment, it was the animosity between Dominique and Daniel.

After about 15 minutes, Dominique walked over to inspect Arielle's artistry. Arielle had sketched two people who stood adjacent to each other. They both had fire where their faces should've been. One wore a dress, which was to represent Dominique, and the other wore a suit, which was to represent Daniel.

Dominique kind of laughed but, at the same time, she kind of felt embarrassed by the fact that she had been so aggressive in front of a child. While Dominique marveled over the work of Henri Matisse's female counterpart, Arielle started drawing a replica of the posters she had seen coming into the office. Noticing Arielle's eye for detail, Dominique got an idea.

Beginning in late November, Mo's Mix would be having a campaign to promote "No Press? No Stress." Additionally, they planned to unveil "Shine On," which would debut at the conclusion of the campaign. The campaign would end just before Christmas so that people would have a lovely surprise from Mo's Mix in their stockings.

Dominique stepped into the communications wing and made her way over to the Design Studio, where the artists debated over whose artwork they would pitch. "They're all ugly," Dominique stated. The artists looked up as if offended. "You don't look like a Patrick."

"Who's Patrick?"

"A new artist." Alex, a creative directing apprentice, explained. "If that's not you, you have no business being down here and I'm going to have to…" Alex paused, gazing at the design in Dominique's hand. "Who drew that?"

Dominique put her hands on her hips. "Excuse you. As an executive assistant, it is my job to oversee every department and give a status report to either Mr. Ross or Mrs. Ross-Cassells. But if you're wondering who drew this…" Dominique nodded towards Arielle. "She did." Alex raised his eyebrow. "First I get a glorified intern coming in here trying to tell me how to do my job then you promote the artwork of a baby? This must be some practical joke."

"I'm not a baby!"

Alex looked down at Arielle. "Where's your mommy, kid?"

"At work. She dropped me off with my Uncle Daniel."

"Daniel...as in Daniel Ross?"

"Yes; she's the boss' niece." Dominique answered. "And this kid's got talent." Alex folded his hands. "Even still, she's just a kid. What am I supposed to do with her?" "You all are struggling with finding a design for the campaign posters, right?"

Alex shrugged. "We're handling it."

"Is that why that garbage can is filled to the brim with balled up pieces of paper?" Alex was silent so Dominique continued, "I have the solution to your creative block."

Dominique showed Arielle's notebook. Alex looked at the sketch book closely before suddenly scooting back. Picking up on this, Dominique figured that Daniel had walked in. She turned and saw him standing behind her with an unhappy look upon his face. "What exactly do you think you're doing?"

"Um..."

"You should not be in here without official--" Daniel paused because Arielle's design caught his eye. "Who drew this?!" "I did," Arielle told him. Hearing that, Daniel cleared the station to make a place for Arielle. "Do you think you can recreate it?" "May....be." Arielle sat on a stool.

"But I might need some paper and crayons, unless you want me to draw on the desk and use my blood as paint." Daniel laughed at Arielle's burgeoning condescendence. "So sarcastic. You're *definitely* my kin."

"I have a doll named Ken and he's married to Barbie."

Daniel sighed. "It was at this point that I remembered she was still four years old." Then he clapped his hands. "Alex, get this girl some paper. Ayanna, find her some crayons, Patrick, introduce yourself, and Dominique, make sure she stays in your sight. Is that clear?" Everyone nodded and got to work.

"Here you go." Arielle finished her third attempt at a drawing but it still didn't look like the original one. "Can I be done now," Arielle wondered. "Not yet," Dominique answered. "It's still not conveying the same rawness as the first." Arielle stared blankly. "What?" "Just try again," Dominique said next. Arielle huffed and got to drawing. Alex glanced over at Dominique. "By the way, I drew one of the pictures that you called ugly."

"Is this the point where you demand an apology because I hurt your male pride?"

Alex shook his head. "This is the point where I ask you your name. I like a woman who's not afraid of her own opinions." "And I like a man who's not my co-worker so, if you're trying to hit on me, quit while you're ahead."

"I love a good challenge." Dominique was attracted to Alex, but she knew she had to control it because he was her co-worker and she had an on again/off again boyfriend who she had to worry about. "That's nice, but we both have jobs to do." Dominique went back to watching Arielle while Alex studied a vision board for possible inspiration.

As Dominque was surfing through her phone and Alex was talking to his fellow artists, Arielle saw an open bottle water and got a sudden urge to knock it down, since it would create the perfect distraction. Arielle pushed the bottle and the water fell inches away from Dominique's phone. Quickly, Dominique moved her phone. "Why would you..." While Dominique was talking, her phone slipped from her hand. Luckily, Alex caught it before it could hit the ground.

"Since I just saved your phone from possible death, you might as well go ahead and put my number in it."

Dominique rolled her eyes. "Not gonna happen."

"Then I guess I'll just have to do it myself." Dominique scoffed. "You don't even know the password." "Good thing it's already unlocked." Before Dominique could stop him, Alex was typing his number in. "I know you like me so there's no reason to be acting shy." Dominique snatched her phone back. "I'll deal with you later. Right now, I need to…" Dominique turned around and saw that Arielle had vanished. "Oh no."

First, Dominique dashed to the media room. "Have you seen a small child?" Everyone shook their heads to say no so Dominique tried Finance next. No luck there either. Dominique thought about the tech wing next, since kids tended to gravitate towards gadgets. No luck there. Finally, Dominique tried security, though she highly doubted Arielle would've gone downstairs. Still, it was worth a shot.

As Dominique descended the staircase, she had a flash back to the fire. *Can anyone hear me?!* Abigail had been calling out for help but Dominique had run away at the first sign of smoke.

Although Dominique did call the fire department, she felt slightly guilty that she hadn't been of more assistance to Agent Abby. Dominique was reminiscing when Arielle skipped over licking an ice cream cone.

Dominique looked down. "Where'd you get that?" Arielle pointed to a nearby vending machine. "I saw a sign that said 'vending machine' and I followed it. I'm sorry for leaving and for knocking the water bottle over and for making you almost drop your phone." Dominique exhaled and took Arielle's free hand. "All will be forgiven as long as your uncle doesn't find out I lost you."

While they were walking, Dominique thought about something. "How old are you?"

"4."

"And you're already reading well? Kudos to your parents." Arielle nodded. "My mommy said it was 'fundamental' to start young – whatever that means." Arielle hopped up the stairs licking her ice cream cone. Daniel, who had seen Dominique roaming through the office, was standing at the top with his arms crossed.

"Tsk. Tsk. Tsk. I expected more out of you, assistant."

Dominique sighed and went through the door. "I don't get paid to babysit." "Lose my niece again and you won't get paid at all." Dominique took a deep breath. "Should I take her back to the studio?"

"That won't be necessary. I'll have my assistant care for her for the rest of the day."

"I thought I was your assistant."

"That's what you get for thinking." Daniel walked off laughing. He had decided to promote Brian Gatsby, the former marketing intern who had pitched the name "No Press? No Stress." Since Monique was back, Dominique would assist Monique while Brian assisted Daniel and they would share the office that Dominique had once solely resided in. "What is this, battle of sexes," she questioned.

Monique said, "Mr. Ross tells me that you two were clashing heads so he decided to make some changes. Although you are no longer his assistant, you are still required to answer to him. And, if you have an issue with the way Mr. Ross 'snaps' at you, then you either go to Yasmine and she'll bring it to me or you contact me directly. You should not have been raising your voice at a supervisor."

Dominique sighed. "I know I lost my temper and I could've handled the situation better." Monique appreciated the honesty so she touched Dominique's shoulder. "I will be talking to Mr. Ross later on because one of the core values here at Mo's Mix is respect and it is not respectful for him to snap and expect you to come forth as if you're one of his pets. Next time something like this happens, talk to me, okay?" Dominique nodded and went to her office.

Monique looked at her niece. "Hey, busy body. What's this I hear about you running around the office?" Arielle wore a sheepish grin. "I'm sorry, auntie. But I was *so* hungry." Monique looked at the paper from Arielle's ice cream cone. "I see. Where'd you get money?"

"My daddy gave me this for emergencies."

Arielle held up a coin purse that was filled to the brim. "How did you know how much money to put in," Monique wondered. "My daddy taught me how to count money and told me how much each coin was worth." Monique nodded. "James is brilliant." Arielle grinned. "I'll tell him you said that." Monique took Arielle's hand. "Now, why don't you tell me what you were doing?" Monique and Arielle went back towards the studio while Arielle chatted a mile a minute.

Later in the day, Monique pulled up an old employee picture of Evan. "Was it this guy?" Camille shook her head. "No. I recognize that guy from somewhere but not my apartment. The one at my apartment was a little bit shorter and he had this kind of demonic look in his eye." Monique sighed. "Why would he visit you, though?"

"He said that I could help him destroy you or be plowed down in the destruction of your business."

"He really said all of that?"

Camille nodded. "Yeah. It creeped me out, honestly." "Why is April doing this? Because her mom used to own this building?" Camille sighed. "It has to be more. Who sold the building to you?" Monique thought about it. "Nathaniel something."

"Is it Nathaniel Ewing," Camille asked while she looked at the day's paper. "Yeah; that's him. Why?" Camille held the paper up for Monique to see. "He just became the CEO for Summerland Corporation." Monique looked closely at the paper. "That's the guy who sold me the building. What do you think his angle is?"

"A pawn in John's chess game." Monique raised her eyebrow. "So John and April are working together?" Camille shook her head. "More likely, April found out about her daddy's misdeeds and she's passive aggressively taking her anger out on you."

Monique sighed. "I can see why she's angry. He stole from his employees and he might've *raped* one of them? How sick is this man?" She took a pause. "Who would've guessed buying and remodeling an abandoned building would result in all of this?" Camille shrugged. "You just never know, Mo. And none of this came out until after you started your business."

"What if I moved Mo's Mix," Monique wondered. "You think that would end all of this?"

"Uh-uh. You eliminated Cocoa Puff on top of the fact that the building you operate from used to be her mother's beauty school before it was torched by her uncles."

"It's all so convenient." Monique vocalized. "This just doesn't make any sense." "How did you even find this building?"

"My mom told me about it," Monique admitted. "Next, am I going to find out she's somehow involved in this too?" Monique and Camille starting laughing because they thought the prospect of that was just ridiculous. While they chuckled, Attorney Mosby walked into the office. "Mrs. Ross-Cassells, I'm here to--"

Kaitlin paused when she saw Camille sitting there. "I didn't realize you were busy." Camille stood up. "What are *you* doing here?" Monique raised her eyebrow. "Cam, this is Kaitlin Mosby, the courtroom attorney for Mo's Mix. Do you know her?" Camille rolled her eyes. "I have the misfortune of being related to this woman; she's my sister." Monique looked from Camille to Kaitlin and back. "Oh, now I see it. How come you never talk about your siblings?" "I don't associate with them," Camille noted.

"Until you need legal help," Kaitlin countered. Monique raised her eyebrow again. "What's that supposed to mean?"

Kaitlin, who was trying to remain professional, folded her hands in front of her briefcase. "Camille, you should leave. There's important business to be handled." Camille warned, "Kaitlin cannot be trusted. She's a money hungry opportunist and I didn't really want to contact with her but I felt that I had no other choice."

"Why do you need legal help?" Monique queried. "We'll talk about that later," Camille replied as she left. Kaitlin sighed. "She resents the fact that I rose my stock while hers remained the same. Please don't listen to anything she says."

Monique didn't like the way Kaitlin was dismissing Camille so Monique told Kaitlin, "You didn't even need to comment on that situation. By doing so, you are proving yourself to be unprofessional; professionalism is a requirement here at Mo's Mix. If you wish to continue representing this business, I suggest you remain professional at **all** times."

Kaitlin took a deep breath. "I do apologize. But, I'm here about Samuel Lee." "What's the latest," Monique asked, skipping over Kaitlin's empty apology.

"After our outstanding performance in court yesterday, the jury's decision was almost set in stone. However, at the attorney hearing today, Lee's attorney pulled a tape of you and Mr. Ross discussing the upcoming case and Mr. Ross suggesting that you all dismantle the video cameras? This has created reasonable doubt. The jury doesn't believe that *you* had any involvement in the fire but, Mr. Ross, they're not so sure about."

Monique exhaled. "What tape are you talking about?" Bree had received a nice paycheck for recording the conversation and sending the tape to Lee using a dummy email. But, this was private information so Kaitlin didn't produce an answer. Monique continued, "Daniel clearly stated that he only wanted to dismantle those cameras to protect the reputation of Mo's Mix." Kaitlin said, "Mrs. Ross-Cassells, in order to effectively represent you, I need to know all the facts. You can tell me if this was an insurance scandal."

Monique shook her head. "This was *not* an insurance scandal. The fire was caused by a vindictive ex-entrepreneur." Kaitlin raised her eyebrow. "The court believes it was the work of disgruntled employees, though." "They were hired by April Spring – the vindictive ex-entrepreneur. She sent her pawns in to destroy Mo's Mix."

"If what you're saying is true, this definitely sounds like a revenge plot," Kaitlin mentioned like she didn't already know.

MO'S MIX: *Queen-dom*
(Part II)

Chapter XI – *In a few months, Andre has become a stay-at-home dad while Monique continues to protect her Queen-dom. Meanwhile, Camille and James hit a rough patch.*

4 MONTHS LATER

Monique was up late working on some annual reports when Emelia started crying. Because Monique didn't want to stop her work, she didn't move. Andre rolled over. "Mo, the baby just woke up."

"I know, but I'm busy."

"Doing what?" Andre opened his eyes and saw Monique over at her desk. "You're *still* working?" "The board is expecting these reports first thing in the morning." Andre sighed. "You can't pause for five seconds to see what our daughter needs?"

"Can't you do it?"

Andre groaned. "Of course I can. It's not like I don't do everything else around the house." "Dre, don't be a baby." "If I were a baby, you wouldn't care about me." Andre left the conversation there while he went to care for Emelia. When he got back, Monique asked, "What does that mean?"

"It means Emelia's your hobby, not your priority, which is what I feared."

"I took two months off to care for her."

Andre shook his head. "2 months is hardly even a starting point, Monique. This is your child, meaning you're gonna be caring for her the rest of your life." "No, I won't. You do all the work, remember?" Monique spat sarcastically. Andre exhaled. "Now, who's being the baby?"

"Still you."

Andre sighed and got back into bed. Not 25 minutes later, Emelia was crying again. 45 minutes after, she was crying again. Two hours after, she was hollering. Each time, Andre had to get up and console his child because work was more important to Monique. "It's Thursday," he noted in the morning. "What does that mean?"

"You forgot already – not surprising," Andre replied. Monique raised her eyebrow. "Forgot what? Your birthday's not until next month." Andre closed his eyes to remain calm. "You said, and I quote, 'I will take Thursdays and Fridays off to care for the baby'." Monique looked at her calendar, which she had marked accordingly.

"You're right, Dre." Since Monique didn't pick a fight, Andre decided he wouldn't either. "I'm sorry if I get angry with you, but it takes two to parent." Monique picked Emelia up. "I know." Monique looked down at Emelia. "Good morning, beautiful. You hungry?" Then, Monique got on her motherly duties.

Later in the afternoon, Monique was reading an article and Emelia was crawling in the living room. Suddenly, Monique heard something fall and her maternal instinct kicked in. Although Emelia wasn't hurt, Monique moved the baby away from the TV for fear the TV would crush the baby. "No," Monique said. Monique sat as a barrier between Emelia and the TV. "Don't crawl past mommy." Still, Emelia went towards the TV. Monique pulled her baby back once again. "No," she repeated. To prevent it from happening a third time, Monique placed Emelia in the playpen.

Emelia didn't like this so she started crying at the top of her lungs. Monique sighed and pulled Emelia out. When placing her daughter back on the carpet, Monique made sure to watch Emelia carefully. But, when Monique's phone rang – meaning Monique was distracted – Emelia crawled back towards the TV.

"Yes, mom, everything's fine. Emelia's…" Monique paused and snatched her daughter up from the TV area. "I told you no two times already. 'No' means no! Let me call you back, mom." Monique hung the phone up and hit Emelia's leg. "Maybe now you'll understand the concept of 'no'." At first, the pain didn't register. But, when it did, Emelia made sure the world knew.

"Where did that money come from?!"

"It was tips from the shop."

Camille shook her head. "I had narcs asking me if I knew Pedro Manning." "I don't know why you're coming to me about that. I don't mess with drug dealers."

"Not anymore, right?"

James let out a deep breath. "The shop was suffering so I took a loan from my buddy Damien. But, that was a one-time transaction. It's over with now." "I swear if I get taken in, I will name you." James groaned. "You won't get taken in. I promise you that wasn't drug money."

"Then why do I have narcs trailing me?!"

"I don't know!!"

"Don't scream at me!"

"You started it!"

Camille threw her hands up. "Because I lost my job! After all the failed job searching, I finally got a fulltime position and I lost it when the police began asking my boss about my affiliation with Manning." "I had nothing to do with that," James stated assuredly. "Maybe it's one of the guys you sleep with. You have like ten a month, after all."

Camille was not in the mood for James's smart mouth. "Get out," she ordered. James quickly thought about what he said. "I'm sorry. I didn't mean that." "Get out," Camille repeated. James tried to kiss Camille's neck but she squirmed away. James put his hands on her hips but Camille shoved him. "Get out!!" "You don't mean that."

Camille huffed. "I do, James. Get out!" When he didn't move, Camille shoved him again. "Get out!!" James grabbed her wrists. "You not gone keep pushing me." Camille yanked her wrists away. "You know I don't play that."

"You put your hands on me first."

"Because you won't get out," Camille pointed out. James looked her in the eye. "I'm sorry you lost your job but I didn't have any part in that." Camille shook her head while speaking. "See, I might've been more compassionate if you hadn't made that comment about my sex partners. But, since you did, I'm **done** being nice. Get out!"

James remained standing where he was so Camille charged at him with all her might. Again, James grabbed her wrists. When she felt his grip, Camille had a flash back to her abusive relationship. Thus, she started attacking James as if he were her abusive ex. James tightened his grip so that Camille would calm down. "Relax, okay?" The tighter James's grip became, the more Camille recalled the day she had gotten the scar. "Let go of me!!!!"

James finally let go once he realized he was reminding Camille of Donald. "I was only holding your wrists to calm you down. I didn't mean to scare you." Camille opened the door. "Just leave. Now." This time, James exited. And it was clear from the way Camille slammed the door that he wouldn't be back for a very long time.

"Ahmad Jordan is here to see you."

Monique raised her eyebrow. "Who is this?" "He's an FDA inspector and he's here for a tri-monthly lab inspection." Monique nodded. "Send him in and call my driver, please."

Mr. Jordan stuck his hand out when he stepped into Monique's office. "It's a pleasure to meet you, Mrs. Ross-Cassells." "Likewise, Mr. Jordan. But, what happened to Angela," Monique wondered while shaking Mr. Jordan's hand.

Jordan replied, "She left the agency recently." Monique nodded. "Just wondering. But, I should let you know that our labs have moved." She pulled a card from her purse. "This is the new address for future references." Mr. Jordan took it and put it into his wallet. "Is there a reason you moved?"

When she got a signal from Dominique, Monique stood. "My driver will take us to the laboratory. To answer your question, a fire occurred a little while back and it damaged the old labs beyond repair. So, my COO and I decided to shut those labs down and move to a building downtown."

Mr. Jordan asked, "What caused this fire?" "Investigation is still ongoing," Monique evaded. Mr. Jordan raised his eyebrow. "That doesn't sound too good. Do the police have any suspects?" "Right now, it's being ruled an accident. Evidence shows that some people were smoking behind the building one evening and they improperly put out their cigarettes."

"Were said people employees of yours?"

Monique sighed. "Sadly, yes."

As they walked into the garage, Mr. Jordan glanced at the quarantined former science wing. He focused specifically on a sign: SMOKING **IN** OR **NEAR** THIS BUILDING IS STRICTLY PROHIBITED. ANYONE CAUGHT SMOKING WILL BE <u>IMMEDIATELY</u> TERMINATED.

Ahmad noted, "I was doing some research about Mo's Mix and I found that you hired a number of new employees around January. Does this have anything to do with the fire?" Monique replied, "It does. Some employees left when they found out wages would be reduced. Other employees were laid off based on breach of company policies. Nothing out of the ordinary."

Mr. Jordan nodded. "The article then discussed a man named Evan Armoire and a woman named Donna Roberts, who were apparently let go because of internal dating. Yet, the article furthermore pointed out that that your then-fiancé was the courtroom attorney for Mo's Mix at the time of the firings, which would invalidate any claims of separating business from pleasure," Jordan argued.

"Fair point," Monique acknowledged. "But, given that you are just an inspector, I am not obligated to discuss confidential business matters with you."

Mr. Jordan chuckled. "Talking around the issue. Classic corporate move." Monique motioned for the car to come forward. As Jordan and Monique got into the car, he continued, "After reading that article, I did further research and some allegations claimed that Mr. Armoire and Ms. Roberts were involved in the fire and that's the real reason they were terminated. This correlates with the statements from Samuel Lee, Abigail Newhouse's brother." Monique gave the driver instructions then turned to Jordan.

"Mr. Jordan, I assure you that Mr. Armoire and Ms. Roberts were let go because they breached a company policy. Now that that has been said, I respectfully ask that you leave the subject alone." Jordan would not stop until he got answers. "How did you know they broke this policy?" "I'm not obliged to disclose that."

Jordan laughed. "Of course not. By doing so, you would have to admit that you were checking the security tapes and you saw them shacking it up in a car. But, by confessing that, you would then have to answer the question as to *why* you were watching security footage. I think you were distrustful because you knew something was off, Mrs. Ross-Cassells. Then, that fire made it obvious that someone was out to destroy you. This leads me to my next query: who's after you, Mrs. Ross-Cassells?"

Monique felt that she had given Jordan too many chances. So, instead of responding, she pulled out her phone to text Camille. Monique was silent for about 10 minutes. "Pleading the fifth?" Just then, Camille sent a full profile on Ahmad Jordan.

Monique read, "Ahmad Jordan graduated Magma Cum Laude at the top of his class from Champlain University. How Jordan got to the top is questionable, though. Rumor has it that he cheated, schemed, and destroyed in order to uphold a long held family reputation. Apparently, he has five brothers who all became doctors, lawyers, or corporate managers."

"To keep with tradition, Jordan had to knock down the little guy so that he would make his Muslim father proud. Goes to the Mosque faithfully. Has a wife named Fatima and…oh, what's this? In college, he had a *special* friend named Cecilia with whom he had a long term relationship. But, Jordan could never marry her because, upon registering with the Nation of Islam, Jordan was to take a Muslim wife." Monique took a breath. "Shall I continue?"

Mr. Jordan's face went blank. "Where did you find that information?" "I have my sources. So if you continue sticking your nose into foreign affairs, I'll instruct my source to send *this* picture to your wife." Monique showed her phone to Mr. Jordan. On the image, Jordan and Cecilia were in a very compromising position. "This is dated to last week, meaning that you're cheating on Fatima, right?"

Mr. Jordan exhaled. "I beg you to get rid of this. I apologize for speaking on something that doesn't concern me. Just please don't say anything to my Fatima. She'll be heartbroken." Monique took a deep breath and texted Camille.

Monique: Abort mission.

Camille: He wasn't sent by April?

Monique: Don't think so. He freaked out when he saw the picture.

Camille: Sigh. I'll destroy this info then.

Monique: Thanks, Cam. Ttyl.

While Mr. Jordan looked around the lab, Monique thought about her power play. Monique had never thought herself a dictator until then. *What am I capable of?* Daniel came over. "What's up?" "That inspector was talking recklessly so I had Camille find some information on him to shut him up. I never realized I could be so destructive."

Daniel rubbed Monique's shoulder. "Gotta defend the Queendom, right?" Monique thought on that statement. "Right. Let me see your keys." Daniel raised his eyebrow. "What?" "Let me see your keys. I'll drive your truck back to Mo's Mix and the driver can bring you and Jordan there once Jordan finishes his inspection."

Daniel gave Monique his keys. "What are you thinking of, sis? You have a determined look on your face." Monique smirked. "You'll see."

Monique grabbed the keys and got back to Mo's Mix as quickly as possible. In order to stop April's revenge plot, Monique realized she had to prove that Mo's Mix was there to stay. "Bree, schedule a press conference for Monday morning at 9 AM sharp. Dominique, call Attorney Mosby. Brian, fetch me a snack. I'm in the mood for something greasy and disgusting. Get moving, people!" Everyone got on their respective tasks and Monique clapped her hands. "It's going to take more than that to dethrone her highness," she asserted. "This is *my* Queen-dom and I will protect it at all costs."

An hour later, Kaitlin stared blankly at Monique. "You want to have a memorial?" Monique nodded. "Mhmm. We're coming on a year since Abigail was brutally murdered and I think it's only fair that we talk about it."

"What about your product release and your campaign?"

Monique gasped because she had an idea. "The hair show! The hair show could be in honor of Agent Abby. It can be called 'At Your Service'." Monique clapped her hands. "It's genius."

"It's risky," Kaitlin countered. "Since the jury is getting ready to reach a verdict, they may think this is a final move for you to plead your innocence."

Monique shook her head. "This is just what we need. The world must know that Abigail Newhouse's death was no accident. It was murder – cold-blooded murder facilitated by none other than April Spring, whose real name is Malaysia Summers, daughter of the most notorious white collar criminal ever to smear the streets of this once pristine city. The world must know the truth."

"It's not your job to tell it to them."

"It is, though. April wants to play dirty? I will drag her through the mud by that hideous blonde head of hers. And when she is ruined, she will be reminded that a self-hating biracial can*not* overthrow a Black Queen." Kaitlin put her hands on her hips. "So you're one of those people who think that biracials aren't black, huh?"

"You're hearing me incorrectly, Attorney Mosby. I don't respect Ms. Spring because she will only embrace her blackness to spite her father. April is black for convenience, but white for privilege. Therefore, she is a self-hating biracial. If you feel that any of that applies to you, you're probably just like her."

Kaitlin, who had never been spoken to in this way, put her hands on her hips. "I am *not* self-hating! I love being black." "Is that why you tried to take down one of Willowsville's only successful black businesses?"

Kaitlin laughed because she had been caught. "I don't know what you're suggesting Mrs. Ross-Cassells, but it's untrue." Monique sighed and pulled out the pictures Camille had taken of April and Kaitlin meeting at April's mansion. "Those are all doctored, obviously."

"Attorney Mosby, your time here is up. Please leave this office immediately and don't expect to ever be admitted on the premises again." While Brian escorted Kaitlin out, Monique rubbed her temples. *Just when I thought it was over.*

Meanwhile at Templeton University, Camille shook hands with her new boss. Camille had dug deep into the vaults just to find a viable reference. "My colleagues reviewed your tests and you've gotten some excellent recommendations from those Computer Science professors at Nia University so we've come to the consensus that you will be very suitable to teach at this prestigious institution. It's a shame we never found you sooner. Nonetheless, I'm happy that you'll be joining us here at Templeton-Willowsville..."

As Dr. Owens sang praises to Camille, Dominique prepared to meet her new advisor. Dominique quickly trekked towards the offices and she noticed that Dr. Owens – Dean of Information Science – was talking to a woman. "Guess that's her," Dominique murmured. As she drew closer, Dominique realized the woman was familiar.

Camille turned. "Hi. I'm Ms. Harrison, the newest computer science professor." Dominique stuck out her hand. "Dominique Thornberry." "Any relation to Juwan?" Camille joked. But the names were no coincidence. Dominique raised her eyebrow.

"You know my brother?" Since Dr. Owens saw that Camille and Dominique had much to discuss, she left. Afterwards, Camille responded, "Juwan and I met when I was walking past your father's school." Dominique nodded. "And, let me guess: Juwan tried to hit on you." Camille laughed. "He did, actually. Is something like that common for him?" Dominique rolled her eyes and responded, "Not unless they look like you. Juwan gravitates towards any biracial because he's the only one like that in our family."

"How come?" Camille wondered. Dominique noted, "My dad's first wife was crazy, which is why he only had one child out of Annabelle before getting himself an Angela." Camille chuckled. "You're very personable." "And you're very familiar," Dominique countered. Camille raised an eyebrow. "Am I?" "I work for Monique Ross-Cassells."

Camille let out a deep breath. "Small world." "Truly." Dominique and Camille began forming an advisor-student bond while Monique went home in glee. Emelia was crawling on the floor so Monique picked her child up and kissed Emelia's cheek. Andre laughed from the stove. "You seem happy."

Monique smiled. "I am, I am. We got the venue, so this hair show's really happening, Dre. I'm excited. Overjoyed. Thrilled." "Tell me more." Andre said as he carefully placed his quiche into the oven so that it wouldn't fall like the others had before. "Maybe later. Right now, I want to know why you're treating that quiche like it's Emelia." Andre sighed. "It's always the quiche that keeps messing me up with these auditions."

"How many times has it been now?"

"3."

Monique pulled her necklace out of Emelia's mouth. "And that's $500 every time. This is going to start getting expensive, Dre. You know Mo's Mix is getting back on its feet and taxes are eating up that money from the community center. Are you sure you still want to pursue this dream?" Andre closed the oven door slowly. "I'm very sure. Besides, I'm not even touching our money to pay for auditions. I have another source of income."

Again, Monique had to pull her necklace from Emelia's mouth. "Oh? Do tell." "Georgiana and I have this little venture that--" "Would you stop?!" Monique yelled. For the third time, Emelia was playing with Monique's necklace. Emelia started crying so Andre took her into his arms. "Your mommy didn't mean it, okay?"

Once Emelia was calm, Dre said, "Mo, she's a baby." Monique rolled her eyes. "And this is a $200 necklace. I would rather it not have slobber on it." "You sound so considerate," Andre mumbled sarcastically.

"Don't get me wrong. I love Emelia. I just wish she wouldn't put everything in her mouth."

Andre explained, "That's a part of infancy, which you would realize if you actually took care of her instead of putting all your attention on your lovechild known as Mo's Mix." Monique groaned. "Please don't tell me this is about to be one of your tangents."

"It is," Andre confirmed. "Emelia is just as much your child as she is mine. But, when was the last time you actually spent a day with her, huh? When was the last time you mentally calculated her feeding schedule or programmed your day around her sporadic naps? When did you have to change her diaper three times in one hour because she had diarrhea or change your shirt multiple times because she didn't want to eat? When, Mo? When? Right now, you're acting like you love that business more than you do your family."

Monique huffed. "Andre, I have a duty to my company."

"What about your duty to your baby?"

"Mo's Mix *is* my baby," Monique declared. "Your *actual* baby," Dre countered. "You know, the one you carried for nine months then spent 6 ½ hours pushing out? The one who represents the love that you and I share? What about her, Mo?"

Monique exhaled and put her arms out. "Let me hold her. Please." Andre gave Emelia back to Monique. Monique clutched her daughter tightly. "I love her, Dre. And I love you too. I just *have* to be at Mo's Mix all the time because we are in post-crisis mode right now."

"Isn't that why you brought Daniel in?"

"Yes, but Daniel is very domineering. I fear if I let him have too much control he'll make Mo's Mix his own."

"So, in other words, he's just like you, except a man?"

Monique shook her head. "Nah, Dre. Daniel's a lot worse than me."

"You should've been done a half hour ago! What's the hold up?"

"The delivery truck hasn't come yet and we've run out of materials so we're waiting until it shows up."

Daniel went to pick a phone. "Did you think to call the supplier or were you not taught how to use a one of these?" At the lab-workers silence, Daniel continued, "Furthermore, did you become a lab-worker because you were too stupid to get a better job?" Astonished, the worker quickly scurried off. Daniel started reviewing the performance reports and saw something he didn't like. "MARCUS!!!!"

The head of science came forward. "Yes, sir?" Daniel wondered, "Why does performance stop for an hour on a daily basis?" "In your email, you said that lunch should be taken at 1," Marcus explained.

Daniel scoffed. "I know what I typed but I also specified that lunch breaks were to last only 15 minutes – 20 if the line is slow." "That's not enough time for everyone to eat. The cafeteria downstairs gets very packed because there are three other businesses in this building."

"Then tell your workers to have their mommies pack lunches. I'm sure half of them here still live with their parents anyway!"

Completely speechless, Marcus nodded and went off. As for Daniel, he checked his pulse. "I'm too old for this, man." Daniel's worry lines showed his age better than his birth certificate. Lena, the office intern, came to him with water. "You seem like you might need it." Daniel knocked the bottle out of her hand. "Know your place, intern." Lena quickly darted off. Daniel, who actually *did* need the water, picked it up and drank from it.

"Oh, baby, you're so stressed," a voice said. Knowing the tone anywhere, Daniel turned. "Malcolm, you are not allowed here." Malcolm smiled. "I am, though. Mrs. Ross-Cassells just hired me." "I'll have you fired then."

"But she adores me, Daniel."

"Do you feel validated by love from a woman? I thought you were gay."

Malcolm chuckled. "Honey, I am – proud of it too. But, it gives me great pleasure to know that your sister overrode *your* decision, meaning she's in charge and you're not. She runs you, Daniel." Daniel shook his head. "She does not."

"You all may be in that c-suite together but I assume the pie has been split 60-40?" Daniel didn't answer. Malcolm continued, "Or is it 70-30? 80-20? How much power do you *really* have?"

"Enough to destroy you if you come in here questioning my authority again." Malcolm patted Daniel's shoulder. "Your hubris is cute but we both know who wears the pants in that business relationship. Little hint: it ain't you." Feeling satisfied, Malcolm left. Feeling slighted, Daniel was suddenly determined to exert as much power as he could.

"I think Yasmine needs to go, Dominique and Brian should be regulated to desks, and you need to shrink your tech wing. You have 12 people doing the work of 6."

Monique stared blankly. "We're supposed to be grocery shopping and looking for Christmas gifts, not discussing business." Daniel sighed. "I know. I'm just making some suggestions." "After Thanksgiving, I will take them under advisement."

"Meaning you won't consider them at all."

Monique smiled. "Brother, you know me so well. But I happen to like where Mo's Mix is at now." "Even if it's ineffective? Yasmine should leave because, if our employees need a therapist, they can pay for one on their own time. Dominique and Brian should not be in an office because that makes them feel like they're important when, really, they're glorified interns. Finally--" Monique put her hand up. "Off the clock, Daniel. Talk to me on Monday." Daniel huffed but still decided he would wait before trying to assert his machismo.

James came riding on a pink bike. "You think Ari will love this?"

Daniel shrugged. "Sure. It almost screams 'Sorry I've been cheating on your mommy for the duration of our marriage.'" James cut his eyes. "I bet you would've wanted this when you were her age and you would've asked if it came with a pink dildo so you could practice being a f-." Monique cut her eyes. "James, you know we don't use the 'f' word."

Daniel commented, "For you at that age, we should've gotten handcuffs to symbolize the way you must dominate every woman you're involved with." James scoffed. "That's part of being a man – having dominance. But, you wouldn't know anything about being a man since you enjoy living like a woman."

"Like a woman? That's sexist," Monique asserted.

James put his hand in Monique's face. "This is between me and our *sister*. Stay out of it." Monique moved James's hand from her face. "James, don't be disrespectful. You need to get your misogyny in check."

"Maybe I have to overcompensate because my brother decided to forego his manhood so that he could become someone's personal bitch." Daniel, who had heard enough, socked James dead in the eye. "You owe me over $3,000 for all the times I financed your infidelity. If you don't get that to me in the next few weeks, I **will** come after you."

Angrily, Daniel stalked off. James looked up from the ground and saw Monique's disappointed face. "Aren't you going to help me up?" He asked. Monique, completely outdone, went over to the next aisle. Andre returned from buying gifts for his family. "What's going on," Dre wondered. "I could've sworn I heard someone fall." Then, Andre saw James on the ground. So, Dre offered James his hand. "Thanks," James said while standing up. "How'd you deal with it?"

"Deal with what?"

"Having a faggot brother."

"For starters, I've never called my brother that. Next, I accepted that that's how God made him."

"Why would God create that? If this world's full of gays, then there will be no babies."

Andre sighed. "Which is why not every man likes men and not every woman likes women. The Bible says that God makes us in His likeness and that He loves *all* His children."

Although Andre was making valid points, James didn't want to hear them. "You're blasphemous," James decided while walking off. Monique, who had been listening, came towards Andre. "At least you tried." Andre shrugged. "Some people will forever be convicted into their misguided beliefs."

Speaking of convictions, Camille decided to reassess hers. After work one evening, she took off her shoes, pulled her hair into a ponytail, and dropped to her knees. "Dear God," she began. For weeks, Camille had taken to worship in the hopes that by finding God again, she could find her lost soul. Camille thought about her repentance and promised God she would be His loyal follower if He forgave her. Camille thought that by getting the teaching position, God was granting her a second chance. "I know I don't deserve it but thank you anyway."

She had been able to pay off the loan sharks, give her attorney his money, and even purchase her first car. Seemingly, Camille was starting over. Alas, Camille would soon have a harsh blast from the past. She was in the middle of prayer when she heard loud pouncing on the door. "Camille, open up," Martin ordered. Camille finished her prayer and looked through the peephole. Outside, two officers stood with Martin.

"What's going on?"

"Open up and they'll tell you." As soon as Camille unlocked the door, the officers barged in and arrested her. They had traced money she had spent back to Pedro Manning and now Camille was being taken in for drug trafficking.

This had been perpetrated by April's malicious half-brother. He did some research and found that Teasers was funded by drug money. Instead of bringing down people who meant nothing to April, Devin had paid Camille's ex-boss to say that Camille was involved with drugs and that was why she had left the club after only 2 months of being there.

Since Camille had come from foster homes and had a record of street fighting, the police bought the story. "What do you know about Pedro," one officer questioned. "I don't even know who the fuck Pedro is." "You'd better watch your tone," a second officer warned. Camille sighed. "I don't know who Pedro is," she repeated in a calmer voice.

They held her for hours trying to get information. But, Camille couldn't speak on what she didn't know. So, she remained quiet. "What, you're protecting the profit?" "I am asserting my 5th amendment right, which encompasses freedom from self-incrimination."

While Camille made it clear that she knew her rights, Devin continued with his latest mission. "You need evidence," April told him. "We've got evidence," Donna mentioned. She pulled up a profile of Donald Johnson. She had received his name from Kaitlin, the "money hungry opportunist."

"Donald dropped out of Nia University his sophomore year," Donna stated.

"Where is he now?"

Evan found an article about Donald. "In Vieille Ville, as expected. He and Camille dated on and off throughout high school and Camille even followed him to college although he had another girlfriend at the time."

"Then, he put Camille in the hospital," Devin added as he pulled up a picture. "They got into a huge fight because he was mad about her having an abortion. Next thing you know, she has a gash on her head."

"Is it safe to assume that's why they broke up," April joked. When no one laughed at her dark humor, April cleared her throat. "Tough crowd. Any who, what's his occupation and how can it be used to our advantage?"

"Might work for Pedro Manning, according to these pictures that I found."

April smiled. "Perfect. What's say we send an anonymous tip to the police about Camille and Donald's previous relationship? That would really invalidate her innocence." Donna lifted the phone. "On it." While she called and prepared her fake voice, Evan stood in front of Nicole. "A year ago, I was the fearful and you were the agitator. Much has changed in a year, huh?"

"I'm not afraid of you, Evan. I made you this way."

"A woman cannot make a man something he's not already."

Nicole laughed. "I guess that's why neither Donna nor your wife could make you faithful." Evan slapped Nicole with all his might. When Nicole tried to get up and fight back, he put his knee on her back and asked April, "How shall I handle this indignant creature?"

"Do with her what you want," April stated. "She's worthless to me now." Evan smirked. "Follow me," he ordered. Nicole scoffed. "I ain't following you nowhere." Evan banged Nicole's head into the ground then carted her off to a back room. Donna wore a sad look when she heard Nicole's screams and the sounds of the headboards hitting the walls. April rubbed Donna's shoulder. "Sweetheart, you were the PR – i.e. a rook we had to capture to get closer to the Queen. I hope you didn't think whatever you and Evan had was *serious*."

"He said he'd leave his wife for me."

April cackled. "Men say a lot of things, don't they? But, back to business – did you send the tip?" Donna sighed. "Done. Camille's about to be booked." In that moment, Camille was put in handcuffs. "Where are you taking me?!" Her eyes got big when the prison bars came in sight. "I didn't do anything!!" "Your ex is one of Pedro's workers."

"What does that have to with me?!"

"We have reason to believe you are still involved with him."

This "reason" was the discovery of text messages between Donald and Camille that Devin had retrieved from Camille's phone. Devin had found some naked pictures exchanged from Donald to Camille and vice versa. These were all from many months before, but the time stamp on the pictures matched the days that Pedro had resurfaced. Plus, Camille's old boss had named her. So, the officers threw Camille into the cell. "You'll have one call in 10 minutes," the first officer said. "You can't do this!!" "We have evidence, little missy. I think we can."

"I'm innocent." The officer walked off laughing. Camille's new cellmates cackled too. "We all innocent, sugar," the leader, who was the biggest in the cell, noted.

Camille took note of the grisly appearances around her. "I'm not like you all. I'm *actually* innocent." The large woman stood up. "Just because you 'look' clean don't mean a thing." "This is a misunderstanding," Camille cried. "I shouldn't even be here." As tear drizzled from Camille's eyes, the cellmates could not contain their laughter.

Camille told them, "You're all insensitive because you *chose* to subscribe to your ascribed statuses. I'm **not** one of you." The 4 women didn't appreciate Camille's attitude so they surrounded her. "Keep talking and I'll show you why I got in here," a second cellmate cautioned. The big lady pushed Camille forward. "You better realize who you're speaking to." Camille whipped her head and stepped in the woman's face.

"You better watch who you put your hands on."

"Or what?"

"Push me again and see," Camille warned.

The leader was much, much bigger than Camille so it seemed that the leader would have the advantage. Thus, the hefty woman shoved Camille again. "Do something." Camille usually suppressed her fighter mentality but it came back out that day. Camille kicked the leader in the stomach then grabbed the leader's hair and pushed the leader's face into the cell door. "I told you to back off."

The other inmates didn't like seeing their leader be handled in this way so they grabbed Camille's hair and pulled her to the ground. Then, they started stomping on her face. Once Camille stopped fighting back, the ring leader stomped on Camille's ear so hard that it started bleeding. At that point, Camille was down for the count and the guards came to get her out of there.

"Ms. Harrison, come with us."

"Did someone post a bond?"

One guard laughed. "Wishful thinking, huh? You can make your phone call now." The other guard stood to block Camille's cellmates from escaping while his partner led Camille to the phones. "You all didn't even help me." "We saw the way you slammed that girl's face into the bar. We didn't think you would need any help."

"But, it's your duty as a guard to protect the inmates. Plus, there were four of them and one of me." The guard pulled a tissue from his pocket. "Take this as a sign of my remorse," he said condescendingly. Camille scoffed and snatched it. "Asshole." "I've heard worse." He threw Camille towards the phones. "You got 15 minutes. Use them wisely." Camille blotted her ear and tried to think of someone she could call. Since Monique's number was the only one Camille knew by heart, this was who Camille called.

"This is the longest I've ever been away from Emelia. It feels weird," Andre voiced.

Monique nodded. "It really does. But, my mom was begging to spend some time with her grandchild." "Weren't you supposed to pick Emelia up after we went shopping?" Monique thought about it. "Oh, I was. Let me head over there. You think you can prepare dinner while I'm gone?"

"What would you like, my Queen?"

Monique raised her eyebrow. "Is that sarcasm?" Dre shook his head. "Not this time. All jokes aside, you are my beautiful Nubian Queen and when you took me as your King, it became my duty to provide for whatever you needed financially, emotionally, sexually, etc."

Monique smiled. "I like the sound of that. This evening, her highness would like to be surprised." Andre kissed her shoulder blade then he kissed her. "Your wish is my command." Dre went to start his gumbo and Monique headed to the car. On the way there, she received a call from Willowsville Correctional Facilities. "Yes I accept the charges. Cam, is that you? What's-- Wait, what? That doesn't make any…of course. Of course. Hold tight, okay? I'll be there shortly."

Monique hung up and booked it to her mother's house, where James was selling his sob story. "Ma, I didn't even really provoke him. He just has this chip on his shoulder because he knows the world hates abominations like him." Mrs. Ross sighed. "Yes, but you don't have to remind him of his sin every chance you get." Monique knocked on the screen door. "Hey, mom."

Mrs. Ross rushed over. "Oh, thank God you're here. Your daughter has been crying for a half hour." Monique picked Emelia up and felt something damp underneath the baby. "When was the last time you changed her?

"3 hours ago. I didn't see any more diapers in the bag."

Monique bounced Emelia up and down to calm the baby. "You didn't think to – I don't know – go to the store and buy some more?" Mrs. Ross rolled her eyes. "Monique Laclare Ross, I don't know who you're getting snippy with. For your information, I was baking all day. And, just to be clear, I only offered to watch Emelia because I haven't spent any time with my grandbaby but, if you gone catch an attitude, this babysitting service ends right here and right now."

Monique let out a deep breath. "What about dad? Couldn't he run to the store?" "He didn't feel like it." Monique shook her head and put Emelia into the carrier. Then, Monique quickly started packing everything. "You in a rush," Mrs. Ross wondered. "I have to drop Emelia off at home then run down to the county jail to get Camille out." James sat up straight when he heard that. "Camille's in jail?"

Monique rolled her eyes. "Didn't I *just* say that?" James raised his eyebrow. "What did I do to you?" "Have you forgotten what went down in the store earlier?" Mrs. Ross put her hands on her hips. "Little girl, stay out of that. That's men's business."

"You know, that's why women are still oppressed: women like you don't address unjust shit because y'all are too busy trying to stay in a 'woman's' place." "You watch your mouth when you speak to me," Mrs. Ross ordered. "Shit, shit, shit. And it smells to me like Emelia took a *shit* and you didn't clean it up." "You should've packed more diapers."

Monique opened the side of the diaper bag. "I did! But, knowing you, you were so concerned with your cakes that you didn't think to check the *entire* bag." Mrs. Ross cut her eyes. "Don't you have a friend to bail out?" Translation: Get out of my house.

"I'll be out of your hair just as soon as I ensure my baby doesn't get diaper rash." Monique took Emelia to the bathroom and removed the dirty diaper. As Monique was about to put the new diaper on, Emelia grabbed her feet so that they wouldn't be in Monique's way. Monique thought this was the cutest thing ever. Mo put on the new diaper then held her baby close to her. "I love you so much, little girl. Promise me you won't ending up resenting your own mother." Emelia smiled wide and this gave Monique all the assurance she needed. Monique thought about her daughter's beautiful smile all the way to the front of her parents' house.

In the driveway, James was leaning on Monique's car. "What do you want?" "I want to go with you to see Camille." Monique shook her head. "You don't need to get involved in this." "Why not?"

"You have a *wife*, James." James scoffed. "You say that like marriage actually means something. Marriage is a transaction. You and your spouse sign contracts, aka marriage papers, and then you *belong* to each other. It's a business deal, Mo. A real bond don't exist on paper."

"That's **your** marriage," Monique clarified. James shrugged. "Whatever you say. But let me come with you." "What about your escalade?" "The bank is looking for it so I'm hiding it here for a while."

Monique let out a deep breath. "Wow. Just wow. Get in."

At home, Dre announced, "I'm making gumbo." He looked up from his pot and noticed that Monique still wore her purse and shoes. "Are you heading out again?"

"Yeah. Camille's in trouble."

Andre raised his eyebrow. "Legal trouble?"

"Yep."

"Should I come too then?"

Monique shook her head. "No. Just stay here with Emelia." "Okay. Call me if you need anything." Monique went over and kissed Andre. "I will. I love you, baby." Andre rubbed her back. "I love you too."

Though she was in a rush, Monique lingered in Andre's arms for a while. "Is everything okay?" He finally asked. Monique replied, "Not entirely. James said something about marriage and it bothered me." "As you've pointed out, James is a bothersome person."

This statement opened up a conversation that Andre had been avoiding. "What did he say to you when you all got into that argument?" Monique asked. Andre finally admitted, "I told him I don't lie to you and he told me I don't lie to you yet, that I'm your lap dog, you're marrying a woman, and that my brother is the 'f' word just like his."

Monique shook her head. "James really is something else." Andre kissed her. "But, you know I love you, Mo. So whatever he had to say doesn't apply to us."

"You're right, Dre. Love you too." Monique kissed Andre. "I'll be back." Andre kissed Monique again then put Emelia in her high chair. As Dre finished up his gumbo, Emelia sat and laughed at the way he sang to himself. Loving this precious moment, Monique reminded herself that Andre and James were not one in the same.

Chapter XII – *Monique continues her reign as "Queen Mo" while Andre begins to build his own empire. There are a few deterrents along the way, however.*

ONE HOUR LATER

"LIAR!!!"

Posing as Camille's attorney, Monique used some lawyer lingo she learned from Andre to plead Camille's case. In under an hour, Camille was released on the basis of hearsay. The evidence presented, Monique had argued, was vague and therefore could not be used to incriminate Camille. Despite the fact that she was out of police custody, Camille still had words for James in the car. "You told me it wasn't drug money!! You liar!"

"I'm not, though!"

Camille wasn't hearing it. "I could get fired, James! Do you not realize how bad this looks on a professor?"

"I'll have Brian clear your record," Monique offered. But, that wasn't what Camille was really concerned about. Someone she trusted might have gotten her thrown in jail. "How could you just betray me like this, James?" "It wasn't me!" James screamed. "Then who was it?!" As Camille yelled back, the bandage on her ear fell off. "Ow," she said. "Mo, do you have a napkin?"

James went in the glove compartment and started to grab one. "I asked Mo," Camille pointed out. James scoffed. "Don't be pompous." He turned back to give Camille the napkin and he bore witness to her fresh wounds. "What happened to your face?"

Camille snatched the napkin. "Jail." "You were running that motor mouth of yours, huh?" "How 'bout you shut the fuck up talking to me," Camille spat. James backed off because he knew she was in no mood for jokes. Monique asked, "What's the problem here? I'm lost." Camille explained, "Your brother set me up. Months ago, he gave me money 'to help me out' and he claims it was tips from the shop."

"It *was*! Why won't you believe me?"

"You're a pathological liar!" Camille hollered. "You lie to your wife on a daily basis by telling her that you love her!" "Leave Laila out of this!"

"I will not! I've allowed you play me for a fool for far too long. I'm done, James!" Monique had arrived in front of Camille's apartment so Camille quickly hopped out of the car.

In her apartment, Camille threw her purse to the ground and cried her eyes out. When Camille had finally calmed down, she noticed that a card had flown out from purse. Since it was the business card from Juwan, Camille took that as a sign from God she needed to focus on her relationship with Juwan and leave James in the past.

"Auntie Mo!!!" Arielle came from school excited as ever to be back at Mo's Mix, which had become her mainstay ever since Daniel learned of her skill. Monique caught Arielle in her arms. "Hey, big girl." Laila stepped forward with three other women. Dominique announced, "These women are Laila Ross, Mahalia Hamilton, Angelique Newman, and Tatiana McNeil. Laila would like to speak you about a business inquiry, Mahalia is interested in becoming a vendor for the expo, and Angelique and Tatiana are hair models who would like to walk in the show."

"Who got here first?"

"They all arrived at once."

Since Monique didn't want to be partial, she did eenie-meenie-miney-mo in her head and landed on Mahalia. "Ms. Hamilton, please step inside. Ms. Newman, Ms. McNeil, and Mrs. Ross, you all may sit in our waiting area and Brian will get you some water." Arielle looked up. "What about me? I didn't hear my name." Monique smiled and waved Dominique over. "Dominique will show you your tasks for the day." Arielle skipped off with Dominique and Monique got down to business.

Once Mahalia and the models were filling out applications, Monique called Laila into her office. "What can I help you with?" "You've seen the hair that I do, right?" Monique nodded. "I have. If ever I decide that I want another sew-in, I'll definitely come to you. You do great work."

Laila smiled. "Thanks. I'm here because I'm trying to start an online hair shop called Inches Please. It would feature a blog for my different hairstyles, a personal page of testimonials from all the girls whose weaves I've done and also testimonials from the girls I sell hair to. Then, there will be a page for appointments. Finally, I want to have a storefront where I'll sell the bundles I've made."

Monique raised her eyebrow. "You make bundles?"

Laila nodded. "Yes. That's actually how I came up with the name 'Inches Please.' I'm coming to you because I need money to build a high-quality website and to satisfy other initial business expenses. Since Mo's Mix is in the cosmetics industry, I was wondering if you would like to invest into Inches Please. Before you come to any decision, though, I have some things to show you: a record of sales from the shops I've been at, sales for the bundles, and pictures of my very satisfied clients."

Laila placed a binder in front of Monique. "I know you might think that because I didn't finish college I might not be qualified but I seriously think you should consider it." Monique told Laila, "I will. We're pretty busy with the show coming soon so I could schedule a meeting with you on…" Monique pulled up her calendar. "January 8th. Is that do-able?"

"That's perfect. That way, I can show you all the holiday styles I'm going to do."

"It's a plan then."

Monique had Brian schedule the meeting while she rehearsed what she would say to the press. 45 minutes later, Monique announced, "Presently, the jurors prepare to reach a decision regarding the death of Abigail Newhouse. Though some evidence suggested that foul play from this company was involved, there is stronger evidence confirming her death was in no way the fault of Mo's Mix; it has been ruled an accident. Even so, Mo's Mix wishes Abigail Newhouse's family the best and we hope Abigail is resting peacefully.

"To fully assert that Mo's Mix cherishes all its employees dearly, I am proud to announce that our first annual hair show will be in honor of Ms. Newhouse, who was taken too soon. The show will be entitled *At Your Service* and it will run from Thursday December 17th – Sunday December 20th at the Rockwell Convention Center.

"On Thursday, there will be an expo featuring Mo's Mix's sponsors and friends and there will be a meet and greet with the models slated to walk in the show. On Friday, there will be an activity day with events for all ages and, that evening, there will be a benefit concert sponsored by *Sull*-ful Records."

Monique went to her next card. "On Saturday, there will be 4 hair shows and each show will feature a different set of models so tickets can be purchased accordingly. Sunday morning, there will be a memorial service for Abigail Newhouse with words from those of us who knew her."

Monique went to another notecard. "Finally, there will be one comprehensive show on Sunday featuring all models. Single tickets or weekend passes have been made available on our website: www.mosmix.com/hairshow. For further information, please visit this website." Monique went to her final note card.

"To conclude, Mo's Mix deeply regrets the death of Abigail Newhouse and we wish we could have prevented it. Thank you all for listening. Any questions?"

Carlos Lockwood, the constant whistleblower, shot his hand up. "Carlos Lockwood of Trinity Magazine. Mrs. Ross-Cassells, why is it that Mo's Mix took *so* long to address Abigail Newhouse's death?" "In order to avoid hearsay, we preferred that her death was kept private."

"How does her brother feel about this? He's been *so* vocal, after all."

"We have not spoken to Samuel Lee."

"Why not," Carlos wondered. Monique knew what Carlos was doing so she gave him a half-smile and looked towards Margot, the press conference coordinator. "Next question," Margot said. A woman raised her hand. "Percy Ellis of the Times. Isn't it a little convenient that this announcement falls right as the verdict is being made, Mrs. Ross-Cassells? Are you trying to save face?"

Monique replied, "What you view as incidental is a mere coincidence, Ms. Ellis. Mo's Mix has been planning this hair show for months so it has no ties to the jury's decision."

"True, but was dedicating the entire event to Abigail Newhouse a 'mere coincidence' as well?"

Monique gave another half-smile and looked towards Margot again. "One more question and that will be the last one," Margot stated. Monique pointed to man in grey who seemed rather familiar. "Tristan Bell of TVA. Ms. Ross, you've spoken so much about Abigail but not about the allegations concerning your former employees. Then, you had your PR address those claims instead of you addressing them yourself. Care to explain that?"

Monique took a deep breath. "It's Mrs. Ross-Cassells, sir. And, working for TVA, the city's largest TV studio, I'm sure you understand how busy the workplace can get. Mo's Mix's PR only spoke on my behalf because I was handling other business. But since you're so very inquisitive, what would you like to know about those claims, Mr. Bell?"

"Are they true?"

"That was supposed to be the last question."

Monique told Margot, "He's fine. Why does the validity of those claims interest you, Mr. Bell?"

"If they are true, it would expose you as a liar who got rid of those people not because of 'internal dating' but because they started the fire. Admit it: you hired *arsonists*, Ms. Ross."

Monique looked the man in the eye and realized it was Evan, the former CFO. "For the last time, I am Mrs. Ross-Cassells and this press conference is over." Monique stepped down from the podium and went back upstairs. Bree, who had been watching the whole showdown, said, "Job well done. I admire the way you kept your composure while addressing those ludicrous rumors."

"Thank you, Bree. How are ticket sales looking?"

Bree pulled out her Jotter. "They're skyrocketing. I guess I'm not the only one who admires your candor." "Great. Great. This is all great." Monique walked up the stairs feeling good about herself. Alas, James waited in Monique's office with Dominique and Arielle. "There's news," he said.

Since sending Camille to jail had failed, Devin had decided to use another method of torture. He gave the police a tip about Donald's involvement with Pedro Manning and – due to overwhelming evidence – Donald was hauled off to jail.

Devin visited Donald there. Donald wondered why this unfamiliar person was offering to post his bail. "Who are you?"

"Doesn't matter. Take a look at this." Devin showed Camille's mugshot. "She got put away too?" Devin then slid a picture of Camille being released. "She gave a name and she was released."

"Why does that matter to me?"

"How do you think you got in here?"

Realizing what Devin was suggesting, Donald started going into "Don" mode. Don was Donald's maleficent alter-ego. "That lying snitch." Devin saw that Donald's eye had a Mr. Hyde kind of glare to it and this made Devin happy. "You want revenge now, don't you?"

Donald didn't respond but instead nodded to confirm that he and Devin were on the same page. Subsequently, Devin paid Donald's bail, after which Devin handed Camille's address to Donald. That same day, Dr. Owens requested a meeting with Camille; Dr. Owens was troubled by the bruises on Camille's face. "Is everything okay, Ms. Harrison?" "Yes. I just got into a fight."

"That must have been some fight. Those are some pretty nasty scars you have."

Camille sighed. "I thought my make-up had covered them."

"Make-up can't hide all blemishes," Dr. Owens aphoristically noted. But, since Camille said she was okay, Dr. Owens let the issue go. After signing out, Camille dashed home to prepare for her date with Juwan. 45 minutes later, she was skipping down the stairs. Before Camille could even get to Juwan's car, though, Donald was charging at her. "You said we were cool, you lying ass snitch!" Donald jumped on Camille and pushed her neck into the ground.

"I told you I was sorry for all the times I hit you and you decide to pull this?!"

Juwan hopped from his car. "What do you think you're doing?!" He dashed over but, by the time Juwan got to Camille, Donald had vanished. Completely astonished, Camille held her neck while the trauma set in. In the hospital, she continued to hold her neck in the same manner. "She's been like that for hours," Juwan stated. "PTSD at its finest." James mumbled as he pushed a sleeping Arielle up onto his shoulder. Monique stood in shock. "Cam, who did this?"

"D...D...."

"Donald?" Hearing that name, Camille burst into tears. Monique sat next to Camille on the bed and hugged Camille tightly. Over in the corner, James looked Juwan up and down. "Who are you?"

"Juwan."

"Why are you here?"

"For moral support. Is there a problem with that?"

James sighed. "There's no problem. I've just never seen your face before."

"You might want to get used to it," Juwan asserted. While he and James shared an awkward silence, Camille cried into Monique's shoulder. Realizing that the friends needed a moment alone, James and Juwan migrated to the waiting area. "Are you her boyfriend?" James asked to break the awkward silence that had only gotten worse by the minute.

"Yeah. It's only been a few months so at least I know early on about her baggage."

James shook his head. "Camille doesn't have 'baggage'. Donald is just a guy from her past who clearly isn't over her." Juwan raised his eyebrow. "How would you know that?" "We've been friends for years." This was mostly true, but Juwan could see a longing look in James's eye. "Are you all *close* friends?" Juwan wondered. Though he had Camille's attention, he knew her heart was elsewhere.

James let out a deep breath. "That other woman in there is my sister and she's also Camille's best friend. That's how Camille and I know each other." Juwan nodded. "Oh okay. Just wondering."

James replied, "You'll never have to worry about Camille betraying you. She's loyal because that's the kind of treatment she wants from a man. Camille may have this really tough exterior, but she's a sweetheart once you get to know her. She's very loving. She's also funny and…and smart. Quick witted too.

James sighed. "Let me tell you something about Camille: most of the time, she's running that slick mouth of hers but she's serious when need-be. That's the type of woman you get to be with."

"It sounds like you've already been with her," Juwan pointed out. James was revealing himself, he realized. Because he wanted Camille to be happy – even if that wasn't with him – James stopped his mind from thinking of all the reasons he loved Camille. "How'd you know to call Monique anyway?" He asked to change the subject.

"Her assistant Dominique is my sister and I texted Dominique about it. How'd *you* hear about what happened?"

"I was going to Mo's Mix to pick up my daughter and Dominique relayed the news to me." At that moment, Arielle came running over. "Here you go, daddy!" Ever since James had taught her how to use a vending machine, Arielle was eager to use every vending machine she saw. She brought James back some chips. "Aw, thanks baby girl. Did you get yourself anything?"

Arielle showed her empty coin purse. "No. I ran out of money." James laughed and opened the chips before handing them to Arielle. "Take them." "Thank you, daddy." Arielle eagerly ate her chips while Monique stepped out of the room with Camille. "The doctors said that because there wasn't a lot of physical damage, Camille can go home."

"You want me to drive her?" James wondered. When Juwan raised his eyebrow, Monique said, "*I'll* drive her." She and Camille left together. Afterwards, Juwan looked at James. "So you and Camille are *just* friends, right?"

"That's right."

"Let's hope I don't find out otherwise." With that said, Juwan disappeared. Arielle looked at her father. "Is Camille sick?" "No. She just got hurt."

"She has a lot of booboos on her face," Arielle noted.

"In her heart too," James lamented.

"Where have you been?!" Lester yelled. Juwan was Lester's only son and therefore the only eligible heir to the Thornberry Academy empire whenever Lester decided to retire. "The candidates are waiting on you."

Juwan signed in for the day. "I was at the hospital with my girlfriend, which I put in the text you probably ignored."

Lester shook his head. "If I pass this school down to you, I need to know that you're going to be focused on what's important." "Carrying on *your* legacy, right?" Lester rubbed Juwan's shoulder. "It's *our* legacy, son." Juwan shrugged his father's hand off and started putting on his uniform. Lester, who knew his son's heart was elsewhere, just sighed and walked away.

After the candidates spent 45 minutes cooking, Juwan walked down the row and tasted each dish. To himself, he thought: *Dish 1: So bland. Dish 2: That almost murdered my taste buds. Dish*

3: That made me want to throw up. Dish 4: This dish is... Juwan paused because one dish finally hit his taste buds in the right way. "Exciting," he mumbled. "It's exciting." Leanne, Lester's other daughter, raised her eyebrow. "Do I spot a winner?"

"Let me taste the final two." Juwan tried the other dishes but they paled in comparison to the fourth. His father and Leanne tasted the dishes themselves and they seemed to come to the same conclusion as Juwan. But, they had to deliberate before making a final decision.

While the judges spoke in hushed tones, Andre prayed that his dish would be chosen. In his 4th try at getting into the school, Andre had finally made a Quiche that didn't fall apart in phase one and he had passed all the tricky tests in phase two. When Andre received his final test results, he also received a hat with a "4" on it, which the judges collected before the competition started.

Lester, Leanne, and Juwan finally came to a consensus so they picked a hat from a pile and put it onto a silver tray, which they then covered with a silver dome and gave to Julianna Fletcher, host of *Chef Boot Camp*. Lester had left out the fact that the final 6 candidates would appear on his show; he decided to keep this part a surprise. While looking at the audience, Julianna shook the platter.

"Who's it going to be? Mary, the southern belle who hopes her Louisiana style crepes will wow the judges? Andre, the stay-at-home dad who combined lady fingers with butter cookies in an attempt to make a more contemporary butter finger?"

The audience laughed and Julianna continued, "Will it be Walter, the 19 year old skater dude who hoped his cranberry cornbread had a nice kick? Could it be Andi, the girl next door whose crumb cake is supposed to take the cake? Is it Remy, the single dad who put a creative spin on peanut butter and jelly? Or is it Shawnee, the modest homemaker who believes her toffee flavored pudding will sit just right with the judges? Who will it be?"

Julianna shook the platter once more then pulled out the hat. "It's chef number 4: Andre!" When Andre heard his name being called, he was more than excited. He was stunned. Julianna gave him back his hat. "I believe this belongs to you." Andre placed the hat onto his head and smiled towards the crowd. After the show, he picked Emelia up and kissed her face passionately. "Hey, pretty girl. You happy for me?" Emelia just smiled because she didn't know what was going on.

Andre put Emelia back in the stroller and kissed Monique. "*You* happy for me?" "Of course I am." He hugged her tightly. "I was scared you wouldn't make it because you were at the hospital." Monique motioned to Camille. "I brought Cam with me."

Andre looked at Camille. "You okay?"

"Define okay."

Andre let out a deep breath. "I'm sorry to hear about what happened." Camille put her hand on her neck. "One thing I ask is that nobody pity me. I am fine." But, James did the exact opposite of what Camille wanted. He stopped by her apartment with food later on. "I thought I made it clear that I didn't want to see you anymore."

James placed the food into Camille's hand. "You look like you haven't eaten all day." "Well, I *was* in the hospital for several hours. Or did you forget that?" Camille opened the door and put the food on the counter. James stepped inside. "I swear I wasn't messing with drug dealers. You gotta believe me."

Camille threw her hands up. "Why should I, James? You're a *liar*." James groaned. "I'm telling you I didn't do it." "Then who..." Camille paused because the outfit from the club stared at her. "Rob," she murmured.

"Rob?"

"My ex-boss – Roberto. I always wondered why he only paid us in cash."

"Why would he lie on you?" James asked. Camille pulled out her phone to call Monique. "Good question."

Monique was playing peek-a-boo with Emelia when a lump rose in Monique's throat. She ran to the bathroom to barf into the toilet stool. *What is going on?* Monique remembered the last time she had gotten sick like that was when she was pregnant with Emelia. "This is a joke, right?" She looked down at her stomach. "Please tell me I just ate some bad food." Emelia, who was eager to know why her mom had run off so fast, crawled towards Monique. Since Monique touched her stomach, Emelia did the same. Monique laughed and Emelia did too.

"Are you imitating mama?"

Monique thought that she saw Emelia nodding so Monique bent down. "You silly goose." Emelia said, "Goo." Monique, realizing Emelia was imitating sound too, grabbed a bottle. "This is a bottle." But, Emelia didn't repeat the sound like she had at first. Monique sighed. "I guess that was just wishful thinking." Emelia continued to crawl around and Monique just watched. *Being a mom's not that bad,* she thought. While Monique basked in the glory of Emelia, Daniel called her.

Monique exhaled when she saw who it was. "Daniel, you know I take Thursdays and Fridays off to spend time with my baby. What is it?" "Great news: the campaign will begin as scheduled." Monique let out a sigh of relief. "I was looking at the performance reports and I got worried."

"I took care of the slow performance."

"In other words, you struck the fear of Machiavelli in them?"

Daniel chuckled. "Sister, you speak so ill of me. I'm not a tyrant." "Brother, when I was five, you told me if I didn't let you watch the TV you would cut my pigtails off and sell them to a cancer patient." Daniel gave off his most sinister laugh. "Maybe I am a little intense at times."

Monique scoffed. "A *little*?" Daniel laughed again. "I'm headed back to Mo's Mix to see how things are moving there." Monique nodded. "Cool beans. Have Dominique call me with a status update."

"Can I use Brian instead? You know your assistant and I don't see eye-to-eye." Monique sighed. "Sure." After hanging up, Monique played with Emelia until the phone rang again. "Monique Ross-Cassells. How may I help you?" "Hi. It's Hagen Sullivan of *Sull*-ful Records."

"Hi, Mrs. Sullivan. What can I do for you?"

"For our benefit concert, I have a few more people who would love the publicity." "Names?" Hagen said, "Drumma is an up and coming rapper who developed a love of music when he played the drums in his high school marching band. He's released 3 mixtapes and will soon release his first album, 'Drumma no Boy'.

"In addition, Drumma performed as an opening act for some of the hottest names in rap. Next, we have Bria Love; this is a singing group who's been making a splash with their hit song '18 Problems.' Thirdly, Marius Hughes is a fledgling producer who's trying to get his name out. He's more than willing to DJ. Finally, Dantavius is a soulful singer who hasn't gained much traction but he should. You can find all these people on YouTube and call me back if you like any one of them."

Monique pulled out her Jotter. "Will do." Almost as soon as Monique put Emelia in the play pen, Emelia started crying. But, her tears stopped once the music came on. Emelia paid close attention to the beats and seemed to be analyzing the structure of the songs. Monique wondered, "Is this an allusion to the future?"

Daniel was locking up the science building for the day and he noticed that one person had not turned off their station light. "That's ten cents off your next check," Daniel murmured. When he walked over to the station, he saw that the nametag was placed on the desk. **Devin**, it read. Daniel started putting the nametag back into its rightful slot but he noticed words on the back. **It's not over**. These words made Daniel feel uneasy. *Is this some kind of cryptic message?*

Because Devin was a lab worker, Daniel feared that Devin had put something into the bottles of Mo's Mix that would cause a phenomenon. At first, Daniel thought of ripping through the boxes and pouring out every last drop of "No Press? No Stress" that was in existence at that point. However, Daniel realized that Devin could have been playing a trick so Daniel cautioned himself not to act hastily.

Daniel imagined what would happen if he disposed of harmless products. "What do you mean you threw them all out?! Do you know how much money you just wasted?!" Mo would yell. Daniel would rub his temples, responding, "I know, but I was worried that he had put something in them."

"Who?!"

"Devin."

Monique would then try to calm herself. "Who the heck is Devin?!" To Monique and Daniel, Devin was a name with no face. To Camille, he was a face with no name. But, to all, he was a force to be reckoned with. Of course, Monique wouldn't know this so she would then ask, "How many boxes did you empty?" Daniel would respond, "Only three. We're awaiting official approval from Johnson Cosmetics before we go ahead and make the rest."

Monique would take a deep breath next. "How much is our profit loss?"

"About $1,000."

"$1,000?! How are we going to cover that? What will we put in the books?" Daniel would argue, "**I don't know** but let's hope I stopped another situation from happening." Monique would rub her head. "It sounds to me as if you've started one. You should have…"

Daniel came back to reality. *What am I going to do?* The next logical option would be testing all the bottles.

"We have strict orders not to open them. If we do, they're no good," Marcus explained the next morning. Daniel sighed. "Do the workers mark the bottles after completing one?"

Marcus shook his head. "No."

"Then can I have about 50 bottles drawn at random? I want you to note that I'm testing them so that the money can be withdrawn from my next check." Marcus nodded and made a note of this on his clipboard. "Is there anything else you need, Mr. Ross?" Daniel searched the office for someone who seemed suspicious. "Where's Devin?"

"Right over there."

Marcus nodded towards the station that Daniel had gone to the night before. Daniel stepped over. "You're Devin?" Devin nodded. "I am."

Daniel knocked everything off of Devin's desk. Devin raised his eyebrow. "Can you explain why you just did that?" Daniel yanked Devin's nametag out of its slot, preparing to catch a criminal. Alas, the back was blank – thanks to the fact that Devin had replaced the nametag when no one was watching. "That's impossible!" Daniel yelled, "There were words on here yesterday!"

Devin raised his eyebrow again. "Words? What words?" Daniel, who knew Devin was playing Daisy Buchanan dumb, pushed his finger into Devin's chest. "Let me find out you're working with April Spring; I'll make sure you regret ever getting involved with a bottle blonde bimbo *desperately* in need of some sunlight." Daniel walked back over to Marcus. "What's Devin's last name?"

Marcus looked at his roster. "Summers." As soon as Daniel heard that, he rushed back over to Mo's Mix.

"Brian, find out if Ursula has a brother." Brian looked up. "And by 'Ursula,' you mean April, right?" "No, I mean your mom. Of course I mean April!" Daniel stormed into his office and began pulling up his research. "April Spring must be stopped."

"This is my brother Andre." Miguel's boyfriend Max stuck out his hand. "I'm Max." Andre shook it. "Nice to meet you. Are you a freshman too?" Max nodded. "Yeah. Miguel and I met in our Honors English class."

"Cool. What are you studying?"

"English and Political Science."

"In the hopes of becoming a lawyer, right?"

Max smiled. "Yes. How'd you know?" "You remind me of myself when I was your age." "If you're a lawyer, do you think you could put me in contact with some firms that offer internships?"

"I'm actually not a lawyer anymore but I could call on some of my attorney friends and have Miguel get back to you if they have anything."

"Thank you so much." Max's phone started ringing so he kissed Miguel goodbye then went on his way. Andre said, "He seems focused. That's a good thing." Miguel sighed and put his trunk into the back of the truck. "He's way more focused than me." Andre nodded. "I heard mamma had to get on you about those parties."

Miguel laughed. "It's college, Dre. That means freedom. Self-expression. Purpose." "Just because you're an English major doesn't mean you have to utilize every word in the English language." Miguel laughed again. "I have to get used to it if I want to be a novelist."

"What kind of books do you want to write?"

"Action."

"You do love you some actions movies."

"If guts ain't spilling, I ain't watching." Andre chuckled and asked, "Is that everything?" "Yep. Where to next?" Andre shut the trunk. "Off to Georgia State to get Karen then Florida to get Georgie." Miguel raised his eyebrow. "Why's Georgie in Florida?" "You know Jamir goes to FAMU. He invited Georgie to his homecoming. He offered to pay for transportation too."

"Mamma *actually* said yes?"

Andre shrugged. "Yeah; I was surprised she did. She's been so laid back ever since papà died." Miguel said, "She was always laid back, I think. She just had to be uptight for papà." Andre realized, "And now she can be who she wants." Miguel nodded. "Definitely." He and Andre continued with this casual conversation through the rest of the trip.

Meanwhile, Monique cooked ravioli while Emelia played with a toy. The toy made noise every time it was hit. Because Emelia was fascinated, she kept hitting it off the floor and laughing when she heard the sound. Monique didn't prefer the noise, but knew Emelia was just being a baby. So, Monique focused on her cooking. After a while, the sound stopped and Emelia began crying.

Monique placed her spoon down on the stove. "Oh no. What happened?" She bent down and saw that Emelia had accidentally hit the "off" button so Monique turned it back on. When Emelia heard the sound again, she clapped her tiny hands together. Monique smiled. "You are too cute." She finished the ravioli and put Emelia in a high chair. After this, Monique blew on Emelia's ravioli to cool it then placed the food in front of Emelia.

It took all of two seconds for Emelia to make a mess. She got ravioli everywhere – the high chair, the floor, the ceiling, and her shirt, which Monique had paid $50 for. Monique put her hands on her hips. "That was one of my favorite shirts too." While Monique was wiping Emelia's mouth, Emelia put her hands on Monique's chest so that they had matching stains. Monique gasped dramatically and Emelia just laughed.

"You're already turning into a little trouble maker." Once Emelia was fed and clean, Monique put the infant in the play pen with the noisy toy. Then, Monique ate her ravioli. A little while later, Monique napped in her room with the door slightly cracked. Monique wanted it open somewhat so that she could hear Emelia when necessary but she kept it slightly closed as to shut out the annoying sound of Emelia's toy.

Monique wasn't the only Ross having an experience with new parenthood. In Vieille Ville, James was introducing Mrs. Ross to her (second) grandson. "What's his name again?" "K'ron Jon Ross."

Mrs. Ross huffed. "Jesus help that woman. She named my first grandson *K'ron*? How ghetto." James sighed. "Mama, it's not even that bad. And he's not your *first* grandson." Mrs. Ross took

K'ron into her arms. "You know what I meant." James looked at his shoes. "Speaking of which, Cam said the court has seen her dramatic shift and that might work in her favor because apparently Jalen's adoptive parents are headed for divorce. His adoptive dad was cheating on the mom and embezzling money from whatever company he worked at."

"I guess having a good job doesn't always mean you have a good home."

James shook his head. "Not always. You and dad struggled but look how we turned out. Mo and Danny are at Mo's Mix and I'm running granddaddy's old shop." Mrs. Ross nodded as she rocked her grandchild in her arms. "But, James, what you gone do if Camille gets that baby back? You gone leave Laila with two kids?"

"No, but I should support Camille, right?"

Mrs. Ross sighed. "She gave the baby up. She can't expect you to pay anything." "But I pressured her into the adoption." James reasoned. "I said it was either me or the baby." Mrs. Ross stared blankly at her son. "James Stefan Ross, you did not."

"I did."

Mrs. Ross shook her head in disbelief. "It was either you or the baby, huh? And she lost both." She continued to shake her head. "You really are your father's son." James knew what Mrs. Ross was getting at, so he quickly opened the conversation back up to him and Camille. "I regret ever giving Camille that awful ultimatum."

Mrs. Ross rolled her eyes. "As you should. You know, I wanted you to marry Camille – not that bougie broad from Boca."

"Mama let's get two things straight. One: Lai's *grandma* is from Boca; Lai is from Orlando. Two: you have no right to call my wife a broad."

"James Stefan Ross, let me make something real clear: you need to watch that goddam tone when speaking to me." Mrs. Ross hit her son over the head with her free hand. "I'm not your wife so you not gone get away with talking crazy to me."

Mrs. Ross took a deep breath and got back to the conversation. "But, anyways, I never liked Laila. The first time I met her was in the principal's office after her and Mo got into that heated argument. Then, she and Camille ended up getting into a couple fights. Yet you went ahead and married her cause she was the Prom Queen and she came from money. Right?"

"I married Laila because I love her."

"If so, why did you get Camille pregnant?" Mrs. Ross challenged. She then laughed aloud because she knew James didn't have an answer. Mrs. Ross decided, "It's because Camille the one you in love with but you too pretentious to accept her for who she is. Meanwhile, your fairytale princess is trying to produce as many heirs as possible so that if you leave her that child support will be a royal pain in the ass."

James shook his head. "Laila isn't trying to trap me." Mrs. Ross sighed. "You say that now. Just wait until she springs baby number 3 onto you." But, Laila would not be the next pregnant Ross woman.

Chapter XIII – *Monique is hit with some shocking news, Andre plans his next career move, and the hair show is soon to be underway.*

1 WEEK BEFORE CHRISTMAS

Monique stared blankly at Dr. Seneca. "One more time?" "You're pregnant – again. It's a pre-Christmas miracle, right?" Monique thought about the piles of bills she and Andre were still figuring out how to pay. "I'll get back to you on that." After receiving this news, Monique returned to Mo's Mix – where she would encounter some more bittersweet news.

Andre was in Monique's office when Monique arrived. "Hey, baby. My mamma offered to watch Emelia today so I have some time off and I rushed over here because I have something to tell you: we've been approved for the loan!"

Monique tried to smile. "Yay." Dre raised his eyebrow. "Is everything alright?" Monique thought about the ultrasound sitting in her purse confirming that she was with child. "No; we need to talk." Andre sat on Monique's desk. "What's going--" "Mo, you need to hear this!" Daniel interrupted.

He slammed his phone on the desk and played the jury's verdict. "Upon receiving one final piece of evidence, the jury has ruled Abigail Newhouse's death a homicide. Hospital footage reveals Nicole Nicholson sneaking into Ms. Newhouse's room and pulling the plug, thus killing Ms. Newhouse. Nicole Nicholson will be charged with 3rd degree murder and arson. She will face life imprisonment with no chance of bail. Our sincerest apologies go out to anyone who was falsely accused and we hope that this new revelation will grant Ms. Newhouse's family the closure they've been searching for. Thank you."

Daniel threw his hands up in glee. "It's over, Mo. All this madness is through."

"What about Evan and Donna," Monique wondered. "Or April? They're just as guilty as Nicole."

"Who cares? Nicole Nicholson is where she belongs."

"And what about her 8 year old daughter?"

"Raven will go back with her father," Daniel said. Monique shook her head. "Trevor's a nut job. Did Camille tell you that he pulled out a knife on her?" Daniel scoffed. "Why does it matter? April is *done* sabotaging your business; her cronies will now fear imprisonment due to Nicky's murder sentence. It's over, Mo."

Monique declared, "It's *not* over, Daniel. I have a sneaky feeling April set this up." "Why would April send her friend to jail?"

"Maybe Nicole did something that April didn't like."

"Or maybe this has gone on so long you don't want to believe it's over," Daniel suggested. Monique felt worry in the pit of chest. "I'm having a premonition, Daniel. Something just tells me it's not over." Daniel thought about the fact that someone who was possibly related to April had been working in the labs. But, Daniel didn't want to worry Monique with an erroneous suspicion. She had enough anxiety as it was, Daniel thought.

Plus, Brian had found no connection between April and Devin. Devin had carefully removed familial information between him and April once his identity became compromised, but Daniel didn't know this. He just knew that the bottles he'd tested came back showing that they had only the ingredients that they were supposed to. So, Daniel repeated, "It's over."

He picked his phone up and walked away. Andre rubbed Monique's shoulder. "Early this morning, I got an email from Landon George. He says my dish made it to the final round of evaluation, which means that I could have my hands on $20,000 to pay for cooking school added to the $2,000 grant Thornberry is offering me because I scored the highest on my entrance exam. Then, we have the loan for the house. On top of all these *amazing* things, they've finally convicted someone for Abigail's death. The universe is really working in our favor, huh?"

Monique couldn't take Andre's glee because she was inwardly in agony. "I'm pregnant," she confessed.

From the kitchen, Monique and Dre watched Emelia play with a toy. "Are we really gonna do this again? We're just getting used to having *one* child." Andre rested his head on Monique's shoulder. "I would understand if you decided to terminate the pregnancy."

Monique held her stomach and stared at Emelia. "Look at how cute and innocent she is, though. Imagine having two of her running around." "Then imagine screaming and crying 24/7." Monique laughed. "That's Mo's Mix on an everyday basis." Andre put his hand on top of Monique's. "If you want to keep the baby, keep it. If not, don't. It's indecision that complicates these processes."

Monique moved her head away from Andre so she could look him in the face. "Since when were you so dismissive?"

"I'm just saying, Mo. I hated all that back and forth with Emelia. It was so annoying."

"And you waited how many months to tell me this?"

Andre sighed. "It's not that big a deal." "It is. Communication is the key to any healthy relationship." "You're absolutely right so let me communicate this: I want at least two sons and two daughters. I want us to have a big family and I want you to let me take care of you. I hate how much you stress yourself out at

Mo's Mix. But, I will *never* stop you from following your dreams, so I stay silent."

Monique sat on the counter. "I don't like the stress either but that's the sacrifice I make by running my own business. Like you, I would love lots of kids but, since we're both career people, one of us would have to step down in order to raise those kids."

Andre asked, "What if it was me? After I finish school, I could continue working at the center and watch our children in my free time." Monique raised her eyebrow. "You would want to do that?" "I'm good with kids. I practically raised Miguel, David, and Georgiana, after all."

"What about my body though?"

Andre stood in front on Monique. "I know of a workout we can both do." Monique shook her head. "If you want *at least* four kids, the only workout we'll be doing is chasing after them inside this crowded condo." "I don't want to raise four kids *here*, Mo. I want them to be raised in our house."

"The house we can barely afford?"

Andre showed Monique an email. "Three bidders pulled out so the asking price dropped substantially. If we outbid this other couple, we could get the house." "What's their offer?" Andre went down the email and saw the other couple's offer. "Oh, that's disheartening." Monique looked at the number too. "Yikes." The other couple was offering in the 800s and Monique and Andre didn't want to go a dime over 5.

"There's always our second option," Andre said. He pulled up another email. "It's within our budget and we're not on the waiting list." Monique shook her head. "I say we hold our horses. There's something special about that house on Broadway Boulevard." Andre nodded and touched Monique's stomach. "Have you made a decision about this yet?" Monique told him, "I might just take you up on that offer." Before it could be discussed further, Emelia's toy fell and Andre's food was done. So, Monique hopped down from the counter to get the toy while Andre prepared lunch for two important ladies in his life.

Hours later, Monique was watching her team of interns set up for the hair show. *This is all coming together nicely.* As Monique pushed Emelia's stroller around the room, she accidentally bumped into the heel of a man in a business suit. "Oh, I'm sorry." Tomas Phillips turned around. "You're fine." He got a closer look at Monique. "Fine as the small print in a contract."

Monique rolled her eyes. "You *still* using those same tired pick-up lines, Tomas?"

He laughed. "I guess I am. It's nice to see you again, Monique." Monique smiled. "You too. What are you doing here?" "I'm one of the events coordinators here at the center. You?" Monique replied, "I put the 'Mo' in Mo's Mix."

"So the rumors are true?"

"Rumors? What rumors?"

Tomas chuckled. "Daisy voice, right? But I met up with some of our old classmates and they told me you had started a very successful business, which I see now. It makes sense that you would name it after yourself, though. You always were conceited." Monique flipped her hair. "With good reason." When Monique did this, Tomas saw her rock. "Let me guess: Andre's the hubby and this is his daughter?"

"Ding-ding-ding."

Tomas let out a deep breath. "What's her name?" "Emelia B. Cassells." "And you're Monique Cassells now?"

"Ross-Cassells," Monique corrected. Tomas raised his eyebrow. "You hyphenated? That's *just* like an independent woman." Monique chuckled. "I do say so myself."

"But every strong woman needs a strong man by her side. Right?" Monique felt that Tomas was referring back to their relationship so she pushed her purse up on her shoulder. "I'll catch you later." While Monique pushed the stroller forward, she sent a text to Camille.

Monique: Tomas Phillips. Find an angle.

Camille: Tomas your ex?

Monique: Same one.

Camille: There's the angle...

Monique thought about this and vowed to keep a close eye on Tomas. But, since she had a job to do, Monique put thoughts of Tomas on the back burner.

Tomas waited for Monique to go out of sight then he called Bree. "You planted it?" "It's done."

"Monique didn't see anything?"

"She just thinks that her old college boyfriend happens to conveniently work at the center her brilliant PR suggested to her."

Bree smiled. "Perfect. Then she won't know what hit her." Dominique had been coming to ask Bree a question and she overheard this conversation. Quickly, Dominique headed into Daniel's office. "Mr. Ross, I--" "I know we fired Yasmine but no you cannot come to me for relationship advice," Daniel interrupted.

Dominique exhaled. "Mr. Ross, I have big news – like super big news."

"And the news is so *colossal* that you had to say 'big' twice?" Dominique shook her head. "Never mind that. Bree is up to no good and she needs to be fired." "Bree is one of the best PRs Mo's Mix has ever had. What are you talking about?"

"She was on the phone with someone and she said 'Monique didn't see anything?' The other person said something else and Bree replied that Mrs. Ross-Cassells won't know what hit her. She has got to go."

Daniel noted, "Bree is trustworthy, Dominique. Perhaps your hearing is impaired because of all that loud club music. I understand that you're a second semester senior but a party a week? Isn't that a little excessive?"

Dominique raised her eyebrow. "You been keeping tabs on me?" "Everyone is liable to be treated as a suspect, especially someone who was there on the night of the fire yet has not been booted out. Mrs. Ross-Cassells may trust you but, as you have realized, I am *not* Mrs. Ross-Cassells."

Dominique smiled. "Of course not. Mrs. Ross-Cassells actually knows what she's doing."

Daniel chortled. "Under her command, two arsonists were allowed a place in this company and you were allowed to think you can speak to your supervisor any sort of way. So, I beg to differ, assistant."

"You shouldn't speak so ill of your sister."

"Monique and I have different business philosophies and hold our respective opinions about each other. But, my professional opinion is in no way tied to a personal one. I love my sister dearly. I just don't feel she's fully capable of running Mo's Mix. She's too emotional. You see the way she rerouted her entire hair show to memorialize Abigail Newhouse. If it were up to me, I would send the family flowers and call it a day."

Dominique scoffed. "If it were up to you, you would sweep Agent Abby's death under some expensive rug because then it would be out of sight, thereby pushing it out of mind. You only care about yourself and that's going to come back and bite you in the butt."

Daniel didn't like Dominique's dismissal. "That's a write-up, assistant. As I've stated before, I'm your boss, *not* your friend. Speak to me correctly or don't speak at all." "I don't consider Mrs. Ross-Cassells a friend. But, I respect her because she actually treats me like a human being, Mr. Ross. All that I ask is that you show me some respect."

Daniel folded his hands in front of his face. "I've been showing you tons of respect by not saying how I truly feel but, since you've provoked me, here's a little note for the future: don't get too comfortable in any position, don't *ever* sass your boss, don't be too opinionated and, most importantly, don't fraternize with your co-workers!" Daniel slammed a picture on the desk of Dominique and Alex kissing outside of Alex's apartment building.

"Where'd you get that?"

"Doesn't matter. You're fired, Dominique."

"You can't decide that."

"I can, actually. The board has officially made me COO so now my judgment holds as much power as Mrs. Ross-Cassells's. This considered, allow me to point out that your employment contract **explicitly** forbids internal dating. Since you decided that you were too good to follow this policy, I ask that you pack your desk and be gone in the next five minutes.

"Should you ignore these orders, I will instruct the guards to sick one of their rabid dogs on you to imitate the animalistic behavior I assume you must be into because I wouldn't expect anything better from a substandard, self-assured *child* who thinks skipping a few grades qualifies her to work with adults. Your time with Mo's Mix is complete, Dominique. Have a nice day."

As Dominique left astonished, Daniel made a call to Shaney to ensure that Dominique was immediately replaced. Bree, who had heard the entire fiasco, smirked to herself. Though this wasn't an official part of April's plan, it comforted Bree to know that Dominique would no longer pose a threat.

Monique pushed Emelia's stroller into the office. "Dominique, can you come watch the baby? Daniel called me here for an immediate meeting." Monique waited 2 minutes and didn't hear anything. "Dominique?" Brian came in Monique's office. "Dominique isn't here, Mrs. Ross-Cassells."

"She had something to do at Templeton?"

"She was fired," Brian explained. Hearing, Monique stepped into Daniel's office wearing a look of discontent. "You fired my assistant?" Daniel nodded. "Yes I did." "What gives *you* the right to fire *my* assistant," Monique asked.

"She spoke out of turn and, now that I'm the COO, I was merely exercising my 10%."

"You were being a tyrant. I understand that you didn't like Dominique but her employment – or lack thereof – was out of your jurisdiction."

Daniel pulled out the same picture he had shown Dominique. "Even if she was seeing her co-worker?" "Where did you get that?" Daniel shook his head. "Doesn't matter. Dominique broke a rule." "Which qualifies her for a write-up."

"She also sassed me for the umpteenth time. I did what I had to."

Monique shook her head. "You wanted her out so badly. But I don't understand why." "She also accused Bree of treachery, which to me sounds like a load of bologna hanging from the mouth an adolescent too immature to function in this adult environment."

Monique responded, "*I* think that Dominique's firmness threatened you; she was never afraid to stand up for what she felt was right. She challenged you, Daniel. She *constantly* held you in contempt. She..." Monique took a pause. "She reminded you of me," Monique realized.

Daniel threw his hands up because Monique finally got it. "Yes, Mo! She is *just* like you. Dominique will abide by your rules now then overthrow you later. She had to go." Monique sighed as that thought settled in. Brian came running into the office. "I'm sorry to barge in like this but your baby just spit up and I didn't know what to do."

Monique held her arms out. "Give her here." Brian put Emelia into Monique's arms. Monique said, "Fine; Dominique goes. But all other decisions should be run through me first. Got it?" "Got it." Since Emelia was still spitting up, Monique walked back to her own office. She sat on the floor and bounced Emelia up and down. "Baby has her first flu?"

Monique wiped the vomit off of Emelia's mouth. "Mommy just came here for a second, okay? We're going to go back home and put you into your nice, warm crib." Monique started putting Emelia's hat, coat and scarf on when Bree walked past the door. When Monique saw Bree, Monique thought about what Daniel had said.

"Bree, could you come here a second?"

Bree knew she was about to be interrogated so she mentally prepared herself while putting on her best poker face. "Yes, Mrs. Ross-Cassells?" Monique stood up with Emelia then nodded towards an empty chair. "Please sit." Before Monique could even get a word out, Emelia was spitting up again. "Should we postpone this until after the hair show?" Bree wondered.

"We can. Let's talk a week from today."

Bree left and Monique said, "Brian, call my pediatrician." As Brian did that, Monique threw her head back. *I can't bring another baby into this whacky world of mine.*

Although Monique hadn't questioned Bree, it was important to figure out Bree's angle, if she even had one. So, Monique decided to do some research. Since Camille was an expert in all things technology, Monique recruited Camille to help with this task.

"I found something," Camille eventually said. She turned her laptop to face Monique. "Breanna Perry used to work at Nia University before she was fired due to a leadership change. The new President found discrepancies in the books and booted people out accordingly. 3 staff members were canned for embezzling." Camille scrolled down on the page. "It says here that Bree had very 'close bonds' with the students."

Camille tapped her finger on the laptop. "Maybe she was selling game or event tickets off the books so she could inflate the price and gain a larger profit margin than she would have had she done it officially."

Monique sat back. "Good point, but why would she be working with April?"

Camille shrugged. "Profit motive?" "Wait. You said she worked at *Nia*?" Camille nodded. "Yeah. Is that important?" Monique sat up straight. "On Bree's first day, she told me she had worked for her Alma mater for 6 years and that they hired her straight out of school."

"Which would mean she was there when we were there?"

Monique nodded. "I remember her now. Breanna Perry in my Business Ethics 305 class Junior Year. She and I applied for the same internship and she was *mad* that I got it over her."

Camille raised her eyebrow. "You think this is revenge?"

"Could be. How did I not recognize her before?"

"Probably because you didn't know her," Camille offered. "But, I feel like there's more. Why would she seek revenge over a lost internship?" Monique thought about it. "I was getting paid to do research while she was working in the cafeteria."

Camille shook her head. "There were plenty of other internships out there. If she's this pressed over one, she's petty as hell."

Monique shrugged. "These are all just propositions, Cam. We don't know that any of this is true." "You're right." As Camille spoke, Emelia awoke crying and coughing. Camille scrunched her face. "Mo, that sounds bad." Monique picked up the medicine she had gotten. "The doctor said I'm supposed to give her this but she refuses to take it."

Camille grabbed one of Emelia's toys. "I have an idea." Camille distracted Emelia with the toy while Monique stuffed a spoon into Emelia's mouth. Emelia tried to spit the medicine out so Monique put her finger on Emelia's lips and waited for the medicine to go down. At first, Emelia cried; then the medicine started kicking in and she slowly dozed off.

"That was really smart, Cam." Monique complimented. "You're gonna be a great mommy one day."

"That may be one day sooner than you think." Before Monique could question this, she noticed something on Emelia's stroller that didn't belong there. She snatched the recorder off and thought: *There's another snake on the premises.*

"It's all set, right?" April asked.

Bree nodded. "All set. Monique's Sunday show will end with a bang." April clapped. "So devious. I love it." Bree took her payment and went home. There, she had an unlikely visitor.

"Attorney Khan, is this business?"

Malcolm let out a deep breath. "In a way." He explained, "As the attorney for Mo's Mix, it is my duty to guarantee the business succeeds. I do what I have to in order for that to happen. Sometimes, this includes research, such as tapping phones, checking bank statements, paying house visits to sneaky PRs, surfing through hard drives, hacking into computers, digging up hospital records for sneaky PRs, etc. Now, this is not to say that the people I trail are guilty. I just have some suspicions and I use various resources to follow these sus--"

"Will you be reaching a point anytime soon?" Bree interrupted, upset that Malcolm was not-so subliminally calling her out.

Malcolm decided to finally cut to the chase. "I know what you're doing, Ms. Perry." He pulled out pictures of Bree meeting with April. Bree put her hands on her hips. "Have you been following me?" Malcolm nodded. "For days now – ever since Mrs. Ross-Cassells's former assistant came to me with a shocking revelation. You need to stop whatever you have planned."

"If you knew how much money was involved in this, you would do it too," Bree argued.

Malcolm shook his head. "Probably not, actually. I'm an ethics kind of guy, so profit motives don't exist to me." "Nice to know, but that picture proves nothing." "It proves that you were meeting with April Spring."

"Mr. Ross also met with her. Maybe you should follow him too."

"He visited her to stop her."

"How do you know I wasn't doing the same thing," Bree challenged. Malcolm smirked. "Because you just admitted that you were out for profit and I have you on tape." Quickly, Malcolm got into his car and drove off. Bree, on the other hand, called April immediately. "Boss, there's a problem."

"I thought that when I fired you it'd be the last time I'd have to blot my eyes after seeing your hideous face."

Dominique stared blankly. "I'm just here to pick up a check." "Do I look like I handle that sort of thing? Check with one of my subordinates in Finance." Dominique sighed. "Mrs. Hawdry isn't in today so her assistant told me I could talk to you." "Her assistant sent you off. Your final check will be mailed after the holiday."

"But, I need that money to pay for my grandma's flight. She's coming all the way from Seattle to see me walk across the stage."

Daniel shrugged. "Should've thought about before you sassed me." Dominique got ready to respond but Monique came in. "Dominique, what are you doing here?" "As you know, my graduation ceremony is soon and I would like to fly my grandma in so she can see me walk across the stage. I *need* my final check, Mrs. Ross-Cassells."

Monique tried to ignore Dominique's plea for sympathy. "Why are you hassling Mr. Ross? You know checks are disbursed through Mrs. Hawdry or Mrs. Lewis."

"Neither of whom are in their offices."

Monique sighed. "They're at the convention center handling ticket sales. That's right. Come with me." "Where are we going?"

"I will retrieve your check and sign it for you. Come with me, Dominique."

Daniel shook his head. "Mrs. Ross-Cassells, that's not the official way we do things here at Mo's Mix." "Mr. Ross, I am exercising my 40%. Come with me, Dominique," Monique repeated. She overrode Daniel's decision, proving once more that she wore the pants in her and Daniel's business relationship. Ironically, the person who had pointed this out came to Mo's Mix seconds after Monique's power trip.

Brian announced, "Mr. Ross, Attorney Khan is--" "He can handle it with Bree," Daniel interrupted.

"Attorney Khan is asking specifically for you, though." Brian noted.

Daniel sighed. "Send him in." Malcolm showed Daniel enough evidence to incriminate Bree without even saying a word. "I'll be damned. The child was right." "What do you think they're planning," Malcolm wondered. Daniel thought back to the nametag he had seen at the labs. "I'm not sure but it probably has something to do with our products, since that is the central focus at Mo's Mix."

Malcolm pulled out a file. "I was looking at the records of the fire and some of the chemicals involved matched the ones found in Monique's scalp after that attack. Then, if you review your inventory reports, those same chemicals started progressively decreasing around December of last year."

"Which was right when shit hit the fan."

"Would I be going on a limb to suggest that Nicole was taking the products from the lab?"

Daniel shook his head. "I think that's a reasonable theory." Malcolm continued, "I also noticed that Nicole got booted out right before that initial product release. What if she purposely got herself fired in order to send a message? After all, she didn't put up much of a fight when Mrs. Ross-Cassells questioned her, did she?"

"Good point, but what message would she be trying to send?" Daniel asked.

"That April Spring was a name you needed to become familiar with."

Daniel exhaled. "True, but this clashes with the fact that Nicole was sent to jail while the rest of April's revenge squad roams free, including April herself." Malcolm pulled out more information. "I was just getting to that. You see here that Nicole ratted April out. What if Nicole got tired of being April's bishop but April was not ready to let go of her trusted advisee just yet?"

"So she sent Nicole to jail just to show who's more powerful?"

Malcolm sighed. "It's pretty cruel, but not unlikely." "Where does Bree fit into this?" Malcolm showed pictures of Bree and Andre. "Met her sophomore year at Nia and hit it off but, by junior year, Andre had Monique on his arm."

Daniel scratched his head. "You mean to tell me she would join April's revenge squad all over a broken heart?"

"You'd be surprised what people do over broken hearts."

"If you're referring to the time you keyed my car, no I haven't forgiven you."

Malcolm put the evidence away and touched Daniel's hand. Since Daniel was referring back to their relationship, Malcolm thought that that meant Daniel was ready to open up. "Tell me why you really broke up with me," Malcolm requested.

Daniel reminisced about his purchasing of an engagement ring and how he had gone to Maliq Khan's house seeking Malcolm's hand in marriage. Maliq was a devout Christian who did not support Malcolm's lifestyle, and he got angered by the "ludicrous" request. He ordered Daniel to leave the house immediately.

Daniel tried to be courageous and this only made Maliq angrier. He started yelling homophobic slurs that were still etched into Daniel's psyche. *You are a manifestation of sin – the way you go against nature. Do you see two male animals mating?* Daniel decided he would fire some equally hateful slurs. *God gave you your son. If you hate your son, you must hate God too.* At this point in the conversation, Mr. Khan had pulled out his shotgun.

Frightened, Daniel went back to his car. He started to drive off and that was when Mr. Khan shot a bullet through Daniel's back window. Quickly, Daniel had pushed his foot on the gas and he had gone home. Hours later, he and Malcolm were broken up.

Malcolm let out a deep breath when he finally heard the truth. "So you wanted to marry me?"

"We were in love and it had just been legalized in all 50 states. I was excited."

"Would you *still* want to marry me," Malcolm asked.

Daniel looked his first true love in the eye. A part of him wanted to say yes, but Daniel was still scared that Malcolm's father would come for him. "Thank you for all your information and I'll be sure to tell Mrs. Ross-Cassells." "Does that mean the conversation's over?"

"That will be all, Attorney Khan."

Malcolm sighed. "I'm sorry for you, Danny. You drown yourself in so much work that you forget to love." "Loving distracts you from what's important."

"Loving *is* what's important."

Daniel pointed to the door. "Please use it." "What happened to you, Danny? You used to be so warm." Daniel's mind ventured to two years prior; it had been the wintertime when he found out cancer took his Aunt Pamela. A year later, grief took his Uncle Junior. "Life happened."

Malcolm confessed, "I came to both funerals. You didn't see me at either, but I was there. Your Aunt Pamela was always so nice to me. Your Uncle Junior – not so much – but I wanted to be there to support you."

Daniel raised his eyebrow. "If you knew my aunt and uncle died, why did you ask me what changed in me?"

"I was giving you a chance to admit that you're brittle."

Daniel yelled, "I am not brittle!" "Yet, you're yelling at me when I tell you that you're brittle, which further proves that you are, in fact, brittle."

"Get out!"

Malcolm was pushing Daniel out of Daniel's comfort zone; Malcolm knew this much. Still, he shook his head. "I won't. I want my Danny back and the only way to find him is to break through the seemingly impermeable barriers he's put up to guard his heart."

"You're wasting your breath, Malcolm. I will *never* love again. I loved my aunt and my uncle but obviously that wasn't enough for God. He *still* took them just like the way the Bible says we were made in image of Lord yet, in the same respect, the Bible is used as justification for the hatred spewed at people like us. He convinced people to hate us, Malcolm."

"God didn't convince people to hate gays. *People* convinced people of that," Malcolm uttered, "But, the circle of life is as follows: we live, we love, we learn then we leave. You're just skipping the first three."

Daniel cut his eyes. "What?" "You died with your aunt and uncle." Hearing that, Daniel opened his door. "Malcolm, I don't have time for this right now." Malcolm touched Daniel's hand. "I'll wait for you; I'll wait for the Danny who knows how to love. And if he's really gone then I'll be forced to move on."

Malcolm exited and Daniel was left with an open wound – the same wound he had sealed after his Uncle Junior's death. Monique returned from taking care of Dominique and she saw her brother with his eyes low. "Daniel, are you okay?" Daniel sat at his desk crying. "Do I look okay to you?" Monique went over and hugged him. "No. I only asked as a courtesy." She ordered Brian to close the blinds and shut the door so that Monique and Daniel could have a moment alone.

"This is the third time you've moved this year. I can't keep up with you," Raj said. Camille sighed. "It's better to contact me through the phone." He nodded and stepped into Camille's new apartment – one she moved to after the ominous visit from Devin. On the table, Raj saw two unopened candles and two wine glasses. "You have company?"

"Yes. My--"

"Camille, what do you want me to…?" Juwan paused when he saw Raj. "Oh, hi. Who's this?" "I'm Raj, Camille's brother." Juwan stuck his hand out. "Juwan, her boyfriend. Camille never mentioned that she had a brother."

"We don't really talk much," Camille revealed. "Why are you here, Raj?"

Raj let out a deep breath. "The hospital called. They found pops in the bathroom." Camille put her hand over her mouth. "Oh my god. Did he--" Raj shook his head. "No; the nurses got to him before he could. They said he's been sad because he hasn't had any visitors in years. So, I searched for you because I think we should both go visit him as his Christmas present. He might like that."

Camille nodded. "Of course." Since it was clear that he had dampened the mood, Raj put his hand on Camille's shoulder. "Catch ya later, sis." Raj left. Juwan, who didn't know what else to do, wrapped his arms around Camille and let her cry into his shoulder. "Was this one of those things you said we'd get to later," he queried. "Yeah." Camille nodded and sobbed.

Juwan rubbed her back. "At least the lord was watching over him."

Camille said, "You should go."

"What?"

Camille moved away from Juwan. "I just need a moment alone." Respecting Camille's request, Juwan left. But, Camille didn't *really* want to be alone. She just wanted to discuss her problems with someone else. Later on, James took notice of the way Camille stared up at the ceiling. "You still with that guy?"

"Yeah."

"Since you're cheating on him, I guess that makes us even."

Camille scoffed. "Not *even* close." James laughed and rubbed Camille's bare shoulder. "What's wrong? You seem so sad." "My dad tried to kill himself," Camille confessed. James let out a deep breath. "Oh man. Are you okay?"

"I've been better." Camille turned into James. "I feel like it's my fault. When I used to visit him, it would be so sad. Seeing him trapped inside that box was like viewing an animal at the zoo. Still, I know it must be harder for him. His wife left him and his kids won't even visit him. It's as if Raj and I forgot that, although our mom doesn't want anything to do with us, we still have a father who loves us. He has mental health issues, but he's still our father nonetheless and a relationship with him is important."

"Yeah, relationships with parents are important," James noted as he thought about his own fatherhood. Camille let out a deep breath. "James, go home. Your kids need you." Instead of fighting it, James listened to what Camille said. Once James was gone, Camille called Juwan and told him she was feeling better so they had their dinner as planned. At the same time, James went home and kissed Laila then Arielle then K'ron before making dinner for his family. All was well, it seemed.

"I'm here to see Monique," Andre said.

Bree turned around. "I can help you with that..." She almost dropped her Jotter when she saw that it was him. But, Bree quickly composed herself. "I c-can help you with that, Mr..." Andre flashed his pearly whites. "Cassells. You should know that." Bree raised her eyebrow. "Sh-should I?" "Yes," Andre stated. "You're the PR so you should know everything about Mrs. Ross-Cassells, including who her husband is."

"Duly noted." Bree turned so that Andre could not see her birth mark – the one thing that surgery couldn't fix. With shaking hands, Bree pull out her walkie-talkie. "B-Brian, give me an approximate location on Mrs. Ross-Cassells."

"She is in the executive suite meeting with the e-board," Brian replied. Hearing, Andre smiled once more. "See you later, *Bree*." Then, he walked over to where Monique was. "I'm 85% sure that it's her," Andre confirmed. Monique shook her head. "Why would she be working for me, though? And how come I didn't recognize her?"

Andre shrugged. "Beats me, but is there anything else you need me to do?"

"Give me an update on our little one, please." Andre pulled out pictures of Emelia playing with cupcake papers while Siena was carefully frosting some cupcakes. "Karen sent me these. She and Siena are making cupcakes for a bake sale and Emelia's 'helping'." Monique laughed while looking at the photo. "That is too cute. Please send that to me." "Will do."

Monique's phone started buzzing, which meant she had to get back to work. So, she kissed Andre and went back to her meeting. Andre, on the other hand, headed to Apiqua Private School, the high school Georgiana attended on an arts scholarship. When Georgiana got into the car, she handed Andre a flash drive.

"This is the full game from last night?"

"Yes, Andre. You know I always follow through."

"True that." Andre started the ignition and drove towards the drop-off point. 45 minutes later, he and Georgiana were both $500 richer. "This will be put towards my spring wardrobe. Since I'm a junior this year, I absolutely *must* step up my style game up."

Andre shook his head. "They grow up so fast."

Back at the center, Monique's meeting ended and she was ready to confront a criminal. On the expo floor, Bree was checking the booths.

"Molly's Health Foods will go here, Goodies to Chew should be here, Charisma…" Bree noticed that Monique was swiftly approaching so Bree acted as casual as possible. "Charisma Cupcakes is here, and finally we have Touchdown. Everything on this side is where it's supposed to be." Bree turned to the other side to check that each booth was correct. "Apiqua Real Estate. Edmond-Lincoln Insurance. Army Recruitment. Nouville Hair Lab. Open aisle to walk. Techie. *Sull*-ful Records talent search. Grow Some Mo'--" Monique blocked Bree from taking another step.

"Why did you lie about the reason you got fired, Ms. Perry?"

"I thought we had agreed to pick this up after the hair show." "I have reason to believe you wanted this issue to be picked up after the hair show because, by then, the damage will be done."

Bree raised her eyebrow. "What kind of damage are we talking about here? Is there something I should know?"

Monique said, "I think you know more than you're willing to tell me. I spoke to your former supervisor and she said that there were no 'budget cuts'. So, I'm going to ask you this again: why did you lie about why you were fired, Ms. Perry?"

Bree let out a deep breath. "I was never given a reason for the sudden termination. My best guess was just budget cuts. I do apologize for misinformation."

Monique shook her head. "Apology *not* accepted. Attorney Khan tells me that you may be working for April Spring?" "Did Attorney Khan also tell you that Daniel visited April Spring or was I the only liable suspect because I'm not family? Think about it, Mrs. Ross-Cassells. Daniel is an insider. He's privy to more information than any one of your employees. So, maybe you should be questioning him. Now, if you'll excuse me, I have a job to do. Grow Some Mo' Hair Rejuvenating Clinic will be here. Spotlight's..." Bree continued checking booths until Monique was out of sight. This was when Bree texted April.

Bree: Monique knows.

April: Play it cool. Our Sunday showdown is still completely confidential.

Bree: Roger that.

Days later, Andre continued on his mission to find out if Bree really was his crazy ex-girlfriend Bree. He visited Lauren at her job seeking information. "Laurie…" Lauren put her hands on her hips. "I can't, Dre. I could risk jail time if I was to get caught." "This is to help my wife and your sister in law, though." Lauren sighed. "You're only getting general info that you could find from a Google search."

"Any information helps." Lauren looked at the name Andre had written down. Then, she pulled up records on a computer. "There's no coincidence, Dre. It's the same lady. It's just that she had some plastic surgery a while back."

"Which is why I had trouble recognizing her."

"Yep. Is that all?"

"Why did she have the surgery?"

Lauren rolled her eyes. "Uh-uh, Dre. That's all I'm going to tell you. You want to find out more? Report her to the cops and have them bring a warrant." Andre sat on the stool next to Lauren. "Fine. But, why are you so testy?" She shook her head. "I'm scheduled for three surgeries today even after I requested the day off to finally do some Christmas shopping for the boys. My boss told me I would have to use my vacation days and I only have two of those left. This place irks me so much." Andre rubbed her shoulder. "Hang in there."

"How's the firm?"

"I quit," Andre admitted. "I'm starting cooking school in January." "How are you making money then," Lauren wondered.

"I work at a community center as a counselor and I'm also doing this project with Georgie."

"That thing you all won't talk about, right?"

"It's not ethical, per say."

Lauren put her hands on her hips. "Andre Cassells, are you selling drugs?" "How can a woman who prescribes drugs on a daily basis ever hold me in contempt?" Lauren rolled her eyes. "Is that a yes?" "That would be a negative. We may have grown up on the outskirts of Vieille Ville, but neither Georgie nor I know the first thing about running a drug pin."

"Then where is all this money coming from?" Lauren questioned. "That's on a need-to-know basis," Andre evasively answered.

At Apiqua Private School, Georgiana was setting up for her school's Junior Varsity basketball game. Jamal, a varsity player, sat by her. "Coach says we have to keep an eye on you from now on." "Why?"

"He saw you messing with the camera during our game yesterday."

"I was probably just focusing it."

"Or…sending the tapes off to recruiters who want to see us play."

Georgiana raised her eyebrow. "What would make you think that?" "This recruiter mentioned some of my best plays but I've never seen him at any of my games. So, I think someone's been sending him and other recruiters tapes of me and my fellow teammates, although it's against school policies."

Georgiana sighed. "How do you know it's not your coach sending them?"

Jamal shrugged. "Could be but I don't think he's smart enough to get away with it for this long." Georgiana laughed. "You can't talk about Coach Meyers like that." Jamal chuckled. "I would tell him that to his face because he knows it's all out of love." Jamal moved up a row so that he was right next to Georgiana. "Speaking of love, how's Jamir?"

Georgiana rolled her eyes at the sound of Jamir's name. "He invited me to his homecoming and two of the girls he's been seeing approached me to tell me all about the things they had been doing with and to Jamir. I was disgusted." Jamal shook his head. "Freedom goes to some people's heads."

Georgiana hit "record" because the game was starting. "I guess so." Jamal noted, "It wouldn't go to mine, though." "Is that your way of asking me out?"

"And *desperately* hoping that you'll say yes."

Georgiana sighed. "You only asked about Jamir because you wanted to see if you still had a chance." Jamal smiled. "Guilty as charged. But will you go out with me?" Georgiana thought about it. "Okay." For the rest of the JV game, she and Jamal were talking. Afterwards, Jamal had to go warm up for his game. Though Georgiana would have liked to talk more, she knew she had a job to do. When the coach wasn't looking, Georgiana hit a few buttons and the tapes were sent to her email.

Once the Varsity game was over, Andre came to pick Georgiana up. In the car, he asked, "Did you get them?" "Yes, but Coach Meyers is beginning to get skeptical, Dre. I think we should stop this." Andre counted all the cash he had made. "Georgie, do you understand why I'm doing this? The payment plan for Thornberry costs $300 to enroll then I have to make at least a $900 deposit upfront. Monique and I are trying to buy a house, and Emelia's doctor's bills are out of this world. I have to earn money how I can."

"Can you find another way? I *just* said Coach Meyers was onto me."

"But money is tight right now."

"Since when were you so driven by profit? We came from nothing, Dre." Andre sighed. "And I want to make sure that my daughter never has to face what we faced." While Andre was firm in this belief, he knew that what they were doing was risky and Georgiana was having a once in a lifetime opportunity to be at Apiqua Private School. "But, I also don't want you to be expelled from school. I know how much this means to you. If you want to bow out, we can bow out."

"Thanks for understanding, Andre." Georgiana handed him the flash drive. "Last drop off tonight, right?" "Last one." Though Andre and Georgiana were ready to cease their felonious scheme, April had a scheme of her own she was planning.

"You've done well," she told Jamal. While Georgiana had been looking at her phone, Jamal had planted an ear piece inside her purse, which April had listened to and heard Georgiana and Andre's full conversation. "Now, can I have my money?" Jamal asked.

April gave him the $500 he needed to pay his college application fees. Once he left, she turned to Rob, the former owner of Teasers and ex-husband of Nathalie. Monique made sure that Teasers was audited and it was discovered that Rob was really the one working with Pedro Manning. The police were out looking for him to arrest him but April was keeping him hidden until further notice. "You're more trouble than you're worth."

"What does that mean?"

April snapped and Roberto was taken to a nearby alley close to where Andre was dropping off the final tapes. Devin and Evan tossed Roberto to the ground and kicked him multiple times in the face until he was unconscious. Then, Devin stomped on the back of Roberto's head and hopped into the getaway car with Evan – leaving Rob for dead in that alleyway.

"You're watching Emelia today, right?"

It was Thursday, one of Monique's designated "Emelia days" but it was also the first day of the hair show. "Um, no. Unless you want her to be down there with all those people." "I'm going to a required training program for the school. Every student must have a Food Safety and Sanitation license before entering the academy," Andre mentioned.

"Didn't Karen offer to watch her last week?"

Andre nodded. "She did but who's going to drop Emelia off at my mom's house?" "Is it possible for Karen to come down to the convention center?" "Let me call her." Dre got his sister on the phone while Monique bundled Emelia up tightly. "No more flus for you." Once Karen agreed to watch Emelia, Monique and Andre were able to do what they needed to do.

The expo went off without a hitch, and Monique was relieved by this. There were no surprises at the meet and greet. Everything ran smoothly during the activity day. It wasn't until the benefit concert that April decided to enact her revenge plot once more. As previously stated, April wanted Monique to be on her knees begging for salvation from April's vindictive ways.

"We'll get hitched

She'll love that shit

I'll fuck yo bitch

She'll love that shit

All the snitches

Love my shit

Cause I speak truth

And still make hits.

Like Barry Bonds

But I'm more so James.

Remember the name

Drumma ain't no lame

I murdered the game 'fore it could leave the womb

I open up tombs for these dead careers.

Drumma ain't no boy

He the man of the--"

Drumma's mic was cut off in the middle of the line. "Year," his fans yelled to finish it. This wasn't the first, the second or even the third, but the *fourth* time that Drumma's mic had been cut in the middle of his set. So, of course, he took it as a personal slight. "Man, all y'all just jealous cause my shit fire and yo shit weak!" Drumma threw the mic down and stormed off the stage. Backstage, Lola Lavender, Drumma's manager, put her hand on Drumma's arm. "Drumma, it was an accident."

"No! They always do this to rappers 'cause don't nobody like us except for us. They hate rappers, man!"

Drumma went on a rant while Bree came downstairs to see what was going on – although she knew what was going on. "Is he okay? I'm so sorry that this happened." "Just fix it," Lola yelled while trying to calm Drumma down. Bree went to the sound booth. "What is going on here?" She asked like she hadn't texted Tomas just minutes before. The sounds people shook their heads. "We're not sure. The system malfunctioned for two seconds and, next thing we know, his mic was cut off."

Hagen Sullivan stormed into the sound booth. "This is *not* okay! My artist just left the stage in the middle of his set because someone cut his mic off! Which one of y'all cut his mic off?!"

"They say there was a glitch in the system," Bree mentioned. Hagen looked at the soundboard and noticed that one of the cords had been unplugged. "There wasn't no 'glitch' in the system. Someone purposely cut Drumma's mic off. This will *not* go unnoticed."

Hagen was so livid after that. She called Daniel to voice her compliant. "I don't know who you hired to work this event but the board of directors *will* be hearing about this. Who had the audacity to cut Drumma off while he was performing?! This is unacceptable!" As Hagen yelled, Daniel had one thought in his mind: *April.*

"How would she even slip someone into the sound booth? We background checked every last employee."

Monique let out a deep breath. "Maybe we missed something."

Daniel paced the floor back and forth. "This makes no sense. Who was in charge of the booth?" Monique pulled out her Jotter. "Tomas Phillips – an events coordinator at the center."

"Tomas Phillips, as in your ex?"

"Same one. I had Camille dig info or him but she can't find any clear motive for him to be teaming with the revenge squad except that Tomas was mad after the break-up."

Daniel said, "Don't you get it, Mo? It's you. *You're* the motive. Tomas is working with Spring because he's hurt that you stopped coddling his TPS." Monique chuckled. "While you playing, that might actually be true. After all, Bree conveniently suggested the Rockwell center and Tomas conveniently got put onto my event."

"Remind me again why we haven't fired Bree yet?"

"Since Pauper Perry decided she wanted to cross the highest power, Perry's banishment from the Queen-dom must come when she least expects it. Be patient, Sir Daniel."

It was Saturday, i.e. the first day of the hair show, so Monique grabbed her purse. "In the meantime, we must figure out to what extent April's pawns, rooks, bishops, and knights have infiltrated our castle." She hurried off to the center.

Alas, April's next move didn't affect Monique professionally, but more personally. Monique was running around backstage checking to see if something was off while Andre was speaking to a police officer.

"Roberto Harper was just found unconscious in an alleyway and it has been brought to our attention that you and Roberto got into a very public dispute a few years back. Would you happen to know anything about Mr. Harper's assault?"

Andre shook his head. "No. I haven't seen Roberto in years." "But, this picture shows your car near that alley around 10 o'clock P.M. According to doctors, the wounds had to have been placed between 9:45 and 10:15 P.M.

"In addition, security cameras at a local bar found that two men were seen assaulting Roberto then fleeing the scene of the crime and, ironically enough, you and a man were having a meeting in that *same* bar then you sped off in your escalade 10 minutes after Roberto was supposed to have been assaulted."

"I'm going to need you to come with us," a second officer said.

Andre got hauled off to a police precinct while Monique made aimless attempts to fight an essentially invisible force. After an hour of finding nothing wrong, Monique thought that maybe she was just paranoid. Then, it dawned on Monique that April would love it if Monique marginalized a serious problem by deeming it paranoia when it wasn't. As Monique went back and forth in her head trying to figure out a way to stop April, Mo felt a sharp pain in her stomach followed by another one and another one after that. "Oh my god."

Because the pains progressively got worse, Monique ran to the bathroom – thinking that maybe she had eaten some bad food and it was coming back up. Sadly, this pain was different. Monique watched her unborn child drip into the toilet stool. For a while afterwards, Monique sat frozen. *What just happened?* 20 minutes in, Monique cleaned herself up, put Daniel in charge of the show, and rushed to the ER. Here, they told Monique that she had miscarried the child. Monique cried because she hadn't even come to a decision about whether or not she wanted to keep the baby. *I guess the decision was made for me.*

In a courtroom over in Nouville, Camille was hit with some equally saddening news: she would not be getting Jalen back. Because someone (April) had given the opposing side a picture of Camille's stripping days and these pictures were presented in court, the jury decided that staying with the other family would be in Jalen's best interest. Camille started leaving the courtroom and she saw Evan Armoire again. It finally registered that he was the guy from the baby store and the guy Monique had shown Camille. *Scumbag,* Camille first thought. Then, Camille saw Skyler, the boy who had bumped into her at the baby store.

Camille stared Skyler in the face and realized that he was actually Jalen. This was when Camille had an epiphany. *But, if Skyler's actually Jalen, that means his adoptive father was the one who...* Camille's eyes shot to Evan. *Jalen's adoptive father worked for Mo's Mix.* After having this revelation, Camille grew angry.

"You're the reason April got those adoption papers, aren't you?! You gave them to her, didn't you?! So you're an embezzler, huh? Were you stealing money to post bail when you eventually got tried for all your crimes?! You wanna know what I think of someone like you?! You're a dirty, scheming, lying son of a..."

Because Camille had become a loose cannon, the guards escorted her out of the courthouse.

In tears, she rushed to her car. *It's not fair! Why does someone like that get to keep **my** child? I may have been a stripper but I've never killed anyone.* Camille maintained this belief but then thought about something. *Oh wait. I had two abortions. Maybe Monique's aunt was right; maybe it was wrong to rip a child of God from my womb.*

Since Camille was sad and angry and conflicted all at once, she hit her hand on the steering wheel about 5 times. The people outside started staring to see if Camille was okay, so she drove off. At Camille's apartment, it was no better. Camille walked up the stairs and saw someone sitting by her door. Going closer, Camille realized it was Mo, whose eyes were redder than Camille's bruised hand. "I lost my baby and I really need a friend right now."

Camille opened her arms. "That makes two of us. Come here, Mo." Monique got up and hugged her best friend. A week before Christmas, Monique and Camille both needed the gift of a friend.

Chapter XIV – *Although April had been very destructive in various ways, Saturday was merely the predecessor to Sunday.*

SHOWTIME

"Are you sure you're okay?"

Monique blotted her reddened eyes. "I'm fine, dad. I have to go." Mr. Ross took his daughter into his arms. "Baby, you don't have to be tough for anyone, okay? We all know you're hurting on the inside." Hearing that, Monique bawled for the fifth time that morning. She couldn't even start to fathom how she was going to speak positively about death when it was having such a negative impact on her. Daniel stepped up. "Dad, can I talk to Mo alone?" Mr. Ross nodded and went back by his wife. Daniel put his hands on Monique's shoulders. "You did it with auntie, uncle, and Abby, so you can do it now. I know it hurts, Mo. The loss of life is never an easy idea to wrap one's head around. But, you have another child to protect: Mo's Mix."

Monique took a deep breath. "Daniel, I can't speak today. I feel too exposed."

"Monique, there is something bigger than us at work and it's our duty to get a handle on it."

Monique shook her head. "I just can't, Daniel. Go without me." "Mo's Mix is *your* empire, though. You're going to let some peasant overthrow it?" "Daniel, I lost my child! What don't you understand about that?!" Mrs. Ross came by Monique with some tissue. "Mo, baby, calm down. I know you're hurting but listen to what your brother is saying to you. Bumps in the roads like this one help that crazed woman sleep at night. You have to show her you're resilient."

Monique began tearing up again. "Don't tell me what I have to do!!!!" Camille came to Monique's side next, seeing that Mo was beginning to lose it. Camille embraced Monique and whispered, "God sends us challenges in order to strengthen us, right? He wants you to be strong, Mo. He wants you to fight. It's not easy to lose a child but imagine what it will be like to lose a child and your business at the same time. You have to fight, Mo. Fight the pain so you can prosper."

Monique listened to Camille because Camille had survived some of the most trying situations – including two run-ins with rapists (excluding the ones at the club) and, of course, 2 years of domestic abuse with Donald. Yet, Camille overcame these situations – to some degree, at least. So, Monique hugged Camille tightly. "Thank you." Then she looked around the room at Daniel, James, Mr. and Mrs. Ross, Laila, Arielle, K'ron, and Emelia. "Thank you," she said. "I needed this. I needed family." Monique kissed her actual child while vowing to protect her metaphorical one.

"After I finished school, I took on a risky venture by starting a business. Most people want to build up capital and attain resources before they begin but I decided I wasn't most people. So, I wasn't going to wait. Mo's Mix started out as a project of sorts. I recruited 3 of my college friends and, together, one of us bought supplies and mixed the products, two of us promoted, and one of us kept a record of sales. At first, I lost more money than I earned, which caused 2 of my friends to walk away from the business."

Monique flipped to the next page on her Jotter. "But, I kept the faith. I knew I was doing something meaningful. The one friend who didn't abandon me was my boyfriend Andre, who's now my husband the father of our beautiful daughter Emelia. He was so supportive of me then and he's just as supportive now. He gave what money he could to help me and I combined it with the money I made at my desk job. Once I had saved up enough funds, I was able to pay for the building where Mo's Mix sits today. This was a result of keeping the faith."

Monique flipped to the next page. "But today's not about me. Today is about Abigail Newhouse, a woman who was seriously in the wrong place at the wrong time. At first, Mo's Mix wished to respect the privacy of Abigail's family but, seeing as it has been a year since Abigail's death, I think it's finally time to discuss Agent Abby in length. Abigail Newhouse came to Mo's Mix because she wanted a low-stress job that would allow her to get married and have babies. Unfortunately, her fiancé died in a car crash during Abigail's first year at Mo's Mix. However, this never stopped Abigail from doing her job. She was loyal, dedicated and hard-working."

Monique wiped a tear that was coming from her eye. "Most of all, Abigail was courageous and strong. I went to visit her in the hospital before she passed and she was already recovering. I was sure she would make a comeback and continue to protect Mo's Mix. Sadly, Abigail's life was cut short. Even so, I would like her legacy to live on. I dedicated this hair show to Abigail because I want her to know she is loved by Mo's Mix and *dearly* missed. Abigail spent so much time protecting this business that she couldn't..." Monique was beginning to cry again so she took a moment to pause and recuperate.

Then, she continued, "Abigail spent so much time protecting this business that she could not protect herself from the harsh force which took her life – the same harsh force that plagues Mo's Mix to this day. I opened with that anecdote about the barriers I faced when starting my business because, 6 years later, I still face barriers, just in a different form. The business world can be a very competitive place and some will stop at nothing to tear others down. Some will go as far as to create a chess game. In other words, pawns, knights, bishops, rooks, and a king will be sent in to demolish the opposing side's pawns, disarm its knights, obliterate its bishops, nullify its rooks, and – most importantly – decimate its king all in an effort to overthrow the Queen.

Monique took a deep breath. "But, being a champion at the game, I understand that the way to circumvent attacks is to neutralize the opposing party's forces. This starts by learning and anticipating the other person's moves. One must master the art of deception to rise to victory in this chess match. Since chess is a game of wits, may the best Queen win."

Game, set, and match, Monique thought as she stepped down from the podium. Monique hoped that her extended metaphor had made it crystal clear that Mo's Mix was not going anywhere. Backstage, Bree yelled, "What was that?! You told them you have **enemies**, Mrs. Ross-Cassells." Monique replied, "Oh, I do. And I'm looking at one of them."

Bree raised her eyebrow. "I thought you said that you had overreacted." "Did you listen to my speech, Bree? Chess is all about mastering the art of deception."

"What does that mean?"

"It means you're fired, Patricia Samuel's getting a promotion and that Jotter belongs to me." Monique took the company Jotter from Bree and proceeded to the backstage area B – where the models and hair stylists were all prepping for the show while the security guards carefully monitored who came in and out.

When Monique arrived, she said, "I need two knights standing guard at all times. IDs are registered to the system so even if it *looks* official, be sure to double check. We got a throne to protect."

As Monique amped up security, April threw a cell phone at her computer screen. "May the best Queen win?! Does she actually think she can beat me?" Evan came over and massaged April's shoulders. "Relax. We still have Tomas down there." April looked at the text she had just received. Hagen had made sure to get Tomas written up by his boss for the incident during Drumma's set. As a result, Tomas was pulled from the event. "Tomas is out too. Monique is beating us, Evan. She's learned our plays. She's..."

Though April was running out of attempts, there was one move she hadn't made. April turned towards her brother. "Wait a minute. You still have that company ID, don't you?" Devin pulled it from his bag. "Yeah. Why?" "Surely, Mr. Ross kicked you out of the system when he fired you. Perhaps you can find a way back *in* to the system?" Devin smirked. "I like the way you think."

Monique looked at her phone to see if Andre had called back. *Where is he?* She hadn't heard from him in hours and she was worried. *Please tell me April didn't get to him.* Monique called for Patricia. "Mrs. Samuels, I need you to do me a favor."

Patricia stepped forward. "Anything, Mrs. Ross-Cassells." "Find my husband," Monique requested. "On it." While Patricia made some phone calls, Monique paced the floor back and forth. *What could he possibly be doing? He wouldn't cheat on me. He's stopped drinking. What else could it be?* Monique paused.

*Oh, God. Did something happen with his mamma or one of his brothers or sisters? I hope that's not the case. Lord, **please** tell me that's not the case.*

Patricia finally got some insight that would allow Monique to stop guessing. "I just spoke to the Chief of Police at Nouville Precinct. He says that Mr. Cassells was taken in late Friday evening for an assault charge," Patricia discovered. Monique was relieved to know where Dre was but the news didn't exactly put her at ease. *Did he lose control again?*

"An assault charge?"

"Roberto Harper was found in an alleyway and Mr. Cassells was being held as a suspect," Patricia continued. Monique's face went blank. "Was Roberto dead?" Patricia shook her head. "No, no. Just unconscious." Monique let out a sigh of relief. "Thank God. Why was Andre being held?" "Apparently, he was near the same alleyway at the same time." Monique exhaled. *I hope Dre didn't lose control again.*

"The charges were dropped when Harper woke up and said that your husband was not his assailant," Patricia added. But, Monique was too busy trying to get in touch with Andre to hear this part. While she was dialing, Brian's name popped up on the caller ID before Monique could make the call. "Yes, Brian?" Monique asked impatiently. "Dennis Quaver is here at Mo's Mix and he is not happy."

"What's wrong?"

"WHERE IS MRS. ROSS-CASSELLS?!" Monique heard. "I'll be down there immediately," she told Brian. Monique grabbed her purse and zoomed over to Mo's Mix. "Where is Mrs.--" Quaver stopped when he saw Monique. "You!"

Monique raised her eyebrow. "Me. Is there a problem?" "There is! My fellow board members heard your little speech and decided that you were hinting at the fact that I want to decrease the size of this company's board. They concluded that I was attempting to take a controlling interest in the company so they exercised their collective 45% and they removed me from the board! Do you understand how much money I just lost?"

"You have other investments, don't you?"

"None that are as profitable as this one. I had visions for this place. Surely, you understand that, Mrs. Ross-Cassells." When Monique didn't respond, Quaver shook his head. "Of course not.

You resented the fact that I questioned your competence so you used everything in your power to get me out."

"I ended my speech by saying may the best *Queen* win, Mr. Quaver." Monique clarified. "So, unless you have something to tell me about your gender, I don't believe that applies to you."

Quaver threw his hand up. "No one says what they mean anymore, Mrs. Ross-Cassells. But, you got your wish. I'm out. Happy now?"

Monique smiled. "I actually couldn't be more overjoyed. You have a nice day, Mr. Quaver." Monique had an intern escort Quaver out of the building while she went back to the hair show. Noon had hit so the comprehensive Sunday show was just beginning.

But, there was one person who would not be in attendance: Daniel. After leaving his parent's house that morning and passing the church that held his late aunt's funeral, Daniel had a harsh flashback. Subsequently, Daniel made a detour on his way to the convention center.

While Monique was watching the show to make sure everything ran smoothly, putting out an informal APB on Andre, and wondering where on Earth her brother was, Daniel was staring from the cab window at the gravesite for Pamela Ross. Though he had been suppressing his feelings on her death for a while, Daniel couldn't hold them in for much longer. The anniversary of the most traumatic time in his life was that day and he had been crying ever since he realized.

Daniel continued to look at the grave site for Pamela Ross and bawl his eyes out. Then, he instructed the cab to go over to Oakwood Ranch. Uncle Stanley Ross had built it after relocating from Greenwood, Tulsa, Oklahoma following the decimation of Black Wall Street. The ranch had a rich history but once Uncle

Stanley passed away, it went unnoticed. This was until Pamela took an interest in the ranch and decided to revamp it so that it could become a small business offering horse rides, apple picking, lodging, and other previews of country life.

But, Pamela got so sick that she decided to put her dream of reforming Oakwood Ranch to rest; she would just visit the ranch for leisure. Once Daniel arrived at the ranch, he paid the driver and slowly approached his aunt's cabin. Daniel hadn't been there in a year but it was still a familiar place for him. He took in the scents of everything around him and imagined that Auntie Pam was still alive and well.

"You miss her almost as much as I did," Uncle Junior stated. Daniel raised his eyebrow. "You're supposed to be dead." "And you 'sposed to be alive but you're dead on the inside, ain't you?" Daniel grew silent so Uncle Junior's ghost laughed. "You is. Life's for the living, my man, so you better off dead."

Uncle Junior moved to the rocking chair and sat it in. "This remind you of her, don't it?" Uncle Junior went to the oven. "This too, right? Remember how she used to bake those oatmeal raisin cookies that you loved so much? 'member how you used to swing on the oven till she told you to get down? You 'member that?" As Uncle Junior's ghost swung the door back and forth, the memories were coming back to haunt Daniel. He yelled, "Stop! Please stop."

"Let her go, Danny."

These words weren't coming from Uncle Junior's ghost, though. They were from Malcolm. "You have to stop living in the past." Daniel glanced up at Malcolm. "How are you here?"

Malcolm sighed. "I followed you because I was worried."

Daniel looked Malcolm in the eye. "Malcolm, I'm losing it. I've been trying to keep it together ever since my sister brought me into Mo's Mix but I can't anymore. I just miss my aunt so much." Malcolm put his hand on Daniel's shoulder. "I know. I know." Daniel dropped to his knees and cried. "I just want her to her come back."

Malcolm watched in silent agony. *Daniel is in so much pain. I have to do something.* "I know you do," Malcolm said. As Malcolm and Daniel shared this tender moment, James tried to get back to more tender moments with Laila. James said, "I just put K'ron down for his midday nap and Arielle's in the room watching cartoons." Laila smiled wide.

"You're a great dad, James Ross."

"Does this mean you'll let me move back in?" Laila sighed and looked at James's suitcases on the floor. "Yes." James kissed his wife passionately. "Thank you so much, baby. I love you."

"I love you too." James and Laila were finally back to a harmonious living, even if it was only for show.

"I was so worried about you."

Monique wrapped her arms around Dre's neck. "Are you okay?" He nodded. "I'm fine. They didn't have enough evidence to keep me there so they had to let me go." Monique pulled Andre close to her. "I'm glad. I couldn't be alone at a time like this."

Dre raised his eyebrow. "A time like what?"

"I had a miscarriage." These words caused a part of Andre to shut down. He was silent for 10 minutes. "Dre?" "Where's Emelia?" He finally asked.

"With my mom," Monique replied.

Andre started pacing the backstage area. "I have to see her. I have to talk to her. I have to love her. I have to be there for her. I have to--" Monique put her hands on Dre's shoulders. "Take a breath, baby." While Monique was trying to calm Andre, the pain she had been subduing resurfaced.

When Monique saw the hurt in Andre's eyes, it re-registered that her baby was there one minute yet gone the next. She stuffed her head into Dre's chest. "I thought I had gotten a handle on my emotions, but I haven't. I'm trying so hard to hold it together for this show but, on the inside, I break down every single second." Andre rubbed Monique's arms. "This is why we have each other. We will get through this together."

Since Monique was distracted, she didn't see Devin switching a harmless bottle of "No Press? No Stress" with the concoction he had conjured up. By the time Monique looked up again, Devin was gone. As April suspected, Daniel had kicked Devin out of the system but Devin, a mastermind behind a computer, knew his way around an encrypted security system.

Marcus raised his eyebrow when he saw Devin walking into the lab. "Mr. Ross fired you. What…" Devin sprayed mace into Marcus's eyes then went around switching every third bottle of 'No Press? No Stress?' with the product he had created. By the time Marcus could see straight again, Devin had vanished.

Suddenly worried, Marcus called Daniel. But, Daniel's phone had no service since he was still at the cabin. So, Marcus called Monique next. But, her phone was in her purse so she didn't hear it. *I have to tell someone what's going on,* Marcus thought. Fearing there might have been dire consequences if he didn't act fast, Marcus dashed to Mo's Mix. *We cannot have another Agent Abby situation.*

Once Marcus was gone, Devin went back to the lab and began creating another batch of his version of "No Press? No Stress". This one would contain high levels Nair, which would cause substantial hair loss in its users. Across the street, Georgiana took pictures of the entire act. She had found the earpiece in her purse and she had shown it to Andre, who caught Georgiana up to speed. Since Georgiana was a sucker for a good crime drama, she decided to join the one April Spring had created.

Monique heard her phone ringing for about the fifth time and finally answered. "Hello? Yeah. Uh-huh. Okay. Slow down. One more time. That's...Okay, Marcus. Thank you. No, it's not your fault. Thank you. Back to work, please."

At the same time, Georgiana was sharing with Andre what she had discovered. After Monique hung up the phone, Andre showed her his text messages. "Look at what Georgie just sent me." Monique watched video of the altercation between Devin and Marcus. Monique zoomed in on Devin's face. "He obviously works for my labs if he had an ID but what is he doing there?"

"Possibly tainting the products?" Monique nodded and screenshotted a picture of Devin then sent it to Camille.

Monique (from Andre's phone): Cam, it's Mo. Is this the guy who was at your apt? [Media Attachment]

Camille: That's him. He works for you?

Monique: Not anymore.

Monique took Andre's phone over to the security officers. "Have you seen this guy at all?" "Yeah, he stopped in a while ago. He seemed pretty shifty and he knew we were watching him so he was in and out." "Let me see your Jotter." Monique went down the list of employees who had signed in until she found a name to match the face from the pictures. Monique was troubled by what Devin had changed his handle to in the system: **My surname may be "Summers" but I am <u>not</u> sunny.**

Realizing that she was still caught in April's web, Monique rushed down to the security wing of the convention center and asked to see the videos of backstage. On the cameras, Monique saw Devin going over to the stations and touching a bottle, after which he quickly left. She zoomed in and realized Devin had switched out the bottle of "No Press? No Stress" with one that he had been carrying with him.

"Oh. My. God." Monique had solved the mystery but was too late to prevent the storm.

"Patricia, tell everyone to stop what they're doing!" Monique yelled into a walkie-talkie as she bounded the stairs. "I repeat: stop everything. Do not use another product from..." The door at the top of the stairs was locked, thanks to April's newest recruit Tavus, a security guard who had played his role awfully well. Thus, the wicked witch's sly snake would soon slither its way into the Queen-dom, causing great detriment. Monique watched the demolition take effect from the big screen at the top of the stairs. *What more can this nut job possibly do?*

To close out the hair show, the final collection was called NPNS (for No press? No stress) and each model was in a different stage with her natural hair. So, as the models walked out, the audience was able to see the gradual transition. Geegee Sterling, the final model, was always a show stopper because at the end of her walks she struck unforgettable poses.

For that particular show, Geegee decided she would run her hand through her hair while she put on her best resting face. This was all good until Geegee pulled her hand out and ¼ of her hair was in it. "AAH!!!!"

[Cue: Bittersweet Christmas music]

Epilogue – *After an epic show, Monique's job only got harder – given that she was still reeling in the loss of her child. In an effort to find nirvana once more, Monique made some questionable decisions. Resultantly, Monique will face some repercussions.*

9 MONTHS AGO (DECEMBER):

While Monique bore witness to a show-stopping stunt, April was taking a sabbatical in the Swiss Alps. "May the best Queen win, right?" April pulled down her ski mask, ready to go downhill, but she felt a presence behind her. So, she turned around. "You're a long way from home," April told her surprise visitor. "And you're right at home. Bon voyage." The visitor gave one good shove then laughed as April went downhill tumbling and screaming. "The true nemesis is the one you never saw coming," the visitor said from the top of the slope.

PRESENT DAY (SEPTEMBER):

Daniel showed a copy of *Spotlight* to Monique. "What is this?" "Well, that's a magazine. Typically, people read them." Daniel shook his head. "The cover – look at the cover." Monique glanced at the photo of April Spring. "She made the cover of *Spotlight*. Good for her."

"Aren't you going to do something?"

Monique nodded. "Yes, actually, I am. I am going to continue being a stay-at-home mom because that's all I'm qualified for, right?" Daniel sighed. "I know you're still mad about your leave of absence but the board felt it was the best decision for Mo's Mix. After the fiasco with the hair show, you made some pretty rash decisions."

"Are you referring to me firing everyone who seemed like they might've been helping April in the slightest or breaking every last bottle of our product because I feared they were all tainted?"

Daniel let out a deep breath. "Both." "I was trying to clean house, you know?" "Your cleaning house resulted in the lowest grossing quarter in Mo's Mix history." Monique stared blankly. "That was bound to happen because of the fire." Daniel sat down next to her. "True, but there was so much going on that an executive decision had to be made."

"And the best option was to kick out the woman who had the vision to start Mo's Mix in the first place?"

"Think about it from a macrocosmic perspective, Monique. By taking a break from Mo's Mix, you were able to spend more time focusing on your home life. You're finally living in Apiqua, you and Emelia are like besties now, and your hubby is enjoying himself at Thornberry. Those are all positive things."

"What about me?" Monique questioned. "What about *my* contentment, huh? Mo's Mix was my baby. How did I lose **two** children in one year, Daniel?" "It's a temporary leave of absence," Daniel quickly pointed out before Monique started thinking about her miscarriage again.

"Plus, you're still getting paid. Be grateful."

Monique shook her head. "You should be the one who's grateful. I pulled you out of your mental purgatory and nursed you back to sanity all while my business was being taken right from under me. Then, I vouched for you when the board was wondering why you disappeared right after the hair show. I said that you were out scouting for new investors. Where were you *really* at Daniel?"

"I was briefly incapacitated." Daniel replied quickly.

"Mom says you took a vacation." "I was definitely on a trip," Daniel lamented. After leaving the cabin and doing some self-evaluation, Daniel decided that April Spring needed to be eliminated by any means necessary. When Daniel saw April's face on the cover of *Spotlight*, he recalled what he had done. Monique picked up the magazine. "What's that on her head – a wig?"

Daniel laughed. "*No*. It's her hair when she doesn't relax it. April's had a come to Jesus moment; her stint in the coma helped her realize that it was time to get in touch with her roots. She's decided to open Cocoa's Beauty School as a nod to her mother."

"This is a joke, right?"

Daniel opened the magazine. "Read for yourself."

Monique put her hand up. "I'll pass. I try not to delve too much into that business stuff anymore because it always brings me back to my lingering question: how was Queen Mo dethroned by peasants?"

"You weren't dethroned. You still wear the crown."

Monique sighed. "I wish I felt like that on the inside." Daniel patted his sister's shoulder and went to grab some food from the kitchen. "Peasants, that's all they are. I'm the Queen," Monique mumbled while drinking her tea. Though Monique was determined to ignore the article, a little voice in her head told Mo that she needed to read it. A part of Monique yearned to know what April had to say because that same part of Monique yearned to be back at Mo's Mix.

5 minutes later, Monique had finished reading. Although it was a completely garbage piece victimizing an aggressor, in Monique's opinion, there was one line that Monique kept thinking about. It struck her as vaguely familiar but she couldn't figure out why. While Monique sat pondering, Daniel came back with his food. "Do you know what Camille's 'big news' is?"

"Yes, but she wants it to be a surprise so I'll let her announce it."

"Some people live for the element of surprise, I suppose." Daniel noted as he casually ate his Chinese food. When he lifted an egg roll to his mouth, Monique glanced at the tattoo that both her parents had hated because they thought it was too sinister. Then, Monique realized why the quote she had read was so familiar. Daniel's tattoo said: ***The true nemesis is the one you never saw coming.***

[TO BE CONTINUED]

Made in the USA
Middletown, DE
12 April 2022